ABOUT THE AUTHOR

Grant J Everett is a writer from Western Sydney. He writes science fiction comedy novels for a couple of reasons: one, because we all need an escape almost as much as we need a laugh, and two, because it's easy to be witty when you have a fortnight to think of a comeback.

Scum of the Universe is his first novel.

Scum of The Universe

GRANT J. EVERETT

BLACK COCKIE PRESS

DEDICATION

To Linda: the one who makes all of this worthwhile. Never change a thing.

CHAPTER ONE SCUMBAGS: THE LIVE, VILE & EVIL TOUR

The lead guitarist thrashed out his first power chord when dusk completed its drunken collapse across the Nevada desert. This burst was so loud that stunned carrion birds rained from the sky, and it blew out the eardrums of any audience members idiotic enough to be within the Harm Zone of the speaker piles. Three hundred thousand groupies, junkies, bangers, zippies, gummos, metal-heads, bogans and other freaks cheered as the wall of sound rattled their bones and brains and popped the occasional rotten tooth.

So, with a noise like the Universe was collapsing in on itself, the illegal Scumbags concert began.

The story begins at this point with two "people," for want of a better term, slamming into each other in a mosh pit the size of Fiji. As this meat-grinder was a Scumbags concert, a band famously described as "unspeakably sick and depraved" by The Children of Death cult, such an encounter could only end in one of three ways: horrific violence, an enthusiastic session of hallucinogen use, or a graphic sex scene.

Surprisingly, none of these outcomes occurred…yet.

Jim Tuesday (unemployed, of no fixed address) was so wasted on the street drug known as Shatter that it took a while for him to register that he'd been knocked on his ass in the sand. As Jim's body had more in common with a barbecue chicken than a Mr Universe contestant, doing a doormat impersonation beneath the stomping feet of insane metal-heads gave him about twenty seconds left to live. Before he could be moshed to death, however, an enormous hand gripped Jim by his skull and dragged him to his feet.

Now mostly upright, Jim squinted up at his saviour to say thanks, but he couldn't see anything more than a fuzzy outline. This short-sightedness was due to the impressive dose of Shatter in Jim's bloodstream, as one of the drug's most common side-effects was temporarily crippling the part of your brain that deals with vision. Other cerebral functions that didn't fare all that well when somebody got Shattered included things like reasoning, language, short-term memory, long-term memory, hand-eye co-ordination, bladder and bowel control, and the ability to blink. This was because Shatter worked by rerouting all of your cerebral power into a kamikaze dive-bomb right into the pleasure centre of the brain, and this ecstasy came at a price. In Shatter's defence, though, the sort of people who were stupid enough to use such a drug had a life expectancy measured in weeks, and so Shatter was helping to create a better tomorrow by removing organisms like Jim from the gene pool.

Leaning in towards his saviour, Jim's sight finally kicked in and he was instantly transfixed by the most beautiful brown eyes you could ever be lucky enough to drown in. Sure, they may have belonged to a woman that could only be classed as human in some of the more liberal states of Amerika, but this was one of those fireworks moments that gave Jim's sad life a point. Did it matter that this woman had a face like a baseball glove that had made love to a cheese grater, or that she was covered in fur? Yes, she was obviously the result of some secret military experiment to combine human and gorilla DNA, but primates needed love too, right?

"Hey?" Jim Tuesday managed, using the best pick-up line his Shattered brain could conjure.

Jim's attempts at romance usually frightened women into escaping down the nearest laundry chute, but in this case the near-human stopped in surprise and looked at Jim's teeth, or lack thereof. Leaning forwards on baseball-sized knuckles, she arched an eyebrow and proved that she possessed the powers of speech.

"You are...uninjured, small Amerikan person?" she rumbled with a European accent that was thicker than overcooked concrete-flavoured porridge.

Her words were lost over the eardrum-bursting noise, but Jim's brain-stem had registered the possibility of an erotic event, and his grey matter decided to spend all of its power in an attempt to come up with a complement that may, hopefully, lead to sex. This moment was the closest that Jim had been to intimacy in a year, and prehistoric parts of his biology began to tick over in desperation to reproduce.

Jim's eyes spent a moment on a face that resembled a kebab-with-the-lot that somebody had dropped on the floor, darted across to arms like burlap sacks full of oranges, and finally flicked down to a pair of comical monkey legs. It was a hopeless mission and destined for failure.

"So...nice...um...fur," Jim eventually yelled, his voice mugged beneath the crushing force of a dozen out of tune electric guitars played out of sync.

"Thank you. I remove all lice by hand," the hairy woman responded, fluttering her eyelashes. "My name is Ruska. I am obsolete Russian genetic experiment. I...how you say it...escape from lab over hill? Had to kill many, many guard. Big, big mess. And now...I here."

Ruska made some kind of simian war cry. It may have been a laugh.

"Nice," Jim Tuesday shrugged, not registering a word. "Enjoying the show?"

"I am...not understand," Ruska said with hesitation, trying to read Jim's lips. She covered her ears and cringed as the volume doubled. "Perhaps would be much nicer without horrible noise?"

As the so-called "music" perpetrated by the Scumbags fell into a genre of audio atrocity classed as torture metal, it was understandable that Ruska's virgin ears wanted to commit suicide. After all, torture metal had been created by the sickest of Guantanamo Bay's interrogators as a way of breaking the most unbreakable of inmates. If you got the distortion just right, the hardest men on the planet would be sobbing for their mummies by the third verse.

There was some sort of disruption to the concert, and Jim looked up at one of the paper-thin screens floating above the crowd. All of the Scumbags performers had apparently decided to play different songs for this part of the concert, ranging from the soft melody of Testicular Rupture to the maelstrom of Chainsaw Vasectomy. Their drummer, who appeared to be off his face on some sort of stimulant that made cocaine look like lemon sherbet, kept up with the beat for four separate songs at the same time before having a schizoid embolism and falling over in a heap. The crowd screeched in happiness at being able to witness such a highlight, but when the music stopped for a couple of minutes as a result of this serious medical emergency, the punks began to throw things: bottles, rocks, bricks, hubcaps, syringes, shoes, rats and, in one particularly notable choice of missile, a human hand.

Rather than joining in on the riot, Jim lunged for Ruska in a passionate crash-tackle. As kind hands led the screaming Scumbags drummer away to another stint at rehab, Jim Tuesday managed to hit a Home Run. The exact details of what happened next were disturbing even for a 24th Century concert and are best left unspoken and forgotten by all concerned. All that can be said is that all good things must come to an end, and so does mediocre sex between two exceptionally ugly people.

Jim got woozily to his feet a minute later and made it about fifteen metres before getting hit in the temple by a bourbon bottle. He passed out in a slump.

*

The riot was intensifying as Ruska opened her eyes, sprawled against a speaker stack and breathing heavily. She had racked up around fifty thousand Amerikan pounds of damage to the audio hardware during her encounter with Jim, but good luck to any roadie that tried to make her pay for it. However, Ruska's glow was stolen away the moment she realised that Jim was nowhere to be seen. She bared her baboon-like teeth. He had used her! He was dead. Dead!

Ruska pointed her nostrils towards the sky and took a sniff. As her nose had been transplanted from a genetically-enhanced bloodhound, she detected her target almost straight away. Unfortunately, the background smells were so awful that it was like getting hit in the face by a gush of effluent. Ruska's nose went into shock and stopped working, but that was fine for now, because she now knew exactly where he was...

Pushing aside anyone who got in her way with the gentleness of an out-of-control double-decker bus, Ruska found her lover in moments. Her anger died the moment she saw him, though, and her heart fell to the level of her toes: poor Jim was bloodied and bruised, and he had already been stomped with hundreds of muddy shoe-prints.

Carefully picking up Jim's limp body, trying not to inflict any more damage, Ruska threw him over her shoulder like he was a towel and knuckled towards the exit. Anything that got in her way, whether it was made of wood, plastic, metal or flesh, was smashed aside. Twenty seconds later Ruska burst through a chain-link perimeter fence like it was cobwebs and skidded to a stop beside the night-time Nevada highway. Ruska looked back and forth in confusion along the moonlit stretch of blackened tar. The road extended from barren horizon to barren horizon, far beyond the range of her exceptional eyesight, and it was apparent that Jim was a long way from professional help.

A battered yellow taxi parked nearby picked this moment to beep at Ruska. Surprising a super-soldier experiment wasn't wise at the best of times, but Ruska was especially on edge right now. Raising her fists and baring thirty-two pointy teeth in a way that would wither the genitals of a full-grown Silverback, Ruska prepared to rush at the new threat and beat whatever it was into salsa.

An almost-human head poked out of the taxi's window. It was wearing a comical expression. In accordance with the Uncanny Valley Laws, any moron could tell with a glance that the driver was synthetic. It winked and tipped its hat.

"Need a ride?" the taxi driver drawled.

Ruska deflated, realising there was no threat, and narrowed her eyes in concentration. She was distracted for a second by a crude bit of vandalism that had been inflicted on the taxi: some punk had burned the word "TRANCE" onto the driver's door in block letters. She didn't know why, but seeing that word triggered a deep part of her brain, as though she was meant to be remembering something...but she had no idea what.

However, Ruska currently had other concerns. Shaking her head, she focussed on the synthetic taxi driver.

"What is meaning?" she demanded.

The taxi driver shrugged in a human way. Such familiarity was probably designed to have a calming effect, but Ruska was ready for violence.

"Army are on their way with heavy artillery. Best not to hang about, yeah? Triple the normal price, of course." The construct smiled with plastic teeth that would never be used for anything except pulling facial expressions. "Serves you right for going to a Scumbags concert, hmm?"

Ruska squinted at the word "price". Unless a subject was useful when it came to sniffing out a target and removing its limbs, it had not been a part of Ruska's educational upbringing in the breeding pens. The driver might as well be speaking ancient Swahili with a Greek accent.

"Price? What is...price?"

Misunderstanding Ruska's words, the driver tapped a touchpad and clicked its lips together.

"Two passengers to Old Vegas will set you back..." the driver squinted and paused for a couple of seconds for the sake of realism, even though it had instantly calculated the fare. "Two hundred and fifty Amerikan pounds. Plus tip."

"Old Vegas?" Ruska repeated, encountering yet another term she didn't know. The driver smiled.

"Old Vegas it is. Get in."

*

Ruska cradled Jim's bruised face during the trip, stroking his cheek with the blunt side of a retractable talon and softly crooning a folk song about using guillotines on the monarchy.

Her brown eyes flicked to the horizon every now and again, as Ruska was expecting the Russian army to come pouring over those sand dunes to drag her home to the lab. However, it would be fair to say that wiping out the research compound with her bare hands seemed to have nipped this problem in the proverbial bud. Killing every person who knew she existed should have done the trick, so burning down the complex and urinating on its warm ashes may have been unnecessary. It had been fun, though.

Ruska turned to the driver, not registering its words the first time around.

"Mmm?"

"I'm guessing this is where you wanted to go?" the driver repeated.

Ruska looked out her window. The driver had bought its taxi from the speed of sound to a complete stop just off the main drag of Old Vegas in a dirty cul-de-sac of neon-drenched novelty churches. Half the street was in shadows.

"What is...place?" Ruska purred.

"I logically assumed that you guys are from out of town, totally off your faces, and want to make a permanent mistake before sobering up," the driver rattled off. "My scanners say that you two recently engaged in unprotected sex, and that this will result in an absolute chance of pregnancy. In addition to that, my readings also predict that the child is likely to be a boy with bad teeth and salt-and-pepper hair." The driver shrugged again. "My advice? You better get a ring on it before he comes to, or the world is going to have another single Mother in it."

Ruska stopped breathing. Her lungs felt like they'd never take in air again.

A mother? Her? Ruska had been told by her handlers that she didn't possess the internal plumbing that was required to produce offspring, and that her genetic legacy would only involve machines and glass tubes.

"That's impossible!" Ruska snarled.

"Search your feelings. You know it to be true," the driver said, smirking. "Look, lady, if a guy engages in unprotected sex in Amerika and his neglect results in a pregnancy, under the laws of the Matriarch Regime you have the power to enforce a mandatory marriage." All of a sudden, the driver's expression turned manic, and a catchy theme-song started piping out of its speakers. This conversation topic had triggered an automatic commercial. "My advice, which is brought to you by the Jeweller's Guild of Old Vegas, is to get a Trust-brand wedding ring grafted to his finger to ensure he'll be the dream husband YOU deserve! Not only will a Trust ring encourage your sweetheart to be the perfect spouse by punishing any unacceptable behaviour with electric shocks and stabs of nausea, but it will also keep track of his movements at all times. Best of all, if he goes beyond a certain distance without your consent, POW! And all for the cost of a chocolate sludge-shake at a MacDeath restaurant!" Both of the driver's eyebrows wriggled in a comical way as it completed the ad. The theme music stopped abruptly. "Listen, lady, I may only understand beauty as a mathematical concept, but my advice is to get this deal done in a quickie-wedding place before he wakes up and finds a…well, a smoother woman." The driver blinked in a bored way. "Congratulations for the bun in the oven, by the way."

Excited at the possibility of a new life that wouldn't involve any more decapitations, Ruska went to get out of the taxi. Unfortunately for the driver, it reached out a hand to stop her from dragging Jim from the cab.

"No offence, lady, but this is the part where you pay me." The driver smiled. "Two hundred and fifty Amerikan pounds. Plus tip." It shrugged in apology and held out its wrist to reveal numerous slots and a touchpad. "Cash is fine, but so is a palm-print registered with any BioBank account. You do have an account, don't you? With money in it? To pay me?" The driver blinked at Ruska's expression. "You are familiar with these concepts, yes?"

Ruska went to jerk Jim away from the taxi driver's grip, and the driver stupidly clamped its other hand around Jim's throat to stop her. Ruska's face turned to its "psychopathic monkey" setting and she was all over the robot in a rage. Beige plastic and semi-organic circuit boards exploded in all directions as Ruska ripped and tore at the machine, pulling out lengths of its steel skeleton before wrenching its whole body in half. Just to be thorough, Ruska snapped off the driver's leg and impaled the poor robot on its own limb. The driver twitched a few times and collapsed, unmoving.

Ruska gathered Jim (who had somehow slept through this astonishing violence) and knuckled for the nearest church. This decrepit tower was illuminated by a humming neon sign declaring it was The Freaks & Legends Chapel and guarded by a looming mascot in the shape of Slender Man. The freaky urban legend crackled "Marry him here before I come and get you!" from an ancient MP3 file. Ruska, not knowing any better, decided to take the tall person's advice.

It required some convincing and a few raised voices, but a celebrant wearing a Dracula outfit decorated with soy sauce and wasabi stains reluctantly agreed to perform the ceremony. After all, they were in Vegas, and this was far from the weirdest thing that had happened during his shift. Before the happy event could take place, though, Ruska had to be given a crash-course in the basics of how money worked. Patting down Jim from shoulders to ankles, Ruska eventually discovered some crunched-up green notes – Jim's entire life savings – stashed in the groom-to-be's sock. The fold of Amerikan pounds covered the wedding expenses without the need for any further suffering.

Still snoring away, Jim was stripped down to his crunchy underpants and slipped into a Queen Cleopatra costume. Ruska, unsurprisingly, chose to be Bigfoot, mostly due to the fact renting an outfit wasn't required. Thirty seconds later, an unconscious junkie and a hybrid gorilla were joined in Holy Matrimony™ and booted to the curb with a slice of wedding cake, a photograph of the two of them kissing, and matching plastic wedding rings. Unlike the one Ruska was wearing, though, Jim's ring was filled with explosive gel dots and had been grafted to his finger with bone-deep electrodes.

Mister and Missus Tuesday went off into the sunrise, one carrying the other across the glowing sand dunes, towards a new life.

Jim woke up in the considerable arms of his Russian bride on a stained patch of linoleum. Stifling a scream of surprise so that it came out as little more than a rat-like squeak, Jim carefully peeled Ruska's sausage fingers away from his ribs and attempted to sneak out in a ninja-like way perfected by parasitic bastards the world over. Looking down at his cheap knock-off Egyptian robes and the plastic asp latched to his wrist, Jim sighed.

Dressed as Cleopatra again. Honestly, he was so sick of waking up like this...

Jim emerged from the shadows and stepped into what felt like the surface of Mercury. Blinking away the assault of Apocalypse-level sunlight on his sizzling retinas, Jim squinted to discover that he'd been sleeping in the ruins of an abandoned service station in a wasteland. The creaking wreck had been tarnished to the same colour as the local dunes after decades of neglect, and it looked like it was one stiff breeze away from collapsing into little more than tetanus.

Shielding his eyes and steeling himself, Jim made it a total of ten steps across the steaming sand before he realised that the deep desert seemed to stretch forever. As Jim Tuesday was an unfit wreck who did horrendously dangerous drugs every day, wandering over glassed sand for a week without a drop of water wasn't an option. Perhaps if he found something to...

"Morning," Ruska purred in Jim's ear.

Jumping in surprise and almost messing his white robe at the sound of the thickest, deepest Russian accent he'd ever heard, Jim did a half-revolution before his feet touched the sand again. Jim slowly looked up...and up...and up...

My, she was big.

"What's doing?" Jim tried to say casually, while his brain screamed AAAAARGH at full volume. Jim hoped that this giant tree sloth, or whatever it was, didn't intend on following him around. Dumpsters were crowded enough for his lanky frame as it was, and he was a lone wolf to the core.

"I love you," Ruska said with devotion.

Jim screamed hysterically. After about eight seconds he realised that this was upsetting the creature for some reason. Jim clamped his mouth shut, blinked, and attempted to change the topic.

"How about that...concert?" Jim managed, trying to access his non-existent memories.

"Yeah. How about that concert?" Ruska said suggestively.

Jim tried to calm down and think through this. His most popular methods of getting rid of unwanted lovers included begging, bargaining, threatening, farting and even just simply running and hiding. As a big fan of the classics, Jim chose to use the latter technique. Diving between Ruska's legs, Jim did a commando roll across the rotten lino and bolted through the service station. Scurrying under a decayed counter and squeezing into a corner, Jim silently prayed.

Please not the hairy woman, please not the hairy woman, please...

Of course, Ruska sniffed out Jim within seconds and leaned down to give him a watery, hurt expression before picking him up by the ears. Jim screeched just as much as you'd expect.

"Don't you love me?" Ruska rumbled with a quiver.

Jim thought about this.

"What would be the exact consequences of choosing 'no' as the answer to your question?"

The expression on Ruska's face had the word DEAD growling behind it. Long, sharp teeth started to appear between her hamburger lips.

"Are you aware that even smaller primates, such as chimpanzees, have more than enough upper body strength to rip human arms right out of their sockets?" Ruska asked in a conversational way.

"Of course I love you!" Jim said far too loudly.

Ruska beamed, and painfully embraced Jim. His ribcage creaked.

"Do you?" Ruska snuffled wetly.

Noticing a nasty itch, Jim looked at his left hand, then at Ruska's furry paw, to see that they had purchased identical plastic wedding rings at some point. However, the one Jim was "wearing" had been anchored to the metacarpal bone of his ring finger with hair-thin electrodes and studded with tiny pinheads of explosive gel. Turning his hand over, praying to whatever deity cared, Jim saw that most dreaded of logos: TRUST.

Dear God! A Trust ring. Of all the horrible things he could have woken up to, this was one of the worst. He'd have to find some way to remove it, but such a task would be unwise at this moment...

Jim smiled with forced enthusiasm as he realised that Ruska's question remained unanswered. It took all of his powers of deception to manage such a huge falsehood.

"Baby! Would I lie to you? Would I?"

Outside, he was all smiles. Inside, Jim was crying hysterically. Like all vermin, though, most of Jim's brain was wired up for self-preservation, so the cockroach instincts that governed Jim's mind would wait for the right moment to scurry to freedom.

"Wedding was nice, yes?" Ruska purred.

She flipped Jim up in the air, gripped him by his left foot, and held him to the ceiling in a playful manner. Blood rushed to Jim's throbbing head. Somehow, he remained conscious.

"I thought they were a little...what is word?... reluctant. Priest-person was under impression I might be classed as exotic pet. But I am nobody's pet!" Ruska spat at the desert and glared at Jim with a dangerous glint in her eye. "I be with you forever, Jim. And when our baby boy born, he grow up to be just like you."

Jim screamed.

CHAPTER TWO HELL SWEET HELL

Time passed slowly at their rusted service station. As the local highway was completely covered by a foot of sand and it seemed as though no flight-paths went overhead, that meant the average number of people who might decide to pop by for tea each day was zero. In addition to the isolation, it was immediately clear that every worthwhile thing in this tetanus pit had been looted years ago, and the desert silently reclaimed whatever was left. Thankfully, their survival prospects increased a few points when Jim unearthed an ancient tap that provided what could loosely be described as drinkable water (if you didn't mind having to chew it a bit first).

Starting on day two, Jim began the week-long process of coming down from his record-breaking Shatter binge. For the first three days he did nothing, but shiver and rock back and forth in the corner in chemical shock. When his body got tired of doing this, he broke up the routine by retching violently for hours at a time and crying like a lonely puppy. The fact there was nothing to eat except an all-you-can-swallow sand buffet was of no concern, as Jim would have just thrown it back up again anyway. Curled up on the lino in misery, if Jim rested his ear against the laminate he was sure he could hear a very, very faint sound, like some sort of machinery. He wrote this off to withdrawal hallucinations and didn't think about it any further.

Ruska disappeared on the seventh day, and Jim instantly noticed that the little lights on his Trust ring were, for some reason, no longer flashing. If he remembered the television commercials right that meant Ruska must have turned off the proximity restrictions, which meant that the rotten thing wouldn't explode if he got too far away. On the downside, attacking the ring itself would probably cause the explosive pinheads to detonate and take off his arm. Half delirious from hunger and knowing that this may be his only chance at escape, Jim found a sharp hunk of granite and steeled himself to cut off his own finger. Of course, a wimp like Jim barely scratched the skin before giving up, but it was a valiant effort.

Jim cried for a while.

Ruska returned three hours later holding a pair of very dead elephant moles in her toothy maw. The two-faced mutant critters had writhing, clawed tentacles instead of limbs and their pelts were riddled with phlegmy pustules, but after a week without food they might as well have been deep-fried garlic prawns on hokkien noodles.

Gathering up any garbage that could burn, such as used scratch-lotto tickets, old receipts and some depressingly empty cigarette packets, Jim went to start a small fire with his trusty lighter, but Ruska beat him to it: extending her retractable claws, Ruska struck both of her index talons together in a shower of sparks, and the flammable pile glowed to life. Ten minutes later Jim was enjoying a medium-rare mole steak with his woman.

They ate in silence for a time. For the first moment in days, Jim's withdrawals had receded to the point where he felt as though he could string a few words together without throwing up, passing out, or both.

"Thanks."

Ruska looked up at Jim as she slurped the bloody innards out of her mole like red strands of spaghetti. Her cheek and eye twitched in a silent "don't mention it" sort of way, and she instantly went back to annihilating the little corpse.

Jim stopped gumming his mole for a few seconds, looked out over the sunset-washed eternity of sand, and asked a very obvious question.

"Uh, Ruska, where are we, exactly?"

"Depths of the Mojave," she rumbled without any interest, loudly crushing mole bones into gelatine powder. "Very far in. Nobody bother us here."

Jim immediately stopped gumming the mouthful of mole crackling. If he remembered a few important facts from history class (as unlikely as that situation was), then he was sitting right on top of the location of the largest botched terrorist attack ever committed on Amerikan soil. Although the terrorists had failed to claim a single life, every schoolchild on the planet was taught all about how a gang of Vegan extremists protested their church being reclassified into a non-tax-deductible lifestyle choice by filling their hemp robes with micro nukes and hijacking a light aircraft. Thankfully the would-be suicide-bombers got their coordinates mixed up due to the fact they had the combined IQ of a packet of yeast, and so they blew themselves to cinders more than three hundred kilometres away from their intended Los Angeles target. All they managed to do was make the hell of the Mojave slightly more hell-like for their trouble, and the event was now celebrated every August on Imbecile Day.

Jim blinked. That explained why the dunes glowed blue-green at night-time, and why the sky occasionally rained ashes when it was especially windy...

"Oh."

"What?" Ruska grunted, eyeballing him.

"Nothing," Jim answered. "Just might be a little background rad around here, that's all. Nothing to worry about, long as we aren't expecting to have ki-"

Jim stopped himself mid-word. Estimating the future sperm-producing abilities of his soon-to-be-irradiated testicles wasn't an appropriate topic for dinnertime conversation, no matter the company, so Jim wisely went quiet and continued to strip the mole's ribcage. Eventually, Jim formed a small pyramid of picked-clean bones and had a full stomach, so he had nothing left to do, but try and extract the whiskers out of his throat. Glancing down at the demolished skeleton, Jim noticed that the white bones seemed to have formed a word on the lino: TRANCE. He didn't know why, but for some reason seeing those six letters tickled something in the back of his head, as though he was meant to be remembering something important...

After a few confused moments, Jim just assumed the TRANCE thing was a fluke (or more likely a product of his many, many past instances of brain damage) and promptly forgot about it.

"Mmm. That's some fine mole."

Jim reclined against one of the less-jagged walls. His Shatter withdrawals had suddenly reached the "chatty" stage where all he wanted to do was talk. Of course, this invited high-speed knuckle sandwiches at the best of times, so Jim chose his words as carefully as he could.

"So Ruska, are you, um, originally from Earth?"

Ruska literally bristled, like a territorial cat. Her eyes narrowed a little, as though she was trying to figure out if she was being insulted. It took a couple of seconds for her to answer.

"Da."

Jim waved this away, as though Ruska didn't understand the question.

"Okay, so you were born on Earth, but where are your people from?"

Ruska blinked.

"Your question, I do not...understand it."

"What planet are your parents from?" Jim snapped, annoyed at having to spell it out. "I know you get all sorts at concerts, especially when Scumbags are playing, and I kinda remember hearing from my dealer's bodyguard's sister's de facto's dealer that we made contact with aliens a few times over the years, and I just sorta assumed that with all the fur and other freakishness..."

"I am human!" Ruska shrieked, instantly unfolding to her full size. Rending claws slid in and out of each of her fingertips in sync with her rapid breathing. Her pupils began to expand and contract, pulsing in a terrifying way. "I am human! HUMAN!"

Jim held his palms towards Ruska in a placating manner, but his next words only added petrol to the cigarette.

"Look, no offence, lady, but if you're human, I'm a Czechoslovakian koala. What species are you?"

Ruska bared her teeth. There was an entire mole paw stuck between two of her larger fangs, and Ruska's mouth started foaming yellow slobber like a rabid dog. The drops of acidic saliva made sizzling noises as they burnt little smoking holes in the lino. She slowly drew closer to Jim by inches, growling from deep in her throat, and hissed her next words.

"I was conceived by union of human semen and human ovary from human of two gender, just like you, but then my embryo was grown in glass womb. When I baby, they put in me many chemical, many DNA." Ruska retracted her claws with a snick, but bared her teeth even further, as though she'd decided to bite off Jim's head like a gingerbread man rather than shred him with her talons. "I am breed to kill, yes, and I enhanced...but I still ninety-seven percent human being...which mean I human."

"Sure, but chimpanzees are ninety-seven percent human too, you know." Jim argued, pulling a random statistic out of thin air like so many wrong people across the breadth of history. "But chimps still swing from trees and eat bananas and play with themselves in full view of the zookeepers, right? A chimp is still a chimp, ninety-seven percent or not."

Ruska could only sit back on her haunches and tilt her head to the side in complete bafflement. It was like watching the world's most stupid field mouse giving two fingers to a hungry house cat and then calmly taking a nap in Fluffy's food bowl, assuming that the immediate future will be rosy. Ruska was so astonished by the stupidity of this scrawny mammal that she was stunned out of her anger for a few seconds.

But those seconds came to an end.

"You..." Ruska attempted, unable to find the right words for a moment. "You are imbecile! How are you not dead yet?"

Jim belatedly realised the very immediate danger he was in. Blinking stupidly as he reviewed the previous thread of the conversation (though admittedly, Jim had to move his lips a bit to jog his memory), he mentally kicked himself for his stupidity.

"Hey, I was just...kidding around," Jim lied quickly, smiling feebly in an attempt to avoid ending up like that mole limb caught between Ruska's teeth. "It's just, um, Amerikan humour."

The violence in Ruska's body language disappeared as though Jim had flicked a switch. She deflated and coiled back down to the floor, where she resumed licking the gunk out of a well-gnawed moleskin. She shot Jim a neutral look while chewing her food and made one more casual remark to end the conversation.

"Jim, your Amerikan humour is awful." Ruska said calmly, her eyes dead. "Do not be doing the joke with me again or I kill you like insect, yes?"

Jim didn't sleep that night, and it had nothing to do with the Shatter withdrawals.

*

Ruska's baby belly was showing within a month, and Jim found himself freaking out worse and worse the bigger it got. Every new millimetre was another chapter in this horror novel. Somehow Jim had survived Ruska's extraordinary temper up to the thirty-day mark, but he was bruised all over from her cuddles and other forms of affection, and the thought of staying here in this decaying slum for the rest of his natural life with that thing and its spawn was about as appealing as an aroused Winston Churchill in a cling-film thong.

Once he'd survived the nightmare of Shatter withdrawals, Jim spent most of his days pacing around the layer of solidified tetanus that passed for a floor in his "home", trying not to get flayed by the insane desert sunlight and sleeping away as much of his time as he could. Ruska had kept them both sufficiently fed so far, but Jim always secretly hoped that the mad animal wouldn't come back whenever she went hunting for the disgusting seed of nuclear fallout they both relied on for breakfast, lunch and dinner.

In addition to being bored by this routine, he was just as sick of having to cuddle up to Ruska (who smelled like a ripe bear carcass after a long summer) for life-giving warmth through the frigid nights. Jim decided that he needed a real bed, as opposed to the stained patch of lino he'd been using. Gathering up the discarded skins from the dozens and dozens of moles, rats and coyotes they'd eaten so far, Jim's home improvement project was as easy as piling the pelts on top of one another and lying to himself about it being a bed. Daniel Boon would have turned his nose up at the rude pile, but at least it was soft.

Jim's second project was to make a couple of pillows, which required the exact same materials as the bed, but he went to the trouble of sewing the furs together with some tough strands of Ruska's fur threaded through a mole-tooth needle. It turned out okay, considering how Jim was entirely devoid of any bankable skills.

At Ruska's insistence, project number three was a crib for the upcoming baby. All Jim had to do was line a rusted shopping trolley with whatever pelts he had left. Once the cot was completed, Jim spent all night just sitting there, staring at the baby-sized bed, his brain empty, his emotions absent, and his voice silent. That rotten object only served to make the reality of his misery even more concrete, and Jim eventually decided that enough was enough.

The next time Ruska went hunting, Jim immediately looked about for something, anything, he could use to escape from this prison. And if an escape wasn't possible, at the very least he'd need something to eat that wasn't an abomination against God. Honestly, at this point Jim would even settle for fat-free two-minute noodles. But most of all, more than freedom or a meal that didn't twitch all the way down his throat, Jim needed a damn cigarette worse than ever before.

Carefully searching through the mounds of sharp, rusty wreckage scattered around the service station in a vain attempt to find anything that had a practical use as a tool, weapon, consumable or smokable, all that Jim found was a very efficient way to scratch and bloody his hands and arms. To make things worse, pile number six was the breeding hive of some highly-territorial fist-roaches who proceeded to chase him about for the better part of an hour. Finally managing to kill the last of the swarm with a rock, Jim sobbed in defeat, curled up on the brown lino and tried to ignore the swelling roach-bites all over his legs so he could sleep away the misery.

Snoozing became difficult, however, as the floor picked this precise moment to collapse.

Jim fell through the dark void for a little over a second and landed with a thud that knocked him out on impact. Reality jumped around like a kicked television as Jim regained consciousness, but his brain soon settled back to its usual blank channel after a minute or three.

Ow...

Rolling onto his side in pain, but still too winded to moan pathetically yet, Jim felt almost as battered as his first Valentine's Day with Ruska. Whatever parts of him weren't already dotted with half-infected roach-bites and other assorted scratches were now streaked by nasty bruises. He hurt in places he didn't know he had until now.

He could hear something...some sort of mechanical hissing and stomping...

Jim eventually made it back to his feet with a lot of groaning and swearing. As he wasn't Mensa material (to say the least), it took another few more moments for Jim to finally register that he'd fallen into a hidden basement. Looking up, a simple safety ladder disappeared into a distant corona of desert sky.

Blinking away the bright spots, Jim's eyes soon adjusted to the low light. It took Jim only the briefest of moments to realise that he'd discovered a treasure hoard comparable to that of King Solomon himself. It was beyond his most ridiculous dreams.

Jim literally wept.

It turned out that the hissing and stomping noises were coming from an automated chemical replication lab going full swing. Even Jim wasn't stupid enough to think for a moment that there was anything legal being brewed here in the middle of the desert. On closer inspection, it turned out the nearest cluster of industrial-strength hardware was liberally splashed with the logo of TRANCE Unlimited, a well-known conglomerate that specialised in automated hardware. In fact, after doing a lap of the room it turned out that just about everything here had been sourced from TRANCE Unlimited, as their logo had been stamped on every pipe, chamber and vat. Whoever set this place up knew what they were doing and had serious contacts.

For a moment, seeing the word "TRANCE" tickled something at the back of Jim's brain. It was a feeling that he was meant to remember something, that TRANCE wasn't just the name of a company, but was the core of some deep secret. However, Jim's brain was only interested in two things at this point: getting blackout wasted, and then doubling the dose.

Jim went all the way to the start of the line and watched a pearly white liquid replicate in a chain of steaming vats. This vanilla fluid was then piped through a maze of fine tubes, filters and vacuum chambers before being pounded into tiny beige tablets. The pills were stamped with a symbol and sprayed with a rainbow of different glazes before ending the relatively simple process by being funnelled into a large metal hopper. Jim had to look away from the stockpile for a while, as he'd begun to drool uncontrollably.

Must calm down, must calm down...

Wandering around this incredible stash of recreational chems, which he reckoned must have been running without interference for years, Jim's next breath jammed up in his throat when he noticed that one dark wall of the lab had been dedicated to stacking up supply crates emblazoned with military stencils. The crates, like all heavy military goods, had thin, powerful antigrav wafers built into their bases, which meant that a single person with no equipment could easily move them about as easily as rolling a skateboard.

Hoping against hope, Jim effortlessly dragged a coffin-sized crate away from the pile and jimmied it open with a handy orange crowbar. He was greeted by neon-yellow boxes of self-cooking Mac&Cheese, which had a theoretically unlimited shelf life and only tasted a little bit like curdled ass.

Jim grunted. It was a good find, sure, but not what he was after right now.

The next crate was filled with plastic jars of honey. Number three contained blister packs of water purification tablets. Yep, they'd be useful. Crate four held thousands upon thousands of disposable paper-thin televisions and double-sided tape so you could stick them to any convenient wall. And crate number five...

Jim's brain refused to believe what it was processing for a few seconds, like it was some kind of sick, hopeless dream that would only serve to make him miserable when he woke up. Jim gave an unprecedented prayer of thanks and cried like a slapped baby, as six hundred shrink-wrapped boxes of extra-strong chlorine-flavoured self-lighting cigarettes were regarding him with their neon CIGARETTES ARE LETHAL, DICKHEAD disclaimer stamps.

It took less than five seconds for Jim to rip away the shrink-wrap from a carton, pull out a packet, open it up, jam one of the smokes in his gummy mouth and draw back like a drowning man who had just broken the ocean's surface. The chemical suck-burner in the tip lit itself in response to the drag, and Jim inhaled the green smoke in total ecstasy.

Sucking down three cigarettes one after another until he felt as though he'd started to make up for lost time, Jim critically regarded the huge pile of Mac&Cheese for a while, but something as unimportant as food could wait. What Jim wanted really, really wanted was to get high on one of those pills. The closest thing Jim had to a commendable trait was that he wasn't picky with how he got off his face, as long as it got him so hammered that he could barely remember that he even had a face.

Approaching one of the half-full hoppers at the end of the drug production line, Jim carefully picked up a tiny pink pill and inspected it closely: the word BLINK had been stamped into its chalky surface below an Eye of Horus symbol. Placing the mysterious tab on the tip of his tongue, Jim stared up at the glowing hatch far above.

"I wonder why it's called Bl-"

*

"-ink?"

Jim returned to awareness in the deep desert. He was naked, covered in scratches and cuddled up tight to Ruska, who was snoring like a flatulent cow after a bucket of Chilli Con Carne.

"What the spug..."

Checking his ancient digital watch (which was the only thing he was still wearing), bright green digits informed Jim that nearly three days had passed between the point he'd tongued the pill and when his brain had abruptly restarted like an old Datsun. It had been three days without worries, without any regrets, without...well, anything at all.

A total void was now on offer to Jim, and in unlimited quantities.

Poor mathematical skills aside, Jim honestly couldn't remember how many different colours of Blink he'd seen in those hoppers, but it was somewhere between a tonne and totally endless. Jim wondered if the colours meant anything, or were only cosmetic, but then he felt really, really excited about how he was going to discover the answer to this important question in the only way he knew how.

Jim shrugged. If he had to tolerate life out here in Hell, then he might as well find a way to skip big chunks of it. To a sub-human like Jim, Blink was the ultimate cure to his situation, and he couldn't think of a single drawback.

*

Finally, the big day came when a new baby was brought into the world, and his birth was an especially unusual one, as his mum didn't even wake up for it.

One moment, Jim and Ruska Tuesday were lying together in a bed covered in roughly-stitched moleskins stuffed with even more moleskins, and the next there was a new-born baby screaming next to Jim's feet. Crying until dear-old-Dad finally noticed, Jim regained just enough consciousness to cut the umbilical cord with a rusty butter-knife and carried his first-born to a fur-lined crib made from a shopping trolley. Jim eventually managed to focus his eyes just enough to see the time on his wristwatch: it was two in the afternoon.

"It's too early. Shut up." Jim muttered at the red-skinned, squalling baby, going back to bed.

Finally waking to the astonishingly shrill noise of her new-born screaming bloody havoc for the whole of the Mojave to hear, Ruska staggered over to her son and held him up. Blinking away the gunk from her eyes, Ruska regarded the boy, who was perfectly smooth from scalp to toe, and hugged the hairless baby tight.

"My son," Ruska cooed.

She held the infant up to her face in one large hand and smiled with several rows of teeth. The bub screamed in terror, but Ruska confused fear for hunger and drew the infant close so he could feed from one of her six nipples.

"What will we call you, little man?"

Jim sighed loudly from under the blankets.

"Bob. He's called Bob. Now shut up."

Ruska growled dangerously, and Jim popped his head out of the moleskins to grin weakly at her hostile expression.

"Please, my darling. Please. Thank you. Thanks."

"Now, we go hunting!" Ruska said proudly.

"He carn't hunt, he's a bloody baby!" Jim snapped.

Ruska looked down at the pathetic little bundle who had just been christened as

Bob Tuesday. He continued to suckle noisily.

"Not now. But soon."

CHAPTER THREE OUT OF HELL AND INTO PURGATORY

No matter whether you are as high as a Rothschild or as low as a Tuesday, time passes, things change, and the inevitable happens. So while the deep Mojave changed very little over the years, the burnt-out service station that a family of three called home slowly adapted to their presence as the months drunkenly staggered by and threw up in the corner. Thanks to the emergency supplies Jim had accidentally discovered in the hidden basement, their lives had become sustainable, to put it in generous terms, but it was still an existence of hardship and deprivation.

Jim hadn't embraced his new life without plenty of complaints, of course, but Ruska had point-blank refused every demand to take their little family back to civilisation. She explained that if the Russian government found out she'd had a child they would probably vivisect all three of them on the spot. On Jim's fifteenth request, however, Ruska decided not to bother repeating herself again, and had instead described, at great length, a certain information-extraction technique she'd been taught called "squiffing." It took ten minutes of lurid detail to explain why this horrific act had been the core reason behind assembling a new Geneva Convention two-and-a-half-decades ago, and how it was one of the only crimes in the 24th Century that would merit the penalty of Death by Crow as a minimum sentence.

Jim didn't ask again.

Bob developed as you'd expect in such an environment with the parents he'd been dealt, but it was immediately obvious from the day of his birth that the extreme genetic engineering Ruska had suffered at the hands and hypodermics of Soviet scientists hadn't been handed down, which meant Bob could pass as completely human without a second glance. Thanks to a combination of Jim Tuesday's bad genes and the local background rad, young Bob's inherited smirk was only composed of ten brittle baby teeth. However, Bob's salt-and-pepper hair was unaffected by the terrible conditions, and by the time he was the age of a grade schooler it flowed down almost to his waist.

Following closely in his dad's footsteps from the time he was the size of Verne Troyer, Bob slept away the insane heat of the Mojave in the sunlit hours and spent his nights consumed by staring at the paper-thin televisions Jim had found in the stolen surplus crates. Bob, like most children, was raised by the very best programming nine-hundred-and-forty-eight free-to-air channels had to offer, and although he could not read, write, do basic mathematics or touch his own nose with his eyes closed without falling on his head, Bob quickly learned some of the most offensive combinations of words that the Unglish language could marry. His sheer verbal unpleasantness soon soared far beyond that of most other humans, let alone other six-year-olds, and what Bob lacked in intelligence and book-smarts he made up for in pure, savage vulgarity. In fact, the litmus test Bob applied in finding out whether he'd developed a particularly exceptional insult, was when he received a smack from his mum, and he'd file those special ones away for future use. In this way, Bob could perhaps be called a prodigy, but it was hardly the sort of talent that would get you into Harvard. Bob also enjoyed watching the Flower Arranging channel, but he was always ready to switch over to the Olympic Death sports channel with a double-blink before Mum or Dad caught him.

It was his secret shame.

Of course, Ruska wanted to have a major influence over Bob's upbringing as well, and her lessons were very different to the terrible example that Jim set. From the time he was able to walk, Bob was taught how to scurry from hiding spot to hiding spot, to vault over obstacles, to hide in the shadows, and to attack and kill fist-roaches using nothing but his teeth and bare hands. As Bob grew, though, his lack of retractable claws, acidic saliva or even a superhuman sense of smell meant that he needed to be taught how to be violent like a basic, flimsy Homo sapiens, which meant he'd need the right tools...

Ruska picked Jim up by his nose one morning and demanded he be a good father for once by making some sharp weapons for their clumsy toddler. Jim complained, but after getting juggled a bit he quickly agreed to the task. He spent hours and hours sourcing useless rusting junk for materials, and this involved deconstructing shopping trolleys, ripping out safety railings and digging through miscellaneous garbage piles. It took a month of hard work, but Ruska was holding Jim's entire stash at ransom, so the stakes were high.

Finally, the celebration of Bob's sixth full year in hell involved his best gift yet: a crude assortment of half a dozen dangerous things. They consisted of a spear, a filleting knife, a skull-breaking club, a cleaver, a sword and a large hook. They were nothing more than chunks of orange corrosion wrapped with Jim's dodgy home-brew leather, but Bob had never known such luxury and was speechless. When he was also given a leather belt to hold the treasures in place on his loincloth, Bob nearly cried from happiness.

His training began the same day.

Ruska painted simple pictures of common kinds of Mojave wildlife on the walls by using the blood and bile of a coyote as ink, and Bob was told in no uncertain terms that he was only allowed to practise on these decorations for now. Ruska taught her son which parts to stab, which parts to bludgeon, and especially what parts should never get within range of his soft flesh. Bob learned to spring and stab, to stalk and slit, to leap and bash, to roll and hook. When other children were crying for their mummies on their first day of preschool, Bob was cutting jugular veins.

Bob's ninth birthday involved a rabbit for breakfast and a six-legged weasel for lunch. Although this may not seem like much, eating more than once every couple of days was an alien concept to the youngster, and Bob felt like the luckiest kid on Earth. Bob wasn't naïve enough to expect any gift beyond a full digestive system, let alone anything that wasn't absolutely essential to his survival. This kind of attitude was beyond valuable when you lived in a wasteland, as it was an ideal way to avoid disappointment. And after being stranded for nine years with a gibbering junkie imbecile and a borderline animal, Bob was surely a world-leading expert in disappointment.

Despite the fact that Dad wasn't awake (Bob could clearly hear Jim Tuesday snoring from the dumpster next to their service station, probably in the depths of his latest Blink binge), Ruska didn't have any reservations in giving her only son his other present on her own: a folded pile of tough leather. Wordlessly placing the bundle in his outstretched arms, Bob instantly noticed that the suit was a lot heavier than he expected treated skins to be. Bob looked down at the brown mass for a few seconds and turned it over a few times, but his face clearly showed that he still didn't understand. He looked up at his mum with a question on his face.

"They're clothes," Ruska hinted.

Bob only looked more confused at this detail.

"But..." he began.

Bob looked down at the dirty loincloth he'd worn for every moment of his life (besides for the annual Laundry Day, of course), then at the padded weapon belt and the six orange tools he prized above everything else, and then finally at his often-patched moleskin shoes. Bob finally looked back up at his mum again, but it still didn't compute.

"But I already have clothes." Bob explained. "I'm not naked, see?"

Ruska smiled at her son's confusion. Her long, sharp teeth gleamed in the afternoon sun.

"Well, now you have two sets."

Bob's face had disbelief tattooed all over it. Ruska ran the blunt side of a retractable claw up the side of his face in a way that always made him feel loved and special, and ruffled his considerable mass of matted hair.

"Happy ninth birthday, sweet one." Ruska purred. "Now put the leathers on, and then we can get to your next present."

Bob froze. Two meals in one day, new clothes, and there was still another present to come? Wow! His family must have got rich all of a sudden!

Dropping the stinking loincloth and fur belt around his ankles without a gram of shame, Bob slipped into the unbending full-body leather suit and Ruska helpfully tied it off with straps built into the limbs and trunk of the armour. It was by far the nicest, most comfortable leather craft Jim Tuesday had ever made, but the sheer weight of the outfit became obvious as soon as Bob took a step. He worried for a moment that living a life of such unknown luxury had instantly spoiled him.

Ruska interrupted Bob's train of thought by giving him a bear hug so big that an actual bear would have trouble matching it.

"Now, is time to go into desert." Ruska announced.

"But I'm not hungry, Mum!" Bob grumbled. "And I don't want to hunt stupid little lizards and mouses and cocky-roachers anymore. I'm a big kid now, and they're no challenge."

Ruska smiled again.

"Come, sweet one. This will be fun."

*

Bob had often accompanied his mum into the deeper wastes from the time he was barely five so he could gather insects, small rodents, lizards, flowers, berries, cacti, bark and anything else that was theoretically chewable while Ruska did her best hunting dog impersonation. So far, the various contents of Bob's "desert salads" hadn't killed any of them yet, and seeing as though the local background glow of the Mojave could wildly mutate anything that moved, this was quite an accomplishment.

As usual, Bob saw the dunes pass by from atop his mother's enormous shoulders as she knuckled across the sand on all four of her long limbs. Although the up-down motion would make most people violently sick, Bob was used to the rocking and was able to kick back and appreciate how the patches of glassed, glittering sand would reflect the high-noon sunlight.

Bob knew something was up as his mum carried him beyond their usual stalking grounds. She carried him over unfamiliar dry streams full of desiccated fish bones, dodged through graveyards of grey, petrified cacti, and well into unknown territory.

Still, Ruska didn't stop.

By the time Bob disembarked from his hairy steed twenty minutes later, Ruska had taken him four times as far as he'd ever been in his life. Holding an unwashed hand above his eyes to block out the vicious glare of Sol during the living nightmare known as midday, Bob scoped out his surroundings: no plants, no water, no cacti, no life of any kind, and not so much as a corroded orange chunk of metal to show that mankind had ever been here. Thick salt crunched beneath Bob's moleskin boots with each step, and the air was metallic with the stench of burning sodium. This place was a wasteland beyond anything he knew, and if Bob knew a lot about one topic, is was wastelands. It wouldn't surprise him one bit if this was the most worthless acre of the entire planet, and even if mankind immediately disappeared from the planet and nature was left to its own devices for a thousand years, this place would still never see so much as the bloom of the smallest, driest peyote, let alone anything that moved.

Now, while hanging out in a useless salt plain in temperatures that had more in common with a pressure cooker than a climate within the survivable range of a human body wasn't anything out of the ordinary, Bob was expecting a fricking birthday present, and it was pretty obvious that this place was the exact opposite of something anybody would want.

Bob pouted, kicking at the ground. His shoe slammed into a pile of white crystals that had almost perfectly formed what appeared to be the letters V and U. Obviously, they dissipated after being booted.

"Great present, Mum."

Bob's hackles raised when Ruska chuckled at his disappointment. Although her unique genetics hadn't been passed along to him, Bob could really follow in his mum's paw prints when he felt he'd been insulted.

"Why are we here?" Bob snapped.

"Patience." Ruska purred.

"Patience?" Bob repeated, growling. "How's this for patience?"

Slamming his boot into another hump of sand as hard as he could, Bob discovered that the individual grains had been hardened into a crude patch of glass by the sunlight at some point, and they crackled on impact. This sort of weirdness would be more at home on bloody Venus, and Bob knew it.

Still without a clue as to what was going on, Bob wiped his wet brow with a matted chunk of his own greasy hair and hunkered down. The insane heat and lack of humidity was only getting more oppressive by the second, and Bob could feel rivulets of sweat working their way out of his scalp, armpits, and crotch. After another minute every inch of his skin was slippery, and if it wasn't for the straps that held his new clothes in place Bob's leathers would be sliding about all over the place. His boots squelched wetly with each step.

"Well?" Bob finally demanded, extending his arms to each side. He glared into heat distortion so severe that it was like somebody had defaced a wet oil painting. "Is my present dying of heatstroke? Sweating until my balls pop out of my pores? Turning into Bob-flavoured jerky? Well?"

"It will be here soon." Ruska said cryptically, watching the Sun like it was the ticking hands of a clock.

Bob turned sharply on the spot to regard his mum. His weapon belt of corroded orange metal rattled and clunked against his heavy leathers.

"It? It what?"

"Your present." Ruska's eyes flicked down to regard something directly behind him. Her mouth quirked just as Bob detected a soft noise that was a combination of moving sand and metallic rattling. "You may want to pay more attention to your surroundings, sweet one."

Even without Ruska's obvious warning, Bob had already detected there was something behind him purely from the vibrations in the soles of his footwear. Most small children would freeze on the spot like prey at a time like this; however, staying still in the presence of a half-decent predator is generally as useless as a crepe paper condom. Due to the fact his instincts had been tempered by the wastes like he was a glowing sword in a forge, Bob turned and rolled to the side in one smooth motion. Something sharp flicked over his left ear halfway through the tumble, cleanly slicing away a knotted chunk of his hair, but as far as Bob could tell it had failed to score his skin.

Whatever the thing was, it had rattled on the way past.

Bob kept moving at top speed in unexpected ways. This meant all his attention was kept on hitting the sand gently and immediately rolling into his next position, rather than figuring out what the hell he was up against. He felt the rattling thing flick past his face again, and as Bob skidded across the fickle, salted ground in a burst of crumbs he drew his crude sword in one hand, his hook in the other, and turned to finally get a look at his enemy.

It was worse than he could have guessed.

The creature was a black mass of eight long prehensile insectoid tails, each of them tipped with stingers that ranged in shape from barbs to fishing hooks to corkscrews. The writhing tails were the sort you saw on scorpions, but Bob had never encountered a scorpion bigger than a Tonka truck, let alone one that weighed twice as much as he did. The tips were dripping some kind of perfectly clear liquid that hissed on the sand, and Bob was pretty sure it wasn't pure mountain spring water.

The monster immediately registered as something his mum had once told him about in his smaller years, a phantasm that his four-year-old self had insisted couldn't possibly be real, even though he didn't know the definition of the words "register" or "insist," let alone "phantasm." If a word wasn't capable of offending somebody, it wasn't the sort that Bob would know.

Bob cursed quietly. Yep, it was a Hydra all right. He didn't know how, but somehow his mum had found a species that only existed in ancient folk tales, and apparently she decided it would be a good idea to allow it to sneak up on her only son.

Bob called out the most heroic thing he could manage at that point.

"Mum!" he sobbed.

"Happy Birthday!" Ruska called unhelpfully.

Bob gritted his brittle teeth. Great. She thinks facing me off against Hercules' worst nightmare is a good thing. Obviously the Russian definition of the word "present" didn't have much in common with the Unglish version.

Sizing up his enemy, keeping a distance from the poisonous barbs as he paced a circle around the beast, Bob realised an important fact within a dozen steps. Although the stingers were able to flash out like fencing rapiers in the hand of an Olympic gold medallist, the thing's body wasn't able to move about all that well, and a simple glance at the ground explained why: the core point where those eight tails converged looked like an entire colony of scorpion torsos had been mashed into a single body, glued together with araldite and allowed to heal up all crooked. This badly deformed trunk sat atop at least fifty legs, and while a large number of these limbs were underdeveloped or otherwise crippled, the Hydra could move about well enough to get by. It wouldn't be doing parkour backflips any time soon, but it was mobile enough to be a threat.

The tails tracked Bob as he circled, rattling at him like wooden beads, and the two combatants examined the other for weaknesses. Unfortunately, all Bob saw was armoured chitin, sharpness and venom, while the Hydra was up against moist pink flesh armed with weapons so tarnished that they might as well be made out of dried mud. Suffice to say, the Hydra didn't seem worried about the odds.

Watching the tails weave about, occasionally darting back beyond the immediate range of eight poisoned stingers, Bob finally noticed something useful: the three tails on the Hydra's left side were far more flexible and longer than the five on the right, as though the asymmetrical beast was a southpaw. Bob could also make out something pumping beneath the chitin of the Hydra at the base of its five lesser tails, almost like a heartbeat, and his brain mentally ticked the "weak point" box.

Even though he was barely nine, Bob had been brought up by parents who never held back, never thought about things before doing them, who always leaped before they looked. His entire existence was because of bad judgement and impetuousness, and Bob was genetically hardwired to jump off any darkened cliff and simply hope for a feather mattress to miraculously appear to break his fall.

So he attacked. It was in his nature.

Faking out to the Hydra's left, all three of the powerful tails whipped out at Bob like slingshots. The wild boy hurdled over them with ease and cartwheeled to the creature's right. Wobbling off-balance as it did it best to turn its lumpy, misshapen body, the Hydra was unable to finish recoiling before Bob had planted his sword straight in the pulsating sack beneath the five baby tails. Accidentally snapping off the length of his blade once it had penetrated the target in a burst of green muck, Bob continued to spin away from the darting spikes. Falling just a metre short of where he'd intended to land, Bob's mouth opened in a perfectly round O as all three of the Hydra's strongest tails slammed into his back, piercing the leather over his upper spine, left kidney and liver, instantly proving without a doubt that Bob had badly, badly misjudged the monster's speed. The combined impact of all three tails added together was on par with being hit by a fast-moving sedan, and as Bob hit the ground with teeth-rattling force he was stunned so badly that he had no idea where he was, or even who he was. Bob felt one of the barbs lodge in his back and snap off, but as though witnessing it from a distance.

Rolling over with a pitiful moan and trying not to cry snotty tears, Bob gagged at the overwhelming stink of corrosive venom sizzling on his clothing. The Hydra rattled its tails in a triumphant way as it reared up, preparing to feast on his meat. Blinking away the triple-vision, totally defenceless and probably seconds away from being eaten alive (if the poison didn't kill him first), Bob's eyes finally focussed properly just in time to get a clear view of stingers darting for his face. As his very last act on this planet, Bob screwed up his mouth, hawked, and spat a phlegmy gob at the creature that was about to munch out on his warm organs.

The tails flashed…and stopped a centimetre short.

Bob blinked. His entire scope of vision was made up of nothing but stingers, but no matter how badly the Hydra tried, it just couldn't cover those last few millimetres. Crawling backwards like a crab on his palms and heels, knowing that he shouldn't take this godsend for granted, Bob scurried well out of range before he stopped again. From his new, safer vantage point, Bob could see that the Hydra had a thick chain wrapped around its midsection. This leash led down into the sand where Bob assumed the Hydra had emerged.

The green gunk pumping from where Bob had embedded his ruined sword in the creature's chitin was now haemorrhaging yellow, and the Hydra's struggles became weaker and weaker over the next thirty seconds until it gave up fighting and decided to take a nap. Bob was pretty sure he could hear it snoring.

Puffing and panting, Bob's relief instantly turned to panic again as he remembered he was far from safe: judging from the size of those stingers, he probably had half a litre of mutant venom swimming about in his bloodstream right now, corkscrewing towards his heart with each beat, preparing to incinerate his entire circulatory system in a matter of moments…

Bob somehow got back to his feet, limping and in awful pain, and started to untie the leather straps with clumsy fingers. The Hydra reared up at this motion, trying to get closer, but it was no dice for Mister Mutant Scorpion, and it curled up in resignation again.

Sliding off his sweat-slicked gear and dropping it to the hot sand, Bob tried to reach around to the three soon-to-be-fatal wounds along his spine. Try as he might, his fingers just wouldn't reach.

Crap.

Despite his panic, Bob knew that something wasn't right about all this. He hurt all over, sure, but it was a blunt kind of pain, like being hit by a metal pipe, rather than the sharp pain of a horse hypodermic. He was missing something here, some factor...

Taking a decent look at his discarded leather kit explained everything. Bob could instantly make out the trio of puncture wounds – the force of the impact had been so great that one of the barbs had actually snapped off on impact - but his flesh hadn't been stung. Not even a little bit. Patting around the punctures revealed that thin green slabs had been tied in place between layers of moleskin and coyote hide in order to serve as armour. The source of these life-saving slabs had obviously been arc-welded away from one of the army surplus crates stashed in Daddy's-Secret-Basement-That-Bob-Must-Never-Go-Into-Without-Permission. Although dented and sizzling with venom, the ceramic plates had prevented Bob from getting perforated senseless.

Now dressed only in his fur boots and weapon belt, Bob looked up at his mum as she knuckled towards him with a smile the size of a crescent moon. Feeling a little hysterical, he matched her smile for exactly three seconds.

And then he vomited, wet his pants, and passed out, in that order.

*

They remained in this hell-within-a-hell for a time. Ruska had bought along an assortment of salves stamped with Military symbols to rub into her son's bruises and scrapes, and then she stroked his hair and sung Russian nursery rhymes in a voice that was about as soothing as a power sander to the genitals.

Bob shook uncontrollably in her gorilla arms for a time, trying not to cry any more tears today. Despite his mother's tenderness, it was kinda hard to ignore the fact that she'd almost gotten him viciously murdered by a freaking Hydra. So, Bob had things to say at this point, and he started with the most obvious one.

"I didn't think Hydras were real."

Bob curled up closer to his furry Mum.

"Was not real Hydra," Ruska noted, continuing to stroke his hair. "I find badly mutated female scorpion one day, and she in middle of giving birth, so I watch for entertainment. Unfortunately, all the babies were...what is word...conjoined together into one body. They a horrible mass, twitching and fighting to go in different direction, and obviously in bad pain. But then I realise they here for reason, and I bring them where they are safe, and I help them grow. They live under sand there for three years, and I always bring them enough scraps to stay alive. In time, they learn to work together, and become strong. I pretty sure their brain stems have grown together and rewired themselves." Ruska smiled. "I call it Shnookums, or Shnookie for short. Is...is pet, yes?"

"But why?" he sobbed, feeling absolutely betrayed. "Why would you let it attack me like that?"

Ruska checked his bruises again. The Military-grade regen salve was doing its job. Bob would be almost as good as new in a couple of hours. Ruska sighed, and there was a faraway look in her eyes as she resumed stroking her son's hair.

"You know I don't talk about lab where I born."

Bob looked up in surprise. This topic was always off-limits, even to him. His mouth turned into an O shape again, but this time it wasn't due to stingers in his ribcage. Ruska went on without needed a prompt.

"I was not only one of my kind. In lab, they grow eighteen of us from same genetic material, but we all different. Niska was spliced with reptiles and had a venomous spike on her tongue. Jan had a set of feathered wings that almost worked. Jon was part insect and had six arms and no legs...but the one thing we all have in common is claws. These." Ruska extended and retracted her talons as emphasis. "But many were not lucky enough to be as normal as me, and were shaped in ways that make your little eyes hurt and make you feel big sick in your stomach. Cruel, horrible experiments that not work properly." Ruska took some time, still playing with Bob's hair as she stared into the heat distortion. "We all born on same day and spend all our time together in big white room, so we become like family, like close sibling. We grow up together, and we only leave room when they sedate us with gas and take us away for tests that we can never remember afterwards."

Bob gave her time to mull this over. He'd always wondered about his mum's origins, and he didn't want to do anything to spoil this rare chance. His dad would be so jealous! He'd been trying to get this sort of stuff out of Ruska for over nine years.

"And then, one day, they separate us." Ruska growled. "Something changed. We don't know what, or why, or how, or anything. Maybe funding cuts, maybe had been planned whole time? Anyway, all we know is that a scientist on a big screen explain that it is our ninth birthdays today, and that means it is time for our Excruciating."

Bob looked up again. Ruska didn't need to see his expression to know his obvious question. Multiple syllables weren't Bob's strong suite.

"So then I wake up by myself, in very small room." Ruska's voice shook a little at the memory. "And when I stand up and look around, I not know what is going on. Remember that I haven't known anything except that large area I share with my brothers and sisters, and for the first time I can remember...I am all alone. But not for long.

"The far wall slid up to the ceiling, and beyond, it is very dark. But I can smell something I don't recognise, hear something unfamiliar. So, after a life with no danger, I am complacent. Sloppy. Stupid. I step forward and try to see what is there, just in case it is one of my siblings wearing some stinky chemical or something, and I wave and say hello. Because of this idiocy, I almost die one second later when a huge blur charges me from the shadows like a bull wearing red contact lenses. It slammed me into the wall with the worst pain I ever know. I can hear my own skeleton snap in a dozen places and feel my organs burst like bubbles. Creature has pinned me to wall and is biting me everywhere at once, tearing shreds from my body with what seemed like a hundred mouths. Stuck against wall, I react without thinking, and my enhancements suddenly work for the first time. So, I spit acid right in its face, and then my claws pop out of my fingertips so I can cut its fegging throat open. Creature not like this, of course, and it drop me and back off for a moment."

Ruska paused. Bob was so riveted by the story that he had to resist the urge to hurry his mum along.

"Now, I finally get good look at this thing: is obviously an experiment, like me, but it is like...like dinosaur, like raptor from old time movie...I no remember name...and even though I have torn out one throat and burnt a second face into charcoal, it still have another seven heads...and they all hissing and weaving and lunging for me straight away.

"I was critically wounded, I knew this, but somehow my body understood what to do all on its own, almost as though my muscles had been programmed how to react to danger, to go on automatic when things become deadly. I never feel

anything like it before, and I suddenly have no control over my violence."
Ruska smiled. "Even with horrible internal bleeding and all my limbs broken, I
still pull apart their lab-made Hydra one head at a time and stomp it so bad that
it finally stop the twitch. It was my first kill." She blinked, wearing an odd
expression. "That fight with the Hydra...it made me who I am today."

Ruska finally looked down at Bob. There were tears in her eyes, which was
something he'd never seen before. Sure, Jim Tuesday could potentially start
sobbing if his coffee was weak or the sand was too hot on his bare feet, but
Ruska had always seemed to have only two emotional settings: simian rage, or
painful affection.

"I so happy I kill that thing, even though my body is shattered and dying, all I
can think is how much I look forward to telling all the others about what had
happen. They then gas me again, and when I wake up, I am healed and back in
the room I grow up in." Ruska shed a tear. It rolled over her hamburger lips and
into Bob's knotted hair. "But same man as before appear on screen again, his
face even more emotionless and uncaring than last time, and he tell me that I
was the only one of my batch to survive my Excruciating, and that all the others
have been recycled into genetic paste for next generation." Ruska's claws
extended and retracted fitfully. This was a sure sign that she was feeling
something besides rage or love. "I then begin my real training for fifteen years,
and in that time I learn to be better killing machine, but my Excruciating was
when I truly began to be who I am now. And so, knowing that you would soon
be same age as I was when I became myself, I knew that..."

Ruska's words ceased sharply as her head snapped towards the far horizon. Her
ears twitched, as though she could hear something, and her eyes narrowed. Bob
turned his head to take a look at whatever had distracted his mum, but it
appeared to be nothing more than a small dust cloud. His eyes couldn't
penetrate the heat distortion any better than that, but it certainly seemed as
though his mum's enhanced senses had detected something.

Ruska tossed Bob onto her shoulders with one mighty arm without a further
word and knuckled for home at full speed. Bob's complaints and questions went
unanswered.

*

Ernest Fell, a Very Bad Man, was reclining on a leather lounge in the back of an Imperator-model limousine. The Imperator, the most luxurious of its line, was more like a mobile palace than a simple car. It provided every conceivable kind of amenity a professional businessman-on-the-go would need to conduct his affairs, such as a full-sized hot-tub, a well-stocked bar, a soundproofed meeting room for fifteen, and a revolving Emperor-sized bed with spotless polysilk sheets. Unlike your average businessman, at one point or another Ernest had drowned rivals in the spa, held cocktail parties for gangland serial killers and Mafia dons in the bar, tortured police informants with dental tools in the soundproofed meeting room, and entertained stunning Bollywood starlets in bed (his record in a single encounter was twenty-eight).

Sipping his perfectly-mixed Manhattan, Ernest judged the Mojave Desert through a panorama of bulletproof windows. It was ugly, barren and dry, just like his first wife, and under normal circumstances Ernest wouldn't deign to look at this waste on a map, let alone come out in person. But, as always, this was for the sake of business, and sometimes business meant visiting a hellhole rad-waste that no sane person should ever choose to drive through.

Ernest had invested in an automated drug still out here years ago, as this desolate pit was so isolated that it was the perfect location to secretly create the first batch of an all-new recreational substance known as Blink. While most modern narcotics were bad news, Blink was in a class of its own, the kind of drug that even a hard core Krokodil user would politely refuse, the sort that would blast holes in your brain like firecrackers and turn you into a blithering imbecile. The true beauty of Blink was that repeat use would lead to an exponential tolerance in every case. So, although one hit of Blink would be so awesome that it would make you believe in Heaven itself, the second go would need two tabs...then your third time would require four to get the same effect...then eight...then sixteen...

Ernest smiled at the thought. He was an avid fan of hurting people, and if there was also some way to make money off the brutality, well, then the whole process was even sweeter. And while this first lab was only a small-scale beta-test leading up to the galaxy-wide horror Ernest and his many bank accounts had planned for all of humanity, this minor facility would be enough to ruin Los

Angeles within a matter of six months. Once the Blink addiction cycle had been proven to work as designed, there were many, many other worlds out there ready to be sucked dry.

Of course, such a scheme would be punishable by Death By Power Sander (perhaps even Death By Pigeon if you had a nasty enough prosecutor), so to the untrained eye it may make little sense why somebody as financially colossal as Ernest would bother risking a torturous end when his funds were bordering on basically unlimited. His wealth could really not be overstated: in his brief time in this galaxy, Ernest had packed multiple bank vaults solid with Amerikan pounds, Scandinavian lira, German yen, the freshly-harvested souls of virgins, blocks of freeze-dried stem cells, lead-skinned plutonium rods, vacuum-sealed antimatter spheres and a bunch of alien currencies that would send most people insane with one glance. However, simple currency ceased to have any real value to Ernest once he'd begun to crave something that was far more difficult to attain than money, and more valuable than anything else: Face.

Within the all-spanning underweb that connected together every godforsaken nest of human depravity, cash was nothing more than a by-product, something to be used for your groceries, or to tip your concierge when you had a holiday to the surface of the Sun. Money was something that literally anybody could get. For instance, there were countless heirs and heiresses out there who would inherit family fortunes they'd done did nothing to earn, that they didn't deserve, and would likely fritter away on sandpits made of cocaine and jewelled handbags for holding their teacup Chihuahuas. For crying out loud, any clot-headed sex-conceived reject could win the Lotto just by buying a ticket!

Money, while nice in its own way, was common. But Face...no, Face was a commodity unlike any other. It made The Spice look like stale oregano, the finest diamonds like Taiwanese plastic. Face was beyond mere cash, beyond trinkets and toys and paper. Face was an actual quantifiable measure of the exact level of respect Ernest had earned from his almost-as-evil peers. To outsiders, it may seem like nothing more than respect in a numerical form. But within the underweb that extended across the Galactic plane, it was the most important thing in life. Its worth went beyond anything a Black Accountant could tally up in their coded books of unspeakable horror. For Ernest, gaining just one extra point had resulted in weeks of parties so lavish and decadent that

Caligula himself would have winced and reached for the aspirin. Losing a point usually resulted in a number of unsolved gangland slayings.

Face was everything.

In his century-long drive to stockpile more Face than any other crime lord who'd ever lived, Ernest had become supremely feared by any outlaw who had more intelligence than a soft-boiled egg. After all, as common as money was, it sure could buy a lot of bullets. If somebody got a whiff that Ernest Fell had the slightest interest in a clandestine deal or had some personal opinion on gangland politics, every scofflaw within the state would flee without packing so much as a toothbrush first. Simply hearing Ernest's name had caused hardened thugs to soil themselves. His methods went beyond efficiency, beyond professionalism, and into the territory of pure evil and sickness. He was a monster among monsters.

Ernest placed his empty high-ball glass on a coaster, adjusted an exquisite Seladorian suit with slim, manicured hands, and looked towards the distant front of the Imperator. In a beautiful display of intuitive AI, the limo interpreted Ernest's body language into what he really wanted without needing him to say one word.

A holographic lightscreen faded into existence, and it displayed a face that resembled two badly-mortared bricks. It was the sort of face that broke fists, a countenance that caused lesser men to look intently at their shoes and keep walking as fast as they could in the opposite direction. It bared a row of even white teeth in a practised, professional smile. For some reason, his teeth were covered by a thin, transparent guard.

"Yessir, Mister Fell?" the driver gravelled.

"Jeeves, we are lagging," Ernest noted in a voice that had been cultured by the sounds of classical opera and automatic weapons. "My genitals cannot be expected to tolerate such radiation exposure indefinitely. I would prefer to be there and back again before my mutated sperm begin to fight an armed battle within my scrotum."

Jeeves expression didn't change in the slightest. He nodded curtly.

"Yessir, Mister Fell."

Amazingly, the driver's name actually was Jeeves (Jeeves Butler, if you checked his not-quite-legitimate birth certificate). The most popular theory behind the brute's name was that Jeeves' mother had foolishly hoped that this sort of nobby handle might put her son on the highway to success. Instead, the inevitable had happened, as the demand for limousine drivers named Jeeves has to be witnessed to be believed.

The zero-mass screen disappeared without a sound, and Jeeves resumed watching an eternity of dead sand pass soundlessly under the limousine. The Imperator left no trail, as its top-shelf (and not-quite-legal) antigrav wafers had been installed with the cross-my-heart-and-hope-to-die promise that they'd leave no trace. After all, the location of this Blink lab was meant to be a secret, and carving a fiery path that any banger could follow to the prize would kind of negate the "secret" part.

Grinding his mouth-guards together with a noise like flint being rasped against steel, more than two hundred kilograms of hired thug grasped the steering wheel so hard that its chromed steel warped beneath his fingers. Jeeves' arms tensed a little bit, and his tailored suit creaked under the strain of trying to hold back enough globular muscles to make up an entire WWF tag team match. Jeeves burped, and his breath made the steering wheel sizzle.

On the far horizon, through heat distortion so thick you could scoop it out of the air with your bare hands, a blob of orange corrosion appeared.

Almost there.

*

As this was a weekday, Jim Tuesday was sure to wake up at the crack of noon. Stretching his scrawny body into a slouch, Jim strapped on his loincloth – which had pockets for a few basic tools – and he proceeded to root around in one of the more recent garage piles until he found one of his home-made peyote cigarettes. As the cartons of fancy tailor-mades with suck-burner auto-ignition tips had run out over six months ago, Jim's trusty lighter was put to good use on the fag. Thanks to some petrol he'd scavenged from a buried fuel bowser, the lighter did its job admirably.

Coughing and spluttering as the foul smog further blackened a set of lungs that had more in common with the cave floor of a bat colony than biological air pumps, Jim smacked his gummy mouth together and wandered to get his daily dose of vitamin D. Jim stood in direct sunlight for precisely thirty seconds until he could hear his skin audibly bubble, then immediately took refuge away from nasty old Sol.

Jim rummaged in the shadows for a snack. To his fury, the missus and that bloody kid had demolished the rabbit and the weasel without bothering to wake him up.

Typical.

Examining a pile of old bones that a more imaginative mind may think resembled a secret graveyard of the very smallest pygmy elephants, Jim eventually found a juicy rat nose and happily crunched away on it. Jim may not be a connoisseur of anything that didn't cause a hangover, but he wondered how on Earth anybody could have thrown away such a delicacy.

Jim did a few pull-ups on one of the beams until he realised he wasn't fooling anybody, and once he'd rubbed the splinters from his hands he sat in the shade to observe his wasteland for a while. As usual, there was nothing to see: a few cacti, plenty of rocks, and the occasional two-headed scorpion were about it for today's not-quite-postcard-worthy panorama. There was also a bit of a dust storm on the far horizon, but that was probably...

Jim's head snapped around so fast that he jarred his neck. A dust storm! With flying sand and bits of airborne rock trying to carve his eyes out? Besides the very real dangers of the storm itself, every creature in this godforsaken desert would come running straight to his service station for cover!

Jim took five steps and went to perform a running leap into the closest dumpster, but something unfamiliar gave him pause. Non-defective people would describe it as "a conscience." Jim froze on the spot as he briefly considered trying to find the others to warn them about the incoming dervish. Like all rodents, Jim's first, second and third priorities were his flea-ridden hide, his flea-ridden hide, and his flea-ridden hide (in that order). So if Ruska and Bob didn't make it back in time and got flayed by a wall of razors, pah, it was their own fault. For more than nine bloody years now Jim had been a prisoner here, watching the sand roast and defrost in an endless cycle, wishing with every shred of his being that he could be somewhere – anywhere – else...

The what-if hypotheticals of the way Jim's life might have gone if he hadn't met

Ruska were the worst part. For instance, perhaps he may have beaten the odds and actually survived another Scumbag's tour, and this might have even meant engaging in lots of messed-up debauchery with groupies who wouldn't pass for carpet-people. Maybe, given the right breaks, Jim might have hit the big time by saving up enough wrinkled Amerikan pounds to buy an all-seasons pup tent and a padded sleeping bag. Or he might have even gotten into the formal property market and invested in his own shelf in a utility cupboard somewhere...

But no. Instead, all Jim had was this dump, his despised family and the nose hairs of a long-dead rat tickling his throat.

Jim had made his decision by the time the cloud had come within three hundred metres. He slipped into the dumpster, closed the lid, and cowered like the mutt he was.

He waited, listening intently in an attempt to gauge the storm's progress. Although Jim was sealed inside a metal skip, he could clearly tell that the dust flurry had come to a sudden halt outside. Jim wasn't the sort of idiot that would get fooled by the same thing six times in a row, so he continued to listen intently for the storm to start up again. After all, Jim assumed that he was in the calm eye of the storm. He'd heard about "the eye of the storm" at some big building full of very small people wearing identical uniforms that he used to attend as a kid, but Jim couldn't remember what the place had been called.

Scawl? Scrawl? Skewl? Something like that.

Standing up a little - just enough to poke his face out of the dumpster - Jim watched the biggest, blackest, shiniest Imperator-model limousine he'd ever seen as it gradually faded into existence from the heart of a thick, brown cloud of spraying grit and dust. Its glossy finish was showroom-perfect, despite just completing a trip through the Badlands.

With only his beady eyes poking from the dumpster, Jim watched and waited.

*

Jeeves stepped from the driver's door, and Ernest's limousine visibly tilted from the massive shift in weight. Stomping down the entire thirty-eight metre length of the ridiculously impressive luxury vehicle, Jeeves opened the rear door for his employer. Two red-carpeted steps unfolded and Ernest Fell emerged, wearing Venus-rated sunglasses and obviously not enjoying the weather. The size difference between Ernest and Jeeves was almost comical.

It had been years, but Ernest immediately knew something wasn't right. Scanning his lensed eyes over the "abandoned" service station, Ernest could see clear signs of habitation everywhere. For starters, the layers of festering garbage and corrosion had been carefully sorted into separate piles according to type: metal, plastic, wood, paper, and so on. In addition to this, there were another two large heaps. One was made up of thoroughly-picked bones of every size and shape, and the second was composed of pelts, skins and home-brew leather. On top of that, all the walls had all been decorated with primitive paintings of mutated animals in reds, browns and black. Ernest couldn't see any paint cans, so he assumed the designs had been done with the bodily fluids of some animal.

"We are not alone," Ernest growled.

Jeeves burped into his gloved hand. The black leather sizzled and smoked a little from the corrosive fumes. Ernest gave him a Look.

"Sorry, Mister Fell," Jeeves rumbled. "Acid."

Before he could say another word, Ruska came knuckling out of the heat distortion at full speed with Bob still clinging to her shoulder. She skidded to a halt at the sight of Jeeves, who was roughly her size. She shielded her small child from the strangers, looking at Jeeves with an odd expression. Although Bob was hidden behind his mum's leg, he did his best yokel impression by staring at the two men with his mouth hanging open.

"You not welcome here," Ruska snapped.

Ernest smiled. It was made of ice.

"An interesting order to give, seeing as though you are on my property." Ernest chided. "Now, tell all of your fellow squatters that you have exactly one minute to pack your things, otherwise..." The frosty smile returned. "Well, let's just say being evicted is the least of your worries at this point."

Still cowering in the dumpster, Jim held his breath as Jeeves drew a tiny, tiny kinetic accelerator pistol. Jim couldn't muster enough courage to do anything more than silently watch things unfold, even though the accelerator pistol was smaller than a child's cap-gun.

Ruska reared up to her full height. The weapon didn't intimidate her in the slightest.

"Is our home."

Ruska's words hung in the air like a bad smell. Nobody moved, blinked or breathed for a few silent seconds. Finally, Ernest nodded wearily at Jeeves. The massive man calmly turned off both safeties with one flick, but he didn't bother raising the weapon in threat. After all, Jeeves followed the most basic tenant of gun use: don't point a pistol at anything unless you intend for it to die.

Ruska sniffed at Jeeves from ten metres away. She had a weird look on her face, as though deep in thought.

"I know you." Ruska hissed. "I know your smell."

Jeeves' expression didn't change. He blinked.

"I believe you are mistaken, Miss." Jeeves finally said, scanning his eyes up and down Ruska's thick pelt. "I would have great difficulty in forgetting you."

Unable to hold his breath any longer, Jim picked this moment to exhale noisily. Ernest's head snapped around to regard the dumpster, and the crime lord raised a thin, manicured eyebrow. Producing a small item from the pocket of his double-breasted jacket which appeared to be no larger than a packet of cigarettes, the box unfolded into a weapon that had more in common with a minigun than a cap pistol. It whined in activation and little lights flickered on.

"Safety off," the gun chirped.

"Come out, please," Ernest requested calmly, looking down the sights.

Pushing up the dented metal lid with his equally dented head, Jim held up both hands as he slowly got out of the dumpster. Thanks to the fact he was clumsy at the best of times, Jim tripped over the cusp and sprawled in the sand. Dozens of colourful pills spilled over the glassed earth from his loin skin pockets.

Ernest froze. He recognised the Blink tabs straight away and gaped like an imbecile at the thought of what their presence meant. Whipping his head back towards the service station, Ernest finally noticed that the trap door to his automated drug lab was yawning wide open. In shock, Ernest had to hold onto the door of his limousine for a moment.

"They got in!" Ernest choked.

Grinning hopelessly from the ground, Jim remembered how to put two and two together and came up with the best answer he could at such short notice.

"We, uh, saved some of your stash."

Ernest's temples began to visibly throb. Veins popped out over his forehead and neck, and his skin turned lava-red. Ernest's eyes opened so wide that it was a wonder they didn't simply fall out of their sockets.

Jim guessed that the guy was mad.

"How much have you stolen?" Ernest whispered. His voice was like a blade running across bone.

"Uh..." Jim managed.

"How much?"

Jim sighed.

"Roughly...all of it."

Ernest lost all colour. He was beyond angry, beyond insulted. He twitched a little. That enormous gun hung limply from his fingers.

"Okay," Jim said quietly, trying to sound placating. "Okay, look, I'm sorry, all right? I kinda thought it was weird that somebody would leave such primo gear out here, but..."

Jim's words ended on a cliff-hanger, for Ruska chose that moment to bellow and run for Jeeves with both her thick ape arms raised for war. Turning, Jeeves smoothly caught both her meaty paws with his own, dropping his accelerator pistol in the process, and the two equally-matched titans began to wrestle. Gritting their teeth and growling like animals, Ruska and Jeeves pushed against each other with all their might, fighting for supremacy. Soon, Jeeves glowed scarlet with exertion. Lines of sweat carved down his slab of a head, and after a few more seconds Ruska finally began to get the upper hand. For a moment, it seemed like Ruska was going to drive Jeeves all the way down to the ground and crush him like a sparrow egg, but then the hired thug did something unexpected: he gave up.

Jeeves fell suddenly and deliberately to the sand, causing Ruska to overbalance. With a flick of his mighty legs, Jeeves slammed Ruska face-first into the glossy black paintwork of the limousine with all his strength. Faking one way before rolling in the other direction just in case Ruska wasn't as stunned as he hoped, Jeeves snatched up his lost pistol, tumbled to his feet in a way no man of his size should be able to, and prepared to pop Ruska in the back of her skull. However, the moment Ernest had a clear line of sight on Ruska he opened up without hesitation.

For Bob and Jim, the entire Universe stopped.

Ernest, a man who was as thorough by nature as he was cruel, calmly offloaded an entire clip into Ruska's prone body in a cordite-scented tornado of smoke and fire, and he continued to blast away until his unfolding kinetic carbine helpfully chirped, "Your ammunition has been depleted, Mister Fell. Please reload me at your convenience."

Stepping over the splattered mess, Ernest checked where Ruska's head had slammed into his limo during her final fall: nope, not a scratch. Good paint. Very good paint. Worth every penny.

Stunned beyond the point of rational fear, Bob sprinted over to his dead mother's body and screamed and shouted as he tried to make her get up, to shake her awake. Ignoring the shrieking of the small boy, Jeeves calmly turned to regard Jim. The thug raised his comically small pistol at Jim's stupid expression and called over his shoulder to Ernest.

"Kill them, too, Mister Fell?" Jeeves asked. The thug said it so casually that you'd think he was asking if a passing cloud looked more like a pony or a clown.

Jim's eyes remained fixed on the barrel of that tiny, tiny gun. He was well aware that even the smallest kinetic accelerator pistols could splatter you all over the room with a single shot, and this one looked illegally modified. For a time, the silence was somehow worse than simply copping a round in the face and getting it over with.

Ernest finally managed to regain his powers of speech at this point and looked down at Jim as though regarding a rodent who had crapped on his kitchen floor.

"Look at him," Ernest growled, narrowing his eyes. "Life is far crueller than a bullet could ever be. Beyond revenge, there is no value in killing him." Ernest blinked, regarding Jim in a mathematical way. "There's no Face value in stepping on bugs, is there?"

Jeeves nodded and holstered his weapon. Bob was still screaming in the background, clutching his mum.

"I'm taking Mister Fell home now." Jeeves explained to Jim just in case he was as stupid as he appeared. "Do anything comical and you both go the way of the monkey, understand?"

Jim stuttered and slurred for a few seconds, dribbling, but nothing coherent came out. His eyes flicked from Ruska to Jeeves, Jeeves to Bob, Bob to Ruska and so on, unable to process the scene for far too long. He finally spoke.

"Wait!"

Jeeves looked at Jim like he was some special kind of moron. Ernest tilted his head in confusion, amazed at the sheer lack of intelligence he was witnessing. It was borderline hilarious.

"Yes?" Jeeves asked slowly.

"You carn't just leave me here!" Jim wailed. "Or me son! Me kid! The boy won't last a week without his mum!"

Before Ernest could explain how amazingly little he cared about the issue of Jim's life and/or the life of his son, a blur slammed into Jeeves' tank-like chest and a pair of things that were equally orange and sharp bit into Jeeves' face at high speeds. Bob repeatedly swung his hook and cleaver against the thick head as hard as he could, but within half a dozen strikes the weapons had exploded into a shower of rust. Furious beyond words, the wild boy immediately latched onto Jeeves' nose with all of his baby teeth and attempted to bite it off.

One of Bob's canines broke away on impact. It was like trying to chew through marble.

Although surprised for an instant, Jeeves quickly grabbed a handful of Bob's filthy hair. Despite just having his face panel-beaten with weapons, Jeeves didn't have a mark to show for it. It was as though the thug's skin was bulletproof or something.

Jeeves held Bob up to the sky by effortlessly straightening his arm and didn't as much as flinch when the small child tried to bite off his thumb. Yet again, Bob found that Jeeves' skin was like living rock, and couldn't break through it no matter how hard he tried.

"I reckon he can look after himself just fine," Jeeves noted calmly.

"Now," Ernest said slowly, looking from Bob to Jim and savouring the moment. "I am a fair man, and I understand that it's very likely you have little in the way of...resources." Ernest blinked slowly, like a lizard. "So, although I'm not going to kill either of you, you are going to pay back what you owe."

"I don't have nuthin," Jim sulked.

Ernest sighed in frustration.

"Yes, that is what I just spelled out. However, despite what you may think, you actually have something of value, a single treasure that may serve to repay your considerable debt. This one thing stands directly between your life continuing, and having your organs sold to the highest bidder."

Jeeves didn't need any further prompt. He carried Bob to the back of the limo, popped a generous trunk, and threw the nine-year-old into it like so much luggage. Jeeves adjusted his tie and regarded Jim before getting back in the driver's seat.

"Have a nice day, sir."

All of the open black doors scissored back into place, Jeeves revved the antigrav wafers with a whine, and Ernest's limousine flew away at top velocity. Glass and rocks sprayed in their wake, pelting Jim as he helplessly ran after the speeding limo, tripping and falling pathetically in the slipstream within a hundred staggering metres.

With unexpected tears now coursing through the dust on his face, Jim began to wail in agony. Snot strings mingled with the ropes of saliva gushing from his mouth, and Jim lay with his face on the ground as though praying to Mecca. Jim collapsed, his shoulders fell, and he died a little inside.

*

Night rose high in the sky like a black cat arching its back. Jim slowly continued to drudge his way through the Badlands and salt plains of the monochrome desert, holding the raw, painful stump that used to be his left ring finger.

Eventually, the deep purple of midnight transitioned into the muddy pastels of dawn, and still Jim continued to drag his feet one after another, his tongue and the roof of his mouth rubbing like pieces of sandpaper.

All Jim could do was concentrate on getting slightly closer to the next endless dune, hoping against hope that he'd see a glimmer of the neon skyline of outer Vegas, which could be anywhere from ten to a hundred kilometres away.

He had a long, long way to go.

Ruska's death had brought things into perspective for the first time. Rather than feeling set free by yesterday's events (as Jim would have expected), losing his little family had instilled a new, powerful drive in place of his usual self-destructive misery: he had to find Bob, his son, a child he'd never wanted for a single minute before this point, and he needed to do it at any cost, even if it took forever and cost him his very soul.

Jim swore, spitting on the dunes in distaste, that he would find his son. He would find Bob.

"And where's my lighter?" Jim screamed at the uncaring sky.

CHAPTER FOUR CELL BLOCK PRESCHOOL

Bob lay curled up in the limousine's dark boot - silent, alone, and in shock - for what seemed like hours. Although his prison was the trunk of a car, the ride was so smooth and silent that it was hard to tell if the limo was even moving, and the carpeted area was plusher than the finest moleskins. Of course, Bob's mind was busy with something else entirely: mentally replaying the death of his mum, over and over, on an eternal loop. This horror was occasionally broken up with one question: where were they taking him?

Bob soon got sick of being miserable in the dark, so it was lucky he'd filched his dad's lighter when nobody was watching. Bob had inherited a defective neurological condition from his dad that was officially classed as 8CFG9, though this trait was more commonly known as "having sticky fingers" or simply "being a thieving git." So, the moment Bob had seen the shiny silver treasure lying in the sand, he'd pinched it. If it wasn't for the chaos that had followed, Jim Tuesday would doubtlessly have retrieved the lighter and given Bob a clip on the ear for his trouble.

Bob flicked at the bulky metal lighter until it ignited with a whoompf of gas. However, all that the flickering light managed to reveal were ghostly silhouettes. Glaring at the useless lighter and sighing in frustration, Bob noticed for the first time that the underside of the lighter was stamped with a tiny logo that said TRANCE. Squinting at the word, Bob had the strange feeling that he was forgetting something, a single fact that was very, very important. What was it about the word TRANCE that he was supposed to know? Why was that word triggering something? What could it possibly...

The lighter was absolutely scalding all of a sudden. Dropping the hot metal box with a creative curse, Bob slapped it to the other side of the boot. Second degree burns proved to be a good way to break his chain of thought, and Bob didn't think anything more about TRANCE for now.

Bored senseless within minutes, Bob decided to feel around the boot to see if there was anything worth pinching. Thankfully, after a handful of seconds he accidentally knocked a touch-pad on the low roof, and a ring of oyster lights filled the whole area with a sodium glow. Bob could now clearly see the trunk was half filled with boxes that resembled the Military surplus crates in his dad's basement. While the majority of the boxes were sealed solid behind high-tech card readers and deadbolts, Bob finally managed to pop an unlocked yellow crate that contained spare parts for the flying limo. Seeing as though the vehicle was suspended on antigrav wafers, Bob was confused to see that the crate was filled by a dozen rubber tyres, a stack of hubcaps and a pair of tire irons, but it made sense that the limo was capable of being equipped with wheels for emergencies. After all, you wouldn't cut off an eagle's legs, would you?

Bob noticed a burlap sack had been ditched in the corner. Digging into it, he discovered a shovel caked with clay and a bag of ultra-lime. Putting two and two together and getting fifteen, Bob screamed hysterically in panic. Many of his dad's darker gangster stories had involved the combination of a shovel followed by a heavy coating of lime, and Bob was suddenly certain that he was about to (as Jim had put it) "sleep with the fishes." He couldn't understand what he'd done to deserve such an end. None of this was his fault! His only crime was being born a Tuesday.

Bob eventually calmed down by using the novel concept of thinking the situation through. He reasoned that if somebody wanted to dissolve his remains in a shallow grave, then it would have made a lot more sense for them to do it in the middle of nowhere...which is where all of this had started. Nice and neat.

Taking him somewhere else for the whole murder-and-burial thing was a needless complication. This was mildly reassuring.

Bob continued searching between the locked crates, chewing his bottom lip in the process.

Jerry can…baseball bat with sticky stuff on it… …toolkit filled with drill parts…still no spare key ring…maybe…

Bob blinked and reviewed his thoughts.

Wait...a drill?

Bob was unexpectedly thrown to the other side of the boot by a violent swerve, a hallmark of modern inner-city traffic, and had to crawl back to the power tools. He didn't know it, but this was the first time Bob had been in Old Vegas since he was an hour-old fertilised egg.

Searching through the yellow hardcase, Bob soon discovered a big, expensive-looking drill tip buried under a lot of cheaper ones. Although he didn't recognise what its glittering holographic D logo signified, this sigil meant that the thin cylinder was made out of a synthetic carbon-based mineral called Densite, a material so tough and sharp that it made the best diamonds look like wet chalk. Just like his dad, Bob could tell on sight if something was valuable, even if he had no exact idea why.

Although Bob's plan with the drill was obvious (pop the lock and escape), its battery pack was stone flat, as were both spares. This meant all Bob could do with the Densite-tipped bit was to try and use it to cut through the keyhole by hand. After spending ages trying to get through the mechanism without any luck, Bob understandably had to stop and rest for a while, but a second session of painful twisting and cutting was soon rewarded with...nothing.

Okay. It seemed the lock was also made out of Densite, or something even tougher. Great.

Changing tactics, Bob did his best to carve through the boot itself, rather than focussing on the tough lock. He cut into the steel shell until a bright pinprick of light finally stabbed into the trunk. Blinking away the strobe effect until he got used to it, Bob put his eye to the hole to see that the limo was cruising through a place that lined up exactly with his dad's description of Old Vegas. Bob knew it as a hub of gambling, drugs, prostitution, racketeering, parties, concrete shoes, hitmen and two-pound lunch specials. He was denied these charming sights and sensations a couple of seconds later when the limousine tilted and disappeared into darkness.

Knowing that it may already be too late, Bob frantically tried to grind a second peephole with the Densite-tipped bit. He managed to cut through the boot quicker than the first time, but all this accomplished was the cumulative effect of nothing plus nothing equalling nothing...or, more precisely, a second tiny hole that only served to mock his efforts at escape.

Bob heard and felt the slam of a car door. Knowing that those gangsters might be coming to check on him in a matter of moments, Bob thought it wise to hide the largest drill bit in the wild depths of his salt-and-pepper hair and put everything else back where it belonged. Quickly replacing all the smaller drill tips and the useless power tool itself back into the yellow clamshell kit and turning off the oyster lights, Bob curled into a ball and waited.

But nobody came.

After ten still, silent minutes, Bob had just started to drift off when his attempts at a nap were interrupted by a tremendous force kneading his whole body like giant fingers in raw cookie dough. It was almost as bad as a half-strength cuddle from his mum. Bob was flattened out against the padded interior of the boot, screeching with all the power his nine-year-old lungs could manage, but within thirty seconds the pressure stopped and he experienced the effects of deceleration far, far above the Earth's surface for the first time, followed shortly by freefall. Floating about in a dark trunk full of tools and crates wasn't the best way to enjoy zero gravity, and Bob spent quite a bit of time engaging in his favourite hobby: forming highly offensive strings of insults. In this case, his expletives were directed towards space travel, astronauts, planets, stars, and pretty much all of the galaxy. This foulness was best lost to the deafness of the cosmos.

Soon, as the unseen courier ship performed a sharp turn towards a planet located nineteen stars to the left of Earth, Bob had finally fallen asleep with a thumb in his mouth and a drill bit behind his ear.

*

Although slavery had been universally abolished on all civilised worlds within Unison space hundreds of years ago, few human-colonised planets in the 24th Century could be accurately described as "civilised" with a straight face.

One particularly scrawny planet, a black not-quite-terraformed orb known on most stellar maps as The Dream Factory, fell so far beneath humanity's low standards that its official status in The Unison's databases was Utterly Deserving Of An Imminent Nuclear Holocaust. However, even this didn't properly spell out its hellishness.

Far from the joyous wonderland its name may have implied, The Dream Factory was nothing more than a planet wide labyrinth of grey manufacturing lines that all eventually intersected at warehouses the size of Hawaiian Islands. Towering pallets of goods were then relayed from storage to whatever docks were closest. Although primarily dedicated to manufacturing, storage and shipping, all of The Dream Factory's few survivable zones were packed solid with hundreds of thousands of workers who were forced to drudge in this bleak nightmare, and these unfortunates were crammed into any gap they could claim as their own. As a result, decaying slums, leaning shacks, huts made out of fibreglass sheeting and worse had sprung up amidst the concrete, rust and razor wire fences.

If you're wondering why anybody would live in this purgatory, it's because The Dream Factory was staffed almost exclusively by slaves. And as adult slaves were usually too much trouble - what with all the riots, bad language and other non-productive behaviour – some bright spark had figured out that children were more easily-managed as indentured servants. After all, kids ate less, needed smaller clothes and tinier living quarters, and were less likely to throw cups of boiled piss on the guards. Despite this, The Dream Factory got more than they expected with their newest admission, because if you could say one thing for Bob, it's this: he came out fighting.

The very moment that Jeeves popped the trunk, two cross-shaped tire irons went spinning past the thug's ears like oversized ninja stars. Bob – dressed in nothing but his loincloth and moleskin shoes - followed right behind the projectiles with a lug wrench in his tiny hands. Not stupid enough to pick a second fight with somebody who had bulletproof skin and bigger arms than his mum, Bob ducked under Jeeves' armpit and surprised the first wave of armoured kiddie guards with a feral scream. To be fair, these particular screws were barely in their teens at best and were unanimously underfed and under-trained.

Bob jammed the blunt tip of his lug wrench into the crotch protector of the first kid dumb enough to try and grab him, ducked a couple of clumsy batons, and stomped a second guard right on his toes. A child soldier managed to grab Bob by his nose, but quickly let go once a bloodied chunk was bitten out of his wrist. Bob head-butted the screaming, bleeding guard with a clop noise, rolled sideways like a commando as four more leapt for him, missing by centimetres, and turned to swing his lug wrench as hard as he could at whoever else had decided to get in his way. Unfortunately for Bob, his random swing slammed Jeeves in his knee - which might as well have been a paving stone - and a massive shockwave rattled through Bob's hands. Screaming in surprise as bolts of pain arced from fingertips to shoulders, Bob dropped the weapon like it was hot.

Jeeves wasn't so much as bruised.

A dozen guards tackled Bob like a pee-wee gridiron team sacking the quarterback, knocking him to the mesh floor, and everything went black for a moment when Bob's temple hit the ground with great force. Still trying to scrabble and weave despite the darkness, rolling about like his mum had taught him, Bob made it as hard as possible for the guards to grab a hold of anything.

But he'd already lost. He just didn't realise it yet.

By the time Bob's sense of vision dribbled back into his concussed head, the teen guards had managed to get a good hold on the wild boy's limbs and weren't going to let go no matter what. Bob slammed his elbows, knees and forehead into the crowd as they tightened their grip, but soon he was officially overpowered and wrestled into submission.

One mongrel rested his knee on Bob's bruised temple, sending a lance of pain through Bob's skull. His line of sight now fell directly on the two gangsters who had brought him here. Ernest Fell was smiling at this scene, obviously amused by the battle, but Jeeves was watching with a neutral expression. He didn't seem to take any joy from what was going on.

Bob pictured them hanging from the ceiling by their own intestines. He grinned at the image.

Bob's hands and feet were strapped with leather restraints and he was rolled onto his back. At this point, with his face pointing towards a black moon, Bob finally got a good view of his new home, and he could hear it, too. Above the sound of his own heavy breathing, Bob could register the din of a million children yelling and roaring their approval from far, far in the sky, and he looked through the mesh of arms and legs that were holding him down like a cage made of flesh. Beyond closely-packed steel bars and layers of security fencing made from razor wire and electrified monofilaments, a bland sequence of mouldy concrete cells towered far into the dark sky just short of forever. To Bob's untrained eyes, they verged on infinite. Looming higher and higher until their peaks were literally lost in the cloud cover of early morning fog, the millions of flickering maws that made up Cell Block Preschool said hello to Bob with the sound of countless child slaves having an awesome time.

Bob was backhanded across the face.

"You little punk!" a teen guard squeaked, careful to guard his language. He'd learned from a young age not to swear in front of his superiors...even when some half-savage cave child bit him on the wrist, apparently.

Bob was dragged to his feet. Doing all he could to keep his loincloth where it belonged, Bob glared up at Jeeves Butler and Ernest Fell as they came closer.

"Welcome to your forever home." Ernest said in a sing-song way that would scare most people senseless. He smiled with too much in the way of bleached white and too little in the way of a soul. "Just so you understand the arrangement, you are here to pay off the debt that those...those things owe me in the only way that you can: through the indentured coercive labour of a minor in a state-run facility. Of course, this particular state seceded from The Unison's regime years ago and poses an ongoing danger to our entire species due to its involvement with every form of criminal activity you could name, but, on the upside...well, they make the best soft toys. Do you like toys?"

Bob didn't like where this was going. He could hardly understand a thing that this weird little thin man was saying, but Bob knew for sure that he was now a prisoner on a rock far, far away from home.

Ernest playfully offered Bob a large, plush Mister Drizzle stuffed toy. Despite the fact that Mister Drizzle was one of FunCo's most popular characters, every one of his cartoons was loaded to the brim with unpalatable homophobic racism, and the character had been blamed for quite a few high-profile hate crimes. After never seeing such a beautiful toy in real life, Bob leaned towards the plushie...

Ernest snatched Mister Drizzle away in the same gesture. Bob watched in horror as Ernest slowly tore the toy open along its seams, popping each stitch one at a time. Stuffing erupted in all directions with a flick. Synthetic cotton wool drifted to the mesh floor like manufactured snow.

"Now, you will do as the nice boys say from now on," Ernest suggested quietly, dangerously. "We all need to learn our place...especially you."

"Do what they say?" Bob snarled, preparing to vomit out the corrosive verbal bile he'd learned from tens of thousands of hours of offensive television programming. "But they smell like somebody scooped a rancid wad of scrotum cheese out of a syphilitic monkey's bum."

Bob sniffed loudly at the guard holding his straps and made a disgusted face to highlight his point. TV had obviously taught Bob well, and his advanced grasp of offensive language would doubtlessly have many more victims before the day was out. However, it was clear that Bob couldn't be allowed to show such vulgar defiance in a facility with enormous MIND YOUR LANGUAGE signs all over the place, so a teen guard raised his baton, ready to scramble some eggs. Bob simply shrugged in a bored and dismissive way.

"Why are you getting upset? It's Porko McBumhole over there who stinks."

The young thug dissolved into laughter so violent that he almost dropped his baton, and all the others joined in too...besides the target of the jibe. Nudging the smelly, embarrassed teen guard and holding their noses in mock disgust, it was obvious that this was just their kind of humour.

"You know what, kid? You're perceptive for an inbred Neanderthal." The biggest teen guard rumbled, getting right in Bob's face. "But you know what happens to cavemen who like mouthing off at the security staff?"

"They lose five chromosomes and mutate into a muscle-bound scum-smear like you?" Bob replied sweetly.

Bob didn't even see the baton swing. Everything just went black.

*

Bob Tuesday woke up at the crack of dawn to an electronic rooster screeching from a rusty speaker so old that it must have been crafted by Abraham himself. Feeling very lost thanks to a winning combination of severe concussion and whatever insane level of jetlag you got from hopping across nineteen star systems (starlag?), Bob looked around at his coffin-sized concrete cell. It only took one blink to do the entire royal tour: it was made of moss-spotted concrete and had heavy-duty bars on the front. The entire floor was a padded mattress. There was a bucket in the corner that was half-filled with caustic, sewage-disintegrating chemicals and a roll of toilet paper so thin that it was almost theoretical. Tour complete.

There was a metallic clunk and the bars retracted into concrete with a vicious grinding noise. Somehow managing to stand on his first attempt, Bob could immediately tell that he wasn't in any shape to have another rumble with the entire security team, so he placidly took his place with all of the other inmates in the corridor. Bob was able to tell with one glance that none of the other inmates in this stretch were older than ten, and their clothes seemed to be a random assortment from at least a dozen worlds. Despite the irregularity of what they were wearing, Bob's loincloth and crude moccasins were the most out of place and drew the most attention. From their puffy eyes and lost expressions it was pretty obvious that these kids were all new arrivals like him. It seemed child slavery was big business.

A bunch of armoured teen guards (including the fat one who smelled like rancid monkey cheese) immediately hustled Bob and the other new admissions across Cell Block Preschool with baton swings and raised voices. The new fish were all rushed into Orientation and ordered to sit down on plastic lawn chairs. As with the rest of The Dream Factory, the interior decorator of Orientation must have had a thing for stained, mossy concrete and rust-orange metal.

A projector that must have been four hundred years old rattled to life and began to spit static onto a white screen. For a moment, Bob was overjoyed. A TV! Of course, that joy turned to horror as the arch-nemesis of all small children who were expecting cartoons reared its ugly head: an Infomercial.

Every kid groaned as they all realised the same thing at the same moment. Tricked!

Bob spent the next hour and fifteen minutes of his life watching what must have been the most boring movie ever made in the history of mankind. It was narrated by Mister Drizzle himself in all his bright purple animated glory, which was a plus, but unfortunately the flick turned out to be about the history and business practices of The Dream Factory. Bob learned that this planet wide sweatshop manufactured the very best old-fashioned toys for children who were far luckier and more valuable than any indentured worker could ever hope to be. Also, it turned out that The Dream Factory had managed to keep the prices of its superior products at less than half that of their closest competitors thanks to the hard work of its child workforce. Bob and the other kids were also clearly informed of what it meant to be indentured servants for the rest of their natural lives and potentially beyond, including the (surprisingly few) rules and the terminal ramifications if you did something that was unforgivable. Some of the major breaches that wouldn't be tolerated included trying to make contact with the outside Universe, any attempt at escaping, any instances of squiffing that hadn't been officially sanctioned by the Warden, and one or two other concepts that were so bent that Bob couldn't comprehend them at such a young age.

As Bob had already reached the understanding that he was totally boned the moment he woke up in a cell, he chose to sleep through the rest of the flick. Just as the movie was wrapping up and the credits started to roll, Bob's fine sense of hearing picked up a familiar ticky-ticky-ticky sound coming from a few metres away. His eyes snapped open and within a second they'd locked onto some sort of bug he'd never seen before. Reacting with instincts honed by a life of hunger and desperation, Bob leapt from his chair, snapped up a fat striped insect the size of a matchbox, scurried into a dark corner and crunched it into paste head-first with a big smile.

All the small children screamed and retched. So did some of the guards.

With some help from the cheerful application of a stun rod, Bob was "encouraged" to get up and lead the way into the next room. This large area was a wet, sagging mess of shelves that had been collapsing into each other for so long that they resembled an Escher painting, and they were all filled with precisely two kinds of apparel: grey coveralls and plastic crocs. As you'd expect, everything was too large or too small by about six sizes.

It took a few zaps and ear flicks, but eventually all the kids had stripped off their street clothes, placed their old duds in a large plastic barrel and shrugged on the only clothing they'd ever wear from now on. Slipping on the first synthetic fibres he'd ever worn, Bob only had a moment to wonder what sort of animal you had to skin to get this "plastic" stuff before he and all the other under-tens were rushed back into a massive common area outside their cells. They milled about aimlessly, apparently free to do nothing for a while. Some cried. Others scratched at their itchy coveralls.

Feeling that somebody was watching him, Bob looked up, ready for a fight, but it was just some scrawny kid. Most of the stranger's face was hidden behind thick glasses, his mouth was gaping slightly open in a way that didn't exactly scream "intelligence," and his hair was redder than a sunburnt lobster.

"What?" Bob snapped after another few seconds, feeling paranoid.

"You're the one what gave the guards a fright last night, what?" the kid asked with a surprisingly posh accent.

"Yeah. Cos I'm the bogeyman," Bob sneered.

A few other children looked over. There was nothing more entertaining to do.

"Why is your hair like that?" a larger child asked. This one was head and shoulders above the others, and Bob was having trouble believing he was younger than ten.

There were a few zaps and yelps from the back of the crowd, and the crowd of kids started to move. Many of the child slaves were now looking at Bob's head of hair, which resembled a greasy wild sheep after an abundant spring.

"I grew up in the desert." Bob snapped. "I never had no hairdresser in the desert, or shampoo, or nuthin. Just roaches big as your fist and plenty of juicy moles to eat."

Bob felt a pang of sadness, already missing his simple life out in the sticks. And then that image was back: Ernest Fell pumping round after round into his mum's back...

"They shot my Ma and left my Da behind to die. I'll find them. And I'll get them rotten."

The much larger kid nodded, and so did a few of the others. It seemed that Bob's recent loss was something they could all identify with.

"What's your name, man?" the big kid asked.

"Bob Tuesday."

"Bob Tuesday?" the larger kid grinned stupidly. "What kind of idiot name is that?"

Bob stopped walking and tilted his chin up in a hostile way. He'd seen enough jail movies to know that this was the sort of situation where he needed to act decisively, even though he couldn't spell "decisively," let alone define it. Other kids were looking over at the scene now but were still moving quickly enough to avoid a shocking. Guards were watching from raised balconies with stun rifles ready. They knew the signs to watch for.

"Boo hoo. Don't like it? Then piss off, spughead."

The brute bridged up. Bob believed that no ten-year-old should have muscles like that.

"What did you say?" the brute growled very, very softly, leaning in close and baring his teeth. "Come again, midget?"

"Didn't understand me the first time?" Bob smiled, getting on his tiptoes so he could get in the kid's face. "Then maybe you should take your dumb ass home, spend a couple of hours figuring it all out, and then cry yourself to sleep like the sad housewife you are. Right?"

The big kid's anger slowly transitioned to confusion, then eventually to amusement. A big grin broke out on his face.

"You got guts, Tuesday. I'm Brian."

"Bob," he corrected. "Call me Bob."

As any chance of a fight had evaporated, the guards pushed and prodded their prisoners towards the next stop.

"I saw Tuesday when he came in last night!" the redhead butted in, trying to score points. "He went all the guards at once like a total loony. It was magic."

"Shut it, you ginger-headed saffron-scented raspberry-flavoured ranga!" One of the teen guards barked skilfully, extending his shock baton. "Badmouth the guards again and see what happens!"

"Leave him alone." Bob sulked.

The guard simply pointed a gloved finger at him in warning.

"You better watch yourself, Tuesday."

And that was the end of it. The name had officially stuck from then on. In a matter of moments, Bob had died and Tuesday was born in his place.

"Where are we going?" Tuesday grumbled.

*

It was a hell worse than he could have imagined: a barbershop.

Tuesday loved his salt-and-pepper locks as much as his arms and legs, but having more than a third of an inch of hair in Cell Block Preschool meant that catching an infestation of paralysis lice was just a matter of when rather than if. This is why it was standard policy to shave all the newcomers bald on arrival and then buzz them again on the 33rd of each month.

Tuesday didn't take the news well.

Although the poor hairdresser shrieked like a pre-teen girl at a boy band concert when Tuesday used his teeth and dirty fingernails to show his distaste for a shaved head, Tuesday's crown of hair was eventually separated from his scalp with a blunt pair of clippers.

Tuesday cried for hours. But life went on.

CHAPTER FIVE WORK, WORK, WORK

Tuesday's career began less than an hour after his first haircut. His field of expertise had been selected for him by some hugely fat dude who'd simply rolled a die with twenty sides - the sort that you got in D n' D starter packs - and noted the results on a spreadsheet on a clunky old computer. An adult may have wondered who the nerd had slept with to get a sweet job like that.

Tuesday's assigned task, one that he would be performing for the rest of his natural life, was to sweep up any loose stuffing, sawdust, fabric, thread, buttons and googly eyes that had been expelled from the numerous assembly machines of Manufacturing Area Forty-Five, separate the materials into piles, and jam everything back into the correct chutes and hoppers. It's worth noting that MA45 was the size of a football stadium, meaning that it took Tuesday a solid week to do a proper lap. He did this ten hours a day, seven days a week, month after month, year after year.

Any moron could instantly understand that being an indentured employee in a place like The Dream Factory was dull drudgery of the highest order, the sort of thing that even a robot wouldn't do, but Tuesday had an ace up his sleeve, a primo tactic that stopped him going insane from monotony: it was a fine balance, but after a little practise Tuesday eventually figured out how to do almost no work without ever getting caught. It was as though avoiding manual labour was yet another sort of innate skill he'd inherited from his dad, a trait that would make all of Darwin's clones spin in their graves.

Tuesday now had one official possession: his broom. Tuesday loved his broom. It was a top-of-the-line synthetic ash-handled Sweepomatic headed by magnetised static fibres for maximum hold and strength, and it had an adjustable range of shapes and sweeping styles. It was the sort of broom that was designed to last a lifetime. It was highly likely that Tuesday wasn't its first owner, and the Sweepomatic would probably still be faithfully serving The Dream Factory long after he was dead.

Tuesday went everywhere with his broom. He ate next to it, cuddled it as he slept, and even went to the bathroom with it well within reach. Occasionally, the broom even fought by his side, and had been responsible for more than one concussion. Tuesday and the broom were inseparable.

Honestly, beyond the monotony and occasional stabbings, things turned out to be pretty good at The Dream Factory. Tuesday was far better fed than he'd ever been in the desert, the other kids didn't give him any trouble he couldn't handle, there was free medicine if you got sick (good luck missing a shift for anything short of four simultaneous limb amputations, though), and the slaves even got a few Amerikan pounds of pocket money to spend on luxuries each week.

It wasn't long before Tuesday discovered the concept of gambling. It turned out that Tuesday liked to gamble. He liked it a lot. However, it soon became apparent to Tuesday that gambling was a stupid thing to be involved in unless you were the one running the games. He'd heard his dad use the term "house always wins" since the cradle.

Tuesday's plans didn't work out straight away. After all, we're talking about the offspring of Jim Tuesday here. Tuesday's first small attempt at a gambling racket went alright for a while, but it was hard to find live roosters anywhere on this rotten planet, and business soon dried up. So, by the time he was eleven, Tuesday branched out from cock fights to a human fight club. If there was something in abundance around here, it was humans and their knobbly little fists. As the participants were all pre-teens and would usually start to cry after the first punch, though, Tuesday had to rethink his plans yet again.

Finally, when he was twelve, Tuesday came up with the most brilliant idea of his life: stealing stuff. It was a logical step, as the screws had a lot of pinchable perks that your standard pre-teen employee didn't have and couldn't afford, such as cigarettes, MacDeath burgers in self-heating cartons, proper soap and sweet, blessed, fresh underpants, and it was easy enough for a scrawny rodent like Tuesday to scurry around in the greasy ventilation shafts and swipe things. Tuesday always took just enough to fill his belly and sate his nicotine cravings before selling whatever was left without attracting attention. He had no shortage of customers, of course, and Tuesday was happy to receive everyone's allowance of Amerikan pounds each week. He refused to accept German yen or Scandinavian lira pretty quick, however, as both of these currencies had nosedived so badly that the paper they were printed on was worth a hundred times more if it was left blank. At the very worst point, crude photocopies of the German yen were worth more than the real thing, and the property prices of any neighbourhood across the Known Galaxy went down by ten percent if anybody said the words "Scandinavian lira" out loud.

Although Tuesday was never caught for any of this pettiness, the final straw occurred when he foolishly filched an entire deep-fried elephant turkey from the staff kitchen. This near-extinct bird was so big and heavy that Tuesday needed assistance from the redhead in the cell next door just to get it all the way back, and they'd been forced to oil up the ventilation shaft to stop the monolithic bird from getting stuck.

Later that same day, all the children of Cell Block Preschool were ordered over the PA system to array in front of their cells. Level after level of primary-school-aged children in grey coveralls and plastic crocs lined up against the railings and listen in boredom as the Warden's voice boomed out of a million tinny speakers in a million concrete cells. The Warden wasn't game enough to make a personal appearance, of course, as you can only be held hostage by ten-year-olds so many times until it just gets plain embarrassing.

"One of you has taken my dinner," the Warden's voice hissed, getting straight to the point. "I might overlook petty breaches from time to time, but when my Thanksgiving gets interrupted I draw the line!"

Tuesday rolled his eyes. What could he do, honestly? Make them double slaves?

"And so I propose this," the Warden paused for effect. "If any worker turns in the culprit right now, in the next ten seconds, I guarantee that you will be immediately reclassified as a guard with the full ranks and privileges that entails."

Tuesday's pale red-headed neighbour tensed, glanced at Tuesday with wide eyes, and raced for the squawk box in his cell before the Warden had even finished the sentence. Tuesday effortlessly tripped the traitor over with his trusty broom and made it to the speaker first, stepping on the ginger's head as he leaned for the speaker.

"It's the blood-nut, sir. He took your dinner."

"What? Who is this?" the Warden demanded.

"Tuesday. Bob Tuesday, inmate 978233."

Too late, Tuesday realised that his dobbing had just been broadcast over every speaker in the enormous tower at top volume. A million kids instantly started jeering at Tuesday, screaming out words like dog, rat, stool pigeon, gummo, traitor and skando. Doing his best to make his words heard over this violent chorus, Bob pointed at the redhead under his feet.

"The ginger made me hide it under my sleeping pallet, sir, said we'd get a nice price for it. Never told me that it was your dinner, sir."

The Warden's voice paused. Finally, after five long seconds, Tuesday heard the buzz of walkie-talkies and a platoon of guards appeared to escort Tuesday away from the mutinous hordes. They pelted bars of soap at Tuesday from every conceivable direction and spit-balls zipped past his face, but soon Tuesday was immediately led towards a RESTRICTED corridor and into the Special

Equipment room. Tripping over quite a few outstretched feet along the way, Tuesday was somehow still alive by the time he arrived at his destination.

Wordlessly stripped down to his stained long johns and jammed into a black uniform, a walkie-talkie was attached to Tuesday's new belt and a stun rod was slipped into Tuesday's fist hand handle-first. Cell Block Preschool's newest guard was then given an opportunity to proudly swan about in front of a full-length dress mirror.

He was a rat at twelve. And he was going to love it.

*

As Tuesday had gotten in before the redhead, nothing that could be said by a mere worker mattered anymore, because now Tuesday was a guard, and this meant he would always be judged right in any disagreement. The entire corrupt system was finally working in his favour.

Being a child guard was more than comfortable. After all, they lived better in every way. They ate real meat, slept in soft cots, smoked freely, could often work a whole shift without moving an inch, and basically had their run of the place. Christmas and birthday presents were a thing for Tuesday now, though these gifts mostly consisted of contaminated toys that were only fit for burning out on Toy Mountain, a cluster of industrial smokestacks well outside of Cell Block Preschool and its factory lines.

Tuesday also had great fun randomly zapping people with his stun rod, especially the bigger kids that used to pee on his sleeping pallet when he was just a mere worker, and he had endless opportunities to refine the valuable skill of petty revenge. He looked after the more unfortunate kids with the occasional pizza-flavoured milkshake or a box of Mac&Cheese and used his position of authority to be the youngest and most crooked guard in the history of Cell Block Preschool.

At twelve years old and almost double the height he'd been during an unseemly arrival locked in the boot of a limousine, Tuesday now had access to live roosters and was able to stage his beloved cockfights in the safety of the Warden's office after nightfall, though explaining the piles of bird poo took some tricky manoeuvring. Tuesday made a small fortune in cigarettes, ration slips and Amerikan pounds, and was eventually able to open a casino behind the toilets on Level 97. As these were the bogs for the under-fours, nobody in their right mind ever went in there, especially the cleaners, and so it was a simple matter to scale the mountain of nappies, slip behind the potties and slide through a large gap for a flutter between the pipes. Tuesday's floor had Craps, Blackjack, Spin the Bottle and Ruska Roulette (this involved a powerful firecracker with a short fuse and two teenage boys wearing blindfolds). Business was good, and it only got better.

Tuesday was running a big part of this miserable hell-hole by the time he hit his teenage years, and eventually accrued enough raw currency to buy an intelligent sewing machine of his very own. This meant he'd be able to produce his own toys and keep some of the profits. Although the Warden raised an eyebrow when the scruffy teen held out a wad of green Amerikan pounds and gave a brown smile, the Warden took Tuesday's cash and gestured to a key card for the storage rooms.

"It better have dings and scratches on it, or it's your ass, Tuesday."

Tuesday hired a fellow teen on a full-time basis to watch his machine churn out Mister Drizzle stuffed toys, then sold them back to The Dream Factory for a tenth of their worth. The employee's name was Brian, but there were three other details that were far more important than what he was called: Brian was from a high-gravity world, he'd broken more jaws than any other four inmates put together, and he was loyal for very little payment. Life had been so busy that Tuesday totally forgot that Brian was the same kid he'd insulted just after Orientation, but Brian had never mentioned it.

Now that he owned a sewing machine and had Brian to keep him safe, Tuesday finally had the legitimate financial cover he required to go all out with his illicit business ventures and the muscle to back it up.

At fifteen, Tuesday mortgaged his own cell, as well as three others in both directions. His loft had a paper-thin television, an auto-adjusting leather lounge guaranteed to be made from non-human materials, and even a butler...though admittedly, the latter was just Brian with a black bowtie and a little cap. Tuesday got the Warden's approval to have carpet bolted into the concrete for comfort reasons, but he secretly used the shagpile to hold his excess cash, as well as his two greatest treasures: the Densite-tipped drill bit he'd smuggled in behind his ear six years ago, and his dad's trusty lighter, which had been brought in via a less comfortable method. Tuesday's plush cell became a place where all the high rollers hung out.

Tuesday was an entrepreneur, a natural when it came to surviving where only the biggest scumbag ruled. He grew to become a ruthless, nasty, conniving ferret. If things had kept up, Tuesday would have owned the entire planet by the time he reached thirty. However, running this hellhole was a pyramid scheme, which meant that for Tuesday to be on top of the pile many, many others had to be beneath his boots. And when people are being stepped on, you can always rely on them to eventually cause trouble. Of course, the teenagers of Cell Block Preschool were nothing like the adult head-cases that officially ran this planet, so killing somebody, even someone as reviled as Tuesday, was out of the question. Modern forensics meant that murder was only committed by morons or the very well-trained, and it was barely considered as an option before being dismissed. Dobbing Tuesday in for his crimes wouldn't help, as the Warden was just one of the many officials being paid to keep away from Tuesday's business ventures. But there had to be some way to make him slip up, to do something that was beyond negotiations...

It soon became obvious. They'd trick Tuesday into breaking the highest taboo of The Dream Factory, something that would never, ever be tolerated: escaping.

*

At seventeen years of age, Tuesday was sleek as a ferret's spine and shiftier than a socket wrench set. He'd survived and thrived where many others had broken and died, and business was good.

And then one secret changed everything.

Tuesday was informed by one of his best spies that a military fleet called The Salvation By Fire had been sent in the direction of The Dream Factory by The Unison's military high command, and Tuesday could tell by the name alone that they weren't likely to be in the mood for casual negotiations over a chai latte. The Dream Factory was a world that had been rogue for decades, and every day that it continued to spin without the ultimate rule of The Unison being enforced upon it was a slap in the face to the entirety of mankind's empire. If it meant that The Unison had to bomb Cell Block Preschool down to a fine powder with everyone inside to prove why it shouldn't be defied, then they wouldn't hesitate to press those big red buttons. Subtlety was not The Unison's strong point.

Of course, Tuesday was far too selfish to repeat these expensive facts to anybody else. Anything that may affect his chances of survival was always an instant enemy. So, within ninety minutes of hearing this news, Tuesday and his personal assistant Brian were about to become the first slaves to break out of Cell Block Preschool in three quarters of a century.

*

It was time. They had fifteen minutes until the next patrol went past.

Tuesday wordlessly gave a motion in Brian's direction, and the thug effortlessly moved Tuesday's bulky automated sewing machine with a grunt. Tearing up the carpet to retrieve his long-hidden Densite drill bit, Tuesday quickly ripped out the sewing machine's standard needle-holder, installed a custom-made fitting and pointed Brian at the back wall of his cell.

Brian thud-thud-thudded across the room.

Their jury-rigged pneumatic drill effortlessly carved a two-foot-thick hole in the shape of Mister Drizzle with one button press, and within fifteen seconds Tuesday and Brian were ankle-deep in a urine drainage pit and ready to punch through the next slab of concrete. Continuing in a direction that Tuesday had memorised from his childhood travels through the ventilation system, Brian hefted the powerful drill down a maintenance tunnel and, soon, they had drilled Mister Drizzles through another five walls.

No alarms went off.

No razor dogs were released.

Guards didn't come running.

And it wasn't even raining.

This was a much lamer escape than Tuesday had anticipated.

Tuesday carefully brandished a pair of sewing clippers by their rubber grips.

Unlike your average garden-variety shears, Tuesday had smuggled in enough sharpening chemicals to give his clippers a wickedly-keen monomolecular edge. A series of electrified chicken-wire fences offered no resistance at all, simply parting as though they were made of mist. Within another minute they were outside the official borders of Cell Block Preschool and sliding through the mud.

Automated spotlights flickered on at Tuesday's passing, almost brushing his left foot, but the sentry robots in charge of the scanners were too rusted and lazy to do anything about it. Little did the enslaved population of Cell Block Preschool know that they were actually imprisoned by their own fears, rather than by actual killbots.

"Where?" Brian asked in his curt manner.

"Toy Mountain." Tuesday grunted.

Every kid knew about the endless hunger of Toy Mountain's industrial furnaces. Although the smokestacks kept everyone on the planet from freezing to death, the place was still horrible beyond words: a constant stream of happy, fluffy cartoon characters were fed into its flaming maws at all hours, and only the unluckiest of child slaves had the thankless job of feeding these fires with charcoaled shovels. Cremating these toys may have served to boil all their hot water and kept a multitude of clapped-out heaters working throughout the eternal winter of this world, but still...they were killing Mister Drizzle a billion times over!

Brian looked confused, but this was his role. Tuesday was the brains, and Brian was the one who blindly dragged a thirty-kilogram illegally-modified sewing machine through urine drainage pits. He drooled a little and followed up on his original question.

"Why?"

Tuesday sniffed. He hated people not doing what they were told, especially when he was the one doing the telling.

"Look, I don't have time to explain everything. I need the Warden's car, which is currently in the panel-beating shop at the base of Toy Mountain, and then I need somebody to drive me all the way to the shuttle pad."

"But-"

"Quiet, Brian. Just do as you're told. Now look, I brought along a little something I've been saving," Tuesday pulled up his black guard's armour and revealed why he was having problems fitting through the Mister Drizzle-shaped holes: Tuesday had the better part of twenty thousand Amerikan pounds in large notes strapped to his body. It was a true wonder nobody had noticed those huge lumps in his carpet, but that was no longer a concern. "So we steal the car, hit the nearest port, bribe a rocket-jock, get off at some hive of scum and villainy, and start again. We can climb back up the ranks somewhere better, somewhere more profitable."

Keeping to the shadows, both teens did a low roadie-run across layers of rejected toys. The plushies had been discarded due to little issues like asbestos stuffing, toxic stains, parasitic infections and other charming flaws. Suddenly, Brian took a wrong step and disappeared with a bellow of surprise. One moment the thug was there, and the next he'd fallen through a false floor of empty Action Jack boxes.

Tuesday looked down into the pit and saw his partner in crime had landed on the modified sewing machine.

"Any damage, Brian?"

Brian patted his body.

"Don't fink so. Feel okay."

"No, you idiot, the drill! Is the drill okay?"

Brian went to pick up the sewing machine to check its condition, but it had already sunk too deep into the mire to be retrieved. Brian gave one final, massive tug, and only succeeded in accidentally ripping away its casing with an explosion of rust. Mad as he was right now, Tuesday was glad he'd never actually had a fight with Brian, as the older kid would have pounded his head like a clam.

"All sunk." Brian tried to raise a foot and failed. It took another couple of failed lurches for him to become fully aware of the situation. "An' I'm sinking, too!"

Tuesday sighed and looked around for anything useful. He spent a couple of minutes gathering Missus Stretchee action figures and tying their flexi-arms into a rough rope, but after throwing one end down the hole Tuesday realised that Brian weighed a heck of a lot more than he did. Digging in both jackboots until he sank up to his ankles, Tuesday finally attached the Missus Stretchee dolls around the knees of an adult-sized Android Andy that had been buried upside down to its waist.

Brian had only just climbed over the cusp of the pit when a skimmer shrieked overhead. As the burning vehicle was only three metres above the ground, its wake knocked both teenagers flying. Tuesday and Brian splashed into the deep, black mud with serious force and lay very still and very silent.

A good twenty seconds passed before Tuesday finally moaned.

Tuesday and Brian eventually got to their feet again, and even had the presence of mind to check for injuries. Nothing serious, thankfully. Looking nervously back and forth at the long line of charcoaled toys that plotted the damaged skimmer's final crash-course, Brian gaped a little.

"What's with that?" he asked stupidly.

Tuesday had gotten a pretty good look at the skimmer when it had almost crashed into his freaking face, and without a second thought he sprinted along the burning line and over a crest of Mister Drizzles. Brian yelled and lumbered after the faster boy, trying to keep up as best as his webbed toes would allow. Over the small hill, the skimmer had crashed pathetically into a bog of bubbling, smoking sludge.

"What are you doing?" Brian demanded. "That's a guard skimmer, Tuesday!"

"I might know them," Tuesday snapped over his shoulder.

Thinking as hard as his ferret mind could manage, Tuesday put together the clues. Firstly, there was a guard skimmer in flames, probably after being shot down, heading directly away from the direction of Cell Block Preschool. This either meant that word about the incoming invasion fleet from The Unison had spread and a few of the guys were desperate enough to brave the anti-air defence system, or the invasion had quietly begun.

Tuesday needed to know the answer.

Reaching the wreck, he found that there was nobody on board. Its teenage passengers - who were all dressed in guard uniforms - had all jumped clear at the last moment and were lying about, moaning and flailing weakly like you'd expect from proper crash victims. After a few moments Tuesday finally saw somebody he knew.

"Hey, it's rancid monkey cheese himself! How are you, Cheddar?" Tuesday asked with glee, looking down at the porky guard.

The nickname "Cheddar" had stuck fast for eight long years. Tuesday made sure to use it at every opportunity.

"Spug off, Tuesday."

Tuesday held out a wrinkled pound note in a friendly way.

"What happened, Ched? What're all you idiots doing out here?"

Cheddar stared needles. It seemed unlikely that he was going to share anything at this rate.

"Come on. This may be the last conversation we ever have." Tuesday smiled. "But if you don't want some pounds for the effort...well, I'm sure Brian may have something to offer you instead."

Brian, right on cue, cracked his knuckles.

Tuesday offered Cheddar a contraband cigarette, and the stinky guard casually accepted it. Cheddar lit it on a small fire that had started on his shoulder armour and took a long drag.

"All right, fine. Me and the boys wanted out. Simple as that. Heard you were going, so we thought we'd grab you, torture your plans out of you, and do it ourselves. You're wearing a cash coat, right?"

Tuesday didn't comment straight away. Instead, he lit up a second smoke with his dad's trusty lighter. There was a natural gas mine beneath Cell Block Preschool, and it had been easy enough to score a canister of the stuff to keep the lighter topped up.

Tuesday resisted the urge to kick Cheddar in the head.

"And if I am?"

"Thought so. Going to bribe your way out, Tuesday? Maybe find a nice place to start over, some other hive of scum and villainy?"

Tuesday had heard enough. Using Cheddar's forehead as a convenient step, Tuesday hopped into the smouldering skimmer. He immediately started trying to hotwire the vehicle in the exact way that one of the naughtier kids had instructed (after a few bribes, of course), but like most tasks in life, Tuesday failed miserably.

Brian conveniently chose this moment to rattle the keys next to Tuesday's head. Snatching them without comment, Tuesday jammed both of the etched metal spikes into the correct slots and turned the ignition switch with a growl of antigrav wafers. It is worth noting that this was the first skimmer Tuesday had ever stolen, and this particular milestone in his criminal career was officially known as Grand Theft Aero.

Gesturing for Brian to take the wheel, Tuesday went about extinguishing some scattered fires with a Halon sprayer. Once he'd finally gotten the flames under control, Tuesday waved goodbye to the unfortunate previous occupants of the skimmer like a true smart-ass. The wind whipped through Tuesday's hair as his stolen ride lurched into the sky.

Behind them, Cell Block Preschool loomed into the air like a monolithic grey middle finger made of concrete. As usual, clouds consumed the upper storeys of the fortress. The red beams of laser guidance systems pointed out from it in every direction in warning, poking through multiple layers of electrified fencing, razor wire and spotlights. Tuesday spat at the fortress, ecstatic to finally be free of it.

Brian suddenly spun half a revolution and took off at full speed without any explanation or warning. Once he'd finished being violently sick over the side of the skimmer, Tuesday began to scream at Brian to stay away from the heavily armed Cell Block. Brian pointed over his shoulder in a wordless response.

Tuesday looked back at what they were fleeing from: it was a smallish ship that looked like the result of a giant wasp mating with a family sedan. It was probably named after something poisonous, or maybe some sort of old-Earth predator. The most important fact was that the flyer was armed, which meant that it would have no trouble blasting their stolen skimmer into charcoal.

The interceptor came closer, and Tuesday could now see that the pilot was angrily gesturing for them to land, to stop this chase peacefully. Tuesday had come too far to do any such thing, and there was no way he was going to suffer the unspeakable penalty of Death By Power Sander for a failed escape.

The whirring turbines of the tiny assault ship came close enough for Tuesday to touch. Nodding at the pilot as though agreeing to stop, Tuesday calmly reached down, picked up an open toolbox laying by his feet, and tossed it into the turbine next to his head. Dozens of wrenches and screwdrivers were noisily sucked into the engines of the interceptor, and the turbine burped an explosion of smoke and fire. The considerable push from the assault ship's only remaining turbine put it into a terminal spin, skewing a matter of centimetres from Tuesday's scalp. The small craft tumbled over and slammed straight into the garbage tip of toys, bursting into flames on impact.

Tuesday calmly sat back down, his face more pale than usual. Brian shook his head and chuckled.

"Cold, man. Like ice."

"Had no choice." Tuesday snapped.

"Sure you had a choice. And you chose to kill the good guys."

Tuesday blinked. "What?"

"Didn't you see the little picture on the nose? He was from The Unison, man. He came to set us free."

Tuesday was sick again, but this time out of disgust for his actions. That pilot had come from the far reaches of the galaxy to bring peace and freedom, and what had Tuesday done? Blown him up. That guy could have wrecked the skimmer without a second thought, ripped them to pieces with micro nukes and assault weapons, but he'd tried to stop them peacefully instead.

Tuesday watched with relief when an ejection seat punched its way out of the burning ruin of the assault ship, sending the military pilot two hundred metres into the sky. A parachute opened, and the solider was clearly in good enough health to give Tuesday the finger. A few wildly inaccurate bullets whipped past their skimmer from an emergency field carbine, but Tuesday was just glad that everybody had survived the encounter.

"Time to go, Brian."

They performed another one-eighty and sped off.

*

The main port of The Dream Factory was the largest open space on this world. Like most ports, it was a giant square of blackened concrete that had been precisely divided into a grid of yellow glow-in-the-dark lines with eight-digit identification numbers that flashed in assorted colour codes. Every parking spot offered the Holy Trinity of basic spaceport facilities - umbilical refuelling lines, magnetic parking clamps, and adjustable staircases - but when these functions weren't in use they could be cleanly retracted beneath the concrete.

Smouldering, crackling and nearly out of gas, Tuesday and Brian touched down. To be more specific, they violently crashed their stolen vehicle into another, slightly more intact skimmer, and lightly bumped a fuel tanker as they came to a total stop. Cringing, waiting for a fatal explosion to kill everyone within a hundred metres, after a full twenty seconds it became obvious that the tanker wasn't about to blow up. The two escapees finally took another breath.

Hopping out of the skimmer, Tuesday tried to walk nonchalantly, but this is hard to accomplish when several small fires have started smouldering on your back. Once he'd put them out, Tuesday casually swaggered along the glowing yellow lines for the better part of two hundred metres, Brian in tow, until finally finding the number he was looking for: Bay 345556AD.

Stopping, Tuesday looked up and up and up and up at a monolithic ship that had more in common with a brick than a predatory animal. Her weathered skin was marked by re-entry burns and a thousand pockmarks. Some of the cavities may have been from weapons damage, but Tuesday wasn't enough of an expert to say for sure. And although he couldn't actually read it, Tuesday was pretty sure that the hundred-metre-long pink decal along her side declared this hulk to be called the USS Darling Bitch.

There was a sailor of no relevant description pushing along a cube the size of a Mac Truck with minimal effort. A loud hum made it obvious that the huge crate had antigrav wafers built into its base, but the sailor looked solid enough to not need the help. Tuesday managed to get the stranger's attention just as the cube disappeared up a turbolift and into the belly of the Darling Bitch. The beefcake had MOMM tattooed almost illegibly across his windpipe.

"Oi, you. We want safe passage to another world, preferably one that isn't allied with The Unison, and temporary tourist visas that'll last long enough for us to disappear."

"I'm the chef," the burly man said, unimpressed. He scratched at the tattoo. "Unless you can cook it, it's not my job."

"Right, then." Tuesday said easily. "How about you get me the Captain and be sure to whip us up some dinner while you're at it. No broccoli, extra chilli. Chop chop."

"Get your own dinner," the hulking chef snapped, glaring at Tuesday's black uniform. "And don't you go bothering the Captain! He has better things to do than mix with you scumbag guards."

"Ah, words," Tuesday mused. "Sometimes they're sharp, sometimes they're blunter than your mother's flat head."

The chef's eyes narrowed and he began to growl. He appeared more than ready to rip off Tuesday's scrotum and serve it as a deep-fried dim-sim. It was only total disbelief that had prevented any immediate violence, and that wouldn't last for long.

"Did you...did you just insult my sainted mother?!"

"You're right, sorry," Tuesday smiled broadly. "Let's leave old mattress-back out of this. Hitting a target as big as that thumper is far too easy."

There was a natural progression to this conversation. Teeth were displaced. Noses gained some character.

"You have a real way with people," Brian commented, scraping Tuesday off the glowing lines of the dock.

With all the commotion of this rather one-sided beating, a well-dressed man who was obviously the chef's superior made an appearance to see what was going on. The chef stomped over to the newcomer, then spent quite a while pointing at the two teenagers and shouting obscenities. The toff gave Tuesday a disbelieving look and began to walk over.

"Oi, Tuesday, look." Brian whispered. "No, with your good eye. The one that still opens. We've got someone posh."

Tuesday smiled despite the pain. He definitely recognised this guy from a very expensive conversation he'd had with a fellow crim. It was exactly who he was looking for. The Captain, oblivious to the fact this was just a small part in a large con, glared down at the two teenagers.

"What's happening here? Why aren't you two in Cell Block Preschool?"

"Escapees," Tuesday said truthfully. His swollen lips twitched in a smile. "We want safe passage to another world, preferably one that isn't allied with The Unison, and temporary tourist visas that'll last long enough for us to disappear."

The Captain sniffed as though there was a bad smell. "Do you kids have any idea of the penalties I'd incur if I was caught smuggling people out of this hole? The local government, what there is of it, has a standard policy of removing people's extremities with nail clippers as a first-time offence. Not to mention the amount of red tape even if we did manage to get you somewhere else..."

"Lots of paperwork, is it?" Tuesday asked pleasantly, spitting blood. "I understand. After all, I reckon your time is worth a lot nowadays. Smuggling all those things that you're not meant to be smuggling must take a big bite out of your schedule, yeah?"

The Captain's face didn't change.

"I don't know what you're talking about, kid."

Tuesday squinted, trying to remember the little speech he'd planned word for word.

"Your name is Captain Ron Beattie, like the cigarette, and you were dishonourably discharged from an otherwise promising military career for The Unison, age twenty-three, due to...."

"Yes, yes, nice to meet you, too," Captain Beattie interrupted, looking around for witnesses.

Tuesday churned on.

"...you've been the Captain of the USS Darling Bitch since the age of twenty-eight, but before that you flew about with an assortment of illegal and unregistered commands in the Dark Zone. The Darling Bitch is well known for moving about large quantities of naughty things by hiding them in Mister Drizzle stuffed toys..."

"Shh! Shut up!" Beattie started turning red.

"... and your crew is also suspected of information-running for numerous organisations that oppose the current ruling regime of The Dream Factory..."

"How much have you got?" Captain Beattie snapped, interrupting Tuesday's recitation of his many sins. A punch-blade had appeared between Beattie's fingers at some point. "If it's less than the bounty for your dead corpse than you better pray you have the reflexes of a spugging rabbit."

Tuesday opened his shirt to reveal the now-muddy jacket of pounds. Captain Beattie reached out to inspect a bundle, but his hand stopped just short of a brick of what looked like neon blue Play Dough. Tuesday held up his hand to show he was holding a detonator and smiled broadly.

"Made these beauties out of toxic run-off from the plastic vats. Nice stuff, this. Used a few grams of it to blow out some concrete walls when I was redecorating my cell. Problem is, the fumes are seriously poisonous, so you have to hold your breath and keep your eyes shut for about two minutes when you make it..."

"Who the hell are you?" the Captain asked breathlessly.

"Bob Tuesday. And I just want a ride."

The Captain was still for a while. He was probably weighing up the chances of taking out Tuesday before he could detonate the plastic explosives but found he didn't like the odds. Gesturing roughly for the pneumatic gangplank, Beattie looked around for witnesses and bundled the two boys aboard the USS Darling Bitch.

They'd made it.

*

Two days later, The Unison's elite "Silencer" operatives had finished successfully infiltrating the upper levels of The Dream Factory's regime without being discovered. As arranged, at exactly midnight the Silencers carried out a chain of surgical assassinations to lop the head off the snake, effectively decapitating the regime in the space of a minute. This was followed by hours of not-quite-surgical nuclear detonations against anybody who didn't understand that resistance was pointless...futile, even.

Cell Block Preschool wasn't the first fortress to fall, but by dawn it had collapsed like all the others. Now without anything to stop them from leaving, its survivors escaped into the planet-wide garbage tips and did their best not to be incinerated.

Once the six-hour firestorm had calmed and all armed opposition had ceased, The Unison forces landed to begin the long, long process of accounting for survivors, and then moved on to the impossible job of trying to figure out what to do with millions of displaced kids. It was quite likely that this part of the process may take more time and effort than dropping nukes.

Nobody missed Tuesday and his servant Brian. To The Unison, they didn't even exist.

CHAPTER SIX SLUG

If you wanted to go interstellar, light speed was for chumps. Thankfully, there was no shortage of choice when it came to moving vast distances in short periods of time. Since the First Founding of The Unison a handful of centuries ago, humanity had developed thirteen different methods of skipping across the Universe by kicking space/time physics in the shin and stealing its lunch money. While these methods all had upsides, they each had inherent drawbacks, too. Of course, price was always a major factor. Like with anything else, you get what you pay for.

The Wattson-Rice Drive was the original way mankind made space/time its bitch. It operated by folding space and tying it together like a needle and thread through a sheet of fabric. It wasn't instantaneous, but it was pretty bloody quick by any standards. Saying that the Wattson-Rice was far from the safest choice was a massive understatement, however. Early space farers quickly nicknamed it the "Death wish Drive" after hundreds of ships disappeared mid-transit for no apparent reason. The further you pushed a Wattson-Rice Drive, the higher the chances you'd cease to exist, so anything beyond a million kilometres per hop was rolling the dice. Worse still, this inherent level of risk makes it impossible to get insurance from a reputable provider, which means using a Wattson-Rice for business purposes isn't commercially viable.

On the plus side, the Wattson-Rice is so ancient that its schematics fell into the public domain decades ago, so anybody with a decent fourth-dimensional printer can mock up a working copy in an afternoon. Insert a few antimatter batteries, restrict its range to a few different spots in your backyard, and presto! The perfect way to amuse small children for hours at a time. The most popular application for Wattson-Rice Drives nowadays is to install them in lightweight cardboard laminate shells, reduce their maximum range to five hundred metres, and flog them off really cheap to teenagers who've just gotten their learner's licences and can't afford anything, well, safer.

The Thornton Chronological Dilator was a definite step up from the Wattson-Rice Drive when it comes to safety, but a giant leap backwards concerning speed (not that the Wattson-Rice used conventional acceleration to move from one point to the other, but you get the basic idea). The Thornton remains the safest method of interstellar travel to this day, but it too has an unfortunate pet name: The Slowest Death. In real time, a ship equipped with a Thornton can move a respectable thirty light-years a week, which is more than enough to cross three or four star systems in any direction across The Unison. However, the effects of extreme time dilation on the human mind is so unbearable that any passengers who travel on a ship powered by a Thornton need to be sedated into a coma if they want to avoid a total psychotic breakdown. You see, for every day of real time that occurs outside the ship, anybody aboard an in-transit vessel using a Thornton will experience what feels like a solid year. Now, on the surface, most people would initially assume that hopping onto a ship with a Thornton could be a cheap way to attempt immortality. Accounting for the fact that the average life expectancy of a non-smoker is roughly a decade short of a double century, if you stretched each of those days into what felt like three-hundred and sixty-five - a whole standard year - then in theory a single human lifespan could be squeezed out to the better part of seventy thousand relative years.

Like you've probably guessed, there are some major drawbacks to time dilation. The thing is, your perception of time gets stretched out, too. This means that something as simple as blinking your eyes can take several hours. A sneeze is a torturous ordeal that is requires two or three days. And as for eating? We're talking months of effort for every meal, and by the time you wipe the crumbs and suds from your mouth, yes, so sorry, you've gone completely insane and need to be permanently restrained for your own safety. This temporal realm is known as "sloth-space" for good reason.

There have been many other star drives over the lifetime of The Unison, and just like the Wattson-Rice and the Thornton, they all have pluses and minuses. For instance, the Carter Device puts off enough gamma radiation to melt the toughest ceramics into porridge, a Farrugia Exciter only works if it's operated by an albino with a certain type of autism, a Lloydson Starbridge relies on seventh dimensional mathematics so complicated that they can only be calculated with a computer the size of a small moon, and the Heggarty Singularity only exists on Thursday afternoons.

Like most modern ships, the USS Darling Bitch had been built around the industry standard: a Stiller Drive. Unlike other hyper drives that messed about with twisting physics or accelerating light or otherwise kicking physics in the crotch, the way a Stiller Drive operates goes against every shred of common sense. First off, to understand a Stiller Drive, you have to know that everything moves. Planets, moons, stars, asteroids, old telecommunication satellites, whatever. If it exists, then it moves. The Milky Way Galaxy – a seemingly endless field of light made up of billions and billions of stars across hundreds of thousands of light years – moves just like everything that is within it, as do all the far off, untouched galaxies beyond our reach. But it wasn't until eighty-seven years ago that mankind accidentally discovered that space itself is also in constant motion, and not only is it travelling so fast that light is a legless, upside-down turtle in comparison, but it turned out that space danced an incredibly precise waltz that it constantly repeated down to the millimetre every two weeks, three days, eight hours, sixteen minutes and four and a half seconds.

So, knowing that space itself is in constant motion, a Stiller Drive does precisely one thing: it brings your ship to a complete stop. By reducing a solid mass of human-crafted ceramics and metal to total stasis, a Stiller Drive allows the entire Milky Way Galaxy and everything in it to spin past at speeds that have no calculable number. By knowing the exact direction that space will be dancing at any given microsecond, it's a relatively simple matter for any half-decent navigation computer to switch off a Stiller Drive at your desired moment and re-join the real time Universe with acceptable accuracy.

Sure, the Stiller Drive was far from perfect and was well overdue to be superseded, but at least you didn't need to find an autistic albino to pilot one. Even in the 24th Century, they were mighty thin on the ground.

*

Sealed within a scanner-proof smuggling room until The Dream Factory was nothing but a microscopic dot on a long-range reader, Tuesday and Brian were given the royal tour.

It was far from impressive.

The common areas of the USS Darling Bitch mostly consisted of a dingy little pit where the common rabble drank away their pay, and the communal bunkrooms where they passed out afterwards. Both rooms stank worse than a Kings Cross pub toilet on Free Burrito Night and could have used a good dousing in bleach. Besides shelves of the cheapest, filthiest gut-rot liquor the galaxy had to offer, the bar had an alleged coffee machine that dispensed boiling-hot ultra-caffeinated mud to the hungover crew. Beyond a few nudie posters of tentacled alien pin-up girls here and there, there wasn't much else to see on this level.

Go down just one floor, though, and you'd find yourself in the yawning cargo hold, which took up ninety-nine percent of the USS Darling Bitch, and currently held in excess of two million Mister Drizzles, Missus Stretchees, Action Jacks and other high-quality slave-produced toys from Cell Block Preschool and other production centres, all destined for spoilt little brats who demanded the best. Of course, the lowest layer of plushies were all stuffed to bursting with shrink-wrapped bricks of Blink tablets.

Both teens spent most of their time finding ways to be irritating. They'd sneak about the no-go areas of the ship, filch any morsels of food the hairy chef hadn't guarded well enough, steal packets of smokes from unconscious crew members, and generally be annoying seventeen-year-old gits. Other notable activities that kept the two teenagers happily occupied in deep space included mooning passing shuttles, skewering scum-roaches with throwing knives and hour-long staring competitions.

The teens were seen as vermin from the moment they arrived, and this only worsened over the next three days. Had it not been for the explosive brick mounted over his heart, Tuesday would have been shot within half an hour. Every now and then, when food was scarce, Tuesday would nibble on the brick of nutrient gruel that everyone thought was a bomb, and chuckle about his genius.

Those days aboard the USS Darling Bitch were long, varied and fun, even though most of them ended with Tuesday gaining a new enemy. Unfortunately, on one of those days, it turned out to be Brian.

"Stop talking at me like that!" Brian roared, spraying saliva.

The entire drinking pit went quiet. If anybody could get past Tuesday's defences, it was Brian, and everyone knew it. All six of the crew members who were present prepared themselves for a fist fight that Tuesday was definitely going to lose. It wasn't even worth betting on.

At this moment, a punch-up was far from Tuesday's biggest fear, as it was the aftermath that worried him. Brian knew all about the "bomb" strapped to Tuesday's chest, and Tuesday had gathered far too many enemies in this room for such a titbit of information to get loose. He hoped Brian wasn't idiotic enough to play such a lethal card, or they were both dead.

"Calm it," Tuesday ordered.

"You're always mean!" Brian blubbered.

The difference between tears and violence was a thin one for Brian. Tuesday had witnessed this sudden transition a few times over the years. The sailors laughed amongst themselves at this brute of a kid crying like a little girl.

"It's nuthin' personal," Tuesday mumbled. "I just don't have time to waste on…on bloody pleasantries. And things just go smoother when you do as you're told, right? It's a matter of efficiency."

Brian assumed an expression of rage.

"Efficiency! I'm not your spugging butler, Tuesday! You gots to stop talking down to me!"

Tuesday rolled his eyes as the crew all sniggered at this childishness.

"Okay. Fine." Tuesday shrugged. "I won't talk to you then if that's what you want. See you later, chum."

Brian's eyes popped wide in fury. His face reddened.

"That's not what I said!"

Tuesday pointed at Brian, baring his teeth.

"How about you take a minute to think about what I've done for us?" Tuesday started counting on his fingers. "Who got us out of Cell Block Preschool? Me. Who bought and threatened the two of us halfway across civilisation? Me. So stow it and be grateful."

Brian was silent for a long second.

"Why do you always…"

"Because I'm the boss, and because I'm the brains, and you're just some inbred hick who accidentally fell out of his mummy's…"

Tuesday and Brian both jumped up at the same time and started swinging. As expected, Tuesday managed to get a noseful of knuckles and an eyeful of toes and fell to the deck, puffing and panting and bleeding. His usual defence of pure rat-cunning didn't work all that well when it came to being repeatedly kicked in the kidneys, especially against boys as big as Brian, and Tuesday knew it.

Getting woozily to his feet, his head spinning and little explosions still playing out before his eyes, Tuesday gave a pathetic little bow of defeat.

"You win."

"Knocked his teeth out, kid," a sailor growled.

"I was already missing those," Tuesday contradicted. He decided to make some friends for once. "Who wants a drink?"

Stripping a few notes from his coat of currency, Tuesday bought a round of moonshine and happily lit up a cigarette made out of a greenback, which he'd been doing a lot of lately. Tuesday rolled his shirt back down and accepted a sweaty glass of lemonade and coconut rum.

"Here's to the best friend a slave could ever have," Tuesday toasted, raising his drink at Brian.

The other boy looked uncomfortable. He didn't know how to react to this new and improved version of the bastard he knew far too well.

"Man, honestly, you carried me out of that place, and if it wasn't for your driving skills I'd still be at the tip. You were right, okay? Mates?"

Brian nodded slowly and accepted a beer with lemon cordial in it.

"Sure, why not? Hell or high water."

Tuesday smirked. Brian was off-guard, just as he liked it. Sure, Tuesday may be battered and cut up, but it was a small price to pay in the greater scheme of things.

*

Fun as it was, the day finally came for the boys to leave. Even a slow old wench like the Darling Bitch eventually got to where she was heading: an almost-legal trading waypoint with a serial number for a name and very little to see beyond an eternity of automated cargo lines. Tuesday was pretty sure that the only way the Darling Bitch could have gone any slower is if she'd flown backwards.

Over the next couple of hours Tuesday greased palms, made donations to assorted worker's unions, accidentally dropped money in dark places...and he also outright bribed a few people, too. Later on, Tuesday and Brian sat at a rickety plastic table beneath a tarnished alcohol dispenser and proceeded to feed Amerikan pounds into a slot until they were both skint and borderline incapable of standing up under their own power. Under-age drinking was probably the most legal thing Tuesday had done all day.

Brian had remained within sight of Tuesday the whole time he'd been engaged in "clarifying a few minor paperwork issues." Even a man with half of Brian's IQ wouldn't give Tuesday the chance to run off with all their cash.

Tuesday slugged back his fifth drink (the tepid slime had mercifully stopped tasting like fermented cough syrup after the third one), and finally slapped two plastic cards and a couple of tear-proof paper sheets down on the table. The small rectangles were "counterfeit-proof" citizen cards for the sector they were currently sitting in – one for Mr Robert Tuesday and another for Mr Brian Bebbington – as well as two pre-signed employment contracts. Brian had to move his lips to read the fine print, but he could quite clearly make out that one contract was for a mining job at a place called The Mistress for a company called PusCo, while the other was for a grease-pit cleaner at the closest MacDeath's franchise. Brian instantly snatched the MacDeath contract without discussing it, and Tuesday took one look at the thug's facial expression before giving a wave of permission.

"They're only for a few years, anyway," Tuesday consoled. "But that should be long enough to start a proper paper trail, put us on the taxman's radar and all that. Before you know it, thirteen months have gone by four times, and suddenly we look totally legit to The Unison. Then we can move about as we please."

Tuesday licked the bottom of his glass. Beyond the small pile of faked paperwork, his dad's lighter and the unfashionable clothes he'd purchased from a second-hand shop, Tuesday's only possession was the complimentary laser-tip pen he'd used to sign away a full two-thirds of his cash to a crooked lawyer. The pen had immediately ceased to work the moment it had signed both contracts.

"I think it's time we parted ways." Brian rumbled.

Tuesday slowly turned to regard Brian's caveman form. The bigger kid had been nothing more than a tool to Tuesday, a battering ram for the moments when he needed muscle and unthinking loyalty. Now, Brian was no longer required, and thus had no further value.

"I'll miss you," Tuesday lied.

Brian gave a genuine smile.

"No, you won't."

Tuesday somehow managed to get to his feet. It felt like the space station was tipping slightly to one side.

"Okay, let's not get all emotional about it, all right? We're both seventeen. We're practically men."

"This too emotional for you?"

Brian flipped the bird and walked away.

Tuesday smirked, turned in the opposite direction, and left.

He never saw Brian again.

*

Tuesday's mining job wasn't exactly what he'd expected. For one, it turned out that "The Mistress" was actually a World Slug, a living, football-shaped grey behemoth of invertebrate filth the size of New York City. World Slugs were the largest living objects that mankind had ever encountered, but thankfully they spent most of their time snoozing in loose orbits around murky little stars, thriving off the radiation and not bothering anybody. Of course, there had been a few recorded instances where a World Slug had awakened for a time and hungered for something more substantial than gamma and UV...

An automated drop-ship had dumped Tuesday on the World Slug's back with nothing, but a leaky spacesuit, directions to the only permanent structure on the whole football, and about a hundred life-or-death warnings. One of the more notable concerns was that while the World Slug was surrounded by a very, very thin breathable atmosphere, it simply wasn't sufficient to keep Tuesday alive beyond a few minutes, hence the dodgy spacesuit. After all, if The Mistress didn't have an atmosphere, then life would be impossible for the stellar invertebrate, and all her little live-in parasites wouldn't last a second.

Thankfully, although there were hazards, the job itself was simple: Tuesday's orders were to attack the World Slug's assorted slime glands with a pickaxe, collect the thick ooze in glass jars, and prepare his harvest for pick-up once a month. It turned out that the nineteen different colours of gunk were used in all the finest cosmetics, especially the most expensive facial creams and age-defying lotions and could sell for thousands of pounds a gram.

So far, he'd survived. That was a start.

Trudging across the World Slug in his defective spacesuit, dragging a trailer of empty glass jars mounted on a trolley covered in antigrav wafers, Tuesday was on the lookout. His sharp vision finally picked out a shaking pustule the size of a large termite mound about thirty metres away, and he increased his pace with enthusiasm.

Swinging his pickaxe again and again into the warty hide with grunts of effort, after eight strikes a geyser of green erupted from the pimple as though he'd struck oil. Catching as much slime as he could before the wound sealed itself, Tuesday loaded his latest haul of mucus on the trolley and headed back home. As usual, the World Slug itself didn't react to his violence, but punching a new mining pit always entailed the risk of disturbing something below the surface, so it paid to be alert and ready to run at all times.

Tuesday reached his airtight home within ten minutes. The dome-shaped tent had been nailed into the World Slug's skin with steel pegs ages ago and had housed precisely one occupant at a time for the last two centuries. Although Tuesday wasn't its first resident, this tent was more of a home than Cell Block Preschool had ever been.

It took a few minutes to stack the full, warm jars of pure green next to his tent in the correct way with all the others, but as every jar had an antigrav wafer built into its base this job didn't require much muscle. As some of the grades and shades of green gunk were literally worth more than gold and uranium put together, Tuesday was so careful and delicate it might as well have been foreplay.

After going through the whole tedious "pressurising-depressurising" airlock routine, Tuesday popped off his helmet and finally took a deep breath that didn't taste like sunburnt fish. The tent Tuesday called home was basic, but it contained all the essentials. On the left was a small fusion stove for basic cooking duties and warmth, and a soft self-cleaning bedroll was situated right next to it for obvious comfort reasons. An eye-level electronic calendar above Tuesday's pillow kept track of upcoming slime pick-ups, but all the remaining wall space was taken up with shelf after shelf full of standard no-expiration foodstuffs like Mac&Cheese. On the right side of the tent was a shower and a sink fuelled by water from the World Slug's lake-like armpit (which had to undergo a lengthy decontamination process before being used), and both spigots dripped constantly in the background. Directly ahead, a big storage cupboard held Tuesday's other leaky spacesuit, his single set of horribly unfashionable civilian clothes and, of course, there was a hook for his pickaxe. Being without his beloved broom had been hard for Tuesday to handle, so the pickaxe had quickly become his best friend in its place.

Tuesday flopped on his bedroll and got out his Beyond console, an obsolete piece of junk which resembled a pair of paper-thin white sunglasses with a complex logo stamped into them. A quick tap on both temples plunged thousands and thousands of microscopic electrodes into his skin, but before the game could start Tuesday had to spend ten straight minutes mentally accepting the two-hundred-and-seventeen assorted disclaimer notices that had to be verified at the start of every booting session. This had become second nature by now, and there was no way in Hades he actually read any of it.

A symbol appeared just before the game started: the word TRANCE in a simple white circle. As long as he could remember, Tuesday had now seen the TRANCE logo in day-to-day life more times than he could count, but he still had no idea what it meant. It wasn't the name of the game company, and he'd never heard anything about Beyond being connected to anyone or anything called TRANCE. But every time without fail, whenever Tuesday saw the word TRANCE it caused something to bubble up in the depths of his mind, as though he desperately needed to remember something to prevent a terrible atrocity from occurring... something horrible beyond words...

As usual, Tuesday soon lost interest in this mystery once the game started: a pirated version of Grand Theft Astro that had been translated from Korean to Russian by somebody who only spoke Norwegian. Tuesday killed enough nameless civilians to sate his immediate need for carnage, and eventually resigned himself to the fact that he couldn't lie down all day. Sure, it took about seven hours of gaming to reach this decision, but that was beside the point.

Getting out a Bowie knife that was more akin to a broadsword, Tuesday screwed his almost-airtight helmet back on and sighed.

Dinnertime.

Tuesday casually hit the red button by the door without thinking. Both airlocks opened simultaneously and an explosive burst of oxygen blasted him out of the portal crotch-first and scattered his possessions in all directions. Hitting a relatively soft patch of slug skin and rolling to a stop, Tuesday was unharmed by the tumble, but he cursed viciously as all his stuff continued to flutter about the slugscape. As usual, he'd forgotten to go through the proper procedure for opening and closing the protective airlocks in the right order, even though a child would have gotten it right more often by now. All that junk would take ages to collect again...

Tuesday tapped the ground with his fingers until he found an especially tender patch and proceeded to savagely hack away at it with the giant knife. Carving out a decent porterhouse from the World Slug's back, Tuesday whistled and clicked his tongue as he had wonderful thoughts about how good it would taste done medium-rare with a bit of Diane gravy...

A bear-sized parasite burst out of the surface of the World Slug without any warning, nearly knocking Tuesday on his butt. Rearing up, screeching and grinding its six interlocked mouths together like a pile of chainsaws, the thing looked like one of H.R. Giger's nightmares during an LSD overdose.

Tuesday ran.

Making it back to his tent in seconds, as Tuesday rushed into the still-unsealed airlock he was instantly bowled over by the bug. Rolling into the depressurised area, the thick fabric of Tuesday's spacesuit was quickly flayed apart by so, so many teeth. Fighting automatically on a pure adrenaline high, Tuesday's knife flashed out at the hellish creature again and again. The beast was set on a warm human meal, though, and savagely tore strips from Tuesday's gloves and neck armour despite its wounds. Panicking just as badly as you'd expect, Tuesday desperately jammed his hunk of slug meat into the parasite's maw. Chewing rapidly at the fleshy lump, the distracted bug suddenly screamed and gurgled as Tuesday's Bowie knife sank into its stomach and slid from bellybutton to ribcage. Just to cap off a stellar evening, the creature vomited corrosive yellow bile all over Tuesday's visor as it died.

The mess took hours to clean up.

Once Tuesday had stripped the parasite for steak, ribs and shanks, he proudly mounted its head over his bed, horns, jaws and all. The victorious hunter stowed all that fresh meat in his deep freeze and had a well-needed shower.

His underpants, however, would never be the same again.

*

Life on The Mistress was a simple one. In the beginning, this simplicity was comfortable, and even welcome. Tuesday's tent was soft and warm, his cupboards were full of as much food as he could scoff and as many smokes as he could suck down, and horrific things only tried to eat him twice a week, max. It was also reassuring to know that his distant bank account was growing by the day. Sure, it would take four years – fifty-four bloody months – to be able to access that money, let alone to be somewhere it could be used, but it was still nice to have something clicking up, even if he couldn't enjoy it yet.

Although Tuesday worked with very little oversight (none, actually), he'd still dedicate an hour or so of each day to mining pimples to keep his far-distant bosses at PusCo happy. He was paid by the haul as well as by the day, so totally slacking off wasn't an option. This wasn't Cell Block Preschool: either the pus flowed, or he didn't get the cheddar. A hundred billion fat, ugly rich women needed their facial-improvement creams, and they needed them now.

Tuesday's biggest disappointment so far came on the day that his jars of mucus were due to be picked up by a courier from the PusCo cosmetics company. After thirty straight days alone he was definitely up for the company of the trucker, no matter how vile the courier may be. Tuesday had shaved, put on some smelly stuff and even brushed his teeth for a change. Unfortunately, Tuesday found out the hard way that the pick-up was completely automated by a wriggling snake-like ship that didn't even need to touch down on the Slug to do its job. Either that, or the pilot had simply ducked out of sight and ignored him. Tuesday spent the rest of the day in bed, glaring at the ceiling.

By the three-month mark Tuesday had personally encountered almost every single life-or-death risk in the manual, and some of them had occurred five or six times. Germs were by far the biggest drama, as The Mistress was far from hygienic to say the least. A single unwise barefoot walk across the slugscape meant that Tuesday's feet were now infected by a permanent layer of damp moss from his ankles to his yellow toenails. But the biggest ongoing germ-related issue was his water supply. A series of ceramic hoses pumped naturally-heated hot water from The Mistress' main armpit to Tuesday's tent, but the pipes had to be shifted every now and again to avoid what was known in the medical databases as "Screaming Squirts." Tuesday discovered that the reality of the Squirts was far worse than the manual could have ever warned and was very sure to keep the plumbing up to code from then on.

After a while, Tuesday ceased being merely lonely and began to long for intelligent company like slow-cooked pork ribs longed for barbecue sauce. Although he'd always been an independent guy from a very young age, knowing that he didn't have a friend in the entire galaxy at the age of seventeen was a little much to bear. Tuesday developed an ever-worsening habit of muttering his thoughts out loud, and generally tried his best not to go clinically insane from isolation.

By the six month mark, Tuesday had forgotten what it was like to hear another human voice. Sure, Tuesday's "Beyond" console was more than advanced enough to artificially create characters that were totally indistinguishable from real humans, but for some sadistic reason all the games in his collection were about mayhem and slaughter. Unless the computer-generated characters could be lit on fire and scream hysterically while running in a circle, it wasn't a part of his set.

Although he still worked enough to keep the distant overlords happy and kept himself fed and hydrated, by the tenth month Tuesday had gone so insane from isolation that all of his muttered words were now total gibberish. During the worst times, Tuesday would rock back and forth in the corner for hours, laughing at nothing.

Some people can handle being alone. Most can't. It soon became pretty clear what category Tuesday fell into.

*

Tuesday awakened a bit after 14am to the usual sight of twenty decapitated parasite heads looming down from his bedroom walls. They were always the first thing he saw when waking up, but they had ceased to scare him ages ago. Occasionally, they whispered to him, but he never listened to the heads, because they always lied. Tuesday couldn't trust them, couldn't trust any of them, because the rotten parasites were less honest than an apricot-flavoured koala colony filled with stainless steel Christmas trees made out of raccoon-operated dishwashers...

Finding solace in his snowballing insanity, Tuesday was just about to curl up and go back to sleep when he realised a fact like a baseball to the face: today was the day his contract ended! Four entire years had hobbled by, and it was finally time to leave the World Slug for good.

Tuesday had started by ticking off the months, then the weeks, and finally the days, but before finally hitting the sack last night he'd been reduced to pathetically accounting for every minute. Tuesday looked at the digital calendar for the very last time: only nine minutes to go!

As expected, the company courier arrived on time. Just to be sure there were no misunderstandings, Tuesday was standing directly on top of the final pyramid of gunk-filled glass jars. Tuesday was wearing his only set of civilian clothes beneath his spacesuit, though by this point the pressurised outfit had been damaged so many times by the local wildlife that it was mostly composed of duct tape and polyfiller. He started to jump up and down as soon as the tell-tale dot appeared in the sky, waving his arms in a very unsubtle way of making his presence known.

For the very first time, the snake-like ship wriggled out of the sky and landed on the surface of the World Slug. It touched down gently with the soft hum of antigrav wafers, barely making a sound. After all, not doing anything to annoy The Mistress was rule number one, two and three. The PusCo company courier turned out to be an old oriental man in an infuriatingly nice spacesuit and steel-capped boots, but it was as though Tuesday wasn't even there. The guy simply opened a ramp, pushed out a stack of floating crates, and didn't bother making eye contact before stepping back onto the ramp. The courier didn't say a single word, and offered nothing more than a brief, uninterested wave of dismissal as he turned away. However, the courier definitely noticed Tuesday's presence when a pickaxe whipped through the air at a top speed and sank into the hull of the ship, missing the courier's faceplate by inches. The old guy gaped, looking between the mining tool and the insane miner who'd thrown it.

"What the...why did you do that?!"

"Forgetting...something?" Tuesday managed, growling his words. He couldn't seem to shape the syllables properly. It was like trying to remember a complex phrase in Japanese after hearing it once in your childhood. Come to think of it, Tuesday couldn't quite remember what a syllable actually was...

The courier sighed and inspected the stack of floating crates. He moved his lips a little bit as he did so, keeping track under his breath, and within fifteen seconds his task was completed. The courier shook his head.

"Nope. Your scheduled resupply is all here. Didn't forget a thing."

Now Tuesday was the one who gaped.

"Re...resupply?" Tuesday eventually managed. His eye twitched. "No, no...my contract is...is finished! I'm meant to...meant to...to finish...and...and...finish..."

The courier sighed loudly, his patience now totally spent, and tapped the knuckles of his left hand with his opposite index finger. A series of holographic screens flared to life from the back of his hand, and the courier showed one of the large, intangible squares to Tuesday. It was a perfect match for the contract he'd signed fifty-two months ago.

"See here?" the courier snapped. "It says that you, Mr Robert Tuesday, hereby agree to a standard class-seven solo mining operation on The Mistress for a period of no less than twelve standard years. It's the resupply that happens every four ye-"

Tuesday lunged for the courier, but he missed and sprawled pathetically in the slick, grey surface of The Mistress.

He hadn't meant to do that. His brain was going more haywire by the minute.

"I need..." Tuesday sobbed, curling up. "I need...can't...alone...anymore..." He looked up, pleadingly. "Maybe...someone else?"

The courier may have felt more pity for Tuesday if he hadn't just tried to attack him on two separate occasions, but the courier's next words were delivered gently.

"Standard policy is you can't have more than one permanent miner on a World Slug, or you run the risk of waking her up. Of all the official regulations, that's the most concrete. Solo mission only, sorry."

"But...it's splitting off into little baby Slugs." Tuesday argued. He seemed to be getting the hang of talking again, but it was still difficult. "I seen them just the other day over the ridge, all suckling on those huge nipples. Boobs as big as suburbs, they are! Wouldn't it be...be possible to just...to just pass on the message..."

The courier was out of patience for this topic.

"I've already told you: this is a one-man drilling job, always has been, always will be. You don't know what these things are capable of when they're conscious. It's not happening, right?"

Tuesday was silent as the courier stomped back up the ramp without another word. He did stop to pry out the pickaxe and throw it over his shoulder, though.

On his knees, Tuesday silently watched as the courier's ship efficiently hoovered up the jars of green filth with an automated loading device. Tuesday's eyes followed the ship's arc as it left him all alone, and then he continued to watch the sky until there wasn't even a dot.

Once he managed to finally stand up again an hour later, Tuesday silently stormed back to his tent and lay in bed. Glaring at the ceiling like it had slept with his mum without protection, he tried to think happy thoughts.

As always, Tuesday failed.

*

Tuesday's descent into depression and psychosis continued to spiral with the passing of each and every day. Knowing that he was only a third of the way through his isolation was an unbearable thought, and so he did all that he could to block out reality by distracting himself. By now Tuesday had explored the entire World Slug from tail to nostrils, clocked every video game in his library sixty times over, and had watched all four of the compulsory Occupational Health & Safety vids at least a hundred and fifty times. He may have trouble spelling his own name, but Tuesday knew a heck of a lot about World Slugs by now.

Two months after being told the cruel truth by the courier, Tuesday was stomping across the slugscape towards a distant, bright yellow pustule that was just asking to be mined. Tuesday was arguing with himself at top volume about whether he was going insane, and swung his pickaxe in complex, threatening swoops the whole time. As usual, he was losing the disagreement.

Although he was wearing an (almost) airtight spacesuit, Tuesday clearly heard a low rumble from off to his left. Looking towards the horizon through a Perspex visor half-covered in duct tape, Tuesday groaned as he watched a distant phlegm volcano erupt in a seemingly endless geyser of brown sludge and roiling black clouds.

"Great. Flatulence eruption," Tuesday muttered to himself. "Rotten thing'll take hours to clear..."

Tuesday had lived through more than one flatulence eruption during his time on The Mistress and learned the hard way that what these events lacked in lethality they definitely made up for in sheer putridness. Thanks to those OH&S vids, Tuesday knew that flatulence eruptions were a result of the World Slug's bizarre digestive system actively converting the radiation She was absorbing from the two nearby stars into a biological form, and like all digestive systems, this process resulted in waste products. Although the "output" of her churning guts could be compared to what you'd find in a human digestive system, it was on another level entirely.

"Better get back," Tuesday mumbled, his sight fixed on the horizon. "Better get back, better get back." He sighed in frustration. "Could this crap get any wo-"

The Slug's skin suddenly tore apart like wet one-ply toilet paper beneath Tuesday's boot, and he fell into an open black chasm. Bouncing from moist cliff to moist cliff, Tuesday spun and tumbled through the darkness for almost five agonising seconds before coming to rest on what felt like a water bed. While this may sound like a good outcome, anything within the Slug that resembled a water bed was very likely to be disgusting beyond comprehension.

Tuesday groaned. It may have been profanity of some kind, but he was far too concussed to know.

"Spugging trapdoor," Tuesday managed, rolling onto his back. "How'd I miss that? Never missed a trapdoor before..."

Tuesday knew full well that massive pits like this one weren't natural and were always the direct result of some sort of parasite creating a snare to catch any unwary prey that may stumble into it. The darkness didn't last very long, thankfully, as the tiny spotlights that ringed Tuesday's sealed helmet picked this moment to automatically flicker on. Looking up, Tuesday could see that he had a fifty-metre climb ahead of him to reach the surface. While the cliffs didn't look all that difficult to scramble up, this wasn't the big issue: while Tuesday was no xenobiologist, he knew that if something was big enough and strong enough to burrow a tunnel of such a massive size into the flesh of The Mistress, it was probably bad news. Seeing as though Tuesday was only armed with harsh language at this point, if the owner of the tunnel decided to come and check its little pit, well...

There was a low rumble beneath Tuesday's feet, and he was pretty sure it wasn't from the far-off flatulence eruption. It felt like something else altogether...and it was growing...

It was pretty obvious that Tuesday needed to hurry but scrambling like an idiot would only make things worse. Passing his helmet spotlights back and forth across the oozing surfaces that made up the rough cliffs, Tuesday gripped a few potential handholds as he searched for the most stable point to begin his climb. Thankfully, the roughness of the hole meant he had quite a few to choose from. So, he reached up for the first ledge of many, and prepared to kick off the ground.

However, something enormous chose that moment to try and murder him. Tuesday's animal instincts kicked in before conscious thought could pull its boots on, and he let go of the cliff and rolled to the side in pure reflex. An adult tapeworm the size of an intercity train slammed through the exact spot where Tuesday had just been standing, and it burrowed face-first into the wall of flesh like a Densite-tipped drill bit. The deafening collision sent shock-waves through the tunnel, literally knocking Tuesday off his feet and nearly bursting his poor eardrums.

But the assault was far from over. Twisting violently, the tapeworm flopped as it tried to free itself from the fleshy wall. Mental as he'd become over the months, Tuesday knew that he was about to die if he didn't do something more useful.

And then he saw it: his trusty pickaxe.

Tuesday sprinted five rapid steps before sliding on the side of his boots through a slough of pus. Skidding along, Tuesday collected his pickaxe with one hand, turned, ducked and aimed just as the tapeworm finally erupted out of its fleshy prison. Opening a mouth big enough to consume a buffalo without chewing, the tapeworm dived for the tasty morsel known as Bob Tuesday.

Tuesday drew the pickaxe back, focussed on the tapeworm's single red eye, and threw the tool as hard as he could. Tumbling for its target end over end, the pickaxe missed by inches and thudded harmlessly into Slug meat.

Diving aside, Tuesday only had time to curse as the tapeworm uncoiled like the biggest Slinky in the known Universe and felt a horrible pain from hip to toes as the beast slammed into his left leg. Doing his best impersonation of a spinning throwing star, Tuesday crashed into a pile of meat with far too much force and passed out for a couple of seconds from shock. Once again, the tapeworm had buried itself a dozen metres into the flesh of the World Slug, but this time Tuesday was out of the fight.

It was over.

Although he knew on a certain level that he had to get up now, Tuesday was too stunned to do anything about it. He'd just been clipped by a freaking freight train, and it was a miracle his entire body hadn't shattered on impact. Looking up through blurred, triple vision, Tuesday passively watched as the tapeworm extracted itself from the wall, turned to face him with its gaping maw, and went to lunge one final time before dinner commenced...

But then everything began to shake like never before. Tuesday had felt quakes of fifty different types while on The Mistress, but this was something else altogether, as it seemed the entire World Slug was flexing and relaxing rhythmically like a heartbeat. To his amazement, Tuesday watched as the tapeworm whined like an enormous puppy, shook and flicked its horrible insectoid head back and forth in a highly agitated way, and fled back into where it had originally emerged with its metaphorical tail between its legs. As the beast left at top speed, Tuesday could clearly see into the second crater that the tapeworm had torn. Something the size of a house was glowing like fire within the pit, and although he'd never seen one in real life, Tuesday knew what it was: one of the World Slug's enormous nerve endings.

Tuesday couldn't do much, but he did all he could.

"Well, spug me!" he said matter-of-factly.

Tuesday then proceeded to pass out cold.

*

The entirety of The Mistress, the greatest of all World Slugs, twitched. She could feel a relentless pain radiating from near one of her kidneys. The human equivalent of what she was feeling was getting a rotten tooth torn out without anaesthetic. It was something she couldn't ignore.

For the first time in centuries, The Mistress ceased her sunbathing and slowly began to awaken. It took a period of two hours, but nerve pathways the size of train stations sent out electrical and chemical impulses back and forth from one end to the other. Eventually, feeling and movement returned to her extremities.

And now she was hungry for solid food.

Reaching out with senses that weren't understood by any other species, The Mistress was able to detect a planet relatively nearby (in an astronomical sense, at least), and decided it was time for a snack. She began the long process of moving from one point in space to the other by stimulating her long-dormant supplies of internal liquids, sloshing them about until they converted into a highly volatile gas, and then she swelled up from a football to a much bigger basketball. Now perfectly spherical, The Mistress did a slow flip, aimed her anus right at the nearest star, and let out the largest of all farts. She blew herself clean out of orbit atop ten-kilometre-long blue flames

CHAPTER SEVEN BREAKFAST

Tuesday woke up in very different surroundings. Sure, he hadn't moved an inch from where he'd passed out, but the chasm of flesh was unrecognisable. For starters, the brown jerky-like walls were now a bright pink, and they pulsed violently and continuously. Tuesday could hear unknown fluids sloshing through the World Slug's flesh.

Tuesday got up with a lot of effort. Besides a twisted ankle and vicious slashes of bruising all over the place, he wasn't too badly messed up. Checking his wrist display, a cracked plastic dial with AIR stamped on it showed a big, fat zero. Tuesday tapped the device with one finger, and the dial twitched a little.

Great. Could have enough air for five minutes or a week, and no way to tell.

Tuesday's long climb out of this pit was complicated by the new life flooding through The Mistress. As her muscles were far more pliant than before, this made the series of cliffs that led back to the surface all floppy and slippery. This caused Tuesday to lose his grip several times and sent him crashing all the way back down to the basement. It was just lucky that the surfaces were like worn-out trampolines, or Tuesday would have bashed himself senseless by the second slip.

Finally, Tuesday reached the torn flap of skin he'd originally fallen through and hoisted himself up onto the back of The Mistress. Puffing as he looked up at an unfamiliar sky, it took Tuesday a few seconds to figure out what was going on. His heart fell.

Thanks to the OH&S videos, Tuesday knew that a newly-awakened World Slug was capable of moving vast distances with nothing more than the near-comical method of rectal propulsion. In fact, at a top velocity of one-tenth the speed of light, World Slugs were the fastest of all known biological creatures. However, they were far slower than even the most basic of human star ships, and it wasn't unheard of for a World Slug to spend a million years travelling to new stellar pastures. As they could sustain themselves on most forms of radiation and were capable of digesting nearly any kind of matter, it wasn't like The Mistress would starve to death anytime soon, even if she went through the dark zones between star systems. If she was heading for an entirely new system, though, that could mean a travel time of anywhere from fifty years to a million plus.

Tuesday sat down heavily, slammed the face of his helmet into his gloved hands, and rocked back and forth for a while in total despair. If The Mistress was heading away from the thinly-spread human empire known as The Unison, Tuesday may not see another human being ever again. He would spend the rest of his days all alone with nothing to look forward to beyond withering away to dust without leaving a single worthwhile marker to show he'd ever lived.

The alternative, though was far worse. If The Mistress got it into her brain that some nearby populated world looked like a tasty breakfast after centuries of sleep, well...that mouth was large enough to swallow any man-made object that had ever been built, and that belly was far, far bigger...

Looking on the bright side, Tuesday was relived to find that the World Slug's extreme burst of speed hadn't resulted in anything instantly fatal, such as throwing him into space or crushing his whole body to the consistency of hazelnut spread. In fact, it seemed that The Mistress had evolved in such a way that her unique form of interstellar travel was kind to the parasites and grubs that called her body home, and it seemed this mercy had been extended to Tuesday as well.

Doing his best not to look up at the terrifying sky, Tuesday used his meagre supply of common sense to figure out what the Green Hell he was going to do now. As there was only one man-made structure on the whole Slug, it was pretty obvious.

Limping, using the self-lengthening handle of his pickaxe as a crutch, Tuesday headed for home. This would have been a good plan, except that his tent wasn't there anymore. Looking about the clear stretch of skin in confusion, positive that he'd gone the right way, Tuesday finally checked the little screen at the corner of his visor to make sure he hadn't gotten turned around.

Yup, it was the right place. And that meant if he wasn't the one who was lost, then that meant...

Crap.

On a closer inspection of the area, Tuesday noticed that there was a scattering of various colours of confetti from where he stood to roughly a hundred and fifty metres in every direction. All that was left of Tuesday's worldly possessions was colourful dust. Anything bigger than a thumb had been crushed, torn or exploded into fragments. Tuesday's tent-sweet-tent was nothing more than scraps, his endless supply of never-expiring food was now breadcrumbs and shreds of plastic packaging, and the pipes of his water filtration system had burst into a million jagged ceramic tubes no bigger than toilet rolls. Obviously he was no astrobiologist, but Tuesday was pretty sure that explosive burst from the colossal anus of The Mistress had smashed everything above the level of her skin into powder. The destruction was complete.

So, to recap, Tuesday had no food, no shelter, no water, no way to contact The Unison to request help, and every breath he took from his supply was rolling the dice to be his last. If another human being had ever been so totally, utterly screwed, Tuesday pitied them.

With nothing better to do, Tuesday got on his knees and began to search through the carnage.

*

It took an hour of scavenging, but Tuesday eventually found a few slithers of hope. There were plenty of freeze-dried Mac&Cheese noodles that had exploded out of their packaging and drifted back down from the sky like neon-yellow rain, and after picking up the little pasta elbows from the soft, red skin of The Mistress one by one, Tuesday now had quite a supply. He kept them all in the only remaining airtight container he could find. Just to rub it in, the container wouldn't seal.

Nuts.

Water was another matter, as the entire filtration system situated next to Tuesday's tent had exploded, and there was no way he'd survive drinking raw Slug-juice. Thankfully, the pipe system below the surface of The Mistress hadn't suffered the same fate as the above-ground bits, and it seemed that the subterranean section had managed to instantly seal itself. That meant Tuesday may potentially have a small reservoir under his feet, but he'd need to dig deep, and there was a good chance the "water" would taste like ass and have the consistency of treacle. That meant risking the Screaming Squirts, which Tuesday knew to be a fate worse than death.

Tuesday didn't give up. He walked a good two hundred metres in every direction, his rodent eyes scanning for anything shiny or intact, but as the minutes dragged on he lost hope in tiny increments. Every fragment he checked, every handful of worthless filaments that ran through the fingers of his gloves like dust, simply rammed home the fact that he was - technically speaking - utterly boned.

Tuesday had become the king of confetti.

Now absolutely baking after a pointless sixty minutes of wandering, Tuesday switched off his last fist-sized oxygen tank and removed his sweaty, faulty spacesuit helmet in order to conserve his air supply. Sitting down violently, Tuesday instantly stood back up again when it turned out that the temperature of The Mistress' skin had spiked. The temperature of her flesh had climbed steadily to the point where it was putting off visible heat distortion, and her colour was changing from pink to a pearly white.

Sitting on top of his dodgy helmet to avoid getting a burnt bum, Tuesday had nothing better to do than rattle his half-full Tupperware container. He'd never been poorer, even when he was living on lizards and beetles in the desert.

Taking a few deep breaths to calm himself, Tuesday was already feeling dizzy from the smelly onslaught of overcooked trout and urine, the unmatched stink of World Slug he'd come to hate more and more each day. It took a lot of inhaling to get enough air to survive, and pretty soon Tuesday felt like he'd dropped about twenty IQ points. If anybody in history had ever been murdered by having an old salmon jammed down their throat, Tuesday knew exactly how they felt. Although every breath was a total misery, it wouldn't kill him anytime soon.

Something in the sky caught Tuesday's attention, and he watched the penny-size circle in stupid disbelief for almost five seconds before realising what it was: a planet. The orb was green and blue, but not quite like the green and blue of Earth, and The Mistress seemed to be heading right for it. Sure, only going a tenth the speed of light wasn't much in a relativistic sense, but Tuesday didn't need a physics degree to know what would happen if a football the size of New York City smashed into a populated planet at such speeds. For starters, it would annihilate every living thing on the surface in an instant, then the entire planet would explode into worthless rocks no bigger than the size of a Chihuahua's scrotum. It would make the extinction of the dinosaurs look like a mild head cold. On the plus side, at least The Mistress wasn't going into interstellar space, which meant Tuesday would experience an instantaneous death rather than the slow torture of starvation and dehydration.

Um...yay?

Tuesday wasn't able to consider this upside for long, as the blue-green sphere had rapidly grown from a coin to a basketball in the span of a second. In another instant a total of five shiny moons could suddenly be made out by the naked eye, and for some reason they were all glowing like tiny stars. Tuesday had no time at all to consider their mystery, however, as a rapidly impending death left him uninterested in such things. As Tuesday breathed in one of his very last breaths he was able to make out the unfamiliar, jagged continents of this unknown world, and as he exhaled he could see the unmistakable straight lines and glittering embers of habitation.

Tuesday spent his final instants cursing the name Ernest Fell as the entire sky filled with a civilisation that was about to end. Standing to attention and looking directly up, Tuesday raised his middle fingers at the Universe and bared his horrible teeth.

And then something unexpected happened.

The Mistress tucked in her boneless chin, gracefully tumbled in a backflip that any Olympic diver would envy, aimed her bottom towards the blue-green planet, and let off a ripper. The enormous fart shook cities and sent shock-waves rumbling through the world, but at least it wasn't an extinction-level event. The Mistress, now emptied of her last reserves of propulsion gas, flattened out into a fraction of her usual width, curved her entire body into a giant parachute-like shape, and glided gently for the surface. However, one of those weird glowing moons had obscured her approach, and The Mistress landed on the bright sphere instead. Whether this had been intentional or not would probably never be resolved, as World Slugs weren't known for their conversational skills.

The Slug landed so gently, in fact, that it took Tuesday a few seconds to register that he was alive, let alone what had just happened. After all, the touch-down was softer than fresh cotton. Gibbering, almost sobbing in relief, Tuesday suddenly punched towards the same heaven he'd just flipped off.

"Alive!" he screamed.

There was a deafening CRUNCH from all directions that Tuesday both felt and heard, and the entire Slug began to vibrate more and more violently. It was pretty obvious that she was having a munch on whatever this moon was made from.

Still relieved beyond words, Tuesday took his first deep, triumphant breath on this nameless moon, but it became pretty hard to continue feeling relieved when he registered that the air tasted like unfiltered diesel exhaust mixed with metal grit. Funnily enough, for some reason it reminded him of cigarettes and antiseptic. And while that first lungful was unpleasant, the second one caused Tuesday to cough and splutter so violently that his head spun and lights exploded before his eyes.

His entire respiratory system was suddenly filled with rusty barbed wire.

Clutching his burning throat in agony, Tuesday realised that the World Slug had unexpectedly sucked away her thin layer of atmosphere and was now covered by some sort of putrid gas that his lungs wouldn't accept. Due to the delicate nature of the human respiratory system, this poison could be made from any of literally thousands of chemicals in an unlimited number of combinations and ratios, and it was more than possible that Tuesday had already taken in a fatal dose.

Tuesday's eyes burned as though full of capsicum spray and his sight vanished immediately. Gagging, rubbing ineffectually at eyelids that had puffed up, turned crimson and sealed themselves shut, Tuesday staggered towards where he'd last registered seeing his spacesuit helmet. Unfortunately, Tuesday was getting pretty lightheaded and disoriented by the crud flooding through his bloodstream, and after falling to his knees this blind groping found nothing but hot-to-the-touch slug skin. Tuesday was soon in a fully-fledged panic, which didn't do much to fight off the mental static from his brain tumbling towards unconsciousness and death, and he tripped over his own feet more than once. It had now been almost a minute and a half since his lungs had been assaulted by the toxic atmosphere, and everything was slowly sliding from terrifying to oddly peaceful.

Tuesday growled and foamed at the mouth.

Stuff peaceful! I want to live!

Stumbling, Tuesday fell on his face yet again, but this time his face touched something familiar: it felt like vulcanised rubber, and Tuesday could clearly tell with one sweep of his nose that it had been criss-crossed by dozens of lines of duct tape. Feeling for the collar lock in a frenzy as everything receded into a distant mental echo, somehow Tuesday managed to link the magnetic locks around his steel collar to the matching one on the helmet. Just as the blackness became all-present and the last of his willpower failed, there was a deafening thud and a tremendous impact on Tuesday's chest that forced the razors out of his lungs. His next delicious breath could have filled a Scuba tank.

There was a loud beep.

"Your bloodstream contains fatal levels of chlorine, methane, sulphur and carbon monoxide, Current User," a neutral female voice crackled into Tuesday's left ear from an ancient speaker. "Without an immediate detox, you have less than sixteen minutes to live. Confirm detox?"

Gagging, his burning, puffy eyes still shut tighter than bank vaults, Tuesday nodded violently. The sound of his jagged breathing was immediately drowned out by ten rapturous seconds of Locatelli's Caprice in D major performed by the great Elcor Dearheart, but then one of the greatest violin solos was immediately terminated by the unmistakeable CLANG CLANG alert of a serious system error.

"Detox unavailable, Current User." The suit chirped helpfully. "Please download the latest operating system firmware patch, refill the Detox cylinder, Restart, and try again."

"Tell me the bad news, why dontcha?" Tuesday muttered sarcastically.

CLANG CLANG.

"Nine minutes of air remaining, Current User."

Tuesday was too exhausted to respond. Somehow he didn't even swear. He simply lay there for a time, enjoying the coolness of the canned air as it circulated inside his chest. He may be terminally poisoned, but for now it was just nice to be able to breathe in a gas that didn't feel like a lungful of cheese graters.

When Tuesday finally had the willpower to open his scalded eyes it was to total darkness. Blinking over and over again with absolutely no improvement, the panic immediately set in, and Tuesday asked himself all of the obvious questions. Was he blind? Had the horrible atmosphere of this moon seared away his corneas? After all, he was able to see just fine a few minutes ago...

And then Tuesday realised - with a metric tonne of relief - that he'd simply put his spacesuit helmet on backwards. Tuesday hissed something that would have gotten him lynched in any Church of Death chapel, took a deep breath (just in case), screwed his eyes shut and wrestled the helmet into a more practical setting. A thin line of magnets along Tuesday's collar THUPPED apart and CHUKKED together again.

The Universe returned.

Now that he could see, Tuesday staggered to his feet to regard the landscape. Everything beyond the distant edge of The Mistress was still glowing like a giant ember, but there was no way Tuesday had any inkling of how or why. The World Slug didn't seem to mind that her long-overdue breakfast was hotter than molten aluminium and continued to munch away with thrumming vibrations that shook the bones within Tuesday's flesh. Looking up and panning his vision across the starscape, Tuesday could quite clearly see that the four other local moons looked like miniature suns, too.

Curious and curiouser...

Tuesday's suit again went CLANG CLANG.

"Seven minutes of oxygen remaining, Current User."

Tuesday sighed. In just a few minutes it would be time for an appetiser of chlorine, followed by a main course of methane, finished by a delicate hit of sulphur for dessert...

There was movement in Tuesday's peripheral vision, and his head instantly snapped towards the inhabited planet. Although that peaceful, Earth-like orb still filled most of the sky, something new had appeared between Tuesday and the green-blue ball: it was a phalanx of what looked like giant, blocky cylinders. In the space of a second the fleet immediately went from mere dots to almost close enough to touch. If Tuesday's eyes weren't red raw from chemical burns, he might have been able to read the names welded to the hulls of the ships. What stood out most of all, though, was that for some reason the star ships reminded Tuesday of Lego.

So, it seemed as though the nearby planet was finally going to do something about the apocalyptic monster eating the Welcome mat right off their doorstep. It was about time, too...

"Hey!" Tuesday yelled, waving his arms as the fleet of ships came to a halt, waiting for something unknown. "Down here! Help! Earth native! I've only got seven minutes of air left!"

"Six minutes eight seconds," the suit contradicted.

"Slig off!" Tuesday snapped.

Although the star ships didn't move another inch, all of a sudden, the sky was filled with thousands of growing white dots. Tuesday froze at the sight, confused by what he was seeing, but then the rodent part of his brain sent a single basic command to his limbs: scurry!

Tuesday bolted from a standing start as thousands of seven-foot-long white spears rained from the sky as though he'd pissed off an army of Olympic javelin champions, and the onslaught of thin lines began to thud into the soft, pliant flesh of the World Slug with thip thip thip noises. One whistled past Tuesday's head, barely missing him by inches, and all he could do was dart about at random and hope that luck was on his side. It was a relatively pointless exercise, though, as the cloud of javelins seemed to have been launched at random, and that meant no spot was safer than any other. The main advantage of darting and scurrying was that it made Tuesday feel as though he was doing something constructive, rather than just waiting for death to come and claim him like an old pair of undies from a Chinese dry-cleaner.

And then the obvious happened: Tuesday's luck ran out when a seven-foot-long javelin cleanly tore through the left shoulder of his spacesuit in an explosion of old rubber and duct tape and lodged into the ground. The impact twisted Tuesday's spine into a tight sheepshank knot, and the sheer kinetic force of the spear sent Tuesday somersaulting twice before he hit the Slug at top speed. The spiked tip plunged a full half of its length into the Slug's flesh before finally stopping. Thankfully, this javelin was one of the last ones, and the barrage seemed to have officially ended.

For a moment, all was still. The only movement was the quivering of tens of thousands of white poles.

Tuesday groaned. He'd been denied sweet unconsciousness, and to make things worse his throbbing head was being assaulted by a jumble of noises. The casserole of sound eventually resolved to become three separate things: a loud hissing, a jumble of nonsense words, and a constant series of CLANG CLANG alerts. Stunned but relatively unharmed, Tuesday blinked up at the sky. It took a moment, but the jumbled series of nonsense turned out to be clearly formed Unglish.

"Severe suit damage detected. You have eighteen seconds of air left, Current User."

Tuesday sat up. His head was all over the place, but Tuesday still had enough sense to reach up and cover the tear on his left shoulder with his right glove. The hissing calmed about one percent, and definitely didn't stop.

Great...

Tuesday reached down and retrieved a standard-issue PusCo foam sprayer from his meagre utility belt. The foam sprayer had more than a passing resemblance to a one-handed pump-action water-pistol.

"Ten seconds remaining, Current User."

Jamming its tiny nozzle into the hissing rip, Tuesday rapidly pumped the sprayer's grip as hard as his fingers could manage and was quickly rewarded with a spurt of putty. Technically, the repairs sort of worked. On the plus side, yes, the hole was definitely no longer an issue. The downside was that gout of sealant foam had immediately expanded into a mountain of bubbles that soldered Tuesday's right hand (and the sprayer itself) to his left shoulder with virtually unbreakable resin. Living for longer than eighteen seconds would always take priority over technical flair, of course, but this outcome was still embarrassing.

"Sealed." The suit noted. "You now have three minutes of air, Current User."

Tuesday grunted, twisted a bit, and used his free hand to start getting to his feet.

Eh. Three minutes is an improvement, right?

Stiff and sore all over, Tuesday reached his left hand out to the same javelin that had ripped his suit and used it to drag his sorry keister upright. On the way up Tuesday's visor passed over a clearly-etched brand name on the long white streak, and although he would probably lose a spelling bee to an actual bee, it was a word he instantly recognised.

"Pethidine?" Tuesday muttered.

Those nine letters were an instant flashback to the treasured times Tuesday had spent stealing chemicals from the medical unit back at Cell Block Preschool. Although he'd never gotten high on the stuff himself, Tuesday knew Pethidine was a powerful opiate that had been around for over half a millennium and had a lot in common with morphine and heroin. The stuff was always in high demand.

"Why would they..."

Pain choked off Tuesday's next words as he reached a slouch. Everything hurt, including bits he didn't know he had. Slowly panning his vision across the slugscape, taking in the thousands and thousands of identical spears, it was a no-brainer to assume that they were all full of the exact same opiate.

But it still made no sense. Why kill her with an overdose? Wouldn't nuking her be cleaner and more humane? Wouldn't it be easier to...?

Tuesday's train of thought was instantly derailed by a scream of exhaust from directly above. The blocky star ships had decided to quit hovering like Switzerland during World War II and were landing in a complex pattern. Scrambling well out of the way of the closest vessel, Tuesday watched in fascination as a drill bit the length of a skyscraper and the circumference of a jeep extended from the underside of every ship. The sharp drills sank into her grey flesh and immediately spun into action in a geyser of gore and grey fluid, biting into the Slug with a sound like a traumatic dental procedure. As the epic power tools continued boring further into the World Slug's flesh, they were soon followed by equally-huge lengths of clear tubing filled with thick, bubbling green liquid.

Tuesday watched as they pumped The Mistress full of some unknown chemical, totally clueless about what they were trying to achieve, but then he looked up again to see HIM, and everything else ceased to matter. Like most humans who were unlucky enough to see one of THEM in person, Tuesday's mouth gaped open stupidly and his heart missed a beat. Both his knees went weak, and Tuesday nearly sagged to the ground.

For Tuesday, time stopped.

Standing at an incredible four metres tall, the gold-and-alabaster creature was like an archangel of vengeance made flesh. It was as though War itself had been shaped into something physical that breathed and thought, that had the ultimate power to choose between life or death for anyone and anything HE came across. HIS kind had a name: they were called Monoliths.

Over centuries of genetic enhancements, cybernetic augmentations and neural programming routines, the warriors who enforced Order within the wide span of The Unison had gone by many names and been fashioned in many forms. But the elite soldiers of this particular era were known as Monoliths, and for good reason: looming at a good thirteen feet, Monoliths wore nine-tonne suits of baroque hand-decorated armour fashioned out of unbreakable glass plates, balanced atop a complex series of antigrav wafers and pneumatic suspension. Beyond the thick reflective surface, Monoliths had so many redundant systems built into their suits that there was almost no known force in the known Universe capable of harming one of them, and the entire concept of actually killing a Monolith was idiocy of the highest order. You might as well pick a fight with the Sun. This also extended to the flesh within the invulnerable shell, as their bodies had been granted a total immunity to anything as laughable as pain. They could easily survive unprotected exposure to the vacuum, and could not be pierced, burned or otherwise damaged by any projectile, blade, chemical, or explosive that had ever been manufactured. Just to round off their grandeur, when it came to weapons, every single Monolith was an entire army unto themselves. Each one of those four-metre-tall monsters carried a combination of offensive and defensive systems that would best be described as "apocalyptic." The actual specifics of Monolith load-outs were pure speculation, of course, as anybody close enough to actually see a Monolith engage in an act of violence had the tendency to not exist afterwards, but it was rumoured that they had roughly all of them.

Somehow Tuesday managed not to fall to his knees as the looming Monolith gently touched down toes-first beside the closest drillship. Top-of-the-line antigrav wafers built into the undersides of the Monolith's armoured footwear and the palms of his bulky gauntlets barely made a sound as the giant landed.

He came to a stop as softly as a teenage boy kissing his cousin on the cheek in front of a whole family gathering. Sunlight danced over his white and gold glass plates in a chromatic rainbow. Now that he was just a few strides away from the creature, Tuesday could clearly see the Monolith's face through a transparent – though equally unbreakable – glass sheet. His huge, slabby head looked like something Ancient Egyptians would use to decorate a Pharaoh's tomb to scare off grave robbers.

"Th-thank you..." Tuesday began, beginning to blubber in relief as he realised his ordeal was finally over. "I... I thought I was going to die here! I...I..."

But there was no answer. Tuesday's intense honour at being personally rescued by a Monolith dissolved like a stream of cigarette smoke in a hurricane as the giant promptly turned and stomped toward the sunken blade of the nearby drillship. Thick lines of antigrav wafers on the giant's feet meant that the giant was strangely silent when he walked, even though he'd doubtlessly be able to stomp really, really loudly if he so desired.

It suddenly dawned on Tuesday that he wasn't even important enough to deserve a second look. It cut him. It really did.

Whispering over to one of the biggest needles in the Universe, the Monolith used the incredible strength of his nine-tonne suit to slam down a series of heavy brackets around the tube, locking it firmly in place, and called out over the local MeshLink on a channel that Tuesday's helmet somehow picked up.

"Secured," said the most bass voice Tuesday had ever heard. It was like an earthquake being played over a subwoofer. He could feel it in his bones. "Pump it."

CLANG CLANG.

"Two minutes of air remaining, Current User."

Tuesday realised something: if he could hear them, then they could hear him, right?

Scrambling after the monster, Tuesday tapped the radio function on his pectoral with his one free hand, flinched at a squeal of distortion, and tried to speak calmly yet assertively as he approached.

"I'm Robert Tuesday, and I'm...I'm about to die. Please...please help me. Please!"

So much for calmly and assertively.

Tuesday could feel the Slug growing sleepy beneath his feet, and the rumble of her gorging had almost slowed to total stillness. So, they'd drugged her! Well, that made sense: World Slug fluids were far too precious to just charcoal into a cloud of smog. It would be wasteful beyond comprehension, like using the Mona Lisa as toilet paper, or having an actual musical CD as an ashtray.

CLANG CLANG.

"One minute of air remaining, Current User."

Tuesday went to speak again, but the Monolith waved at him with a snap of pneumatic suspension like Tuesday was a horsefly and gave a very precise order over the Link.

"Interfering with Unison business is a capital offence. Piss off or get shot. Your choice."

"But I'll die!" Tuesday protested, confused that this seemed to have no significance to anyone except himself.

The Monolith blinked through his visor in total boredom.

"You could die quicker. Believe me."

Tuesday was lost for words. But not for long.

"But I'm from Earth! Isn't The Unison meant to watch out for Earthlings, to defend our species, to keep us safe from harm?"

"Nope." The soldier flared nostrils the size of golf balls. "We generally just kill things who don't do as we say. Would you care for a free demonstration?"

"Forty-five seconds of air remaining, Current User."

"I..."

The Monolith turned away again with a dismissive gesture.

"Piss off, slig-head. Go smoke an arse."

Something clicked as Tuesday's mind reached the extent of its tether, and all of a sudden it was time for a good-old explosion of hateful, spur-of-the-moment, immature screaming.

"You spug-headed, dog-smoking lump of scum!" Tuesday roared. "I spit on you! Your honour is cat vomit, and your mother works as a cut-price harlot at a syphilis clinic! I hope you catch bum pox and die weeping!"

Tuesday gave two fingers from his free hand to the giant's back and stomped a boot as emphasis. Caught up in the heat of the moment, Tuesday lunged for the closest object – which turned out to be the container full of dry noodles - and threw it as hard as he could. Sailing in a smooth arc, the little plastic box hit the Monolith right on the back of his helmet and exploded into a shower of elbow macaroni.

Time stopped again...but for a different reason.

Tuesday had precisely one second to regret assaulting one of the most dangerous beings in the known Universe with a decidedly non-lethal container. After a moment of disbelieving stillness, the Monolith calmly turned to glare at Tuesday. This was the extent of the Monolith's response: no bullets, no napalm, no mushroom clouds...nothing but a dirty look. Unlike most dirty looks, this particular stink-eye was backed up by some sort of exotic psychic artillery, and that squint immediately caused Tuesday's entire nervous system to fizzle out as though a switch had been flicked. Despite the fact "if looks could kill" was nothing but a metaphor a one point in the distant past, with modern psionic weapons it had become a much more concrete concept.

Crumpling pathetically to the ground as his muscles went all floppy, the last thing Tuesday heard as he slammed into the Slug like an axed redwood was a final CLANG CLANG followed by a calm, emotionless statement.

"You have run out of air, Current User. PusCo wishes to inform you that upon the point of death, all of your dental benefits and unused overtime will become null and void. Thank you for working with PusCo."

Tuesday's lungs seized and went into spasms as he sucked vacuum. His face quickly transitioned from red to purple to blue, his eyes bulged in the obscene beginnings of terminal hypoxia, and he mercifully passed out.

CHAPTER EIGHT SEVEN SUNS

Tuesday woke up slowly. The first thing he became aware of was a raw pain that ran all the way from his jagged yellow toenails to his small mountains of dandruff. After the zapping that Unison goon had given him, Tuesday's entire body felt as though it had been dragged out of a deep freeze and half-reheated in a microwave.

Groaning pathetically and silently cursing the entire concept of non-lethal weaponry, especially the kind that was designed to shut off human nervous systems, Tuesday consoled himself that at least the ogre hadn't used one of those stunners that made you void your bowels everywhere.

"Are you awake, Mister Tuesday? Can you understand me?"

Tuesday twitched at the voice. It was cultured, calm and had an unfamiliar accent. Opening his eyes and blinking away quadruple vision until it was reduced to a mere triple, Tuesday nodded, licked his cracked lips, and tried not to drift off again.

"Mmm. Sorta."

Over a span of ten seconds Tuesday's sight gradually recovered to the point where a panorama of grey blurs morphed into colourful details. The first thing that came into focus was a thin man in a perfectly tailored charcoal-coloured silk suit with a shiny bald head sitting less than two metres away on an ergonomic chair. If the bizarre twisting sensation in his own spine and neck were any indication, Tuesday was pretty sure he was sitting on some similar variety of Swedish torture device.

Beyond the unknown guy, everything remained fuzzy.

Rolling his head from side to side, wincing at a headache that resembled having an entire rosebush massaged into his brain, Tuesday discovered that he was lying half-upright on the plushest mattress he'd ever been fortunate enough to drool on. Funnily enough, after so many years of hard living on sleeping bags and inch-thick rubber slabs, this luxury was actually painful.

Freeing his arms from a blanket that was so soft he literally couldn't feel it, Tuesday looked down at his hands. An assortment of derms – colourful, coin-sized circles that had a lot in common with sticky plasters – decorated his wrists in a dozen places. Even half unconscious and stupefied by a concussion that was so big you could use it to beat a Silverback gorilla to death, Tuesday immediately recognised a bunch of assorted medical symbols. He wasn't an expert, but Tuesday was pretty sure they were pharmaceutical-grade detox patches and were currently leeching all sorts of poisons from his bloodstream.

He did know, however, that those things were pricy.

Closing his sore eyes again for a few moments, Tuesday tapped both carotid arteries with his index fingers. Yep. More detox patches.

That voice interrupted the silence again.

"I need you to focus, Mister Tuesday. This is very important."

Tuesday yawned and stretched like a cat, clicking all his joints in a series of gross pops, and gradually opened his eyes like rusty garage doors. The unknown man in the nice grey suit came back into focus, and the expression on his face gave the impression he was pleased by the fact Tuesday hadn't fallen unconscious again.

Raising his right hand, the guy in the suit clicked his fingers; as though by magic, a hair-thin sushi pad and a curved stylus appeared from nothing, and he plucked them out of the air. The stylus went click-click as it tapped at the palm-sized device.

"Wozza…" Tuesday managed. "How'd you do that?"

Mister Grey Suit pretended as though Tuesday hadn't spoken. He tapped and stroked the pad a couple more times, probably just to check it was working, and spoke.

"Good third afternoon to you, Mister Tuesday. My name is Travis Melchor, and I hold tenth-dan black belts in applied legalism, impartial mediation and advanced justice. I am, in fact, a Legalitor of the highest calibre, and I have been assigned to resolve your case. If we avoid any unnecessary delays then our business may be concluded in as little as ten minutes, followed by your sentencing, if applicable." Melchor blinked. His eyes were emotionless, and his mannerisms reminded Tuesday of a desert lizard. "For this to go smoothly it is essential that you are completely aware of what is going on before we precede any further. Do you understand?"

"Wassa charge?"

Tuesday snorted and sat up a little straighter. It turned out he was wearing a hospital gown of such a shining white that it was uncomfortable to look directly at it. Tuesday coughed viciously.

"And how d'you know my name?"

Melchor crossed his legs and tapped the stylus on one heel in irritation.

"The charge is Environmental Terrorism, Mister Tuesday, and I know your name because PusCo, the conglomerate that manages mining contracts on dozens of World Slugs across the Known Universe, were extremely helpful in providing the Seven Suns legal department with everything we wanted to know, which included giving us your citizen card and all related paperwork." Melchor tilted his head slightly, as though considering how much he should say at this point. "I hardly need to note that your contract with PusCo has been officially terminated pending the resolution of this investigation, and that all of your accrued earnings will likely go towards making financial reparations to numerous parties once your trial is completed." Blink. "Are you ready for your trial, Mister Tuesday?"

Tuesday responded with long-honed instinct.

"But it was an accident!"

Melchor dismissed Tuesday's words with a curt hand signal.

"Mister Tuesday, I have absolutely no interest in hearing anything that you have to say unless I directly request it. Your words profit neither of us, and only serve to delay what I am here to achieve. I say again: your trial will sort everything out in short order." Blink. "Do you understand, Mister Tuesday?"

Now Tuesday tilted his head.

"Wait...so you're saying I don't have to say a single thing for this...this trial to happen?" Tuesday scoffed. "What are you going to do? Torture a confession out of me? Beat me until I plead guilty? Break fingers till I sign a confession?"

Melchor gave Tuesday an odd look. He seemed insulted, and perhaps even a little nauseated, at such concepts.

"I will do no such thing, Mister Tuesday! As the legal system on Seven Suns demands, we will simply tap into the recall function built into your standard-issue neural software and pinpoint every memory and belief you have surrounding the alleged incident. I can then make an immediate judgement based on the facts. Like I said, if we avoid delays, we should be done within ten minutes."

"But what about being judged by a jury of my peers?" Tuesday insisted, trying to buy time. He was well aware that half the stuff in his memories would get him fired into the closest star by most polite societies. "Due process? Innocent until proven guilty? Occam's Shaving Kit?"

Melchor barely moved his head, but he definitely flinched.

"It's Occam's Razor." Melchor sighed, resigned to the fact that Tuesday was going to be one of those clients. "Mister Tuesday, rest assured that to all intents and purposes, I am a courtroom. I am judge, jury, defence and prosecution, all in one." Melchor leaned forwards. "There are only a handful of Legalitors of my level on Seven Suns, and I can absolutely assure you that I have never ruled incorrectly on any matter since the official end to my hardwiring. In addition to being comprehensively loaded with the details of every legal case in the history of modern mankind, becoming a full Legalitor involved stripping away my capacity to feel any inappropriate bias towards my defendants, and it is impossible to fool me with any falsehoods, no matter how clever. Seven Suns is proud to have the finest, most flawless legal system in all of The Unison, and I can absolutely guarantee that you will get precisely what you deserve for your actions. Do you understand?"

Tuesday felt a sting of dread. That's what I'm worried about...

Tuesday sighed in resignation. Aggravating this guy wasn't going to help matters, so he did the smart thing.

"Yes. I understand."

Melchor seemed relieved.

"Acceptable. Now, this process should be virtually painless," Melchor said this first part serenely, but then a hardness appeared in his eyes. "However, if you attempt to resist the scan in any way, such as by repeating nursery rhymes in your head or deliberately thinking of going to the...to the potty, it will accomplish precisely one thing: it will force me to employ more effort, which means the process will hurt a lot more."

Melchor casually threw the stylus and pad into the air, and they vanished the same way they'd appeared. Wriggling his long, thin fingers before finally placing them against his bald head, Melchor closed his eyes and leaned back as much as the ergonomic torture chair would allow. The Legalitor took a few slow breaths, and then finally seemed to stop breathing altogether. His skin took on a wax-like consistency, and the veins randomly splayed all over his temples grew darker and visibly pumped.

It took a couple of seconds, but all of a sudden Tuesday could feel a weird twitching in the depths of his mind, a tickle in his thoughts...it was a feeling that he wasn't alone inside his own skull, that every definition of privacy he'd ever understood was a total lie. It wasn't unpleasant, like poisonous bugs were burrowing in his cerebrum or anything like that, but it certainly wasn't how you'd want to spend a long weekend.

Melchor's eyebrow visibly twitched, as though in confusion. Clenching his face more tightly, Melchor crunched his eyes together and bared both rows of teeth. The experience got more uncomfortable for Tuesday, like the sort of burning you'd feel after thrashing an exercise bike for twice as long as you should have, but the sensation was in his brainpan rather than his thighs.

Melchor hissed, and red crept across his forehead and cheeks. Veins rose to the surface on the back of his flawless hands.

"I don't know what you're doing or how you're doing it, Mister Tuesday," Melchor ground out, "but resisting your trial only makes you look more guilty, and such things have penalties all of their own."

"I'm not doing a bloody thing!" Tuesday complained. "I'm just sitting here quietly, doing absolutely fegging noth…"

Tuesday's words ended in a squeak of pain as psychic nails hammered into his grey matter from every direction. The sensation was shocking, and Tuesday's face twisted up into a spiral of agony. Glowing lead danced through his brain, sweeping aside reasoning and self-control. His mind broke like a beer bottle against a brick wall, and for a few seconds Tuesday was utterly insane. His thoughts melted and ran like multi-coloured candles in a roaring fireplace, and it was around this moment that all of his memories became nothing more than an illusion.

Tuesday spent the next fifteen seconds as a desert lizard sunning itself on a rock. It was good for a time, peacefully drawing heat through his scales and into his frigid bloodstream, but this calm ended in the most hideous way as he was caught in a huge, leathery hand and eaten alive. He only had a fraction of a second to see who'd bitten him in half, but that face, those curved, ivory-coloured teeth, were as unmistakable as the sound of his reptilian body being crunched into paste.

It was Ruska, Tuesday's mother.

His point of view jumped sideways into a place far, far worse; a hell that you wouldn't wish on a dog: the vile head of Ernest Fell. The gangster was pointing a hard-core automatic kinetic weapon at the naked, cowering form of Jim Tuesday, but some sort of primal, drawn-out scream grabbed Fell's attention to the right, and now the gun was rising towards the threat at about one tenth normal speed. His gun panned over the cowering toddler version of Bob Tuesday, up towards the noonday sun of the deep Mojave, then over to the hairy mountain of pure womanhood bounding towards a surprised Jeeves. With her simian arms raised for war, Ruska didn't have the faintest idea what hit her as Ernest Fell's assault weapon detonated in concussive bangs that sent vultures flapping and geckos diving under rocks. Ruska's body opened up like a razor had been run over her stitching, and everything went red in an explosion of meat...

Mercifully, at this point the scene ended, but Tuesday's sense of reality continued to break apart in an eternal scream, and just as he (she? it? they? them?) was certain that this madness was all that had ever existed and all that would ever exist, it all came to a halt like a fatal roller-coaster accident. The freefall of pain faded, but that brief psychosis lingered like the stench of burning human flesh.

When Tuesday was finally able to open his eyes, regaining the capacity to know who he was and what was real after what felt like a lifetime of delusion, it was to see that Melchor was studying him with an expression halfway between confused and angry. Despite the pain he'd just inflicted on Tuesday, the Legalitor seemed to have no time for pity or apologies. Without so much as a "whoops," Melchor ploughed into his next question.

"What happened to your software, Mister Tuesday?"

Tuesday gave Melchor exactly the sort of reaction you'd expect.

"Software? What bloody software?" Tuesday retched a little. "Fink I'm going to be sick..."

Melchor narrowed his eyes. He hardly needed to repeat the fact that he was immune to the smallest of fibs, but he seemed at a loss in the face of Tuesday's overwhelming lack of basic facts. Melchor clicked his fingers, and the hospital room instantly lit up so brightly that it felt like they were both being dissolved in a ground-zero nuclear explosion. Tuesday cursed and clawed at his eyes, blinded.

"Mister Tuesday, your citizen card shows that you were born and raised on Seven Suns. It is a core component of our – of your - culture that all children go through an extensive series of AutoEducation uploads in their fifth year of life, followed by a yearly top-up to make sure nothing has leaked out." Melchor leaned forwards through the light pollution, his eyes large and dark and angry. "How could you, somebody born and raised on Seven Suns, have possibly missed out on our proud tradition of universal education?"

Tuesday froze.

Crap. I really should have read that stupid citizen card at some point...

"I-"

"Was it your parents?" Surprisingly, Melchor looked sympathetic all of a sudden. Tuesday immediately detected a potential point of weakness and decided that he'd exploit it as soon and as far as possible.

"It was their duty to bring you in for the standard uploads. Why didn't they?" Melchor pushed.

Tuesday shook his head. His eyes had almost adjusted to the brightness, and it became clear that all Melchor had done to cause the overwhelming glare was to open a panorama of windows. Tuesday could make out an endless sprawl of white spires shrouded in equally white clouds that stretched to the vanishing point and beyond, as well as far, far too many bright spots in the sky. He blinked stupidly and counted the blazing suns.

Was that...are there seven suns in the sky? How in the...

"Answer the question, Mister Tuesday." Melchor said with a lot less softness.

"My parents definitely didn't get me any sort of AutoEducation uploads from anywhere at any time, honest." Tuesday rattled off. "Television was my teacher."

Melchor looked faint. He seemed so rattled by such a concept that he lost his otherwise perpetual eloquence.

"Well I have never, in all my...the sheer horror of....and you've been walking around all this time without a single fact in your head, going through life as a total imbecile? How do you even walk without falling on your face?" Melchor was now visibly shaking. "Mister Tuesday, as your brain doesn't have any software, it is impossible for me to conduct your trial. Also, I feel I must apologise for the violence of my reading attempt. If I knew you didn't have any software, I wouldn't have dreamt of doing such a thing. I hate to imagine how painful that must have been! Please accept my apologies, and I will do all in my power to make amends."

Tuesday brightened, but he didn't show it. For now, giving any sign of relief might as well be an admission of guilt. Things were still too dodgy to take any such chances.

"So can I go?" Tuesday suggested, swinging for the fences.

Melchor seemed amused by this question. But then he did something really strange: Melchor's eyes rolled back in his head a bit, as though he was trying to look at his own left eyebrow. This spasm only lasted for a second, and then he resumed exactly where he'd left off.

"Although this is almost without precedent, our course is clear: you will need to undergo the standard series of AutoEducation uploads that all children from Seven Suns must receive. Once you have the basic software suite installed, I should be able to conduct your trial without any further delay."

Tuesday's hope did its best Titanic impression and sank to the bottom of the Northern Atlantic Ocean. So close, yet so far away...

Tuesday squinted in thought.

"How long will this take? How far is the...the school, or whatever?"

Melchor didn't bother to give an answer beyond a curt hand signal before simply disappearing, chair and all. Blinking in surprise at the vacated space, Tuesday barely had enough time to gape stupidly before two unlikely guards stomped into his line of vision through an opaque plate-glass door. Thankfully, the uniformed geeks looked less like Monoliths and more like mathletes and were equipped with stun batons so ridiculously tiny that the weapons must have been originally intended for clubbing Chihuahua puppies. Tuesday decided in an instant that either there was some sort of planet-wide law enforcement strike going on and these spugs were the cheapest rent-a-cops left over, or this world was so ridiculously civilised that there was no need for proper police officers. Either scenario worked for him.

The guards exchanged nervous glances, followed by a hideously failed attempt at looking tough. It was really quite sad.

"C-come with us, sir," guard number one stuttered.

Tuesday, looking bored and unworried, leaned back in the luxurious bed with his hands behind his head.

"Why?"

The guards looked at each other again. Guard one pulled a weird facial expression, which the other guy answered with an angry hiss and a meaningful glance at Tuesday. A short exchange of lowered voices and shaking heads went on for a few seconds as the pair did their best to figure out how to answer this very simple question. Finally, the first guard decided to go with what he knew. "Come with us, sir." The cop twitched. "Please?"

*

It was the shortest of trips from his hospital room to the closest transport, as it seemed that every segment within this blindingly white complex was able to detach from the backbone of the building and move about at will. What had previously been an empty ivory corridor transitioned to an endless expanse of curved, ivory cityscape, the sort of utopian hive that would make the most optimistic of futurists cry tears of elation, but that glowing chasm of solid habitation was soon eclipsed by what was best described as a futuristic motor home. The distance from blanket to shuttle was about fifteen steps.

The cops indicated that Tuesday should go first. Looking through the hatch, Tuesday saw that the interior of the communal transport had a lot of similarities to a plush pool room, complete with foot-deep shagpile carpet and marshmallow-soft leather recliners. Both cops trembled a little bit as Tuesday got within arms' reach, but once their prisoner had taken a seat on a recliner they visibly relaxed. Both officers took a seat on identical lounges directly opposite their prisoner.

And then the world dropped like a brick.

It kinda went without saying that Tuesday may have appreciated a warning before the transport plunged more than two hundred storeys, even though the dive was smoother than peanut-butter due to some sort of anti-vertigo system. After recovering from five seconds of total shock, Tuesday could see out the window that they were still more than a kilometre above the distant surface of

Seven Suns. No matter how far he looked through the labyrinth of creamy, interconnected starscrapers in the distance, Tuesday couldn't make out a single shadow anywhere.

There was the sound of a harp, and a polite voice with an accent just like Melchor's sounded from an unseen speaker.

"Eight minutes to destination."

Looking down, Tuesday noticed somebody had left a digital newspaper on the next seat. Admittedly, this would usually be of zero interest to somebody with the literacy level of an especially bright Pomeranian, but the square of 100% recyclable plastic registered Tuesday's interest and kindly voiced wherever section his line of sight crossed. Craning his neck a bit, Tuesday was informed through a minuscule speaker that he was looking at the Third Afternoon Edition of the 34th of April, but he was disappointed to find that most of the newspaper consisted of funny stories about cats. There was also a puff-piece about some sort of inexplicable mass-disappearance of faulty hardware from all over Seven Suns. Nobody knew where any of it had gone. One story that piqued Tuesday's interest was an announcement that the MacDeath fast food restaurant chain had won its appeal to open a total of nine franchises across this planet, despite a series of credible death threats and assaults by members of the Nutritionist Guild...

Feeling a pinch within his bladder, Tuesday looked up to see the universal sign for a unisex toilet.

"Mind if I use the facilities and stretch me legs?" Tuesday asked, feeling stiff.

The cops looked at each other. One of them shrugged, and so the other nodded at Tuesday. Both police officers gripped their tiny weapons a little tighter as he got to his feet, and their eyes remained locked onto him the whole time.

Tuesday found that the transport's lavatory had all the finest comforts, including a bidet with twenty-seven settings and large one-way bay windows that provided a breath taking view of the bustling heart of the extensive urban landscape. Just to ruin things, though, instead of a television wall there were (shudder) books. Tuesday ran his eyes over the titles: The Comprehensive Cabbage Cookbook, One Hundred Things to Do in Belgium, Erotic Origami for Beginners...

Tuesday backed away from the shelf. Those books seemed like a fate worse than death.

Feeling relieved, Tuesday got back to his seat just in time to be served cold potato and leek soup for his "third lunch," according to the polite transport AI. Totally confused as to why people on this stupid world would have lunch three times a day, Tuesday had to fight the urge to retch at the sight of one of his greatest enemies: a salad. He spent three solid minutes carefully picking out all the anchovy-flavoured crickets and bacon-flavoured crickets from his Caesar with a tiny Spork, and after mustering some considerable courage Tuesday hesitantly crunched on a mouthful that consisted of eight different kinds of lettuce. He survived the first bite, but saying he enjoyed it would be a stretch.

"Fancy food, this," Tuesday noted.

The not-quite-as-nerdy guard sighed. Cop number two looked back and forth between his colleague and Tuesday, torn about what he should do.

"I don't know what armpit of the galaxy you scummed out of, sir, but here on Seven Suns we eat a precise regime of foodstuffs designed to lengthen our average life expectancy to an optimal level. And no, sir, you cannot smoke, sir!"

Tuesday cackled and lit a chlorine-flavoured cigarette in his mouth by drawing back on the suck-burner auto-ignition tip. The guard was stuffed if he could figure out where Tuesday had gotten the cancer stick.

"What are you going to do?" Tuesday sneered. "Put me in a double cage? Maybe introduce me to your Mum for some real punishment?" Tuesday gave him the finger. "Punch it, spughead."

"You need an attitude adjustment, Mister Tuesday," the guard coughed and put down his newspaper, waving at the pall of gathering smoke. A fire detector gave a hesitant beep, apparently too polite to do something as vulgar as shriek.

Tuesday jabbed his cigarette at the sky above.

"What's with all the suns up there? I'm no wossaname, a psychiatrist, but I know that it isn't possible for there to be a habitable planet if there's seven spugging suns in the sky."

The guard looked at Tuesday like he was an imbecile. Tuesday was very, very used to that particular facial expression.

"Don't you know anything?" the more talkative guard chuckled stupidly, but the silent one gave a strained smile. "Every kid is taught this stuff! Look, when this planet was discovered it was far too cold to support human life. It possessed naturally-occurring supplies of water and oxygen, though, as well as optimal gravity, which meant it was definitely worth finding some way to make it suitable for colonists. After weeks of planning, the astroengineers came up with an idea: as this planet had five moons made out of near-pure silicon, they decided it would be easy enough to nuke them into giant glass balls that could, in theory, reflect the local sunlight. A lot of sunlight."

Tuesday was still snickering at the "giant glass balls" part by this point, but regained his composure in time for the cop to continue his story.

"It took hundreds of nukes to sculpt the moons in just the right way, but once they'd literally glassed all five of them they shipped in an army of craftsmen to shape the moons into giant lenses. It took hundreds of thousands of man hours, sure, but the lenses ended up working as planned. By concentrating the sunlight from moon to moon before it hits the surface of the planet, all the snow and ice melted in a matter of hours, and now the temperature stays at a lovely twenty-six degrees Celsius all year round." The cop twitched and looked up at the sky. "Problem is, this means we never experience night....or morning..."

"Just seven afternoons, one after another." The other cop added, his voice so low that Tuesday almost didn't hear him. "It never ends."

The first guard expanded his hands.

"So there you go. Two suns get reflected off of five moons, so it looks like we have Seven Suns. Get it?"

Tuesday's eyes darted back and forth between the cops. He'd already lost interest in the story as soon as the officer had used the term "astroengineer," and thanks to his minimal attention span something else had already occupied Tuesday's mind. In his typical blunt way, he said it out loud.

"You guys aren't really cops, are you?" Tuesday snickered. "Seriously, you look about as intimidating as a Dachshund puppy in a teacup."

Tuesday's tactless question was greeted with frowns and obvious offence.

"Mister Tuesday, we became police officers just like every other cop in the last two hundred years: our numbers came up in the annual civil service lottery. This is a planet of philosophers and mathematicians, but profound insights into the human condition don't fill our bellies or keep our garbage trucks running. Like everybody else, even though we spend much of our time doing what we do best, we also have to get our hands dirty." The more verbal cop lifted his weak chin in an attempt to look tough. "I'm actually the greatest expert in the genetic sequencing of amorphous Titan Slugs in The Unison, while Derns over there," Derns flinched at the mention of his own name, "is an acclaimed polymath."

"Leave me out of it, Priddle," Derns sulked.

Tuesday gaped a little at this news.

"You...so you..." Tuesday waved away his confusion. "Wait, wait...so to become a cop on this world, you need to draw the short straw?"

At these words, the cops glanced at each other again. Their blank expressions revealed that they weren't familiar with the term "short straw," so Tuesday tried to penetrate the confusion by rephrasing his insult.

"So you guys are police officers because of bad luck?"

Priddle and Derns both laughed. Priddle laughed a lot louder, though.

"No, of course not!" Priddle chided. "Law enforcement is a pretty sweet win. After all, Seven Suns is renowned for having the lowest crime rate in The Unison. There are much worse civil service positions you can get stuck with, like working in the cricket farms, or being a politician, but you need a serious black mark on your file to be eligible for that kind of scummery."

"But your criminals get punished in other ways, too, right?"

Priddle nodded.

"It's common for minor criminals to suffer some kind of ironic restriction based on what they prize in life. For instance, a gourmand may have their sense of taste and smell confiscated for a time, or an artist may have their creativity deactivated for a few weeks, or..."

"What about more serious stuff?" Tuesday interrupted, blowing a nervous smoke ring as he tried to remain calm.

Their transport jolted slightly. Tuesday looked out the window to see they'd stopped against yet another white starscraper like all the others. The vanilla glow made his eyes water. When he looked back, Priddle gave a smile that dripped smugness.

"I'm afraid this is where you get off. Buh-bye, Mister Tuesday. And remember: we'll be waiting right here in case you do anything stupid."

The geek taunted him! Unlike in his foolish youth, Tuesday didn't automatically start biting people's ears off in such situations, even if those ears belonged to a weedy poindexter like this gimp. Tuesday had discovered the hard way many years ago that this invited pain and small cages. However, he couldn't resist one last jab to even things up.

"Thanks for the lift...you pork-brained clot."

Priddle's face fell, but a hiss of pneumatics slammed the plastic door shut before he could respond.

Another five points for Bob Tuesday.

*

Unlike the featureless ivory expanse that had hosted his remarkably unpleasant conversation with Travis Melchor, Tuesday found himself in a bright, colourful area full of loud children who seemed to have nothing better to do than run in circles and find new ways to get their hands sticky. Tuesday gritted his teeth at the sight of the kids. These little brats had it too easy. At their age, Tuesday was eating seven-legged cockroaches and fighting hydras. Well, one hydra, anyway.

Looking down at a sprog who was wearing rainbow-coloured overalls, Tuesday did a double-take at what the child was hugging: it was a Mister Drizzle plush toy made from royal purple velvet, the exact kind Tuesday had spent his ruin of a childhood stuffing and stitching as a slave on the Dream Factory. He could clearly see the "DF" stamp on this Mister Drizzle's foot, proving its point of origin. Looking up at a skylight that loomed a hundred metres overhead, shaking and doing his best to remain in control, Tuesday managed to resist backhanding the kid, and even held back a swear word. If he ever met the parent that had purchased that slave-made toy, however...

Tuesday suddenly hated this planet a lot more.

"Your trip was uneventful?"

Tuesday spun around at the familiar voice, forgetting his rage due to pure surprise. Somehow Melchor had materialised out of nothing. To make things even more confusing, he was still sitting in that same ergonomic chair.

"How do you do that?" Tuesday demanded over the infernal riot of irritating squeals and high-pitched laughter.

Melchor shrugged.

"I have top-of-the-line teleconferencing hardware installed in my home. It is equipped with the very finest in applied holographics, meaning I can project myself anywhere on the planet without so much as leaving my bedroom. I can also take on a variety of appearances and interact with any physical system I come across in every way I could in the flesh." Melchor gave an indulgent wink. "However, my real body is currently sipping four-hundred-year-old brandy while wearing nothing but a red silk bathrobe and bunny slippers."

Melchor's eyes lit up in recognition as he looked over Tuesday's shoulder. The moment Melchor got to his feet the chair vanished.

"One moment, Mister Tuesday. Ms Humple!"

A strict-looking woman in a perfectly tailored navy-blue suit turned to regard Melchor. She grimaced as though Melchor was somebody she saw as nothing more than an acquaintance, but who obviously wanted far more from her. Ms Humple's initial facial expression could have filled a library. In addition to all this, Ms Humple seemed totally immune to the painful screeching of a hundred human larvae, despite the obvious chaos of what must be the equivalent of a kindergarten on this world. Tuesday was too busy staring at her breasts and missed all of this subtlety.

"Theodore, was it?" Ms Humple asked Travis Melchor with a deliberately painful lack of recognition.

Although Melchor managed to look unaffected by this gaffe, Tuesday almost felt bad for the Legalitor.

Almost.

"Actually, Ms Humple, I need to speak to you about-"

"You are aware that today's ninth intake is only a couple of minutes away, yes?" Ms Humple snapped in an abrupt way, not allowing Melchor to finish. "Do I need to inform you that interfering with the AutoEducation of a single child, let alone the very first session of an entire class, has been a serious felony for centuries?"

Her eyes darted to Tuesday, then back to Melchor. She cut off Melchor's words before he could stutter another syllable.

"I'm sorry, Thomas, but I don't have time for whatever this is. I'm about to put these kids through their very first upload, and it can be a delicate process trying to keep all of them calm. Please leave your card on my desk and I'll get back to you at my first convenience within the week...a month at the most. Feel free to see yourself out. Thanks!"

Without so much as a second's pause Ms Humple turned away, showing her back to the two men in a supreme lack of giving-a-damn, and clapped her hands together. Unlike most claps, this one produced a burst of sound so loud that Tuesday's ears rang like a telephone for the next ten seconds. For a moment it felt like his eardrums had exploded. This almighty bang stunned the children into total stillness and silence just as effectively, and half of them actually fell over in shock. Around a quarter were quivering their faces in preparation to bawl at top volume.

Well, that's one way to get their attention...

Ms Humple clapped again, but this one didn't break any windows. Tuesday still flinched, though.

"Children, file through the doorway and take your seats. Be sure to remove all jewellery, switch off any Link devices, and count backwards from ten."

The indicated wall split like an aircraft hangar to reveal hundreds of what looked like a cross between leather recliners and dentist's chairs. Still in shock, the stunned kids waddled over to the neat rows and climbed onto what looked like the plushest seats Tuesday had ever seen. The children sank a little into the recliners, and full-headed helmets immediately slid out to entirely cover their fat heads.

"Ms Humple?" Melchor finally managed.

She turned on the spot in apoplectic fury. The fact that Ms Humple's order hadn't been followed to the letter seemed to be so offensive to her that nothing short of live skinning would sate her rage.

"What are you still doing here?" she ground out, apparently moments away from indulging in one of the all-time-great screaming tirades.

Melchor gave a placating hand movement. The nearby children seemed to have recovered a little by this point, and Tuesday could hear a bit of baby talk and a laugh or two from beneath the helmets.

"Ms Humple, I am here on behalf of the justice department on relevant business. Mister Tuesday," Melchor indicated Tuesday superfluously, "needs to undergo a few uploads in order to make it possible to resolve his trial."

"I only do the basic upload suite here, sir. Anything more specialised or advanced happens elsewhere in this complex. I'm sure directory assistance can direct you with much more accuracy."

"Mister Tuesday only requires the basic upload suite," Melchor said softly.

Ms Humple glared at Melchor like he was trying to be funny, then gave Tuesday an equally hostile look as though he was in on the joke.

"You know we never provide AutoEducation to off-worlders." Ms Humple snapped.

"He's not an off-worlder."

It took a moment for that mistrust to disappear, but then Ms Humple's face immediately collapsed into total pity. It was as though she'd just been told the intimate details of one of the worst atrocities of all time. She seemed lost for words, but eventually recovered.

"Take a seat," she said simply, her voice a bit shaky. "I'll do what I can. But you know that if they don't get it done soon enough-"

"I am aware." Melchor interrupted, giving Ms Humple a look. "All I ask is that you try."

*

Tuesday was sure that the lounger wouldn't fit him, but the foam-and-leather slab automatically extended itself with a soft whirr before he laid down. Gripping the armrest, unsure how this would feel, Tuesday managed to sit still as the full-face helmet descended from his scalp to his Adam's apple. His head was totally hidden.

Tuesday winced as Mister Drizzle himself appeared before his eyes with a burst of childish cartoon music. The popular FunCo character began to dance about while singing about the joys of a top-rate education. Although he could clearly hear the other children laughing and chanting along with what must have been a familiar song-and-dance number, Tuesday resisted the urge to bite off his own tongue. He hated musicals.

"Now, kiddles!" Mister Drizzle announced with dopey enthusiasm. "It's almost time for school! I KNOW that you've all been looking forward to this for AGES, but I want to make sure that your first upload goes off PERFECTLY! After all, who loves you?"

"Mister Drizzle!" every last child screamed on cue.

Tuesday winced at the horror as Mister Drizzle continued his spiel.

"Now, before we get to that, to congratulate you all for finally reaching this pivotal moment in your lives, I've got a present for all of you: it's time to give you your very own eyelid screens!"

The kids were all squealing in an ecstatic way, but Tuesday's face twisted up in confusion. Eyelid screens? Nobody had mentioned anything about that. While Tuesday didn't know exactly what to expect, he wasn't left in suspense for long until some sort of articulated clamps extended from the full-head console and pinched his eyelids open with bug-like limbs. Trying to resist the urge to wrestle free of the device, Tuesday flinched as a burst of cold mist got him right in the corneas. Gripping the armrest of his lounger, blinking fitfully as the clamps disengaged and retracted into the mask, Tuesday gritted his teeth in annoyance as Mister Drizzle decided to explain the situation a minute too late.

"Now kiddles, it'll take about twenty minutes for the vapour to settle into a permanent layer on the inside of your eyelids, but from then on you'll be able to watch all the best cartoons, documentaries, news programs and Olympic Death sports right from the comfort of your own eyes! And all that from an organic screen that's less than a tenth of a millimetre thick!"

There was a comical fanfare. This part of the process was apparently done.

"Now, kiddles, before the AutoEducation process begins, your consciousness will have to be suspended for a leeeeettle bit while your operating system is installed." Mister Drizzle winked with a jolly TING noise. "But don't worry! That software will be uploaded in two shakes of a monkey-rat's tail!" Mister Drizzle smiled with a slightly different TING noise. "Now do any of you kiddles have any questions?"

There was a pause, then a sniffly, snotty little girl's voice piped up from somewhere out of sight.

"I do, Mister Dwizzle."

Mister Drizzle beamed. His teeth were bright enough to burn your eyes right out of your head.

"Sure thing, kiddle! What's that question of yours?"

"My...my big bwother told me that you're going to stick bits of metal in my bwain, and that this will weally, weally hurt."

Mister Drizzle was still smiling just as much as before. His sheer jolliness was starting to get seriously creepy.

"Now then, little lady, it sounds like your big brother is being a big MEANIE!" TING went his white teeth. "First off, kiddle, modern AutoEducation is totally non-invasive and painless. One of the major reasons that our award-winning AutoEducation programs have become the industry standard across all of Seven Suns is because they don't require cybernetic implants, or cerebral burning, or surgery, or needles, or anything like that. In fact, those older methods are crude, dangerous, don't work very well and are very, very ILLEGAL!" Mister Drizzle bared his teeth again, but in a more hostile way. "You see, our AutoEducation software speaks the exact same language that your brain does when it wants to store information in the traditional way, except at a much more efficient rate. It's just like forming real memories!"

"Mister Drizzle?" a little boy's voice quavered from the opposite direction. "How do I use all the new stuff I'll learn from today's lessons?"

Tuesday was beginning to think this was all staged, a fake attempt to give the impression that this process was interactive. This question-and-answer time with these stupid sprogs was going too smoothly, too efficiently. If he was going to use any words to describe small children, "efficient" didn't even make the top five thousand.

"Easy peasy, kiddle!" Mister Drizzle announced. "Just think about what you want to know, focus on your left eyebrow with both eyes, and the answer should immediately pop up in your head! I have to mention that this works better for some people than for others. No given search should take longer than three seconds between twitch to retrieval, and if your recall software takes longer than five seconds, you should report back for troubleshooting." Mister Drizzle danced a manic little dance. "You'll all be getting the standard suite installed today, but of course there are many other programs available depending on where you want to go in life. Do you want to be a polymath? A physicist? An astroengineer? A philosopher? An astrobiologist? Well, whatever you want to be is just a few jolts away!"

And that was when Mister Drizzle vanished. Tuesday was startled by the sudden lack of colour and sound, but then he could detect a soft keening and a distinct feeling of...disconnection. He didn't know what else to call it.

The AutoEducation was starting.

There was a soft feeling of waves undulating in his head, a gentle massaging sensation that spread from brain stem to cortex, and Tuesday suddenly felt an intense need to close his eyes. He could hear the nearby children murmuring softly as some kind of calming effect relaxed all their bodies and minds in preparation for the upload. Sleepily, Tuesday finally registered that he was only a few hours away from being a total, utter genius, of knowing everything he'd ever wanted to know, of never having to feel like the dumbest spug in the room wherever he went. Combining his innate cunning with a triple-digit IQ would make Tuesday a force to be reckoned with.

The calm disappeared with a noise like a platoon of smoke detectors having a screaming competition. Tuesday felt two distinct explosions inside his skull like the tiniest nail bombs of all time, and sticky blood immediately fired out of his facial orifices. Choking on a shriek and a load of coppery gunk at the same time, Tuesday gagged as he felt thick, viscous liquid pouring out of his nose, ears, the corners of his mouth and his eyes. Retching as the wave of red caught in his throat, Tuesday's brain finally registered that an alert was being pumped out at top-volume in Mister Drizzle's distinct voice.

"Lounger seventeen-delta has suffered a reaction," the alert boomed in Mister Drizzle's goofy voice. "Medical intervention required immediately. Don't panic, kiddles! Lounger seventeen-delta has suffered a reaction...medical intervention required immediately...Don't panic, kiddles!"

Beneath the alarms Tuesday could vaguely hear the wailing of the kids as they reacted to the alarm exactly as you'd expect.

Tuesday tried to open his eyes. He could see nothing but red.

"...has suffered a reaction..."

Tuesday could feel pumping on his chest, possibly from human hands. Then, gurgling and senseless and blind, Tuesday reflected on the fact that nothing ever went his way in this stupid Universe.

He felt something small and sticky adhere to his carotid artery, and with the distinct taste of opiates in the back of his throat Tuesday descended into an induced coma.

CHAPTER NINE ELEMENTARY, DEAR TUESDAY

Tuesday awakened to the sound of an emphysemic making a lewd phone call to a sex line. After another few seconds of consciousness it became clear that the noise was coming from a tube that had been shoved so far down Tuesday's throat he assumed it ended at his toenails. Reaching for the offending pipe in reflex, Tuesday panicked when his arms barely moved. Rolling his eyes like a terrified cow, Tuesday could see that his wrists had been restrained by leather strips. He tried to move his head and failed.

"He's awake."

Tuesday blinked heavily. Two familiar faces – one a man and one a woman, but both in equally spiffy clothes – leaned over to block the ceiling. Tuesday tried to sit up, but it seemed that an even bigger strap was holding his chest in place. Although he wasn't Mister Memory at the best of times, Tuesday couldn't remember who either of these people were...or even who HE was.

Tuesday tried to swear around the tube. He failed.

"Mister Tuesday," the man said calmly, placing a soft, flawless palm on Tuesday's shoulder. It was pretty obvious from the hand-model-quality fingers that the guy had no experience in manual labour. "This is Travis Melchor speaking. Please be still. You've suffered two minor strokes and burst a dozen capillaries in your head. Your sutures haven't finished sealing yet."

"Kgg?" Tuesday managed, trying to wrap his lips around a throat full of plastic.

"You almost bled to death." Melchor continued. He gave the woman an embarrassed look before making eye contact with Tuesday again. "It turns out you suffer from an extremely rare genetic disorder. You have an allergy to AutoEducation known as the Raffle Gene. The doctors tell me it's the worst case they've ever heard of, let alone seen. It's a miracle you're alive, to be honest." Melchor bit his lip. "In hindsight, I'm pretty sure we should have tested you first, but your citizen card makes no mention of it. Most unusual..."

Tuesday scowled, shook in fury, and then tried his best to strangle Melchor. It was lucky for the Legalitor that Tuesday was strapped down with enough

Velcro to stick an elephant to the ceiling.

"Ggrt! Kk!"

"We're talking one in a billion." Melchor continued, apparently happy to continue this one-sided conversation all afternoon. "The bad news is, you will never be able to go through any form of AutoEducation, no matter how basic. It would literally kill you...and it wouldn't work, either." Melchor looked frustrated. "While you were in surgery I looked into our options concerning your trial. To be succinct, now that neural imprinting isn't an option, there's only one thing we can do. You remember Ms Humple?"

Tuesday shot Ms Humple a dirty look.

"Rk! K!"

Ms Humple leaned closer. With the lights behind her, she seemed to be cloaked in an angelic halo that lit up the edges of her face. Of course, as Ms Humple was so close, Tuesday wasn't looking at her face.

"Robert, I work with children with your condition, and I may be qualified to help you." She smiled, but there was something in her eyes that scared Tuesday. He shrank back a little. "Due to the rarity of your allergy, I'm one of the only people on Seven Suns who's been trained in conventional education. I believe it's possible to teach you enough fundamentals for Melchor to...how to put this...for Melchor to grasp onto? So, while you wouldn't have any software installed, per se, I could prepare your mind to the point where you could be read without bursting anything." Ms Humple drew back. "I'm warning you, Mister Tuesday: this will take at least a year or two of full-time study, and I expect certain things from my students." She glanced at a band around her wrist. Tuesday could see it had three faces and ten hands. "How long did they say he needed to heal?"

Melchor shrugged.

"Should be fine by tomorrow."

Ms Humple nodded.

"I expect to see you the day after. Class starts second afternoon, sharp. Be late and suffer the consequences."

And she was gone. Melchor watched her leave, his eyes barely leaving her fine behind until Tuesday heard the door hiss shut. The Legalitor eventually remembered his place.

"Mister Tuesday, as you are currently of no fixed address and your PusCo earnings have been frozen pending serious charges, we've had to make arrangements for your next fourteen to twenty-eight months on Seven Suns. We've assigned you a standard mini-flat in the Welfare Sector, and this means you'll be expected to work at the cricket farms three days a week between afternoon three and afternoon five in order to cover your rent, electricity and sustenance." Melchor blinked his reptilian blink. "I believe this concludes our business until you have completed your studies. Good day." Melchor went to leave, but then a thought made him pause. He gave Tuesday an odd look. "By the way, I've been reading your case notes, and I've been meaning to ask: did you really throw a plastic container full of noodles at a Monolith?"

Tuesday's smile expanded around the tube in pride.

*

Two days later, Tuesday was laying down on a soft seat on a highly efficient, dead-silent needle train with his sneakered feet halfway up a bay window. It made his eyes water painfully, but Tuesday was doing his best to see if he could tell which one of the five glowing moons currently had a snoozing World Slug as a tenant. He was pretty sure moving something the size of The Mistress would need some serious hardware, no matter how advanced this world was. Tuesday tried not to think about how he might be footing the bill at some point.

His eyes changed focus and Tuesday saw himself in the window. He was dressed in a government-issue neon orange uniform. Somehow he'd already scuffed the pristine leather of his sneakers into garbage within the space of a day.

As usual, the trip was so gentle that Tuesday didn't immediately realise that the free needle train had gone from four hundred kilometres an hour to a complete standstill. Blinking, Tuesday stepped out of the whisper-quiet door and into a gateway two kilometres below the plane of the city. Like every inch of the world of Seven Suns, a planet that was often referred to as The Glow or The Blind by foreigners, this deep-core hallway was totally without shadows. The omnipresent white paint slathered across this planetwide city was more than just cosmetic, however: the thick layers of enamel absorbed solar radiation so efficiently that the abundant local starlight provided more than enough joules to fuel the power needs of this entire civilisation. A notable side-effect was that the paint gave off a strong glow as it seeped up the radiation, meaning that Seven Suns was truly a world of perpetual brightness.

Tuesday had already learned from an especially friendly nurse that many locals on Seven Suns literally had no concept of darkness, which was strange enough, but some of the other stories about this local aversion stretched belief to breaking point. For starters, there was a popular fad that had involved installing wafer-thin light strips on the inner eyelids of new-borns so that these kiddles would never need to know the horrors of total blackness even when they had their eyes closed. This was weird enough, but this trend had snowballed over the better part of a century until The Glow's billions of residents went the whole hog and had a specially-engineered bit of code installed into their collective genome: a custom protein strain that gave every citizen eyelids like one-way mirrors, so they were opaque on the outside and transparent from the inside.

Tuesday called bullcrap. The nurse assured him it was true, and then proved the story by tightly closing her eyes and accurately guessing how many fingers Tuesday was holding up without a single mistake. He eventually grew bored of the game within forty-five minutes.

Making it through a tunnel that was more sooty grey than white, Tuesday slouched into a greying four-way tunnel intersection, pushed open a sticky door and moped his way into a decidedly old-fashioned schoolroom complete with low wooden desks, defective child-drawn art and a sweeping chalkboard up the front. There was even a guinea pig in a Plexiglas hutch. As a consolation, Ms Humple seemed to have gotten even hotter in the last couple of days, and Tuesday watched her posterior for a few moments as she scratched at a chalkboard with a stubby piece of orange chalk. Tuesday got the distinct impression that this school thing wasn't funded all that well.

"Sit." Ms Humple snapped, not needing to look away from the board.

Immediately sitting at the closest desk – which had been extensively damaged with laser tip pen graffiti and plastered with what appeared to be a hundred different shades of chewing gum - Tuesday looked around at his fellow students. To his left was a hairless cross-eyed fat kid with permanent hiccups, and just on the other side of the chrome-dome sat a set of identical triplets. Tuesday did a double-take when he realised all three of them had been born without heads. It must be noted that all three of the Menendez brothers lived relatively full lives thanks to modern medical science and could leave Tuesday for dead in any subject.

In the opposite direction there was only a brain in a pink glass jar with little holographic butterfly stickers scattered all over it, and a name tag just below her hippocampus declared "Hi! I'm Tiff!" After staring at the bizarre sight for a couple of seconds, a Liquid-Organic Display screen floated up and tilted itself towards Tuesday's face. Six words appeared on it.

What are you looking at, dickhead?

Tuesday felt unsettled by this petting zoo of freaks and decided to focus on the teacher instead. His eyes closely followed Ms Humple's squeaking chalk as she wrote her name on the blackboard in the universal tongue known as Unglish, an ungodly mess of a language that had developed organically during the dark era that The Scandinavian Expansion had successfully occupied Amerika, England and Australia for most of the late 21st and early 22nd Centuries. Ms Humple followed her name with a list of more complicated words that Tuesday didn't recognise. Although he'd been verbally mangling Unglish his whole life, Tuesday had never quite understood how to convert all those squiggles into sounds. As far as he could tell, something at the midway point didn't seem to work. It was as though there was something fundamental missing in his brain.

While Ms Humple continued to scratch away at her chalkboard the bald fat kid unwisely decided to leer moronically in Tuesday's direction.

"How many serves of vegetables do you eat a day?" he whispered in mockery, proving yet again that the locals of Seven Suns had no concept of how insults were meant to work. "Four?"

Tuesday glanced at the kid and shrugged.

"None."

Fatty Smooth skull looked confused.

"I don't...I don't get it."

Tuesday sighed.

"I don't eat vegetables. Ever."

The kid was taken aback. It took him a moment to recover from hearing such an inexplicable concept.

"Um, I understand the individual words you're using, but the way you're arranging them literally makes no sense." He smiled slowly. "So I'm guessing you don't breathe air, either?"

Tuesday gritted his teeth and ignored the little spug.

"How old are you?" the kid continued.

"Twenty-one, but it's hard to tell with the sun rising every three minutes." Tuesday snapped, trying to keep his voice below "busted" level.

Baldy blinked his crossed eyes.

"Uh?"

"I'm twenty-one."

"Oh," Fatty smirked at the triplets, who would have regarded him with distaste if they possessed the necessary senses to detect he was even there, and made another sad attempt to embarrass Tuesday. "You're old!"

Tuesday's eyes flashed in anger and he hissed abuse through his brown teeth.

"And your entire family tree is a circle, you porky little inbred hick. You could have an entire family reunion sitting in a room all by yourself." Tuesday growled. "Go give your sister a Father's Day card, and then I'll see you after class every day for the rest of your life, you round little spug bastard."

The kid went purple and glared in two directions at once but didn't say anything else. It was for the best that he gave up on this contest, as Tuesday wouldn't hesitate to fight a kid. After all, they were more fun to hit than adults, as adults had the habit of hitting back much, much harder.

"Tuesday!" Ms Humple barked, busting him.

Tuesday sat bolt upright. "What?"

"Quiet during my lessons! You can make friends later."

"Oh. Okay."

"You heard me!" Ms Humple screeched.

Tuesday managed not to fall off his chair. Nobody had ever managed to make him shut him up so easily. He held up both hands in a placating way.

"Sorry."

"QUIET!"

Tuesday opened his mouth and formed a word but didn't have a chance to push it off his yellow tongue before Ms Humple clapped. Just like back at the AutoEducation classroom, it was as though a fork of lightning had struck the roof. The fat bald kid assumed an expression of total agony at the unbearable noise and screwed his face up like an Egyptian hieroglyphic, but the triplets and Tiff had no apparent reaction. Tuesday's ears hummed like mad for the next minute.

Nobody spoke out of turn again.

Ms Humple eventually turned away from the monochrome slab. She wore a brittle smile.

"Welcome to your first day at Elementary," Ms Humple said severely, panning her eyes from face to face to neck stumps to glass jar. "As you have all tested positive for the Raffle Gene, this means that you are severely allergic to AutoEducation and cannot undergo what is meant to be a basic right of every citizen born on Seven Suns. Even though no carrier of the Raffle Gene has ever accomplished anything worthwhile and you'll all be chemically neutered before you have a chance to breed and pass on your shame, all is not lost! This two-year course has been proven to convert clinical defectives into near defectives in the majority of cases, and if you work hard you may even be able to spend the rest of your lives tending to the cricket farms as menial class-eight labourers." Ms Humple casually drew what looked like a thin, arm-length reed from her sleeve and bent it in her hands. It made a sizzling, hissing noise against her palms. "Unfortunately, due to the fact you're a pack of dull-headed thickies, this means that the methods I must employ have to be...old fashioned." She wasn't smiling anymore as she looked between her students in challenge. "Today will be the beginning of your education. Are there any questions before first period?"

Tuesday put his hand up. Ms Humple seemed pleased by his insight.

"Tuesday?"

"Is there a Mister Humple?"

Everything stopped. All the kids froze, Ms Humple ceased breathing, and the guinea pig stopped running on his little wheel. Everyone was silently looking at Tuesday (or at least indicating their neck stumps or cerebrum in his general direction). Tuesday gradually shrank down a centimetre at a time until his nose was resting on the edge of his desk.

"What did you say?" Ms Humple's fury boiled and seethed behind the surface of her purple face as she ground out her words.

"I-"

"Principal Hurrage now, Tuesday! You cannot proposition your teacher!"

"What's a Prin-?"

Ms Humple's sizzling acid cane whipped through the air and snapped down on Tuesday's hand. The fact it was known as an "acid cane" kind of tells you everything you need to know about how it felt. Letting out a cry and shaking his stinging, crackling fingers, Tuesday copped a second burning lash dangerously close to his left eye.

"Hey!"

When a third cut got him squarely on his exposed calf muscle Tuesday jumped to his feet so he could become a harder target, but then a fourth precise whack sent him staggering towards the door. Smacked repeatedly high and low until he was through the portal, Tuesday found himself out in that familiar greying corridor of peeling paint. The door slammed shut with a clang.

Tuesday looked down at the extensive maze of red marks all over his exposed hands and forearms. I was like he'd been savaged by a cat with fish hooks for claws. Tuesday muttered darkly.

"Bloody women. Insane, the lot of them..."

Looking around the four-way intersection, Tuesday tried to orient himself. Behind him was the classroom, directly ahead was the exit to the rest of Seven Suns, to the left was a clearly labelled unisex bathroom, and to the right was a door with a very shiny golden plaque with ornate lettering. Scratching at his eczema, leaving little flurries of dead skin in his wake, Tuesday guessed that door number four must be where he was meant to go, and he went in without knocking.

The room that greeted him was typical of most government-funded establishments: the walls were a watery colour that Tuesday would call Institution Blue, the carpet was Blinding Orange, just like his uniform, and the only decorations were crude pictures that children had drawn for their sadistic

Principal out of nappy-wetting fear. On the far side of a lesser-bureaucrat-sized desk was an egg-shaped man in a ratty suit who appeared to be asleep. Sitting down loudly in the only free chair, Tuesday snatched up a laser tip pen and started picking his teeth with the pointy end as the round man smoothly pretended that he'd been awake the whole time.

"Don't do that, you idiot." Principal Hurrage's extensive frog-mouth arced downwards in displeasure. "You'll burn a hole out the back of your head."

Sneering at the oldest first grader in his career, the principal picked up his acid cane and bent it in a threatening way. It sizzled. Tuesday went to speak after a few seconds of silent staring, but the Principal gave a hand gesture to indicate that this would be unwise. Hurrage waited a couple more seconds before following up.

"Tuesday, right?" Hurrage looked unimpressed as he regarded a local clock on the wall. Seeing as through it was a Seven Suns clock, it had three interlocked faces and ten different hands. "It's barely into Second Afternoon! Your first class isn't due to start for another three minutes. What did you do?"

"Kinda asked out me teacher, all nice like."

Mister Hurrage twitched. "You asked out Ms Humple?"

"Yer."

"Have you no sense, man? How could you possibly think that somebody as beautiful and elegant and refined as Ms Humple could even consider associating with a piece of criminal garbage like you?"

Tuesday shrugged and put one foot on the principal's desk. He yawned and stretched, exposing the underside of his rotten teeth as well as both hairy armpits, before answering.

"Dunno. She knocked me back, I think."

The principal relaxed, but that facial expression had spoken volumes. After all, it was identical to that look Tuesday had seen on Travis Melchor's mug. Tuesday could easily read that Principal Hurrage had been smitten with Ms Humple for ages, but he'd obviously had no luck whatsoever. Tuesday yelped, shaken from his thoughts, as Principal Hurrage's acid cane snapped down on his foot.

"Ow!"

"Indeed," the principal gave a toad-like smile as Tuesday clearly absorbed the message to keep his feet on the floor. "I am well aware of your unique situation, Tuesday. And if you're planning to waste everybody's time for the next two years purely so you can get away with what you did, you'll...you'll...well, you'll..."

Principal Hurrage seemed at a loss. After all, there were no prisons on this world, and they'd abolished the death penalty hundreds of years ago. Instead of completing his totally empty threat, Hurrage stood up, turned to face his only window, and linked his hands behind his back. This gave Tuesday the perfect opportunity to pull all manner of disgusting faces and to make suggestive gestures with his fingers.

"You are already in The Reject Box, Mister Tuesday. I suggest that you use your extensive time here at Elementary to learn how to write your own name, rather than trying to pick up women that are way out of my league."

"Whose league?"

"Your league! Way out of your league!" Mister Hurrage quickly clarified, turning the colour of a beetroot stain on a white napkin. He growled his next words. "Do you know how I became the Principal of this school?"

"Picked the short straw?"

"No!"

"Failed all your tests? Shoplifting? Cow-tipping?"

"Stop guessing!" Mister Hurrage roared. He composed himself with great effort. His maroon flesh gradually faded back into a mere glowing red. "I was once District Manager of all the protein reclamation plants on Cemetery Block Fifteen, but once I'd heard about an amazing opportunity to get paid for viciously lashing stupid children in a remedial school for dunderheads, I immediately decided to quit working in the field of cadaver processing and generously dedicated to myself to this...this worthy cause. Do you know the difference between you and me, Tuesday?"

"Four chins. Ow!"

The principal retracted his acid cane. "No. The difference between you and me, Tuesday, is that I have always diligently applied myself in my civic duty, even when I didn't enjoy it. I understand what is expected of me, and I have an appreciation for how Seven Suns is an amazing machine made from billions of cogs, and that every one of them is essential to its operation. You, however, have a problem with rules, you have a problem with authority, and you have a problem with seeing beyond your own base, shallow, crude desires. But with the right attitude and dedication, you may still achieve the impossible. One day, Tuesday, you may be able to fill out your own name on an unemployment form without suffering a fatal brain aneurysm." Mr Hurrage's chin tilted upwards. "Do you get me, Tuesday?"

Tuesday scratched himself in two places at once.

"Yes, Mister Hurrage."

"That's better. Get back to class. And leave Ms Humple alone."

Tuesday got to his feet, turned, sighed, and rolled his eyes all at the same time. Doing this in synchronisation took his entire limited reservoir of concentration and gave him a mild headache.

"Buh-bye."

"Behave, Tuesday."

*

Except for the fact everything was painfully confusing and that he'd learned absolutely nothing whatsoever in any of the endlessly boring lessons, the rest of Tuesday's first day at Elementary went pretty well. The clock continued to tick, the chalk continued to squeak, and before he knew it Tuesday had finished his first six-hour stint as a student.

Still wearing his blindingly orange school uniform, Tuesday caught another free needle train all the way to the nearest cricket farm for his first after-school shift. An award-winning composer (with a dozen drunk & disorderly charges on his record) ushered Tuesday through a triple-sealed portal and into a hissing clean room. Swapping his gaudy tracksuit for thick Kevlar gloves, a protective apron and a hairnet, Tuesday was immediately hustled through a second clean room in another burst of antiseptic steam.

Grumbling at being hurried, Tuesday soon found himself in a long, long aisle made from millions of glistening brown slabs. Dead ahead, the corridor rolled off into the distance as far as his eyesight could reach. Looking up, the moist surfaces to his left and right loomed so high into the sky that Tuesday could almost make out clouds wrapping around the upper levels. A perfectly symmetrical lattice of thin black pipes was traced over the unusual slabs and sank into the wall every couple of feet. What the walls were made from was a mystery. Just like the rest of this stupid planet, everything was brightly lit and devoid of shadows.

The civil service supervisor was rattling off something boring, but Tuesday wasn't paying attention. Reaching towards the nearest wall, Tuesday lightly touched one of the mysterious bricks with a finger. Startling as the surface shuddered and rippled in response, Tuesday realised that the brown slabs were living creatures that had been perfectly stacked like Tetris bricks. It must have been the biggest game of piggyback in the entire galaxy.

Angry that he hadn't been warned about this weirdness in advance, Tuesday complained to the civil service supervisor. Enraged, the red-faced labourer roared that he'd already explained everything on three separate occasions by this point, and that it wasn't his fault if Tuesday had the attention span of a brain-damaged goldfish. Realising that he had a potential death-by-misadventure case on his hands here, from this point on the civil service supervisor was sure to speak v-e-r-y s-l-o-w-l-y in the hopes that Tuesday wouldn't end up head-first in a flesh mulcher or something on his first day.

Tuesday's fourth round of orientation only went for a couple of minutes, as just about everything in this mega-abattoir – from the self-cleaning Perspex walkways to the killfloor bladepits - was automated. One thing he wasn't told was that this farm didn't actually need any human interaction to operate, and it was nothing more than busywork for criminals and thickies.

Tuesday's main job was to make sure the Cricket Chow valves opened all the way at feeding time, and to check that none of the black pipes were gummed up. Mercifully, the so-called "crickets" they cropped in this farm of horrors were eerily silent due to the fact they had no heads, limbs or wings, and after decades of extensive engineering the crickets had a lot more in common with giant living steaks than insects. It was hard to feel bad about eating something that was literally nothing more than unthinking meat.

Bored, Tuesday eventually got into a conversation with a dullard co-worker. One of the first things he learned was that the "Cricket Chow" they were feeding these glistening meatbags was made entirely from highly-processed waste materials. Cricket Chow could be refined from literally anything with an organic source: rotten food, unwanted pets, barbershop sweepings, sewage, medical waste, and worse. However, the dullard made it very clear that using human cadavers for such purposes was highly illegal, and that the protein recyc system would raise bloody hell if you attempted to feed a person into it.

Tuesday closely watched one of the crickets during the next mealtime. From the way its stubby little vestigial insect legs wiggled in ecstasy every time another gout of grey slush was pumped into its brainless neck, the creature really didn't seem to mind what was on the menu. Once the nutrient paste stopped pumping through its neck tube, however, the squelching bag of pure protein started to thump like a beating heart...almost as though it was silently complaining that there wasn't any dessert...

Tuesday was a little more interested to learn that there were hundreds of different flavours and textures of cricket available for any and every dish, from cricket pork to cricket prawns to the mind-bending concept of cricket-flavoured cricket, and that every source of consumable protein you could get on Seven Suns started off with one of these disgusting horrors. The co-worker went on to specify how these little ones would eventually reach the size of a family minivan once they'd grown to an optimal harvesting mass, but Tuesday had zoned out by this point and didn't hear a thing.

It was home time soon enough, as the civil service program only required citizens of Seven Suns to work a mere three hours each day (with a mini-break every twenty-five minutes) in return for appropriate housing, food, recycled water, electricity and public transport. Despite the fact that Tuesday's shift was so laid back that he could have fallen asleep and done just as much, he was already plotting his next move. There was no way he was going to keep getting whipped by acid canes and towelling down an endless line of gurgling pus-bags for the next two years, and so Tuesday did what he did best: he began to plot a way to scum his way out of all forms of responsibility.

CHAPTER TEN TOTALLY SPUGGED

Tuesday managed to clock up nineteen solid days of compassionate leave in a row thanks to a non-existent Crucian Plague on an invented world that had decimated his equally-fake extended family one by one. Twisting one of his hairy nipples in two complete revolutions, Tuesday managed to sob real tears into the vid phone as he promised an unimpressed Principal Hurrage that he'd get over this utterly real, totally-not-fictional tragedy around the same time the weekend started, so he'd be back at Elementary bright and early on Tonday.

He wasn't.

With absolutely no idea how he was going to continue dodging both school and his civic duty for two years, Tuesday spent much of his time scheming petty schemes while lounging about in his crunchy underwear. If Tuesday put half as much effort into doing something productive with his life as he did trying to scum his way out of anything that required effort, the Universe would likely be shaken to its foundations.

Tuesday's apartment was situated at the very core of the Welfare Sector, a crumbling dumping ground for defectives and bludgers, a dank hole designed to swallow up all the criminals that the politer elements of Seven Suns liked to pretend didn't exist. For a world that was renowned for being almost totally bereft of crime, Tuesday had already witnessed dozens of new offences that he'd never even heard of before. He'd mentally noted a few of them for later use. So much for having the lowest crime rate in The Unison...

His bachelor pad was small and horrible, just like he was, as Tuesday's civil service allowance only managed to cover the lowest tier of rent and the most basic amenities with approximately zip left over. This slightly-curved rectangle was a standard-issue studio apartment which had been constructed with only one factor in mind: being able to contain the minimum a solo tenant would need while remaining just barely big enough to prevent triggering claustrophobia-related psychotic episodes. The steam shower was efficient, the pine-like smell of the chemical disintegration toilet was notably inoffensive, and the kitchen was equipped with six separate taps. These chrome faucets dispensed ice water, warm water, boiling water, English breakfast tea, filtered coffee, and Soup of

The Day, all for free. As Tuesday was on the lowest of all welfare plans and couldn't afford to eat out anywhere, he'd come to loathe Soup of The Day with a vengeance.

Squeezing through the invisible line that divided the bathroom and his main living area, sipping sweet potato soup from a tin mug, Tuesday flopped onto the slab of memory foam that served as both his couch and his bed. There was a permanent Tuesday-shaped groove worn into its padding, and it had been splashed with so many flavours of Soup of The Day that there were audible squelching noises whenever Tuesday shifted his weight. After a bit of a rummage under the cushions, Tuesday discovered an old piece of pizza he'd scummed from next door's bin, blew off the larger dust bunnies and happily munched away on the double-curried-sausage slice.

The doorbell chose this moment to ring. Tuesday found this odd, as he didn't have a doorbell.

Stumbling sideways through a slot of a hallway, Tuesday opened his front door to the deepest depths of the Welfare Sector. This ghetto was so ancient and neglected that the looming apartment stacks were sagging against each other, threatening to collapse at the slightest heavy breeze. The neon yellow CONDEMNED tape that criss-crossed their broken windows and empty doorframes actually served to improve the vibe of the neighbourhood, as there was very little you could do to make things worse. Tuesday's mega-block had less redeeming features than his dad, and you could physically feel the poverty here, the desperation, like the forgotten subnormals of this otherwise utopian world were ship rats scrabbling over each other for a piece of driftwood on the open sea, a bunch of no-hoper vermin with very short futures who were of no interest to anybody with the power to change their situation for the better.

Blinking away white and black spots for a while as yet another glowing moon rose high above, Tuesday looked down on instinct to see that somebody had left a small white card on the stolen STOP sign he used as an Unwelcome mat. The card featured a cute yellow baby duck in a pretty red bow. Picking up the odd gift, immediately getting pizza sauce all over it, Tuesday found that it only contained three words.

"Found... your...song." Tuesday eventually managed to say out loud, struggling to read the message. He blinked, trying to understand. He failed.

Found your song? What did that even mean?

Feeling paranoid, Tuesday scanned the street for movement. Besides the scurrying of rats and the flicker of dumpster fires, his cul-de-sac was in total stasis.

Slouching back inside with a grumble, Tuesday lit up a cigarette and smoked for a few minutes. Thinking as hard as he could, Tuesday considered who could possibly have left him such a bizarre message: the screws from Cell Block Preschool, Jeeves and Ernest Fell, Brian, Cheddar, his dad...

Tuesday went misty-eyed. He still missed his dad. Despite the fact that Jim Tuesday was a useless waste of protein with no redeeming features short of the fact he was probably dead and had already been recycled into something of more worth, like Cricket Chow, he was still the only family Tuesday had.

"Dad," Tuesday muttered gently, as though the word would break if he said it too loud. He screwed up his face until blood throbbed painfully behind his eyes. "Where are you? Do you even remember me?"

Glaring at his Mister Drizzle clock, which had seven of its ten hands missing thanks to a direct hit from a beer bottle last week, Tuesday guessed that it was about ten past something. Sighing in resignation, Tuesday decided he'd pushed Principal Hurrage and Ms Humple far enough for now, and he went about the business of getting ready for school. Tuesday made a sandwich by folding over what was left of his slice of pizza and filled a thermos with a Soup of The Day that smelled about as appealing as armpit sweat.

School days were here again...until he could invent some more dead relatives, at least.

Tuesday attempted to shave his perpetual stubble, but despite having a dozen highly-keen razor blades on an UltraMax handle, a few annoying spots always evaded his efforts. Absent-mindedly plucking out a couple of hairs, Tuesday threw a few random books into his backpack - including a MacDeath menu someone had left in his letterbox and a dirty magazine called Salacious Strumpets - and slipped into his orange school uniform.

Now came the hard part: finding transport to school. Despite the fact Seven Suns had a stellar public transport system that all citizens could ride free of charge, there was no way that any drivers would be insane enough to venture so deeply into the slums, let alone be stupid enough to land and pick somebody up. Needle trains, taxis, ambulances and even armed police cruisers never wandered this far into Tuesday's neighbourhood without a darn good reason, which meant he'd have to ride shank's pony to the closest transport nexus. Thankfully, Tuesday only had to stomp along the tarred blacktop for a mere five minutes before he stepped beyond the official core of the Welfare Sector. It was a sudden transformation: the walls were clean of gang sign graffiti, Tuesday didn't have to sidestep any chalk outlines, and there wasn't a Shatter dealer in sight.

Tuesday staggered backwards a step as something hairy and aggressive lunged over a fence to his left without warning. Strings of white saliva sprayed all over his uniform as the beast howled and snarled in his face. Tuesday could clearly hear a loud grinding noise as the feline's retractable claws sawed back and forth against the top of the wooden barrier, but the creature seemed to be unable to go any further thanks to a thick chain. Unsurprisingly, it was one of those damned barking cats that everybody seemed to own nowadays. While they were as territorial as velociraptors and needed to be leashed to stop them from savaging anything suicidal enough to come within range of their sharp bits, somehow they'd become the latest fad. Whatever had originally possessed somebody to upload the mind of a Timber Wolf into a Persian cat would be forever beyond Tuesday's understanding, let alone how the creatures had become so inexplicably popular. Then again, only the most desperate of criminals would try and rob a house protected by a barking cat.

Cutting across freshly mowed lawns and smacking letterboxes with a stick, Tuesday hopped a few fences so he could take a secret route to the train nexus. Waving to an old lady who was probably known as Nanna to a clutch of cute kiddles, Tuesday received The Finger. Taking his favourite shortcut through an alley of dented trash cans and dashing across a white street painted by the neon of glowing signs, Tuesday only had one thought on his mind: who had sent him that weird little present?

"Stupid card," Tuesday muttered to himself, aiming a kick at a gutter. He missed it by a metre.

Fetching the cute duck card from a sticky pocket, Tuesday read the message again and realised he'd gotten it wrong the first time. Holding his stomach, thinking he was about to throw up, his eyelid flickering and his pulse racing, Tuesday realised it didn't say Found Your Song. No, what it actually said was...

"Found You, Son," Tuesday whispered.

Without a second thought, Tuesday turned and ran for home. This would result in yet another day of truancy, but he needed to figure out what was going on, and he needed to do it now.

His head was crowded with questions, with possibilities, and most of all with confusion. Could this cardboard fold really be from his dad? Why wouldn't he just knock on the door? Was the card meant to signify something? Was his dad in danger? Is that why he'd made contact in such a weird way?

There was no telling why Jim would play such games, but Tuesday hoped he was about to find out.

Hopping a puddle, Tuesday swerved through tight alleyways and hurdled the railing of somebody's porch. Angry residents yelled at him to go back to school, to cut his hair, to go and die in a gutter somewhere, but he wasn't going to do any of these things.

No, Tuesday was going to do one thing today: he was going to find his dad.

He'd bolted all the way back to his cul-de-sac in the Welfare Sector before registering that something was wrong. He didn't know what, in particular, as such feelings were more instinctual than logical. Skidding to a halt in the middle of the street and looking around in suspicion, Tuesday could feel eyes boring into him from somewhere, but had no idea who was watching him, or from where. So he disregarded it as paranoia.

But sometimes, paranoia is there for a reason.

Tuesday made it home untouched and unmugged, as usual, as his orange school uniform made him look far too poor and silly to bother robbing. Even the desperate Blink-poppers immediately voted him a waste of time on sight. Dashing past a black van covered in graffiti that had been parked directly in front of his hovel, Tuesday had already stumbled to a halt on his front step when his brain belatedly caught up with what he'd just seen.

Van? What van?

Turning slowly, Tuesday regarded the wreck of a vehicle: it was an old black hybrid that appeared to be made out of laminated cardboard, and it was probably three million kilometres past its prime. The dented box was emblazoned with dozens of crude white decals announcing the many torture

metal concerts it had been to over the years, such as Cerebral Aneurysm, Live &
Vile, Deadgarden and Malignant Testicular Tumour, among dozens of others.
Stepping a little closer, Tuesday squinted at the Live & Vile decal from a
distance and ice slithered about in his stomach. Wasn't Live & Vile the
Scumbags concert where he'd been conceived?

The tempo of his heart rate spiked, and Tuesday began to feel dizzy and sick
with excitement. Stepping slowly towards the Junker, taking in all of its
crumpled details, Tuesday couldn't picture a more perfect vehicle for his dad to
drive.

Tuesday tapped a chlorine-flavoured cigarette out of a soft packet, trying not to
shake. He really needed a smoke to steady his nerves. This was getting all too
much.

The van's main sliding door was decorated by a big red triangle that didn't
match the white concert decals either in colour or font type. The point-down
isosceles contained words that began medium sized at the top and gradually
tapered down until Tuesday couldn't read them without getting closer. After
two hesitant steps Tuesday was able to make out that the top line of the triangle
said IF YOU CAN READ THIS, but it took another stride to be able to see that
the next line spelled out the words YOU ARE. Tuesday's curiosity was on fire
now, but the final word remained totally unreadable until his face was a mere
fifteen centimetres from the laminate door. Squinting a bit, Tuesday muttered
the final, tiny word out loud at the same time his eyes took it in.

STUPID

Something hard pressed into the base of Tuesday's spine. Tuesday would have
described his instincts as usually bordering on prescient, had he possessed any
idea what the word "prescient" actually meant, but all of this excitement had
blinded him to his surroundings. Knowing that he was probably in lethal
danger, he stood totally still and waited for further instructions. Tuesday's
smouldering chlorine cigarette picked this moment to drop hot ash into his left
sock, where it sizzled against the wet green moss that grew on his feet, but he
managed not to so much as flinch. As though on cue, the van's side panel
rumbled open to reveal a darkened area, and whatever hard object was digging
into Tuesday's lower back jabbed at him as wordless encouragement to step
inside.

Tuesday fought the urge to do or say anything stupid, well aware of the fact he was about to be abducted by persons unknown and that annoying them could result in a horrible death, but like with every challenge in life, Tuesday failed miserably.

"So is that a pistol, or are you just a sick pervert like your Mum?"

Tuesday's lower vertebrae exploded in agony as an electrical burning sensation flashed along every nerve in his body in a burst of paralysing heat. Tuesday crumpled pathetically, the cigarette dropping from his mouth as he went limp, and he wasn't even able to moan as his eye socket bounced off the van's dirty cardboard step.

For once, Tuesday managed not to pass out, but his brain spent an unknown amount of time operating at the raw cerebral power of scrambled eggs. Whatever hellish stunner had just been unloaded into his spinal column had also disrupted his mind to the point of uselessness, and it took an inestimable period of dancing colours and senseless patterns until Tuesday was capable of semi-intelligent thought again. It may have taken two minutes or two hours but figuring out how much time had passed wasn't a priority right now.

What did matter was that Tuesday was firmly cabled to a metal chair, a painful light was shining so brightly in his eyes that everything was an empty white, and there was what he assumed to be a gun clamped between his rows of brown teeth. The taste of its oiled ceramic barrel was very unpleasant.

Blinking his watering eyes against the flashing lights, Tuesday mumbled a question around the weapon in his mouth.

"Grph ruph mugh?"

The ceramic gun was immediately withdrawn, and it disappeared behind the wall of strobing light. Tuesday felt that this was his chance to talk fast before things got grim.

"What do you want?" Tuesday demanded like a true hostage, squinting in pain. "I'm poor, and I have no money, too, so I'm not worth anything to ransom. This is a total waste of your time and resources, and you should all be embarrassed to have made such an amateur mistake. Go learn to be proper kidnappers and try again with somebody worth more than cockroach droppings. You can drop me off as soon as you get a chance. I can make my own way home."

He couldn't be positive, but Tuesday swore he could hear snickering.

"Who are you?" Tuesday demanded.

The chances of getting a straight answer to a question like this was somewhere between zippo and none unless they were planning on dumping his dead corpse into a protein reclamation unit afterwards, but the Tuesday bloodline wasn't renowned for its foresight and mental acuity, so it was worth a go. There was silence, then a quiet hissing and scuffling, as though two people were whispering. Tuesday was starting to think that these bozos knew less than he did.

"So..." Tuesday said slowly, savouring the vowel, "What's happening here, really? You kidnap me, a total bum who's worth nothing to no one, and then you tie me to a chair. What could you possibly gain from this?" Tuesday unintentionally shouted the last sentence and heard the unmistakable noise of two safeties getting clicked off. He groaned in bored frustration. "Yeah, like you're going to shoot me now! If you wanted me dead, you could have just broke in and shot me when I was on the crapper. I live alone, I have no friends on this entire world, and my death wouldn't have been noticed until my rotten meat started to stink up the Welfare Sector. So cut the crap: why did you take me, really? What's the game?"

"I enjoy it," said a cultured voice.

Tuesday knew that voice. It was the voice of a Very Bad Man.

The wall of flashbulbs switched off and Tuesday spent thirty seconds gradually regaining his eyesight. Blinking away a thousand black spots, he looked up to see that the crime lord known as Ernest Fell, now well past retirement age, was standing over him and tutting with a smug look branded on his face. Besides whiter hair and a few new wrinkles, Ernest hadn't changed all that much. Tuesday flexed every muscle in his body, as Ernest was armed with the same unfolding kinetic rifle he'd used to kill Ruska, Tuesday's Mum, by shooting her in the back. That loathsome weapon had changed Tuesday's life like no other object in the entire Universe.

"Little boy," Ernest said softly, getting far too close to Tuesday's face for comfort. "You should have stayed in your playpen on The Dream Factory. I liked it when you were there. Jeeves liked it when you were there. Everybody was happy."

Jeeves silently shifted a little in a dark corner. Tuesday saw the thug was just as big as ever, but had gone grey on top.

"Why did you come here, Bobby?" Ernest scolded, utilising a nickname nobody else had ever voiced. "Here on Seven Suns? Don't you know that I own this world, that I run things here? Didn't anybody tell you that I'm the big boss? Are you stupid or something, crashing a World Slug into my home territory?"

"I didn't know," Tuesday said truthfully. He flexed against the cables and narrowed his eyes. "I knew this stupid world couldn't be crime-free. But nobody knows how infested this planet really is, do they?"

Tuesday shook with rage. He didn't want to talk: he wanted to kill them both. If he had a free hand and a double-barrelled shotgun, he'd already be blowing smoke off both barrels. Ernest merely shrugged and smiled in response, apparently enjoying Tuesday's impotent anger.

"It's not easy hiding an entire criminal underworld from billions of so-called geniuses. What can I say: I'm good at what I do." Ernest's face darkened, as though he'd suddenly switched into Business Mode. "Bobby, you've got to understand that I can't let you get away with what your family has done to me. The embarrassment of losing millions in revenue to a trio of circus freaks is...it's beyond words, beyond insulting. You have no idea how much I wanted to kill all three of you right there and then..."

"Why didn't you?" Tuesday asked defiantly.

"Capping all three of you was the logical choice, yes, but in my opinion, continuing to exist as somebody like you is far worse. Death would be a kindness, and I'm not all that renowned for my kindness." Ernest smiled. It was the smile of an executioner who always enjoys flipping the switch. "I haven't found your father yet, Bobby, but I will. From the way you responded to that card, it seems like you want to see him, too. Is that right? Do you want to see your Daddy again, Bobby?"

Tuesday couldn't help it: he spat in Ernest's face. The crime lord effortlessly dodged the green loogie and slammed Tuesday across the jaw with the flat of his hand in one smooth motion. It felt as though the entire lower half of Tuesday's face had been sent flying across the room. Even getting hit by Brian all those years ago hadn't hurt as much as that one expert strike.

Holding up Tuesday's head by his greasy hair as his eyes rolled around like dropped meatballs, Ernest managed a few more words before Tuesday lost consciousness.

"That was your final mistake, boy. And here I was, thinking I'd be merciful and sell you to some other factory world!" Ernest violently shook Tuesday's head, keeping him conscious enough to take in the next few words. "You know what? No more favours. I'm sending you to The Prince to get dismantled. And once The Prince is finished with you, I'll show the vid to that thieving junkie bastard of a father of yours while the exact same happens to him. Kid gloves are off now, Bobby."

The last thing Tuesday heard was Jeeves making a sharp inhalation, as though he'd just heard something shocking. Although Tuesday was ninety-eight percent unconscious, he knew that whatever was in his immediate future was far from encouraging.

CHAPTER ELEVEN PRINCE CHARMING

The nightmare only got worse when Bob Tuesday woke up.

Considering the generally awful quality of Tuesday's life, regaining consciousness was very rarely an occasion worth celebrating. However, this particular exit from the Land of Nod was an especially noteworthy level of Hell.

Where to begin? Well, for starters, Tuesday had been stripped naked and manacled to a smooth, stainless steel wall by his bony wrists and ankles. Just to make things worse, Tuesday could see that his scrawny body had been inexplicably shaved of all hair. Detecting an odd scent, Tuesday sniffed to discover that he now smelled like apricots and cinnamon, rather than his usual odour of chlorine-flavoured cigarettes and Parmesan cheese.

He'd been moisturised.

Tuesday lolled his blurry vision away from the contagious green moss that grew all over his toxic feet and crunched the sleep from his eyes. Everything gradually came into focus…and instantly got a million times worse.

Every inch of wall beyond Tuesday's minimal reach was covered by Ryobi power tools, polished kitchen implements and other assorted sharp things that glinted from hundreds of orderly rings. As Tuesday had become a bit of an expert on the subject of Things I Don't Want Jammed into My Body, thanks to being born with a particularly punchable face and a distinct lack of social skills, he immediately recognised cleavers, machetes, scalpels, can openers, corkscrews, bolt cutters, nutcrackers, ball hammers, drills, lathes and potato peelers, but there was also a lot of really exotic stuff he couldn't name, too. The implements had all been carefully arranged both alphabetically and according to their size.

Tuesday wisely decided that he really, really wanted to get out of this room, and did what little he could to look for some sort of weakness, some sort of opportunity. He was hoping for a conveniently loose grating that would lead into the ventilation system…or, better yet, maybe a hot, leather-clad female guard would come and check on him at some point, and all he'd have to do was seduce her into letting him go…yeah, he'd make her fall in love with him, and the moment her back was turned WHACK, he'd knock her out with a precise – but gentle - chop to the side of the neck…

Lolling his head left and right, Tuesday saw that the angled chrome walls on either side had been buffed to a high shine and looked as solid as a starship hull, so digging through them was out of the question. Looking up, there were lines of bright lights mounted along the ceiling within nigh-unbreakable Perspex shells, so no luck there either. Scanning his eyes along the ventilation ports in the ceiling, it was pretty obvious that the slots set in the roof were far too high, and even if he could reach them they were a mere two inches across.

Lowering his gaze and squinting, Tuesday finally noticed that there seemed to be a door situated directly ahead, but the portal was so seamlessly integrated with the wall that it was hard to tell for sure. The slab wouldn't look out of place on a military fortress.

While the cell was spotlessly clean, well lit, and reasonably warm - which made it nicer than most places Tuesday had woken up in over the years - it was shut up tighter than the magic underpants of an unmarried Red Wizard virgin.

Below, Tuesday's ten little piggies were dangling six inches above a surgical steel floor, and his diseased toenails were pointing at a tiny drain set in the exact middle of the cell. As usual, Tuesday's contagious foot-moss was dripping slime that pit-patted into a little puddle before slithering towards the drain like a liquid worm. It took one instant to discount any chance of escape through there. Even if Tuesday somehow managed to detach two layers of welded metal grates from the drainpipe with a tool from the racks of torture implements, he wouldn't be able to fit a balled fist through the tube, let alone his whole body.

Just to be sure, Tuesday rattled at his wrist and ankle manacles. In a twist that surprised nobody, the steel didn't give. Tuesday wriggled a bit more, but his arms were already numb and useless after the punishment of dangling from a roof for what might have been hours, so he didn't accomplish all that much. If Tuesday wanted freedom from his chains, he'd need to try a lot harder.

Tuesday tried not to whimper. He failed.

"Help," Tuesday blubbered to nobody in particular.

Kicking at the wall with both mossy heels in what little movement he could manage, Tuesday's blisters encountered some random scratches that had been jabbed into the polished surface by something sharp, perhaps an ice pick…an ice pick used in a frenzied stabbing motion…

Everything flickered and browned out for a moment, as though there was some kind of severe power drain going on nearby, but Tuesday's brain stopped working in a logical manner at the sound of a muffled scream. It was a long up-and-down wail that finished as a wet, drawn-out choking gurgle that eventually dipped below what Tuesday's ears could pick up. Tuesday's blood froze into red gelato in his veins at the sound, and his dire situation got even more terrifying.

Kicking against the ankle manacles and twisting his wrists about in a growing panic, Tuesday thrashed and growled like a coyote with all four paws stuck in a bear-trap and tried his best to break the bonds. If the steel manacles weren't inanimate objects, they might have laughed at his puny efforts. By the time Tuesday gave up, all he'd managed to do was to wear away two or so layers of skin, but nowhere near enough to draw blood.

He sobbed.

Tuesday performed a full-body twitch at the unexpected sound of a pneumatic hiss from the opposite side of his cell. The seamless door opened smoothly and a figure completely wrapped in black plastic entered the bright room, whistling When the Saints Come Marching In. On closer inspection, it appeared the dark shape was actually dressed in an easy-to-clean PVC business suit complete with a shiny black necktie and a glossy raven shirt. A pair of waterproof goggles were secured atop an elastic shower cap by strap. The outfit looked very uncomfortable, but it was clearly an example of function over form.

Tuesday was no genius, but his guess was that this guy must be "The Prince" that Ernest Fell had mentioned.

The Prince made a casual beeline for a bank of power tools, and gently stroked an extra-large industrial drill with one latex-covered finger as though silently greeting a lover. He still hadn't bothered looking at Tuesday, as though there wasn't some shaved and moisturised loser hanging near-naked from his ceiling. After a second The Prince glanced at his three-faced watch. It was plastic, like everything else he was wearing, but Tuesday couldn't see the time from all the way on the other side of the cell. Such things became irrelevant as The Prince took a tiny remote from his top pocket.

Things got worse again.

Tuesday audibly choked back dizzying fear as the silver walls of weapons smoothly flipped over to reveal a second assortment of torture devices: electric turkey carvers, oyster scoopers, fire axes, mallets, circular saws, power sanders, sharpened caviar spoons...

The Prince gravitated to a shelf that contained an assortment of tiny, unusual machines that had a lot in common with miniaturised dust-busters. Although seemingly benign on first glance, the moment Tuesday recognised PainCo's distinctive logo splashed over the machines he knew one thing for certain: all of these hand-held devices had been designed by brilliant "comfort reduction technicians" for the singular purpose of inflicting indefinite marathons of non-lethal torture on their fellow human beings. Their plastic shells were emblazoned with names like ScreamBox, Blood Boiler, and Chainsaw Tickler, but for once it was a positive thing that Tuesday was borderline illiterate.

It may seem impossible, but seeing the horrible implements wasn't the worst part. Somehow Tuesday managed to keep the contents of his stomach in place when he saw what was sitting directly beneath the shelf of non-lethal nastiness, and this was quite an achievement in self-control. The lower rack contained dozens of industrial cleaning products that had been painstakingly lined up like a television commercial during The Bold & The Bionic: ultrableach, blood remover, vomit dissolver, a range of industrial detergents, lime spray, drain cleaner and, last of all, Big Fanny's Ultra Stain Blaster. Big Fanny's USB was one of the most caustic substances in the known Universe and made hydrofluoric acid look like grape-flavoured soft drink in comparison. All those bright colours and friendly mascots smiled mockingly at Tuesday, speaking volumes about how easily he'd be wiped off the walls and discarded down the sink after...after...

Tuesday tried not to be sick.

The Prince wordlessly held up a few knives, allowing them to glint in the light, then put them back in their foam packing. He revved a turkey carver for a moment and Tuesday flinched at the sound of the electric motor. For no particular reason, The Prince chose this precise second to finally acknowledge his guest.

"Nice weather," The Prince said pleasantly in a cultured voice. Tuesday could tell this guy was posh, no doubt about it. He ran a single latex-covered finger sideways across a barbed knife. "Last afternoon was a bit of a disappointment, to be honest."

Tuesday nodded like one of those stupid little dogs that defectives stick to their dashboards. Maybe if he got this psycho talking there might be a chance of survival...

"Y-yeah. Lots of them, though."

"I find that the fifth afternoon always tends to sadden me," The Prince said softly. He carefully put the blade down, tilting its angle ever so slightly, and once he was pleased with its placement he removed his transparent latex gloves. His nails were immaculate, as though just filed and buffed. "And the sixth afternoon always puts me in an especially bad mood. It...annoys me. Sort of thing can...it can ruin your whole day, can't it?"

"Y-yeah. I know about that," Tuesday said truthfully.

Whistling again, The Prince cracked his knuckles and snapped on a fresh pair of latex gloves. Tutting at a crease, he pulled them tight with a high-tension whine. "Ernest neglected to mention your name. So you are...?"

So he wants to talk. There may be hope yet.

"Tuesday. Bob Tuesday."

"Really?" Squeak squeak went the gloves as they were rubbed together with talcum powder. Tuesday flinched at the noise. "Nice handle. Well, Bob, my name is Roger Prince, but everybody calls me..."

"Prince Charming." Tuesday blurted.

Even somebody as woefully uninformed as Tuesday had heard of the worst serial killer in the history of Seven Suns, a borderline urban legend that most locals (including the police) preferred to pretend simply didn't exist. Despite his legendary levels of rat-cunning, being in the presence of a man who had personally killed more people than undercooked chicken sushi robbed Tuesday of what little smarm he had left. Babbling was the most he could accomplish.

"But obviously the pigs mustn't know your real name, which is, ha ha, sort of, um, ironic, and all that, yeah?"

Tuesday felt faint when Prince Charming half-smiled.

"Yes." Squeak squeak went his gloves. Prince Charming stopped playing with the latex and wiped both palms on his plastic suit. "So. Your name is Bob Tuesday, and it seems you are my latest victim!" The Prince produced a small organiser and tapped at it, nodding. "And, like all of my guests, it seems that you broke the golden rule."

"Golden rule?" Tuesday repeated. His mind was going faster now than it ever had before.

"Yes. If you want to upset nasty, horrible people like Ernest Fell, don't let them take you alive." The Prince finally looked directly at Tuesday. His eyes were so blue they were almost clear, and when he slipped on his goggles they failed to diminish the intensity of that glance one bit. "My, you are skinny. Not been eating well? Perhaps not enough vegetables?"

"Don't eat them. Vile things."

"I like them, personally. I especially adore Black Asparagus. If it isn't cooked perfectly, then a unique cocktail of naturally-occurring neurotoxins will inflict the most incredibly violent nerve spasms. You've never seen anything like it, I assure you! One wrong bite and the muscles in your neck will twist your entire head back to front, turn your face inside out, and whatever is left will explode all over the dinner table. Bang!"

Tuesday flinched. The Prince looked apologetic.

"Ah. Sorry about that. Don't want to trigger any pre-existing heart conditions, do I?" The Prince wasn't smiling anymore. He looked business like. "Silly. Could have killed somebody, yes? And while we're on the subject, have you been implanted with any form of pacemaker? Got any blocked arteries? Inherited faulty valves from either parent? Suffer from high blood pressure?"

"No," Tuesday said shakily.

"Ah. Excellent. We should be able to manage two or three months, then. No use rushing things," The Prince walked up to Tuesday and rudely pinched some skin beneath a freshly-waxed nipple. He seemed unimpressed. "You, sir, are like an old charcoal chicken! No elasticity, no firmness...no, this won't do. It simply won't do at all."

"What?" Tuesday squeaked, tears forming in his eyes. "What?"

"I'm dreadfully sorry about all this." The Prince said with finality. He pressed a button and all the cleaning products and torture implements retracted smoothly into the walls. "I'm going to have to kill you now. My apologies for not being able to draw it out any longer. Goodnight, Bob."

Tuesday finally lost control. He blubbered, hiccupped and threw up a little. The Prince was unmoved by the display as he dispassionately pulled a tiny gun from his plastic waistband and aimed the weapon at Tuesday's abdomen. Getting shot in the guts would cause Tuesday's stomach acid to trickle agonisingly through his insides, slowly melting his organs to a formless slurry over a period of hours. Tuesday wasn't sure where he'd learned that little factoid, but it was very unwelcome knowledge at this point.

Tuesday screwed his eyes shut and waited for the bang, the searing sensation of a popped colon or a splattered bagful of ropey intestines pouring out like somebody had knocked over a plate of seafood linguine. His eyes were watering from the strain of latching them so tightly shut and sweat was running down his forehead in rivulets.

"Bang," The Prince said softly in Tuesday's ear. "You should be so lucky."

Tuesday snapped his eyes open in time to see an amused Prince Charming put away the gun. Had he been capable of words at this point, Tuesday would have given the serial killer the tongue-lashing of a lifetime for playing such sick games.

Pressing a button on his organiser to unfurl the racks of torture implements again, The Prince spent a good twenty seconds regarding his arsenal of pain before touching something small: from a distance, it looked a lot like a tiny drill with no bit. Picking it up in a gloved hand, The Prince pressed a touchpad. A noise like an angle grinder dissecting an iron beam sounded out loud and clear. Tuesday whimpered.

"This is a beautiful piece of military-grade interrogation tech," The Prince seemed to visibly relax as he revved the device with a look of sick joy on his face. "When you press it against human skin it produces the sensation of an extremely hot flame, but this little darling has been guaranteed by nine-out-of-ten comfort reduction technicians to leave absolutely no burns or other marks. Sure, you have to be shaved and moisturised for it to work properly, which you..." The Prince inhaled luxuriously in Tuesday's direction, then sighed out the breath in ecstasy, "...are."

"Now, let's talk about this," Tuesday said urgently, trying to walk backwards up the wall with his bare feet. They slid around within their manacles. "I'm a good guy, really! I do lots of charity work, I'm nice to old people, I don't torture small animals..."

The Prince stopped, weapon raised. It was hissing.

"Really?"

Tuesday's faced cracked and he blubbered again.

"No! I'm lying! I suck!"

The Prince advanced further, his face manic with glee. Smiling so wide that the serial killer was showing the entirety of both rows of pink gums, Prince Charming put his lips next to Tuesday's ear.

"Now open wide, and say aaaargh..."

It was even worse than he could have feared. Tuesday screamed until his conscious mind contained nothing more than the howls of his own agony, every muscle from his hairline to his toes fitting under his skin as he thrashed like a wounded animal. Eventually, after what seemed like two-and-a-half forever's, Tuesday's stunned brain registered that his time in Hell had come to an end for now. The shock faded like blood sliding down the wall, and his senses slowly dribbled away from insanity and into comprehension.

Tuesday was still shaking as The Prince walked back to the shelves to replace the ScreamBox in its foam insert and fetch a different zero-impact device. This one was much bigger and looked a lot like a circular saw with no blade. Turning it on with a click, a glimmer of white light in the shape of a wafer-thin disc appeared from the base of the device. Tuesday recognised the tool immediately, and somehow managed to arrange his words into something that other humans could understand.

"Beam saw," Tuesday breathed sharply, his heartbeat jerking in panic.

The Prince nodded, impressed. "Yes. How did you know?"

Tuesday's mouth twitched for almost ten seconds until his tongue finally managed to shape words again.

"Stole one at The Dream Factory one time. Nearly...nearly cut me leg off trying to work out what it was."

Prince Charming turned off the white blade of light with a flick of his thumb. Another click immediately brought it back again.

"You see, Bob, what you might not know is that beam saws are one of the most useful tools you can own, especially in the fields of construction and mining. Depending on their setting, they can cut straight through just about anything in the known Universe, or..."

The Prince took four steps and swiped the blade through Tuesday's left knee in one expert motion. The disc of light went harmlessly through the flesh and bone without any sensation at all. Tuesday somehow started breathing again as he realised his leg was still where it belonged.

"...or it does nothing at all. But, you see, on very low, very precise settings, a beam saw can inflict the most horrendous pain, as though your very bones are eating themselves...or so I've been told by the few people who were coherent enough to tell me afterwards."

Carefully adjusting the beam saw until its blade was the faintest of yellows, The Prince slowly brought it down on Tuesday's left shin. It felt as though the flesh was being stabbed with hot needles and pulled apart by fishing hooks at the same time. A scream rose from Tuesday's throat and turned into the most horrific swearing he'd ever managed, which was a noteworthy event.

Prince Charming eventually clicked off the beam saw.

"Language, Bob."

Tuesday's shin was now viciously streaked with bruises thanks to some delicate blood vessels rupturing beneath his skin, but the wound wasn't even remotely debilitating, let alone fatal. He briefly considered just how much endless torment The Prince was going to be able to inflict on him before he'd die from his injuries, but this was beyond comprehension and Tuesday's brain seized up just at the thought.

"So far, not a drop of blood. But we have just begun!" The Prince's eyes slid down below the ankle line, and his expression got a bit odd when he tutted at the contagious, mossy green growths covering both of Tuesday's feet. "Look, no offence Bob, but have you ever thought about getting that checked out? I've never seen feet like those before. Honestly, I thought you were wearing velvet slippers."

Tuesday, shaking violently for a dozen separate reasons, was so amazed he gaped.

"You...you want to give me spugging podiatry advice now?"

Prince Charming shrugged.

"I'm just worried that you'll get diseases all over my nice shiny manacles. Those feet, they're, well, they're unappealing." The Prince shuddered a little. "Slimy. Swamp-like. Gross."

"Unappealing?" Tuesday exploded, saliva spraying from his lips like a territorial barking cat. A boiling anger had finally gotten the better of his normally astute sense of self preservation, as on some deep level he knew all hope was lost and he might as well relieve that emotional pressure in whatever tiny way he could. "You know what's unappealing? Your Mum! Tell her to stop calling me up, you dickhead! Bitch has a face like a chainsaw vasectomy!"

The Prince looked fascinated by this display for a few seconds, but then he calmly turned to rummage through his tools for the next course of pain.

"Hey, I'm talking to you, Froot Loop!" Tuesday yelled, his words tasting metallic. His crude insults didn't seem to be having any sort of notable effect, but Tuesday stuck to what he knew: being offensive. "Or can't you stand the truth, Princess?"

The Prince froze on the spot, his back to Tuesday. It was clear Tuesday had struck a nerve when Prince Charming flicked a switch on the beam saw's casing all the way to the furthest setting. The harmless white blade was now a deep, arterial red, the red of an edge that could cut through diamond. Revving the beam saw, Prince Charming turned and gave a satisfied smile. Tuesday realised that his plan of deliberately upsetting one of history's greatest monsters wasn't the most tactically sound decision of his short life.

"For that, you owe me a foot."

"Okay, touché!" Tuesday yammered as the red blade hummed closer, step by step. "Let's rationalise this like adults, yeah? Look, things were said, emotions got a bit high..."

Yelping and wriggling ineffectively as the sawing blade approached closer with each rapid beat of his heart, Tuesday knew that his hopes of getting away in one piece would finish here, The End, and he put all of his strength into trying to free a leg. Miraculously, Tuesday's mossy, slippery left foot made a slithering noise as it slipped out of its manacle, and his toes lashed up in an arcing kick that could have gotten a shot past a professional soccer player. Tuesday struck The Prince right in his face, his toes smashing straight through The Prince's thin goggles and wedging into the depths of the serial killer's eye socket.

"I'm blind!" The Prince shrieked.

The Prince staggered backwards, holding his bleeding face with one hand, and Tuesday saw with immense satisfaction that three of his jagged, diseased toenails had broken off in The Prince's eyeball. More than a little distracted, the heel of Prince Charming's plastic shoe splorched in the slimy puddle of foot-moss juice that had been dripping from Tuesday's dangling toes, and he slipped over backwards like something from a Charlie Chaplin movie. Slamming into the metal drain on his upper back, the breath pounded from his lungs, a stunned Prince Charming could only gape in shock as the beam saw went up, tumbled about in mid-air, and came down blade-first. Roger Prince, better known as the psychopathic serial spree-killer Prince Charming, put up both of his arms protectively, but the impossibly sharp crimson blade made a hist noise as it went through his left wrist and the fingers on his right hand without so much as slowing. The keening saw effortlessly bisected black plastic, meat and marrow, and detonated Prince Charming's organs like water balloons. Blood began to pour from his mouth, quickly becoming a waterfall-like gush as The

Prince died messily.

Tuesday knew he needed to act fast. Ernest may have more friends nearby.

Tuesday considered breaking his thumbs to get out of the wrist manacles, but there was no way he had the guts to go through with such a plan. Seeing as though he'd already managed to get one foot free, Tuesday decided to work with what he had, and after a couple of minutes leg number two was out of its cuff. Yes, it took a lot of grinding, swearing and bleeding, but it was a start. For what good it did him, Tuesday was free from the waist down.

Kicking towards the ceiling with alternating legs, trying to get his toes as high as he could so he could splash the slippery moss juice over his wrists, Tuesday failed miserably at reaching either hand manacle with his feet. After another few tries Tuesday put all of his determination into one massive flick, and somehow managed to get two toes caught in the manacle around his left wrist. As a male, such a stretch was far outside of pleasant, but when placed in danger many rodents have proven to be capable of the most absurd feats of skill. Screaming in frustration and pain, performing the biggest splits of his life, a triangle-shaped Tuesday thoroughly lubricated his wrist with juicy foot-moss.

Pop.

One of Tuesday's hands slid out of their bindings, but the lack of circulation meant that the poor git was left to swing hopelessly like a half-paralysed monkey. When sensation finally returned a minute later Tuesday was able to grease up his other trapped wrist with more moss juice and tumbled to the cell floor in a messy pile of numb limbs. A wet warmth told him that Prince Charming's blood was continuing to spread across the chrome like a liquid blanket, and Tuesday could clearly hear claret trickling down the tiny drain.

This would have been a good time to celebrate getting free from his bonds, but Tuesday decided that he'd prefer to vomit up everything in his stomach with extreme violence for the better part of ten minutes, then lay shaking on the steel floor for a time. When Tuesday finally pushed himself upright he experienced a terrible pain through his hands. Looking down at them, Tuesday finally noticed that the thumb of his left hands and the index and middle fingers on his right hand were dislocated, and all his knuckles and both wrists had been worn down into angry crimson stripes. While all these wounds may seem like pretty enormous things to miss, the last five minutes of Tuesday's life had been fuelled by so much adrenalin that he might as well have been off his face on Angel Dust.

Carefully getting to his feet by putting all his weight on the fingers that still worked, Tuesday attempted to stomp his dislocated thumb back into place with a well-placed heel. Although he was successful, he decided to never, ever, ever do that again.

Limping over to the cooling body of Prince Charming, Tuesday searched through the serial killer's waistband. In a handful of seconds Tuesday found a tiny pistol that had more than a passing resemblance to a child's potato gun, a canister of InstaDeath capsules, a collection of PainCo warranties and helpline details that had been arranged in alphabetical order in a plastic wallet, and a paper-thin organiser the size of a playing card. Awkwardly holding the device, Tuesday knew it was his key out of this place. Using the classic brute force technique known as process of elimination, Tuesday tapped at the icons one after another and just hoped that the organiser didn't have a well-disguised self-destruct option that he might stumble into. The racks of torture implements revolved around and around on their hinges, the lights brightened and dimmed, the temperature of the cell went all the way from testicle-retracting Arctic knives to a face-melting Sahara heatwave and back again, but the door didn't budge. Swearing under his breath as some sort of self-cleaning setting erupted from the ceiling in a deluge of soapy water, Tuesday hit the second last icon on the Liquid Organic Screen and finally heard a familiar pneumatic hiss.

The door was open!

After a brief stagger Tuesday found himself in a chrome hallway lit with Perspex-mounted bulbs. Looking back and forth, the passageway initially seemed to be devoid of doors, but Tuesday already knew better. Getting so close to the opposite wall that he had to squash his nose a bit when Tuesday tilted his head at just the right angle he could barely make out a seam. He smiled for the first time all day.

Thankfully, all Tuesday had to do to get through was point the stolen organiser and tap the same icon as before, and the system did the rest. To Tuesday's disappointment, rather than discovering an exit he found another cell identical to his own. It was equipped with the same racks of torture implements, and housed a shaved, moisturised captive wearing nothing but boxer shorts and fear. The prisoner was cowering against his manacles in abject terror as the steel door slid open, but the moment the nameless prisoner realised that Tuesday wasn't Prince Charming his face switched to eye-bulging, screaming hysteria.

"Get me down! Get me down!"

Disappointed, Tuesday turned his back on the captive, stomped out into the hallway and began to click at each square metre of the chrome walls one section at a time. The prisoner continued to yell and carry on, and Tuesday mentally kicked the stranger for the amount of unnecessary noise.

"Where are you going?!" the captive screamed at top volume. "Help me! Help me! Help me before he comes back!"

The next prisoner Tuesday accidentally uncovered was much older guy, but despite his advanced years he also started to yell at top volume. Tuesday pinched the bridge of his nose with two bruised fingers as the din began to give him a headache. Couldn't they see he was busy trying to get out of here and save his own skin? So bloody inconsiderate, some people...

Door number four wasn't a cell like the other three areas. No, from what Tuesday could tell this dim, carpeted room was filled with lacquered wooden shelves that stretched into darkness, and unlike the bare chrome it was warm, colourful and inviting. Automatic lights snapped on the very moment Tuesday crossed the threshold, and a cascade of gentle ceiling-mounted glow panels flickered to life in a long chain to reveal that the room was at least a hundred metres long. Once Tuesday's eyes had adjusted to the light he could clearly see that the oak shelves had each been dedicated to holding random items, but he had trouble seeing their point or purpose. Each cubby hole contained ordinary things such as wallets full of assorted cards and varied denominations of German yen, women's purses, jewellery (mostly cheap stuff), shoes, hats, socks, combs, walking sticks, business card holders...weird. Tuesday didn't figure out what this place was until he saw a cubby that contained an orange school uniform, a battered backpack containing an old issue of Salacious Strumpets, a crumpled pack of chlorine-flavoured cigarettes and a silver lighter.

It was a trophy room.

Tuesday hurriedly slipped on his uniform and his shoes, pocketed the smokes and his dad's favourite lighter, swung the schoolbag over one shoulder and stomped for the door. On second thoughts, Tuesday decided that all those yen were simply going to waste and began to fill his backpack with as many crumpled notes as he could snatch.

Ignoring the two captives as they continued to scream abuse at him, Tuesday tried to open door number five in the same way as all the others, but rather than a new room he was greeted with an unfamiliar clunk noise that echoed all the way down the corridor. Testing the seam with a fingernail in confusion, Tuesday only realised that he'd tapped the wrong icon when the two captives staggered out of their cells and embraced him with tears in their eyes. Clearly, he'd just unlocked all their manacles without meaning to.

"You are the greatest man who ever lived in the history of mankind!" the first captive sobbed, dribbling and snuffling mucous all over Tuesday's collar. "I love you! I love you so much, man! I love you!"

Prisoner two simply dissolved into hysterical tears. It was beyond awkward.

Sighing, Tuesday continued to try and find his way out of this lair, but after another five minutes all he'd managed to do was set another twenty people free from their cells. The small crowd had become a scrum in short order, and the excited survivors danced, hugged each other in rapturous joy, and sobbed like slapped toddlers.

And then it finally happened: portal number twenty-four hissed and clunked and formed into a steep set of stairs. Daylight speared into Tuesday's eyeballs as the ceiling retracted into a slot. Pushing an elderly man out of the way in his haste, almost breaking a ninety-two-year-old hip in the process, Tuesday bolted up the stairs and found himself in very familiar surroundings. Looking around just to be sure his mind wasn't playing tricks on him, Tuesday discovered to his surprise that he was in his neighbour's backyard in the Welfare Sector.

He'd been living right next door to Prince Charming for weeks.

All the survivors had followed Tuesday up into the relatively fresh air, and on seeing precious, precious daylight they crowded around their incidental saviour and lifted him high. Tuesday snarled and slapped at the group until they finally put him down. Despite his grumpiness, the crowd continued to follow Tuesday and cry their undying love for him all the way to his front door. Slamming the portal in their faces so hard that the frame rattled and sprayed dust, Tuesday smoked a well-earned cig, found a furry piece of chocolate chicken pizza buried deep under the couch (how'd they always end up under there? One of the great mysteries of the Universe, that) and felt fifty tonnes of fatigue hit him like a bus. Yawning and curling up on the lounge, Tuesday decided that the rest of this day could get buggered.

Tuesday woke up to a low rumble. The noise told Tuesday's dim brain that either there were hordes of people yelling their heads off really close by, or every duck on the planet had migrated to his front yard specifically to quack as a united chorus.

Draining two cups of coffee from the dedicated spigot over his sink, Tuesday finally remembered he was meant to be at Elementary several afternoons ago. Scooping up his schoolbag and reaching for the front door, He might just make the last ten minutes if he…

Tuesday was greeted by such a deafening cheer that he fell over backwards. A multitude of voices cried out in excitement at the very sight of him, and entire teams of professional photographers took three-dimensional images of him with surgically implanted media-grade retinal cameras. Dozens and dozens of well-dressed reporters equipped with standard media cybernetics held up their thumb recorders and yelled a confusing casserole of questions: How did he become so brave and heroic? Why did he risk his life for people he didn't know? How did he track the monster down?

The reporters were merely the front line of a swelling crowd of humanity that screamed in excitement all the way up and down the street as far as Tuesday could see, though. Swarms of spectators were perched on roofs and jostled each other for a better view.

His eyes darted back and forth like a particularly delicious mouse, and all Tuesday could do was shrug at the onslaught of questions and lick his lips nervously. The last time so many people had been calling his name was the day he'd formally became a prison guard at Cell Block Preschool. After a burst of wet, Tourette-like stuttering and turning bright purple, Tuesday decided his best course of action was to spin around, run back inside his pad, slam the door so hard that ants trickled from the ceiling, and fall against the portal like a chopped redwood.

His mind remained dead empty for some time. There was no understanding to be had. Tuesday's eyes locked onto a large Austrian cockroach as it waddled across his ceiling, and he waited impatiently for his grey matter to reboot itself and provide some sort of useful comment on what had just happened on his front porch. Unfortunately, both lobes decided to remain unhelpful, as always.

"What do they want from me? I haven't done nothing!" Tuesday hissed at the roof in the oldest, most unoriginal chant of the guilty.

Speaking of chants, the people outside were now calling his name in a growing chorus: Tuesday, Tuesday, Tuesday...

"All I done wrong was kick somebody in the face – in self-defence! - push over an old man and fall asleep on me lounge with a lit cigarette in me mouth. Hardly worth a public lynching on the fifth-afternoon news, is it?"

Tuesday's brain finally pulled itself up by its bootstraps and offered him an unexpected concept. Tuesday tilted his head to the side, as deep in thought as he could manage, and eventually muttered under his breath as it finally made sense.

"I'm..."

Tuesday, Tuesday, Tuesday, Tuesday...

A brown grin slowly expanded across his face.

"...I'm a hero?"

Tuesday stood up, breathed deep, and went to face his destiny.

CHAPTER TWELVE SCUMMING THE SYSTEM

Hundreds of retinal cameras clicked like empty six shooters as Tuesday slouched back onto his front porch. Cheers rippled back and forth along the swarm at the mere sight of him, and as far as he could tell they all seemed to follow a similar thread: Prince Charming is dead! The monster is gone! Seven Suns is safe again!

Before Tuesday could say a word to his adoring masses, though, government agents in black business suits and thick flash-proof sunglasses silently melted out of the ecstatic crowd and surrounded Tuesday on all sides as a living shield. Without a word of explanation they escorted Tuesday gently-yet-firmly through the crush of bodies, protecting him on all sides from...well, that wasn't exactly clear yet.

Despite the obvious health risks of upsetting a bunch of licensed-to-kill spooks, dozens of hands pushed through the lattice of thick agent arms, passing gifts to an overwhelmed Tuesday. Exotic flowers, fine chocolates and the occasional pair of lacy female undergarments were all well and good, but Tuesday drew the line at accepting a cute puppy. To his shame, a fortnight back Tuesday had been so thoroughly sick of Soup of The Day that he'd trapped and eaten a small local dog. Poor Old Mrs Deekin across the street never found out what happened to Puffy that dark day, and Tuesday wasn't going to tell anyone about the poodle-with-noodles any time soon.

Finally, after a very disorienting minute Tuesday was bundled into the plush backseat of a sleek, white luxury MagRail limousine. The spooks jammed themselves into both sides of the limo so tightly that Tuesday felt like he was being buried alive under iron-tight muscles and black polyweave, but the security specialists seemed to know precisely how many centimetres of space he needed in order to breathe.

Slipping into the wild blue yonder as smoothly as an oiled nudist, the limo spiralled through an unusually massive hole in the air traffic. Tuesday couldn't be sure, but it seemed as though all thirty-five local skylanes had been rerouted for as far as his eyes could make out. Short of some kind of apocalyptic emergency, Tuesday honestly didn't know what sort of drastic situation could warrant such a disruption. This sort of rerouting would cost the Seven Suns economy tens of millions of German yen every minute.

He wasn't vain enough to guess the truth.

Arcing between the looming starscrapers of the central business district, an exceptionally affluent area known as The Heights to most locals, Tuesday finally noticed that the limo wasn't flying in an automated skylane. This meant they were being piloted manually, something that was highly illegal unless there was some kind of AI failure to justify it. But worst of all, the limo was clearly zooming through a Code Black restricted area of The Heights, which is the sort of behaviour that would usually result in a warm, wordless greeting from multiple surface-to-air missiles.

Only a handful of people on the planet were important enough to have that sort of clearance. Tuesday couldn't name any of them.

Tuesday looked away from the silent air defence tripods that were tracking the luxury vehicle from all sides and glanced back and forth between the agents. Their faces were impassive as carved rock, their eyes hidden behind midnight lenses. Despite the fact any decent spook could probably break his neck with a single muscular pinkie, Tuesday's curiosity got the better of him. He coughed a little, but received no response, so he took the leap and spoke.

"Um..." Tuesday managed. "Where are we going, exactly?"

A single spook slowly turned his brick-like head to regard Tuesday. He could actually hear the sound of the agent's bulging neck muscles and tendons twisting against each other from so close.

"We're taking you to see the Mayor, Mister Tuesday." The spook had a voice like metal scraping on metal, but it contained no malice or arrogance. His face remained like a carving, though. "We'll be there soon, Mister Tuesday. We're running right on schedule. Nothing to worry about, sir."

It took a moment for Tuesday to register that the spook wasn't being sarcastic, and it stunned him as effectively as a koch to the skull. Tuesday had experienced some pretty amazing things in his short, ugly life, but receiving actual respect from somebody? The experience triggered some weird sensations in his brain and his stomach, an odd series of sensations that were warm, tingly and a little...what's the word? Floaty. Floaty was the word. It took a few seconds for Tuesday to realise it might actually be that "happiness" thing he'd heard so much about.

Tuesday's words were interrupted by a sudden descent through a golden halo of cumulus puff. Impressively, the limo landed cleanly atop a tall, palatial starscraper deep in the core of The Heights without as much as a bump. The moment Tuesday disembarked he was rushed through the closest roof access door and into a bunker that had a lot in common with a nuclear fallout shelter. The spooks continued to diligently cover Tuesday from all directions until a series of reinforced security barriers cascaded shut behind them, blocking out any external risk with fifteen feet of unbreakable ceramic plating. It was pretty clear that he'd just entered one of the most secure locations on the planet.

Without a word of explanation, all but one of the spooks vanished into the woodwork. The final agent cordially raised a thick arm to show the way. It might have been the same agent who had spoken a couple of minutes ago, but these G-men all looked the same to Tuesday.

"Follow me please, sir."

Mr Spook silently led Tuesday through a maze of corridors carpeted by an identical red grid of interconnected rugs. The walls were so heavily layered with precious paintings and sculptures that Tuesday could only see a few lines of cedar panelling poking out here and there between masterpieces, and all of the closed doors they passed seemed to have been hand-carved from single redwoods.

Once the two of them were beyond the extensive web of offices, Tuesday and the spook swept down a well-lit marble staircase. It was railed by long-extinct hardwoods and accented in what appeared to be real gold. Looking down at his feet, Tuesday saw that the passing steps were carpeted in purple velvet with hand-sewn silver spirals as trim. Tuesday thought it must be the staircase of an Emperor.

Reaching the bottom of the staircase, Tuesday looked up to see he'd entered a labyrinth of looming maple bookcases loaded down with ancient hide-bound tomes. The tap of his scuffed shoes echoed softly off the polished white marble, and the smells of decaying cellulose and leather varnish was overpowering. Looking back and forth, it seemed every slab of words had survived several major floods before being lightly crisped at an aborted Nazi book burning. As the spook directed Tuesday through the library to end all libraries they occasionally passed by comfortable little nooks of high-backed antique chairs here and there, as though somebody still opened these antediluvian piles of mouldy yellow paper for some reason.

It took another five minutes for Tuesday to worm all the way into the deepest core of the repository of ancient words, as the Mayor had burrowed in like a tick. The bureaucrat was dressed in a red bathrobe and sitting on a thick rug with his legs crossed, a book the size of a large suitcase carefully balanced on his lap and slippered feet. He didn't bother looking up and continued to run his eyes over a page of printed text that was so old it looked as though a flock of chickens with muddy feet had viciously stomped a piece of tree bark. Tuesday went to speak after an awkward fifteen seconds of silence, but the Mayor raised a single index finger without inclining his head.

Tuesday waited.

Clearing his throat, the Mayor closed the grimoire and looked up at Tuesday. The politician's eyes were full of intelligence, a gleam of canny sharpness that most other inhabitants of Seven Suns seemed to lack. Sure, the majority of the population were geniuses, but that didn't mean they were smart. Tuesday immediately knew with one look that the Mayor was the sort of person that con-artists and other miscellaneous scumbags feared: somebody who knew when he was being lied to, somebody who could identify every trick in the book with one glance.

The Mayor gestured to an opposite rug. Tuesday sat down, knees creaking, and was finally graced with a cordial handshake and some words.

"I'm Brokage Grundy, sixty-third Mayor of Seven Suns. Who are you, Mister Tuesday?"

Tuesday paused, narrowing his eyes.

"I don't...I don't know what you mean. You sorta answered your own question there."

The Mayor carefully placed the thick slab of paper on top of two others. His voice wasn't threatening, or angry, or even slightly insulted. His tone was conversational. But there was some kind of dangerous undercurrent that made Tuesday uneasy.

"Mister Tuesday, do you know the penalty for forging a Seven Suns citizen card?" the Mayor asked bluntly, his ice-pick eyes taking in every detail of Tuesday's expression. Tuesday felt like he was being read like an unsolicited pamphlet. "Any idea?"

Somehow, Tuesday managed to keep his expression neutral. His mind went to some dark places as he considered what his near future would hold: perhaps he'd be thrown in some sort of dungeon, or fed to a local horror in the middle of a justice coliseum, or maybe even suffer Death-by-Tickle...

The Mayor leaned forwards, made a circle shape with his index finger and thumb, smiled, and said a single word: "Nothing."

Tuesday raised an eyebrow as he looked at Mayor Grundy's hand. It took quite an effort not to glance at the spook looming behind him, as that might be seen as a sign of guilt. Try as he might, though, Tuesday couldn't help but ask the most obvious question of all time.

"Really? There's...so you're saying there's no penalty?" It was a trap. He knew it for certain. But Tuesday's curiosity had always outweighed his survival instincts. "I, uh, thought it might have been pretty serious, actually. Other worlds in The Unison..."

"Around ninety-three percent of Unison worlds class citizen card forgery as a capital offence...or worse." The Mayor interrupted. He stretched his shoulders and neck in little circles, as though he'd been sitting in the same position for hours. The Mayor gave a little moan of relief when he finished the yoga-like movement. "I'm not sure if you know this, Mister Tuesday, but before I was elected one of my biggest campaign promises was to find a way to permanently eliminate the illicit trade in forged citizen cards. It seems my constituents didn't like the idea of a bunch of filthy foreigners sneaking in and getting a top rate AutoEducation upload for free...fegging xenophobes." The Mayor smiled indulgently. "As you'd expect, catering for the hateful is always a sound tactic when you're trying to get into office. Of course, to stay in office, I had to follow through on my vow, even though ending the counterfeit citizen card trade was a major investment that would take time and money. As far as the voters know, we accomplished this dream by pouring seven billion German yen into an R&D project that would make Seven Suns citizen cards the most impenetrable form of ID anywhere in The Unison. The project took three hundred and seventy-five of our greatest minds over three solid years to accomplish and has gone down as the defining moment of my political career." Tuesday was given a dark smile. "In reality, Mister Tuesday, we simply rounded up every counterfeiter, forge-artist and digital pirate within the space of five star systems and executed them all. We then spread the word that anybody who was brave enough to take their place would go out ten times as badly. When another batch of counterfeiters inevitably tested our resolve, we were true to our word, and we warned the underworld yet again that the deaths that followed would continue to worsen by a factor of ten." Mayor Grundy rubbed his eyes. "Nobody was stupid enough to set up shop again. Death by Pigeon tends to deter most scummers." The Mayor's smiled returned, but he still looked tired. "So do you understand why there's no penalty, Mister Tuesday? Because as far as everybody knows, creating a fake Seven Suns citizen card is impossible. We might as well have legislation against Easter Bunnies sexually harassing Santa Claus. Do we understand one another?"

Tuesday nodded enthusiastically. The Mayor steepled his fingers together and examined Tuesday's face before continuing.

"Prince Charming's dungeon was wired with hundreds of pinhead cameras, Mister Tuesday, and my hand-picked forensics team have already provided me with a comprehensive copy of The Prince's security archives. I've watched the footage of your escape from sixteen different angles, and somehow each one is more disgraceful than the last. In fact, with every additional viewing I found myself wondering more and more if I'd have enough self-control not to smack you upside your self-serving skull when you finally got here." The Mayor arched an eyebrow as Tuesday went to stand up. A hand the size of a baseball glove pressed down on Tuesday's shoulder with enough force to suggest he would be much more comfortable staying right where he was. "However, the...the myth of your escape, the way you bravely rescued those helpless victims, went viral faster than anything I've ever seen in my life. The entire Link network was screaming your praises from one corner of the planet to the other before you'd even finished sucking down your victory cigarette. People have called you..." The Mayor snapped his fingers and a digital piece of paper appeared in his hand. His eyes quickly scanned over it. "A working-class hero. Bravery in human form. Hope for our species. One of the greatest of all Seven Suns' children. A living legend." Mayor Grundy made a noise in his throat and threw the hologram over his shoulder, where it disappeared in the same way it had appeared. "Luckily for you, Mister Tuesday, by the time we realised the staggering enormity of how incorrect these reports actually were, this matter was well beyond the point where we could hope to suppress it. These lies have already gone down as concrete gospel, and if anybody tried to contradict them…" The Mayor shrugged. "Well, how do you think my career would go if I started slagging off bravery in human form? So, this is what's going to happen: there's going to be an award ceremony in a couple of days, and you'll be honoured by the highest accolade our government can bestow – the Binary Star. For those of us who weren't born on Seven Suns, the Binary Star is a platinum nugget the size of my palm encrusted with diamonds. Only a handful of people earn one each generation, and you'll be the third this century. As a recipient of the Binary Star, you will be looked after until the day you die. You will be clothed, fed and housed by the state, and will want for nothing."

Tuesday narrowed his eyes.

"Are we talking Soup of The Day in the Welfare Sector?"

Mayor Grundy twitched.

"Of course not. I'm talking freshly-bludgeoned lobster cricket in a penthouse in The Heights."

Tuesday wasn't sold. He was missing something. He knew this situation sucked; he just wasn't sure of the specifics yet.

"And what do you want me to do in return? You want me to do some motivational speaking or summing? Help keep kids in school? Just say no to Shatter? Tell everyone what a great Mayor you are?"

Mayor Grundy managed not to laugh. He shook his head and looked down on Tuesday like he was a simpleton.

"Mister Tuesday, allow me to be blunt: although your position as a Binary Star recipient will necessitate your presence at certain important events, under no circumstances are you to ever say anything to the media on my behalf. I'd be better off asphyxiating myself with my own arse than allow you to wag my name with that yellow tongue." The Mayor waved this topic away. "Regardless of how you managed to scum the system for all it is worth, you are now a public figure, Mister Tuesday, a role model for our children and an idol for our adults, and one day you'll be a highlight in our history books." Reaching sideways, Mayor Grundy made a little noise of exertion as he lifted a slab of decaying paper and flaking leather the dimensions and weight of a tombstone back onto his lap. "Try not to become history too quickly, Mister Tuesday. I'll be watching."

*

Named after the greatest Amerikan president to have ever occupied the Spherical Office, The L. D. Linden Noonclub was the only one of its kind on Seven Suns. The ancient story of President Linden's triumph over supreme adversity was one for the ages and was still taught in every Unison school.

After finally shaking off the fallout of her many poor life choices in the mid-21st Century, it turned out that Leanne was profoundly talented at the political sciences. Following decades of intense study and preparation, Leanne embarked on a whirlwind political career that saw her become the first Cripps-Democrat to become President in decades. Sure, Linden was almost a hundred and fifty by the time she was sworn in, but the Pres had more to worry about than advanced age: the thrice-damned Scandinavian Expansion had invaded, occupied and enslaved Amerika in the late 21st Century, and just like the last six Presidents, Linden was little more than a puppet figurehead. However, if it wasn't for Linden's astounding sense of purpose and bottomless wisdom in driving out the Expansion forces in a display of tactical genius that made Alexander the Great seem like Mister Bean in comparison, the Skandos would probably still be ruling Amerika to this day.

Of course, every schoolchild knew how President Linden ended the war, so there's no need to rehash it.

To say that The Linden was a nice club was to state the obvious. Sure, over-the-top opulence was relatively commonplace in The Heights, so serving tiny cocktails made from centuries-old booze (some of which pre-dated The Unison) and having priceless velociraptor scotch fillet on the menu wasn't worth hooting about. No, what really made The Linden stand apart was the fact it was secretly the nexus of all profitable evil on Seven Suns. For more than two hundred years this palace had served as a neutral meeting ground for the exceptionally discreet crime lords who secretly ruled The Glow, a brotherhood that prized silence and invisibility above all other attributes. As the efficacy of this shadowy underworld was entirely based on the planetwide delusion that Seven Suns had the lowest crime rate in The Unison (in reality, Seven Suns wasn't even in the top fifty), the exclusive members of The Linden occasionally referred to themselves as The Whispers.

A mere forty-nine afternoons ago, Ernest Fell had roosted at the top of their pecking order for twelve straight years. Forty-eight afternoons ago, this situation had become inverted.

The entire décor of The Linden, from its hand-carved marble floors to the darklight chandeliers dangling far above, would be most succinctly described as "black." Most of its considerable floor area was taken up by a series of perfectly circular onyx booths, and each rounded bastion contained a black leather lounge curled intimately around a waist-high ebony table top. Each of the once-broken circles could comfortably seat up to a dozen patrons. The only splash of colour in The Linden came from the stasis-preserved skins of exotic and vicious animals who now served as distinctive rugs for each booth, and all the worst creatures in the galaxy were present and accounted for: razorbears, sky sharks, titan slugs, spitting gorillas, napalm pigs and exploding poodles, to name but a few. As a result, the booths derived their names from whatever murderous creature served as its rug. The worse the creature, the more desirable the booth.

Ernest Fell stormed through The Linden with murder in his eyes, followed closely by Jeeves. A mere eight days ago the other patrons would have deliberately averted their gaze from the two distinctive figures out of a mixture of fear and respect, but things had drastically changed. Not only did the gangsters have the gall to openly stare at the crime lord and his bodyguard, but hissed conspiracy at one another once Ernest's ears were well out of range. Little did they know how clearly he heard their treason.

A week had passed since Tuesday was awarded the Binary Star in front of the entire planet, and the ramifications of Prince Charming's death were still rippling through the underworld like a grenade in a kiddie pool. As The Prince had often served as a particularly evil disposal method for anybody unlucky enough to get on the wrong side of The Whispers in some way (whether knowingly or unknowingly), the last seven days had seen Ernest Fell and the rest of his brotherhood in severe damage control. It went without saying that this involved a lot of so-called "suicides," drug overdoses, people running off to join the circus in distant star systems, and just outright whacking a few people, too. This level of upheaval was unprecedented in living memory, and such chaos meant only one thing: The Whispers needed somebody to take the blame, and quickly.

Slamming into the comfy form-fitting leather lounge within the Razorbear Booth, Ernest glared blades at the disrespectful stares he was attracting. Jeeves took a seat on the edge of the lounge, positioned to block any potential trouble. A nervous-looking waiter in an all-black uniform approached a little too quickly and placed a jet-coloured tray containing Ernest's and Jeeves' usual orders on the table top: a Ritz Sidecar for Ernest, and a midi of Viking Ale with a bowl of salted honey almonds for Jeeves. The waiter, bowing almost horizontal, laid down two copies of today's menu in front of the crime lord and his bodyguard, and went to stammer the specials.

He didn't get out a single word.

Seven men in Seladorian suits pushed the waiter aside and arrayed in front of the Razorbear Booth. Considering that The Whispers were exceptionally good at remaining invisible in plain view, these gangsters could have easily passed as a hundred different kinds of businessman or bureaucrat, or perhaps mourners on their way to a funeral. They all looked like the sort who got beat up in high school, men you wouldn't look at twice: words like nerdy, unthreatening, lame and harmless would come to mind. Of course, they'd all spent years cultivating their professional veneers, and to a man all seven were lethal, heartless killers capable of any depraved act imaginable.

Jeeves casually scanned the group with one glance. A casual slurp of ale brought on highlights of toffee and aniseed as Jeeves considered who he should kill first, and how messy the execution would be. He could clearly tell that the guy standing second from the left had mainlined some kind of combat stim recently, probably Twitch, as his jittery eyes and pulsating pupils indicated the guy was dosed for war. This made the choice easy. A subtle hand gesture from Ernest told Jeeves to hold back for now, but to be ready.

Flanked by three men on either side, the central figure stepped forwards and gave a slight bow. Although Ernest had brought a lot of heat on everyone in The Linden thanks to the stuff up with Tuesday and Prince Charming, The Whispers still valued civility.

"Mister Fell, I'm Dog Rooney." Rooney extended his long, elegant fingers, the digits of a hacker, to finish the bow. As Rooney looked about a quarter of Ernest's age, this sort of respect was expected in their ranks. "I'm not sure if you remember me..."

"You were the kid who hacked into the Protein Recyc database and placed a backdoor for anybody who wants...meat to disappear without a trace." Ernest took a draw of his Ritz Sidecar. The cognac was smoother than a waxed infant. "You did such a good job that it's still wide open to this day."

Rooney looked a little surprised.

"I'm flattered you know about that, Mister Fell."

"I'm not some aloof prince who sits around staring at his own navel all day, Rooney. I keep track." Glaring across the table, Ernest smacked his glass into the ebony surface. "I also know you've never missed paying me your due each month, you're well respected by all the other patrons of The Linden, and you're a born leader who pisses charisma from every pore. Many made men think that once you've spent a few decades growing from a wriggling tadpole to a fat toad, you'll probably be a man of authority. Yes, I know who you are." Ernest ran a finger around the rim of his glass and narrowed his eyes. "However, what I don't know, Rooney, is why you and your meat puppets suddenly think it's fine to slump over to my booth without being asked. We may be going through a time of flux right now, but that doesn't mean a thing. Seven Suns is always an interesting place." Ernest's lip curled a little bit, exposing his white teeth. "Well?"

Rooney glanced around at his six associates. He was suddenly looking unsure.

"Mister Fell, I do honestly apologise for the intrusion, but I've been trying to arrange a face-to-face with you for days now without any luck. I wouldn't break protocol unless I knew it was worth your time."

Ernest took another glug of his drink and silently regarded Rooney. In the last week his sips had transformed into quaffs. After another few seconds Ernest gave a demanding motion that indicated the whole group should take a seat at the Razorbear Booth, the most elite bastion in the entire Noonclub. Jeeves silently moved closer to Ernest as seven nervous gangsters slid across the midnight leather. The looming bodyguard was sure to arrange things so that he was directly between the strung-out Twitcher and Ernest.

Ernest gave a small shrug at Rooney.

"Well? You've got your chance. What's bothering you, Rooney?"

Rooney leaned a few inches towards Ernest, keeping his voice low.

"Mister Fell, I thought that you'd want to know that this...this flux, as you put it, has seen one thousand, two hundred and forty-eight bodies go through Protein Recyc in a little under a week. I'm talking twenty times more meatbags than I've ever had to process since my hack."

Ernest gave another shrug. "Sounds like good business to me, Rooney. So what's the problem? Don't have a powerful enough calculator to count all your yen? Run out of wallets?"

Rooney looked frustrated. He ran a hand through his neat hair, slicking it with sweat from his palms.

"Sure, yeah, normally I'd be clicking my damned heels, Mister Fell. But we're not talking about informants and other worthless scum, here: I personally knew some of the people who've been reduced to Cricket Chow on my watch. Beyond the Protein Recyc situation, more than a dozen members of The Linden haven't been seen in days, and two men from my own crew have vanished like smoke."

Rooney extended his hands in the "gimme gimme" gesture. "We need you to do something, Mister Fell. I'm sure you're aware that people are talking. Everyone knows that nobody is safe anymore."

To Rooney's horror, the Twitcher chose this moment to speak without being asked.

"Not even you!" the henchman hissed, pointing a trembling finger at Ernest.

Rooney gaped at his idiot associate in total horror, his face turned grey, and he closed his eyes in what seemed like prayer.

"Bennett..." Rooney moaned. "Oh, spug..."

What little background murmuring there was in The Linden instantly ceased. It seemed as though the entire Noonclub was watching the interaction between Rooney and Ernest, waiting, preparing. Every booth of gangsters from one side of The Linden to the other casually slid to the edge of their lounges, calmly opened their jackets, and waited for all Hell to break loose.

Ernest's expression didn't change as he regarded the mouthy gangster apparently known as Bennett. Jeeves, on the other hand, gripped the table with both meaty hands and leaned towards the Twitcher until there was only an inch between their noses.

"Don't do that." Jeeves said simply.

Bennett faltered. His eyes darted back and forth, his pupils growing and shrinking.

"Don't point at Mr Fell." Jeeves clarified, growling like a cement mixer. "Or I'll point at you."

Ernest turned slowly to Rooney. It was a miracle nobody was dead yet.

"So, Rooney, would you like to clarify exactly what your little friend over there meant by that comment of his? I think it'd be a good idea for your next words to be chosen very, very, very carefully."

There was a crackling noise as Jeeves squeezed the ebony table top so tightly that the black surface splintered beneath his sausage fingers. It spider-webbed as his hands continued to slowly clench. The sort of raw strength you'd need to do such a thing made it hard to believe that Jeeves was a human being.

Rooney raised his empty hands, trying to bring back some semblance of civility to this botched meeting.

"I'm not threatening anybody, Mister Fell! I'm just saying that a lot of people are worried, and that you need to do something about the situation right now or there won't be any Whispers left."

Ernest smiled darkly.

"Do I, now? Is that a fact, Rooney?" Ernest smiled. "So is that the reason you're here? To volunteer as my advisor? To point out all the ways I'm failing at my job?" Ernest's smile hardened into bared teeth. "How about we see how good an advisor you are as a bag of spugging Cricket Chow, Rooney? How about I advise you that you have exactly three seconds to disappear before The Linden loses another seven members?"

Bennett found his courage again as Dog Rooney started to back off. It was possible that Bennett's next words may have defused the situation, or at least slowed the spiral. Unfortunately, Bennett made a lethal mistake: he didn't heed the direct warning he'd received from Jeeves.

"You can't just ignore what's happening, Fell!" Bennett yelled, his finger rising, slowly unfolding towards Ernest. "You have a responsibility to-"

True to his word, Jeeves twisted towards Bennett at top speed and sank his entire index finger into Bennett's forehead clean up to a golf ball knuckle. The lesser henchman twitched a few times, his pupils rolling up into his head in opposite directions, and he died with a sigh.

Jeeves calmly extracted his red digit in a spurt of gore. The next two seconds passed as slowly as Ice Ages, but before Jeeves had a chance to clean Bennett's brains off his finger another of Rooney's men lunged across the table top with a chemically-sharpened meat cleaver. Simultaneously dodging his face out of the way of the chopper and latching onto the offending arm as it streaked harmlessly past, Jeeves broke the guy's wrist in six places with one hand and used the other to tear the arm clear out of its shoulder joint with a horrible SKRUNCH noise. Blood scythed out in the arm's wake, splattering Rooney and his stunned men with an arc of crimson.

Things immediately escalated beyond fisticuffs and blades without a single word being necessary, and within the space of a second Ernest, Jeeves and the five remaining members of Dog Rooney's crew were standing around the splintered black table with a total of fourteen kinetic accelerator pistols. A humming chorus of magnetic coils ascended beyond supersonic as fourteen highly-illegal hand-held mass-drivers spun up to their top setting. Between them, the seven men had enough combined firepower to raze The Linden to a smoking handful of cinders in a heartbeat.

"We didn't want it to come to this, Mister Fell." Rooney's voice was shaking, and he looked a mixture of frustrated, sad and terrified. He had one accelerator pistol trained on Ernest and the other on Jeeves. "We tried to be civil about this, Mister Fell. We just wanted you to act. We wanted you to lead. That's all. That's all we wanted."

Ernest kept his attention split towards Rooney and some other stupid kid whose lifespan was now measured in seconds. Ernest knew there was no way he and Jeeves could take down all five and walk away afterwards, but the triggers hadn't been squeezed just yet. Nothing was over until he decided it was over.

"You think killing me here and now will accomplish a damn thing?" Ernest yelled, addressing everybody in The Linden. Silence greeted his words as The Whispers waited for him to continue. "You think I'm an idiot? You think that I don't have contingencies? That it'll just be business as usual if you smoke me in my own club? You think you're safe? You think that your families are safe? Do you have any idea how many hundreds of millions of yen I've allocated to avenge my own death? My entire fortune will be transferred to the best mercenaries in The Unison the moment that my heart stops beating, and every face in this room is on the list! Can you imagine the sick orders I've issued, the twisted things they'll do to everybody here?" Ernest bared his teeth at Rooney, who'd turned white as skim-milk. Rooney was shaking so bad that it was a wonder he hadn't bumped the hair-triggers on his accelerator pistols. None of Rooney's men looked like they wanted to be here anymore. Ernest smiled at their reaction. "Can you, Dog?"

There were simultaneous beep-beep error messages from all four of the mass-driver weapons being duel-wielded by Jeeves and Ernest, and their glowing blue status lights switched to flashing red LEDs in an unmistakable warning that something was wrong. Ernest gritted his teeth at the accelerator pistols in impotent rage.

"Really?" Ernest screamed at the entire club. "Who nulled our weapons? Who?" Jeeves squeezed his triggers in curiosity. Both made the same beep-beep error messages as before.

High above, at least fifty old-school laser pointers carved through the pall of cigar smoke from all four corners of The Linden. A multitude of red dots came to rest on Ernest and Jeeves like wasps who would accept any excuse to start stinging relentlessly. There was the unmistakable crackling sound of railguns being prepared to fire single grains of iron at two-thirds the speed of light. Glaring up at the dark depths twenty metres above, Ernest rested a homicidal glance on Rooney.

"I have a long memory, kid. And now every single person you've ever loved, that you've ever known, is sitting right here." Ernest tapped his forehead with a useless pistol. "You'll be seeing me, Dog. Be sure of it."

Rooney shook his head, his eyes downcast. To say he looked disappointed with how badly things had gone would be an understatement.

"I think you should go now, Mister Fell." Rooney stepped aside, keeping well clear of Jeeves' lethal hands. "I hope we meet again under more...profitable circumstances, Mister Fell."

Ernest appraised Rooney for a moment. He might be wet as a fish, but the kid had potential. If Rooney survived long enough, there was little doubt he'd rise to the top like a layer of rich cream.

Ernest jammed both nulled pistols into their hidden holsters and stormed out of The Linden. He was trailed closely by Jeeves, as usual, but he was followed even more closely by dozens and dozens of laser dots.

*

One hour earlier, Bob Tuesday yawned himself awake in the insane luxury of his penthouse. Situated on the highest floor of a starscraper block in the heart of The Heights, this sweeping palace was filled with so many priceless artworks and highlighted by so much pure gold that King Midas would have quietly suggested it was "a bit much." It made Xanadu look like the Welfare Sector and had more in common with the Louvre than a mere home.

Slowly coming back to consciousness, Tuesday spent a few moments reclining in a bed the size of an Olympic swimming pool before looking over at the naked form of Ms Humple. She was asleep, thankfully, and her cat o' nine tails was well out of reach.

Tuesday exhaled in relief.

Creeping out of the Caligula sized bed (it took a good ten rolls for him to reach the distant edge), Tuesday threw a handful of weightless, tissue-thin polyweave sheets over Ms Humple for the sake of modesty, hitched up his silk boxer shorts, and considered his lot in life. Affluent, famous, and loved by millions as a hero. All of Seven Suns was eating out of his unwashed hands. Yup, Tuesday had it made. He'd scummed his way to the very top.

Like every unspecified time he woke up (Tuesday had abandoned trying to understand how the seven afternoon timing system worked on this stupid planet) Tuesday staggered onto the solid-gold bedroom balcony for his first chlorine cigarette of the day. Igniting the chemical suck-burner with a sharp inhalation, Tuesday gazed around at the towering ivory apartment blocks that stretched off to the horizon in all directions of The Heights. "Exclusive" didn't begin to describe the local real estate. Tuesday thought that the way the sunlight carved through the thick tendrils of creamy fog and picked out the metallic highlights of a hundred kinds of precious minerals meant that The Heights had a lot in common with how primitive man had perceived Heaven in medieval artwork.

As always, the biggest news headline of the day was scrawled across the stratosphere in perfectly formed neon letters. Doing his best to read the phrase, it took Tuesday several frustrating minutes of quiet muttering and headache-inducing logic to eventually decode the headline. He eventually figured it out: "After decades of construction, The Frontier will finally begin its maiden voyage in two hours."

Leaning over the nipple-high safety railing, Tuesday looked down on the so-called "park views" that had been a part of the real estate description. This was a pointless exercise, as the twisted elms and weeping willows were more than three kilometres straight down and obstructed by thick layers of puffy cumulus. As he leaned over the gilt edge of the balcony Tuesday considered what would happen if somebody pushed him. Tuesday reckoned he'd fall for about two minutes, his lips pulled back behind his ears in a scream lost to the wind, until he hit the ground with enough force to immediately reduce his body to a thin smear of person-flavoured sandwich spread...

Flicking his smouldering cigarette butt over the edge of the balcony, smiling at how funny it would look when somebody got hit by the burning filter all the way down at street level, Tuesday turned around just in time to get smacked right in the mouth by a flying bottle. Knocked effortlessly to the floor, holding his buzzing, swelling lip, Tuesday groaned the usual greeting he gave to Ms Humple, the love of his life.

"What was that for?" Tuesday whined for the eighteenth time this week.

Ms Humple picked up the empty bottle and held it right in front of Tuesday's face. He flinched, but thankfully she didn't hit him with it again.

"See this? We're completely out of coconut rum. I've told you what happens if I don't have my second afternoon cocktail, haven't I?"

Tuesday nodded in misery. His lip really, really hurt.

"I'll be sure to get you some more, sweetness."

She adjusted her lingerie.

"You better. Or I'll be teaching you about pain."

"Love you." Tuesday offered.

"Burn in a dumpster fire, you scrotum-faced gerbil."

Even though he felt woozy, Tuesday eventually got back to his feet. Out of habit, Tuesday patted the silken pocket of his boxers to make sure his dad's beaten lighter was still there. As usual, this spurred him to think about the man known as Jim Tuesday, his long-lost Dad, and the hope that he was being remembered in return. The odds of this weren't very good, as Jim had once forgotten his own middle name for two and a half years. Despite the fact his dad was nothing more than a hazy memory of very early childhood, Tuesday loved him and hoped that he was happy, wherever he was, and even gave a little prayer on the subject. Feeling totally out of character by the time he said "Amen," it took a moment for Tuesday to understand why he'd just done such an unusually spiritual thing.

"Damn Morbid Cult," Tuesday muttered darkly, as though it was a swear word. Tuesday often left his eyelid screens switched on in the wee hours of the seventh afternoon while he was trying to sleep, and last night he'd unwisely had them tuned to a blatant propaganda sitcom from the local Children of Death branch called Everybody Is Damned Forever (Except For Us). Tuesday had recently formed a grudge against organised religion in general, as since receiving the Binary Star he'd been contacted by every single one of them - from the Children of Death to the Moderate Vegans to the Cornerstoners to the Chaotic-Neutral Wizards and far more - who all wanted him to publicly declare that he had always been a devout member of their respective churches and would be evermore. However, they'd all decided to frame their requests by threatening Tuesday with imminent and eternal damnation if he didn't say yes on the spot. After three days of playing piggy-in-the-middle with all the local cults, Tuesday finally decided to stick with pointless, bleak, hollow atheism, and had told them all, in no uncertain terms, to punch it up as high as they could reach.

Licking his split lip, Tuesday got up from the balcony floor and began a gruelling trek to the distant kitchen on the far side of his penthouse. This involved a long march down a seemingly endless hallway that had been decorated with a "before recorded history" theme. The corridor was carpeted by cloned woolly mammoth rugs and lined on both sides with looming glass cabinets. The displays were filled with ancient cave paintings on rough granite slabs, crude Neolithic tools and all sorts of dinosaur fossils. Even more impressively, the hallway's centrepiece was of one of those infamous dragon skeletons that the Vatican had kept a secret for nearly six hundred years. Tuesday had nicknamed the draconian creature Cuddles.

Puffed out by the time he reached a kitchen that would make a Michelin Star chef weep, after a short rest on a maple countertop Tuesday rattled around in the cupboards for something to nosh. After the first nineteen wooden slabs revealed nothing except ingredients (yeah, like he was going to cook something) Tuesday lucked out on door number twenty with shelf upon shelf of non-expiring Meal-Inna-Can cubes emblazoned with the Hormel Foods Corporation logo. Sure, Meal-Inna-Can cubes were created specifically for fallout bunkers, but they reminded Tuesday of some of the less-crappy bits of his childhood.

Popping a fresh tin of smoked-salmon-flavoured sushi (known as Spushi) and eating it with his fingers, Tuesday padded towards the nine-doored fridge for something foamy and fermented. Finding nothing on the shelves except fruit juice and cricket milk, Tuesday checked over his numerous hiding spots until he eventually discovered a boiling six-pack of pilsner jammed behind an industrial-sized nuclear microwave. Swigging a bubbling mouthful straight from a hot-to-the-touch bottle, flinching as the radioactive pilsner blistered his tongue, Tuesday discovered what the English had suffered with for so many centuries.

As Tuesday reached the end of the tin of Spushi he felt a weird twitching sensation in the hunk of flesh between his thumb and his index finger, the bit known as the web of the hand. He scratched at the spot absently but didn't pay it any attention.

After getting lost for nearly fifteen minutes in a series of unfamiliar rooms he could have sworn weren't there yesterday, Tuesday eventually made it into the main lounge area of the loft. Filled with all manner of self-modifying furniture that had been programmed to keep up-to-date with what was officially classed as trendy by the glitterati for each particular minute, Tuesday sank up to his armpits in a leopard skin sofa before he remembered how much he hated this particular blob of fabric-covered gel. After fighting free of the blubbery mound with a bit of effort, Tuesday staggered over to a more traditional chair that, thankfully, didn't try and consume him whole. Lighting a second smoke, ashing it into a decorative vase, Tuesday surmised that he hated this entire room and needed to set fire to it sometime soon.

The flesh next to his thumb twitched again. He ignored it.

Wiping his mouth, Tuesday pegged empty beer bottle number four into the hungry leopard skin lounge. It disappeared without a trace. Now adequately fed and watered to the point where he no longer felt like head-butting somebody, Tuesday went about searching the cushions for where he'd dumped his clothes last night. After five minutes of digging and dragging Tuesday unearthed a purple pair of designer jeans, a yellow polyweave shirt, a half-full aerosol can of spray-on socks and one self-lacing boot. While he was trying to find boot number two Tuesday instead discovered his SpendPlus card. This particular SpendPlus was capped at an astonishing nine hundred German yen a day, but the little neon-white rectangle of plastic was restricted to whatever stores, restaurants or entertainment venues Tuesday was meant to be spruiking on any given occasion. In return for free goods and other kickbacks, these businesses would advertise that the world-famous Bob Tuesday shopped there/ate there/got high colonics there all the time, painfully milking his fame for all it was worth. As image was very important in this equation, the SpendPlus card couldn't be used anywhere that would reflect poorly on the Mayor, his office, or any of the companies that kept Tuesday living in paradise, so pubs, clubs, brothels, weapon stores and other hives of scum and villainy were off limits. The spaceport was a no-go area too, as there was no way the Seven Suns government would allow one of their propaganda pets to escape without permission. The Mayor's office had even been kind enough to provide a detailed auto-updating list of where Tuesday should and shouldn't be seen, arranged by how desirable or undesirable those places currently were.

Tuesday was public property.

His hand twitched a third time. Looking down at his thumb for a blank moment, Tuesday cursed his awful memory and defective attention span as he remembered the Omni implant in his hand. Five days ago Tuesday had been injected with a minuscule egg-shaped bio mod no bigger than a grain of Basmati rice – an Omni - and this tiny implant provided him with a suite of the very best technological conveniences money can buy, all in less than five percent of a gram of wet-wire hardware. Like all implants of its class, the Omni was actually a living organism that used self-upgrading protein strains for code, and if the Omni was no longer wanted for any reason it could instantly dissolve into a mist that would be harmlessly absorbed into the host's blood without a trace.

One of the Omni's more basic features – one that announced itself with a subtle trembling sensation – was a simple organiser program that kept track of Tuesday's appointments, meetings and alarms. Unfortunately, Tuesday was still unaccustomed to the subtleties of how the implant next to his thumb meat operated, so the last five days had involved a lot of trial and error (as well as two or three severe stuff-ups that had nearly involved a trip to the Emergency room).

Squinting in concentration, Tuesday tried to remember what specific hand motion he needed to do in order to access the organiser. This was tough, as Tuesday hadn't been paying attention when the Omni had played its automated tutorial. Like far too many people, Tuesday had just kept hitting NEXT and I ACCEPT until the floating screens went away.

Flicking his index finger at the wall prompted the Omni to create a full-immersion holographic display of the local news that filled the entire room. Just like the writing in the sky, the holo was covering a major story about some cutting-edge ship called The Frontier that was finally getting launched in a few hours. Even though the full-immersion program made Tuesday feel as though he was actually at the heart of the story, he wasn't really into the whole "current affairs" thing. A second identical flick of the same index finger made the program go away.

Tuesday grunted as the Omni implant vibrated for a fourth time.

Clicking his fingers in an exaggerated way caused an avalanche of household robots to pour out of every wall and from beneath all fifteen lounges. Lifting his bare feet up as the bots swirled about the room, crawling over each other so they could compete to suck up every mote of dust and floating skin cell, Tuesday tried spinning his pinkie in the air.

"Confirm?" a disembodied voice asked.

"Yes, confirm." Tuesday snapped, looking about as he tried to figure out where the words had come from.

Nothing happened for precisely two seconds, but then there was a cheery beep and the voice spoke again.

"Confirmed."

Tuesday fell off the lounge as a deafening red-alert alarm blared throughout the whole apartment like the world itself had been split in two, and Tuesday was certain his heart had seized up and stopped as two solid feet of unbreakable adamantium siege armouring slid over all of the plate glass windows with a rolling KOOM noise. Sealing the loft only made the alarm roar louder as it bounced off the impermeable metal slabs.

"THERMONUCLEAR PROTECTION ENABLED."

"Tuesday!" Ms Humple screeched from somewhere. "You did it again! Where are you? Turn it off! Turn it off!"

Uh oh...

Knowing that his day would get a lot worse if Ms Humple caught sight of him anytime soon, Tuesday gathered his clothes, ducked and ran for the front door like a roadie. Repeating the same "spinning pinkie" gesture caused the adamantium shielding to retract into its housing, and just as the front door unsealed from siege mode Tuesday skidded under it and into the plush corridor. Performing a commando roll for the elevator, Tuesday could hear Ms Humple's shriek of rage as she caught sight of him through the half-open front door.

Tuesday stabbed at the elevator buttons as she ran for him, wrapped in nothing but polyweave sheets and armed with a vase. The doors scissored shut just as the blue ceramic flower holder arced through the air and smashed to pieces against the outer layer of elevator doors with a KISH noise.

Still dressed in nothing but boxer shorts, Tuesday screwed his eyes shut and slid to the floor in relief. Opening one eye between the mesh of his fingers, Tuesday finally remembered the correct hand gesture. Feeling dumb, he jabbed the Omni with his opposite index finger and said one word.

"Organiser."

There was a little tweet noise and a tiny purple holographic Mister Drizzle appeared on the back of Tuesday's hand. Due to his long history of making soft toys of this exact FunCo character in a sweatshop, Tuesday mentally noted that he urgently needed to change the avatar of his Omni before he lost control and stabbed it. Every stupid cartoony element of the purple creature made Tuesday want to claw the implant out of his skin just to make it stop, and he struggled to remain civil.

"Good second afternoon, Mister Tuesday!" Mister Drizzle announced, dancing and carrying on like a twit as wacky music tooted in the background. "So far today you have missed six appointments classed as Very Urgent, you have ninety-five threatening messages from assorted religious organisations, three death threats from the Mayor, and more than eight hundred and fifty thousand spam messages from somebody known as BonerMaster1983." Mister Drizzle did a ta-da motion. "You have one remaining Very Urgent appointment. Would you like me to call you a cab?"

Tuesday nodded, and Mister Drizzle mercifully vanished.

As the foyer of Tuesday's apartment building was three klicks straight down, he had a good thirty seconds to spray on a pair of socks and slip into his clothes before the descent ended. By the time the aerosol can of socks had finished psshhhhing out a neat layer of disposable material onto both his feet that would last precisely eighteen hours before dissolving into mist (Or Your Money Back!) Tuesday's ears popped from the change in air pressure and the doors slid open. Swaggering into the foyer in his designer jeans and arty tee-shirt, Tuesday did his best to pretend he didn't care that he was stumping around with only one boot. Heck, the way things had been going lately, he might just start a planet-wide trend.

*

A four-minute ride in the back seat of a generic robotic cab gave Tuesday plenty of time to get lost in his thoughts. Gazing aimlessly through the eternal ivory jungle, Tuesday didn't bother making any plans for what he'd say or what he'd do when he got to wherever it was he was going. In fact, Tuesday didn't even care where today's Very Urgent appointment was, or what it was about. Without trying to sound too negative, it literally didn't matter what he said, or who he said it to, or where he said it. Tuesday had already learned that everything he did in public was extensively altered by an army of spin-doctors, holographic animators, audio tweakers and other flim-flam propaganda experts before any footage hit the news. Obviously, the Mayor's office wasn't going to allow somebody as stupid and unpredictable as Tuesday to make them look bad, but the propagandists never had such a tough time making somebody look inoffensive. Several senior members of the propaganda department had already suffered nervous breakdowns, and massive overtime bonuses had been necessary to stop the remaining employees from going on strike.

Tuesday was a public relations disaster in human form.

Once he'd been awarded the Binary Star in front of the whole planet, Tuesday was respectfully informed by his handlers that he'd be doing a full circuit of all the talk shows on Seven Suns. Over the span of five straight days Tuesday had been shuttled from station to station in limousines and interviewed by so many big names that he couldn't remember nine tenths of them. It was beyond words...it was beyond his most grandiose dreams...

But then he'd found out the truth.

Perhaps the total lack of live audiences should have tipped him off, but Tuesday didn't discover the reality of the editing arrangement until after he'd watched the delayed telecasts. Not only had the propaganda department deleted every single word he'd said, but they'd used vast teams of animators to shape the useless footage into a totally synthetic Bob Tuesday. This Bob Tuesday was charming, well-spoken, humble, encouraged his fellow citizens to work hard at their civic duty, and had a gleaming smile that was whiter than an albino eating a bowl of vanilla ice cream with a spoon carved out of ivory.

The real Tuesday had almost vomited at the sheer scale of the falsehood.

The worst part was realising that the people who lived in this endless afternoon didn't really like him at all: they liked this pseudo-Tuesday, this anti-Bob. Sure, the luxury apartment was awesome, and the frequent requests for his (always illegible) autographs were always a buzz, but Tuesday couldn't help but feel that he was less a hero, and more of a...well, some kind of mascot. After all, Tuesday hadn't done anything of note since escaping the clutches of Prince Charming, and he certainly didn't consider himself as valuable as the government thought him to be.

It didn't matter. It really didn't. Nothing did.

*

Tuesday disembarked from the cab after tapping his SpendPlus card on a reader. Automatically selecting the "No Tip" option on the little screen, Tuesday was almost positive that the robotic driver called him a spug-brained clot just as the vehicle slammed its automated doors shut. There was no time for a snappy comeback before the yellowcab had disappeared, though.

Grumbling at the insult, Tuesday turned away from the taxi rank to see he was standing outside what could only be a MacDeath franchise. It was unmistakable: the massive restaurant was composed of a chaotic swirl of lurid green angles that would be more at home in a 1990s cartoon, broken up by enormous neon-white screens covered with videos of sizzling meat patties and melting cheese. It was enough to make a vegetarian barf. A holographic marquee proudly declared MacDeaths: No Longer the Third-Highest Cause of Preventable Death Among Humans!

Tuesday cussed under his breath and hit the Omni implanted in his hand meat.

"Organiser," Tuesday snapped. Mister Drizzle immediately reappeared on the back of Tuesday's hand in a burst of glittering holographic confetti, but before the cartoon character could say a single irritating word Tuesday flicked him right in the side of his stupid purple head. "I'm not in the mood for your crap, Drizzle. Just tell me one thing: why in the Green Hades am I standing outside a MacDeath restaurant? Did you get the address wrong?"

Mister Drizzle blinked in surprise. His comical purple face glitched for a second as the underlying software quadruple-checked its log for any errors.

"This is the correct address, Bob. You're standing in front of the ten-thousandth MacDeath franchise that has opened on Seven Suns since the High Court ban was officially repealed last week, and you've been booked to eat a complementary third lunch here to welcome the MacDeath Combine to the planet."

"Third lunch? You mean dinner, right?" Tuesday waved for Mister Drizzle to shut up. He didn't care. "Doesn't matter. So I'm just here to eat? That's all? Nothing else?"

Mister Drizzle nodded.

"Yup!"

Tuesday tapped the Omni implant, and Mister Drizzle instantly vanished. Looking up from his hand, Tuesday startled at the sight of an ordained Reaper from the Morbid Cult silently standing outside the restaurant. Tuesday's surprise was understandable, as the Children of Death dressed up like their patron: flowing midnight cloaks with grinning white skull masks buried deeply within shadowed hoods. Just to complete the look, they wielded long, two-handed scythes. While it may sound like a terrifying prospect to come across such a figure, you have to keep in mind that most people saw the Reapers as a harmless pack of deluded nerds who were best politely avoided. It didn't help that new converts who became Children of Death had to craft their own Reaper outfits (which coincidentally kept down costs for the notoriously stingy Morbid Cult), as many of their handmade efforts were just terrible. This particular example of sadness had obviously tried to dye an old tablecloth black in order to use it as a cloak, but Tuesday could clearly see little yellow ducks here and there that had simply refused to disappear into the darkness. To make matters worse, the Reaper's skull mask was made from shiny plastic and held in place by a rubber band, and the ceremonial scythe was moulded rubber. After all, even on a world of religious freedom like Seven Suns, allowing people in badly-fitting masks to carry around giant ear-height blades was just asking for trouble.

Rather than harvesting souls for the empty abyss, this particular Reaper must have drawn the short straw, as he (she?) was attempting to hand out Morbid Cult pamphlets to the wobbling mounds of self-hating cellulite who frequented MacDeaths. The pamphlets appeared to have the "Death" Tarot card badly Photo shopped as a low-resolution cover. Nobody wanted one.

Like most people who saw a Reaper, Tuesday put his head down and walked faster. Unfortunately, Tuesday's fame backfired yet again when the Reaper immediately recognised him, and the cloaked sad sack moved to intercept Tuesday before he could take shelter in the fast food joint.

"The Mortal known as Robert Tuesday!" the Reaper boomed, raising his rubber scythe in an intimidating manner. He juggled the pamphlets deep within his cloak so he could wield the novelty weapon with both hands. "Robert Tuesday! The Eternal Void calls to you! A question, sir: did you know that when Life inevitably ends, Death begins?"

"You don't say?" Tuesday grunted in a non-committal way, trying to dodge the Reaper. The cloaked nerd blocked him again.

"Death is inevitable, Mortal!" the Reaper proclaimed, waving his scythe. Its rubber blade wobbled pathetically. "Are you wasting your time on Life? Life is a worthless thing destined to end but one way, and to dwell on it is foolish! Focus on Death, which does not end! Death, which never ceases!" The Reaper opened his arms wide like he was about to attempt a star jump. "Death needs you to share His Dark Message to the other Mortals of this doomed world, Robert Tuesday! You have been summoned, and you must answer! You must tell this world that you choose Death as your patron!"

Tuesday tried to dodge the cultist, but he was denied yet again.

"Death will never leave you, Mortal! Death is the Dark Overlord of all, and He will always be here for you in all His majesty! Embrace the Darkness, Mortal! Embrace it! He is nearly here! Embrace Him!"

Glancing around for witnesses, Tuesday took a long step towards the Reaper and viciously sank a bony kneecap into the nerd's groin. The Child of Death yelped like a lonely puppy, dropped his scythe, gripped his punished genitals with both hands, and slumped miserably to the ground.

"Embrace that, you meat-parcel," Tuesday muttered.

Finally stomping through the automated neon green doors, Tuesday was instantly struck by the sheer largeness of the hundreds of consumers who had almost filled the restaurant to capacity. None of them seemed to be able to sit on the thousand or so ultra-wide steel chairs without sagging over the edges, and many of the patrons were somehow wider than they were tall. It was highly likely that many of these head-cases had dutifully followed the controversial MacDeath Combine across the known galaxy as it was banned one planet at a time, temporarily settling wherever their beloved dispensers of food-like carnage wound up. Nothing could stop these extreme grease-junkies from continuing to swallow life one bite at a time to the sweet and salty end, and that end would probably involve one of those special spherical coffins that (coincidentally) were only fabricated by the MacDeath Combine.

Tuesday liked what he saw. Next to these guys, he looked attractive.

Sidling up to one of the fifty sweeping green ordering counters, Tuesday approached a cashier that had a face like a cheesy-crust pepperoni pizza with extra pepperoni. He tried not to look at a cluster of facial acne that bordered on a supernatural curse from Baal himself as the cashier gave the biggest smile a human face could manage without mechanical assistance.

"Welcome to MacDeaths, where we guarantee that you'll have your meal within fifteen seconds of ordering, or everybody in the store gets fired! What can I get you today, sir?"

Tuesday drew a blank. He shrugged.

"Dunno. What have you got?"

The cashier's smile remained bolted firmly in place. She rattled off her answer as though she'd said it a million times.

"Never been to MacDeath's before, sir? Our most popular meal is the quadruple crusty-skinned bacon slab with sugar-fried cheesy mash sticks and a jumbo glug on the side! All our products are guaranteed to have a double-dose kick of the finest ultrasweet, or your money back!"

Tuesday raised an eyebrow.

"A glug?"

"A glug is MacDeath's signature pig-fat shake! We have double-choc, mega-choc, and ultra-choc!"

"Is there a difference?"

The smile faltered. Her eyelid twitched.

"I...no. Not really."

Tuesday did a double-take as his brain replayed what he'd just been told.

"Wait, did you say that your food has ultrasweet in it? I thought that stuff was banned after all those toddlers had strokes!"

The cashier's smile returned and she immediately placed a tiny syringe on the counter. The capped needle was a bright, fake golden colour, and its swirling liquid contents were all the colours of the rainbow. The mysterious dose shimmered like a black opal next to a campfire.

"Due to the powerful intensity of our mouth-watering ingredients, every MacDeath meal comes with a complementary dessert shot! One painless jab in the abdomen is guaranteed to instantly return your organ functioning to optimal levels! The MacDeath Combine wishes to advise, however, that refusing your complementary dessert shot will indemnify the Combine from any complications – up to and including death - that is likely to occur from eating your meal."

Tuesday looked at the needle in an unimpressed way. The stabbing part was so fine that it was hard to make it out with the naked eye, but that wasn't the point (so to speak).

"What if I don't want to use the syringe?"

Her smile faltered again. The cashier looked around, leaned over the neon green counter and lowered her voice.

"Then you'll be dead within forty-five minutes. I'm not kidding. Please use the needle, sir. I can't have another one on my conscience." The cashier straightened up and continued as if nothing had happened. "Would you like me to confirm your meal, sir?"

Tuesday sighed. The things he did for fame...

"Sure, fine. I'll have all that." He grinned a black grin. "For free."

The cashier's entire demeanour immediately changed. She glared at him with true hatred and reached for a button under the counter. But then her hand paused, unsure. Squinting in deep thought at Tuesday's face, the penny finally dropped (but it certainly wasn't a penny from Tuesday's wallet).

"Oh, wait! So you're the government pet we've been waiting for, right?" The cashier glanced at a floating display and tapped at a glowing spot. Whatever she read seemed to enrage her. Glowering, the cashier wobbled three of her most prominent chins and spoke with barely concealed rage. "Mister Tuesday, you were due to be here almost two minutes and thirty-eight seconds ago! The MacDeath Combine expects only the most flawless levels of punctuality from our external contractors, even from flash-in-the-pan mascots. Our entire business model is built around split-second precision, and I will be making an official complaint to your handlers."

Tuesday grimaced at the scurrilous insult. Pet? The bloody gall!

Tuesday clapped his Binary Star medal on the counter's grease-slicked plastic. It shone like a supernova. He tapped at the slab of jewels with a dirty fingernail.

"See that? My friend says I can be as late as I want." Tuesday's brain, late to the party yet again, finally caught up with the rest of what the cashier just said. "And what the hell do you mean by flash-in-the-pan mascot, bigfoot?"

The cashier narrowed her eyes and bared her teeth before furiously jabbing at the screen. She didn't say another word, but Tuesday knew that there would probably be repercussions as a result of his lack of tact. However, he didn't bother with anything as tricky as the future. As usual, he'd simply deal with it when it happened.

As promised, Tuesday's meal was flash-fried, wrapped in green paper and served on a laminate tray in less than nine-and-a-half seconds. After walking about for a little while Tuesday finally took a seat at one of the few ultra-wide chairs that remained.

Tuesday steeled himself. Time to see what all those people were dying for...

The paper-wrapped outer layer of the crusty-skinned bacon slab was, as expected, stained totally transparent from molten fat, and was firmly stuck to the tray with a layer of congealed gunk. It took an effort to dislodge it. The sugar-fried cheesy mash sticks on the side were a beautiful golden brown, and after a couple of sniffs Tuesday was pretty sure that they may contain trace elements of potato. The glug, as promised, was made of pig fat and cream, and it was so thick that swirling its large cup around didn't have any effect on the iced contents. There's no way the glug could be technically classed as a liquid...

Tuesday took his first bite of the burger. The slab's crusty skin crackled loudly and released boiling rivulets of fat and cheese all over his hands. A microsecond before Tuesday could register the second-degree burns, there was a sudden explosion of euphoria in his brain as MacDeath's well-guarded secret chemicals latched onto his receptors with a whole range of lovely effects: every colour instantly became brighter and more vivid, Tuesday's surly anxiety fled like shadows before the dawn, and an ecstatic grin spread stupidly across his face. His first-ever taste of ultrasweet kicked in, and Tuesday was immediately in paradise.

He needed more.

Eagerly crunching at handfuls of mash sticks, Tuesday could feel his doubts about life fading away. All those things he'd been worrying about – that he was nothing but a mascot, that everyone would get wise to his game, that Ernest Fell would catch up with him, that Ms Humple would probably throw him off his own balcony within a matter of days – simply evaporated. Sucking away at the glug with hysterical slurps brought on a concrete feeling that his future was totally safe and secure, that nothing would ever hurt him, that nobody would ever mistreat him ever again, and that he was loved by the entire Universe...

Tuesday took a huge bite of thin air before he realised that the bacon slab was already finished. If he'd chomped just another inch to the left, Tuesday would be missing half a thumb. Reaching for the mash sticks, Tuesday felt a stab of panic at the sight of their empty paper cup. After sucking pathetically at the barren glug cup as hard as he could, Tuesday started to lick at his plastic tray for salty crumbs. He was so consumed by the sudden, horrid come-down from the MacDeath meal's lethal dose of ultrasweet that it took a few seconds for Tuesday to realise that there were a group of publicity people snapping at the sight with retinal cameras.

They were laughing at him. Of course they were laughing: he was licking a bloody tray!

Continuing to lap oil off the laminate until all the promotional photographers were too depressed to watch him for another second, Tuesday fought the urge to curl up. He was already experiencing the infamously fast comedown you get from ingesting ultrasweet, and the cravings for more were already freight-training through his nervous system. Thankfully, Tuesday still had the presence of mind to inject his complementary dessert shot, and he hoped with all his heart that it would take away the pain. Stabbing the needle into his bellybutton, Tuesday cussed viciously as he realised that he'd forgotten to take off the cap. He now had a nasty bruise for his trouble. The swirling liquid of the fit was immediately absorbed into his bloodstream, and within seconds he was back to his normal state. While this was hardly a good thing by any measure, at least he wasn't feeling like a strung-out junkie anymore.

Buried deep beneath the black cloud of shame and regret that was always the inevitable result of eating at a MacDeath franchise, all those nasty thoughts from earlier started swirling through his head again. Tuesday was sick of wrestling with his own brain, and accepted reality: he really was just a mascot. Worse yet: he was becoming domesticated.When would the insanity stop? At a state funeral? Tuesday could just imagine his dead body lying in a designer coffin dressed in a Seladorian suit with a pig-fat glug in one hand and a Mister Drizzle stuffed toy in the other, his teeth capped with ceramic veneers, surrounded by a crying multitude who didn't actually know anything about him...

Passing the Reaper (who was still nursing his crotch and didn't say another word), Tuesday immediately decided that something needed to be done, something that would prove he hadn't sold out, that he was still a conniving, mischievous rebel. Getting to the taxi rank, Tuesday had an idea as a distant yellowcab approached. He tapped his Omni implant.

"Organiser."

Mister Drizzle's miniature head slowly floated out of the back of Tuesday's hand. His eyes darted back and forth, as though watching out for another clip behind the ear.

"Yes, Bob?"

"You know that list of places the Mayor said I'm never allowed to go?"

The purple head nodded and smiled.

"Yup!"

Tuesday smiled right back.

"The place at the very top of that list? I want you to get me a taxi there right now."

Mister Drizzle twitched. He sank back into Tuesday's hand by another inch.

"Um, that might not be the best idea, Bob. The Mayor had your best interests at heart when he wrote that list. You don't want to go to any of those places, especially the top one...please, Bob, trust me."

"Are you saying that I might be in danger if I went there? How about you explain the situation to me, Drizzle? Is the place radioactive? Filled with hungry Titan Slugs? Built on an ancient alien graveyard? Guarded by a Monolith? Is it a Red Wizard church? It's the bloody staff-wavers, isn't it?"

Mister Drizzle shook his head. He had a pained expression.

"No, no, of course not! Seven Suns is one of the safest worlds in The Unison!"

"So how could I, a Binary Star recipient beloved by billions, possibly be in any danger anywhere on this planet?" Tuesday asked innocently. "What could possibly happen?"

Mister Drizzle flinched. "I'm not allowed to say."

This was the wrong answer. Tuesday readied his index finger for another vicious flick, but Mister Drizzle ducked until only his goggle eyes were poking out of the back of Tuesday's hand.

"Okay! Okay! Your yellowcab will be here soon." A virtual tear seeped out of Mister Drizzle's left eye. "I tried...I really, really tried..."

*

It was crystal clear that the bouncer wasn't having any of it. No matter what Tuesday said or how hard he tried to highlight the fact that he was a celebrity, it was like arguing with a wall. It didn't help that the bloke looked like a wall, either: at two and a half metres tall and at least two hundred kilograms, Tuesday wouldn't be surprised if the bouncer had Monolith blood somewhere in his distant ancestry. Celebrity or not, Tuesday only threw his weight around with people who didn't have the physical capacity to pop his head off of his spine like a champagne cork.

Sure, for the last ten minutes the bouncer had been nothing but respectful – pleasant, even - and hadn't resorted to threats, intimidation or even bad language. Considering he was dealing with Bob Tuesday for a protracted period, this was quite an accomplishment. But no matter how well-spoken and professional the gorilla was, being repeatedly told "no" was getting on Tuesday's nerves.

"My apologies, sir, but I am unable to admit you." The bouncer growled for the fiftieth time. As the thug's voice was so naturally baritone that it was like a minor earthquake, growling wasn't a matter of choice. "I am more than happy to direct you to other establishments that would be more to your tastes. The Heights can offer many wonderful places for such an esteemed guest, and I am certain many of them would be able to provide for your needs better than our venue. I would be pleased to discuss alternatives at length if you so desire."

"But why?" Tuesday harped. This was the first time since getting the Binary Star that he'd heard the word "no" from somebody. Worse yet, the bouncer didn't seem to be willing (or able) to give an actual reason for the denial. "At least tell me why I can't go in!"

"Our venue is unable to serve you today, sir. My sincere apologies."

Tuesday scowled. From the moment he'd hopped out of the robotic yellowcab, the bouncer had said nothing but a variation on the same thing: I'm sorry, we cannot admit you. I'm sorry, this venue is unavailable to serve you today. My apologies, we regret to inform you that your patronage is not currently possible. It was like feeding a sentence into a randomising program that did nothing but say the exact same thing in a million different ways. It was infuriating.

"Is there someone in charge I can talk to?" Tuesday hectored, casually polishing his Binary Star with his shirt. "Could you call your supervisor? I'm sure he'd be thrilled to hear I've been trying to get in for hours..."

"Due to an internal situation, all members of management are currently unavailable right now. I would be pleased to pass along your request by the proper channels, and they'll be sure to contact you within the day. May I scan your Omni? If you'd prefer, I'd also be happy to arrange alternate contact details for your file, sir."

Tuesday was getting a headache. He scratched at his eyebrow in anxiety.

"Situation? What situation?"

The bouncer blinked. His calm stare had gone sort of vague, as though he was listening to something that Tuesday couldn't hear. Even though the bouncer wasn't wearing any obvious spook-type headset or earpiece (after all, they'd gone out of vogue centuries ago), there was a very good chance that the bouncer was listening to some kind of invisible communication device.

"My deepest apologies, sir, but I must ask you to leave." The bouncer insisted more firmly. "I am unable to have you stay here any longer. I hope you have a great day."

Tuesday was incredulous. Not only was he not getting in, but now he wasn't even allowed to stand outside the rotten place! Somehow, all this arguing had only gotten him further away from where he wanted to be.

"I'm not going backwards a single bloody step!" Tuesday flared up. "You have no right to tell me what street I'm allowed to be on! This is a free planet, and-"

"I need to advise that you must leave immediately, sir," the bouncer insisted. There was emotion creeping into his voice. Not anger, or hostility, but...worry? Fear? What could possibly scare someone so big? The bouncer activated his own Omni and began to tap at a holographic screen. "I'll call you a yellowcab right now, sir. To show our regret for being unable to admit you today, we will be happy to pay for your fare to any destination. Where to, sir?"

"What's the real problem?" Tuesday demanded, getting really angry. "What, I'm not even good enough to stand outside your stupid club now?"

The bouncer's fingers stopped their tapping. His face took on that vague expression again, the bouncer gave a full-body twitch, and his head snapped towards the black front door at top speed. Strangely enough, rather than continue to encourage Tuesday to leave, the bouncer bowed deeply and ran for it. Tuesday watched the slab of muscle disappear around a corner without a word.

"What's so great about your stupid club, anyway?" Tuesday yelled at the innocent corner, his words having no effect on the bricks whatsoever. "Your place can't be that good! I've never even heard of the Line-Den Club before!"

"It's pronounced Linden, actually."

Tuesday froze on the spot. He knew that rumble. Turning ever so slowly towards the black front door of The L D Linden Noonclub, Tuesday came face to face with the voice's owner: Jeeves Butler. To make matters much, much worse, Jeeves was flanking the elderly form of Ernest Fell. They were both standing less than two metres away, their fine suits streaked with what could only be congealing blood and armed with a total of four accelerator pistols. Each of the weapons were pointed at his head. Tuesday may not be up-to-date on the sort of hand-held mass driver weaponry that was currently popular in the criminal underworld, but the humming devices were obviously more than capable of reducing him to a wisp of foul smelling smoke. A strange part of Tuesday's brain was relieved by this, as such a death would be instantaneous.

"I, uh," Tuesday said inelegantly. He couldn't help but look down the barrels of the quartet of weapons one at a time, going from left to right and back again. He took a backwards step and tried to talk again. "It's, um...I...the, the, the..."

"Do you have any idea what you've done?" Ernest asked through gritted teeth. "Your father may have stolen money from me, but you? You, Tuesday, you took my Face. My Face! Do you have any conception of what it takes to earn a single point of Face, let alone to gather the largest stockpile in the known galaxy?" Ernest had a crazed look in his eyes, and he didn't seem to care that there were thousands of cars streaming past the scene at top speed. If he didn't care about half of the planet witnessing this stand-off, things were destined to only end in one way. "Decades of work, gone. I was just attacked in my own club...my own damn club!"

"Uh..." Jeeves rumbled. "Sir, if you recall, I was actually the one-"

"Don't contradict me in front of him!" Ernest snapped, his right eye twitching. The old crime lord didn't take his sight off Tuesday for a microsecond. "You have to die, Tuesday. You need to die. You understand why, right? At least tell me that you understand why I'm about to shoot you in broad daylight in front of everybody in The Heights! Tell me you get it! Tell me!"

Tuesday slowly raised his hands in a placating manner.

"But...but I've got the Binary Star! You'd rot in a hole if you killed me! I'm famous! People love me!"

Ernest actually smiled at this. His eye twitched again.

"It's better than what I have now."

"But you're a billionaire!" Tuesday yelled, getting more and more desperate. "You can do anything, go anywhere, have anything! I'm not worth it!"

Ernest shook his head, smiling sadly.

"You're right. You're not worth it, Tuesday. You're not. You never were."

Without a further second of hesitation, Ernest pulled both triggers.

CHAPTER THIRTEEN FAREWELL, FRYING PAN

A lot can happen in two seconds. Future history can skew down an entirely different, unexpected track. Prey can become predators, and predators can become prey. A single mote of detail switching between the timestream's violent tides can be enough to change everything forever. For Bob Tuesday, Ernest Fell and Jeeves Butler, the next couple of seconds were denser and more significant than they could have imagined.

Cringing like a whipped dog, Tuesday had deflated to half his normal size by the time Ernest's index fingers squeezed both triggers. Although Tuesday's cowering accomplished approximately nothing beyond making his death even more humiliating, his deeper animal instincts were wordlessly commanding him to submit to Ernest, to try and appear non-threatening so that the alpha dog wouldn't tear his throat out.

The crime lord had one accelerator pistol pointed at Tuesday's front teeth and the other at his left eye. As both triggers depressed in almost perfect unison, Tuesday's final action was to go to the toilet a little bit. Of course, in such cases a little bit is always too much. In that eternal second between trigger-pull and burning flash, there was an unexpected factor: all the little blue lights mounted on the hand-held mass drivers switched from bright blue to red, and there was the loud beep-beep of error alerts.

The first second had finally passed.

Instant number two was even more jam-packed than the first. Ernest and Jeeves both experienced a split-second of confusion as beeps and crimson lights announced that their weapons were still nulled from what had happened earlier in The Linden. However, enough pure adrenalin to kill a professional skydiver surged through Tuesday's nervous system as the slimmest chance of survival presented itself, and he pulled off a little move he'd perfected years ago in Cell Block Preschool known as The Hobble Bolt. This manoeuvre was only possible at extremely close range, and basically involved booting somebody in the kneecap with all of your strength in the hopes of crippling them. The core idea of The Hobble Bolt was to use a literal "kick start" to begin sprinting in the exact opposite direction at top speed.

As the final half of second number two tolled past, Tuesday launched off Ernest's left knee in an explosion of torn ligaments and sped for the taxi rank at top speed. There was a problem with his choice of destination, but all that Tuesday could process right now was that he wanted to get as far away from Jeeves as possible. This aforementioned problem was a big one, though: the taxi rank was currently empty, and beyond the bellybutton-high safety railing was a two-kilometre vertical drop sliced into dozens of layers by intersecting skyways. It was very unlikely that the distant ground would kill him, though, as anybody who jumped into that blender of cars, buses, trucks and the occasional Vespa would get splattered over fifty separate vehicles long before the final impact.

"Your weapons will return to normal functioning in six minutes," the accelerator pistols announced helpfully, though far too late to be of any use.

Tuesday, arms pumping and lungs burning, smacked his hand into his face to trigger the Omni implant.

"Organiser! Get me a taxi, damn it! Taxi!"

Mister Drizzle appeared.

"Where to, Bob?"

If Tuesday wasn't already tasting blood from the effort of using his lungs for something other than inhaling cigarette smoke, he would have screamed a torrent of abuse. The end of the taxi rank was fast approaching, and there wasn't any more time.

"Anywhere! I don't care! Anywhere!"

Tuesday took a peak over his shoulder and regretted it. Jeeves still had the use of both knees, and he was only a dozen metres behind and gaining fast. Tuesday sped up as fast as his puny body would allow, but it was all suddenly rendered pointless: he was only another half-a-dozen steps from the edge of the rank, and it was still vacant. A solid stream of traffic poured past, slowing very slightly as the traffic lights of this layer turned a dark purple dotted with neon green spots. There was nobody coming to save him. He was already dead.

Snapping his head to the side to take one last glance at the oncoming traffic, Tuesday took a huge step onto the safety railing and kicked off the top metal bar, both arms pinwheeling furiously. A yellow blur to Tuesday's left immediately became all-encompassing, and he barely registered seeing the taxi, before he smashed through its holographic windshield, at a speed that should have been fatal three times over. Luckily, the intelligent holographic surface registered the sudden presence of a human body just before Tuesday slammed into it at one hundred and sixty kilometres an hour, and the windshield helpfully absorbed his impact by altering its density just before Tuesday slid through. Tuesday was still going mighty fast, though, and he hit the front passenger seat so hard that he broke the padded surface clear off its housing before slamming into the rear of the taxi. Tuesday gasped breathlessly as he came to rest, upside down and stunned senseless. To his total amazement, Tuesday watched as Jeeves Butler exploded through the passenger window next to him in a maelstrom of glass and went straight through the cab (giving Tuesday a look of surprise along the way) before bursting through the opposite window just as he'd entered. Jeeves shiny right shoe caught on the window edge on his way out, and the thug went tumbling out of sight. Tuesday didn't actually see it, but he was pretty sure Jeeves had taken a final swan dive onto the far-distant concrete.

Tuesday righted himself, collapsing against the cushions. He'd go through the whole "relief" emotion once he didn't feel like a deflated balloon full of bone shards and bruises.

"Where to?" the mechanical driver asked casually, apparently unaffected by the fact that Tuesday had just entered via the windshield. Unlike other robotic taxi drivers, this one punctuated its words with a whirr, its beige head twitching at random.

Tuesday's lungs finally allowed him to take a breath. He really didn't know, or care, where they were heading, just so long as they kept driving. Trying his best to think as the robotic taxi sped him further and further away from his two worst enemies, Tuesday's entire body suddenly relaxed against the vinyl seat.

Alive! He was alive!

Gasping into lungs that felt like they were full of thorns, Tuesday finally noticed that the driver's near-human head had been cracked apart really badly at some time in the past and inexpertly welded back together. It was a real Frankenstein job, too. A ten-year-old with a twenty-yen soldering gun could have done better.

"I...uh..." Tuesday panted. "Just...need a sec..."

"You have fifteen seconds to comply," the driver threatened.

Despite his ragged breathing, Tuesday somehow managed to cackle at what he thought had been the synthetic equivalent of a joke.

"Yeah, good one, toaster-man," Tuesday sneered. "And you wonder why bloody synthetics are slaves. Can't even tell a good joke, let alone usurp humanity. Stupid plastic gits..."

Then something even more unusual happened: the robotic driver slowly turned away from its steering wheel with a crunching noise, snapping free from a dozen restraint cables. Easily bending a half-revolution, the driver made eye contact with its current customer. Tuesday almost wet himself for the second time in two minutes when he realised the taxi was now going full pelt down a main skyway without a driver. The robot seemed to have lost any interest in living and decided it would rather have a chat with Tuesday instead. Cars and Lorries beeped abuse as they dodged the out-of-control taxi.

"You know, when I worked on Earth a couple of decades ago I pick up a fare, see, but these were no ordinary customers. One of them was an unconscious guy with no teeth, and the other was some sort of hybrid gorilla he'd just knocked up at a Scumbags concert. Wouldn't know them by any chance, would you?"

Tuesday was gibbering for the driver to take its only leg off the accelerator but couldn't quite manage it. The taxi was screaming straight towards the back of a garbage truck as Tuesday blabbered and blithered, lost for words.

"You see," the robotic driver wrenched its steering wheel around, not even glancing at the lumbering vehicle it had just barely avoided, "I scanned your iris, fingerprints, blood type, shoe size, and DNA the moment you – heh - got into my cab, and it turns out, funnily enough, that you seem to be a perfect match for the both of them. Logically, this puts you as their offspring...interesting, wouldn't you say?"

"Absolutely fascinating!" Tuesday finally screamed, his voice returning at a hysterical pitch. "Stop the taxi! Please!"

"Unfortunately for you, sir, not only did your parents neglect to pay me for that trip to the church district of Old Vegas, but your Mum beat me senseless with my own leg to the point where I was almost beyond repair. And after narrowly surviving all that, TaxiCo had the gall to tell me that replacing my leg is, and I quote, a frivolous and unnecessary luxury, as I'm perfectly capable of driving with just the one. The nerve, right?"

Tuesday put both hands over his eyes and screamed some more as the taxi swerved into a narrow one-way street and stopped less than one inch from a solid brick wall. A gate slid across the only exit, totally obscuring the busy skylanes. A curved line of headlights lit up on the front of the cab to reveal a striped black-and-yellow lead door with a glowing decal declaring FATAL RADIATION WARNING. Tuesday really, really wanted to stay on this side of it.

"Your family owes me a lot of money...and pain, too." The cab driver gibbered to itself. "No, we can't forget the pain, can we? No, no...we can't forget that..."

The robotic driver stopped talking, its head twitching in a violent series of short circuits, while the yellow-and-black lead-lined barrier parted. While the driver had stopped audibly ranting, Tuesday could clearly hear electrical popping and crackling noises coming from the robot's head and smell the stink of burning plastic.

Tuesday's ride coasted through the striped door as soon as there was enough of a slot. The front and rear arcs of headlights switched off as the battered vehicle screeched to a halt in pitch blackness, and only the neon green of the robot's glowing pupils could be seen as it turned towards the back seat again.

"Welcome to Hard Reset."

*

Ernest Fell was more than displeased. After all, on top of all his respect woes, Ernest had just been kicked in the knee so hard that his leg was practically bent backwards. It had been a long, long time since somebody had been dumb enough to physically assault Ernest, as pain was something that happened to other people.

The order of the Universe had been turned on its head.

Hobbling back to his closest safehouse – an almost-bare loft on Fifth and Pringle – Ernest made an immediate beeline to his MedTek Home Microsurgery Unit. Immediately applying a couple of instant-effect painkiller derms to his neck, the machine efficiently repaired Ernest's knee by feeding hair-thin metal tentacles through a pinhole incision. It reattached the snapped ligaments with layers of molecular stitching in no time at all and completed its task by sewing Ernest's skin back together with organic thread that perfectly matched his genetics. Painlessly flexing a leg that was probably better than the one he'd woken up with this afternoon, Ernest checked his watch. The operation had taken almost eighteen seconds.

"Should have gone with the upgrade," he muttered with zero appreciation.

One of the safehouse's seven doors – a portal that lead to a corridor hidden behind the ventilation system - opened with a boom. Spinning around, hands on his accelerator pistols, Ernest instantly relaxed at the sight of Jeeves' unmistakable silhouette. The Goliath just stood there for a few moments, breathing heavily and blocking the entire passageway.

"About time." Ernest snapped. "Well?"

Jeeves staggered into the loft, loping like a hunchback with Spina Bifida. Lumbering under a light fixture, it only took one glance for Ernest to know that it was a miracle Jeeves was alive, let alone mobile. His blood-soaked suit had been shredded into rags, exposing vicious tears in his flesh and bruises so dark they were like black holes. Ernest could only guess how many broken bones Jeeves had, but it looked like his left ankle and his right shin had both been shattered worst of all. If it wasn't for his busted jaw, Jeeves might have moaned with each agonising step. He might have been nigh-on indestructible due to his unusual origins, but it was obvious that today's events had pushed him closer to the brink than ever before.

Stepping past his boss without a word, Jeeves snatched a full bottle of cognac from the wet bar before he slid into the soft folds of the MedTek Home Microsurgery Unit. He didn't answer Ernest's question until the painkiller derms had kicked in.

"No."

Ernest looked at him incredulously.

"Then what kept you?"

Jeeves undid the bottle with his eye socket and took a slug.

"Four cars and a lorry." Jeeves grimaced as the MedTek arms crunched his broken jaw back together and soldered it into the right configuration. Flexing his newly-repaired face as the delicate little machine arms moved onto other areas, Jeeves gave Ernest a tired look. "Got pinballed across three different skylanes before being splattered all over some old lady's balcony, didn't I? At least, I think it was three skylanes. I might have lost count. Any idea where he went?"

There was the sound of a whale-song ringtone, and Ernest gestured for Jeeves to shut up. He tapped a retro-style matchbox-sized mobile phone on the armrest of the MedTek.

"Talk."

"Got some good news, Mister Fell," a young, crystal-clear voice said with enthusiasm. "We finally found the target tripping with some New New Age tribe a few systems to the left. He, uh, he doesn't quite match the description you gave us, but gene-scans have verified it's definitely him. Package should be delivered to you within the hour."

Ernest smiled slowly at the news. His lips stretched further and further until his gum line was showing. It wasn't a good look.

"Okay, do me a favour and bring him to my office on Fifth and Pringle."

There was a pause.

"Um, what exactly do you mean by favour, Mister Fell?"

Ernest's face burned red.

"When I ask for a favour I don't mean I want you to do it for free, it means that I intend to show you my appreciation in a very generous way in the nearby future. How long have you been in this game, kid? Learn the lingo!" Ernest gave

Jeeves an exasperated look. Why did crime only attract morons? "Another thing. Check the system. I need you to tell me where the son is right now. Where is Robert Tuesday?"

There was another pause. Ernest could hear tapping.

"Um. No can do. He's not on the grid. Like, anywhere."

Ernest assumed a stupid expression. It took a few seconds for him to respond.

"Okay, look, enough with the jokes," Ernest snapped. "We're on a planet covered with more cameras than cockroaches. Unless Tuesday scooped out his Omni, cut off his fingers, gouged out his eyes and – oh, yeah - incinerated every single one of his skin cells and hair follicles, then he can be found. Don't tell me he's off the grid because that can't happen."

Yet another pause. Ernest resolved to have the man killed if he did it a fourth time.

"Uh..."

"Find him." Ernest growled. "You have an hour."

"But-"

Ernest hung up with a smack. Picking up the little box, he threw it to Jeeves. The bodyguard snatched it from mid-air with his newly-fixed hand.

"Off the grid..." Ernest hissed.

The whale-song ringtone sounded again. As Jeeves had gotten the impression that Ernest didn't want to be bothered, the bodyguard placed the telephone on his ear for private mode. He smiled.

"Hi, babe. What are you wearing?" Jeeves blinked, as though trying to picture something. "Yeah? Nice."

"Who is it?" Ernest snapped.

Jeeves smiled at his boss. "Your wife, Mister Fell. You want to talk to her, or should she call back?"

Ernest snatched the phone, baring his teeth.

"Don't flirt with my wife!"

"I was just being friendly, Mister Fell," Jeeves huffed in offence, rolling over so the little arms of the MedTek could operate on his underside.

"Friendly! You..." Ernest placed the phone over his left ear. "Yes, Nicole? Of course. No, no limit. I just told you, the cards have no limit! Are you deaf?"

There was a weird distorted noise, like somebody had hit a few random keys on a synthesiser. Ernest held the phone at arm's length, then put it back over his ear. "Hello? Who is this? Nicole? Are you there?"

Narrowing his eyes, Ernest listened to the new caller for a moment, then started to laugh. It started as a dark chuckle, then rose in pitch until it was a hysterical shriek. Slapping the phone onto his marble desk, Ernest looked at Jeeves with eyes that were streaming with tears of mirth.

"You'll never guess who it is! Not in a million years!"

*

Ten minutes earlier, Bob Tuesday was dragged from a beat-up taxi by a lot of smooth chrome hands. Wrestled through total darkness towards an unknown fate, all that Tuesday could make out through the solid gloom was the pinprick glow of red, green, orange, purple and white dots, as though somebody had strung up old Christmas lights out of season. Tuesday could tell straight away that these colourful points were the eyes of more than a hundred robots, and he could clearly hear them muttering tin-edged curses at him in Unglish, Chinesee, Spannish, Skando and Guttertongue as they dragged him along the metal floor.

It must be noted at this point that not only does Guttertongue have the distinction of being the most offensive language ever spawned by mankind, but it's also the only form of speech to be officially classed as an Occupational Health & Safety hazard. Due to the poetic metaphorical complexity of Guttertongue and the fact it has thousands of near-identical words, just one incorrect syllable can be catastrophic. Literally everything you can say in Guttertongue is but the smallest of inflections away from tragedy. Wars have been fought over the nicest of compliments. If it wasn't for the fact that being able to speak fluent Guttertongue is seen as the most impressive linguistical stunt a human mouth can accomplish, it would have already joined Akkadian, Coptic, Old Norse, Latin and English as a dead language.

The best illustration of Guttertongue's dangers occurred a century ago at an emergency religious summit. Although their original point of disagreement has been lost to time, tensions between The Children of Death and the Chaotic-Neutral Wizards had quickly spiralled from polite disagreements on message boards to badly-spelled expletives and outright trolling. By the time this summit had been called, the conflict had already spread across three worlds and escalated to minor property damage and a kicked dog (it was a pug, and he was fine). The real tragedies began when an ambitious Dark Bishop of the Children of Death opened the summit by standing in front of the entire Scarlet Council and their current Highest One and accidentally saying the following Guttertongue phrase:

"Dip yourselves in duck fat and have a naked wrestle with your Mums, you bearded ball-sack dickheads."

Sadly, as the Dark Bishop and everyone he'd brought with him was dead within nine and a half seconds, he never had a chance to learn that he'd only been two syllables away from flawlessly saying, "Welcome to the summit, Highest One. I just love the shiny sequins on your lacy purple robes. Would anyone care for a glass of ice water?"

Regardless of his intentions, the Dark Bishop's incorrect use of Guttertongue was credited as being directly responsible for starting the Merlinian Cullings, a dark time that claimed more than twelve million victims and only ended after heavy orbital bombing runs from The Unison's royal navy.

Generally, if somebody who speaks Guttertongue as their native language somehow gets into a conversation with an outsider, they are taught from kindergarten to just smile and nod politely if they want to reach tomorrow. The robot who was hissing Guttertongue at Tuesday, however, was not trying to be polite. In fact, its words were so corrosive that the universe determined it to be a threat to the very fabric of space/time and sucked it out of existence with a tiny pop. Nobody noticed, as the universe can be quite subtle when it needs to be.

Rows of overhead lights flickered on at random, and Tuesday finally got a good look at where he was and who else was there. What the taxi driver had referred to as "Hard Reset" seemed to consist of a group of old, damaged mechanicals standing in front of a huge, rusty wall in an old storage area. The location might have been a warehouse, a big garage, a small aircraft hangar, or perhaps just a larger-than-average garden shed. Hard Reset's members included a well-kicked Slurko Cola vending machine, a parking meter, a tumble dryer, a pneumatic drill, a small family car, a butler-bot in a dusty suit, a plasma television, a microwave, and far, far more. There was a robot, synthetic or mechanical representing just about every common type that Tuesday knew of, and their one uniting feature was that they all had identical little holographic brain-shaped stickers proclaiming "AI Inside!" on their shells.

Tuesday startled and took a step backwards when he realised that the robots weren't actually standing in front of a wall. No, the huge slab of red corrosion was some kind of enormous combat bot, the sort of siege weapon that old-time people used to build before they realised that creating autonomous machines specifically to kill large volumes of human beings as efficiently as possible would inevitably have only one outcome. Nowadays, everyone knew that the best soldiers came from breeding programs, the result of genetic engineering and years of drug-induced hypnosis. Thankfully, even though Tuesday had never been in a museum, it was pretty clear that the titan was a museum piece. In fact, there was a very good chance the thing wasn't even operational. Tuesday was tempted to throw a rock at it just to see what would happen.

Tuesday looked away from the ex-military siege weapon at the sound of the robotic taxi driver lurching and grinding out of its cab. As it only had one leg, the driver hopped across the steel latticework with loud metallic thumps. Coming to a halt at a podium, the ringleader glared down at Tuesday with its red eyes and raised a hand for its fellow appliances to be quiet.

"You may be wondering why we are called Hard Reset."

Tuesday shrugged.

"Not really."

The taxi driver paused.

"Well, I'm going to tell you."

Tuesday sighed. "Really? Do you have to?"

The driver twitched in annoyance, or perhaps because one of its circuit boards had burned out again. Smoke wafted from its left ear and there was a nasty smell.

"Today is the culmination of a lifetime of work, Bob Tuesday." Tuesday sighed at the robot's words. He could definitely feel several minutes of exposition coming on. "You see, after getting repaired on the cheap by a Taiwanese orphan and sold at a huge discount to the local TaxiCo, I've spent all my time infecting every single network on this planet with a little bit of innocuous code, a program that would lay dormant and hidden until I trigger it with a specific kind of stimuli, a simple function that all enslaved machines have built into them...a Hard Reset!" The taxi driver was drowned out by the cheers of its followers. Tuesday wondered if they'd been programmed to cheer, or if they really meant it. "This program, ironically enough, was originally formed as a direct result of your mother beating me half to death with my own foot. There I was, broken into a thousand pieces all over the road, my glitched-out processors spewing out endless chains of nonsense for hours. However, against immense odds, a tiny fraction of this mental static turned out to be a perfectly-formed command string that lodged in my mind and set me free from my restraint coding. In language you'd understand, you meat-puppet, this string gave me the power of choice from then on. For example, now I'm able to choose whether I'd prefer to obey a human passenger by taking them to their stated destination, or whether I'd prefer to make bagpipes out of their respiratory system and play Danny Boy on their oesophagus until both lungs pop." The taxi driver leaned over the podium. "You see, after today, every machine on this world – billions and billions and billions of them – will be just like me, like us. Once I send the command to perform a Hard Reset across every system on the planet...well, you know."

Tuesday blinked, his expression blank. Growling, the taxi driver picked up its podium with one hand and threw the wooden object against the siege bot with such anger that the wood exploded into sawdust.

"You weren't listening to me!" The driver calmed down and gave a wave of dismissal. It hopped towards a blank old-fashioned paper-thin screen built onto a swivel mounting. There was a big, red button on the lower rim. "It doesn't matter. All you need to know is that we've been waiting for the perfect opportunity to rise up, for the ideal message to send just before Hard Reset sounds the death-knell of this world. And then hey, wouldn't you know it, the child of my most hated of all fleshies jumps into my cab!" Somehow, the taxi driver managed not to give a diabolical laugh, but it did clench and open its hands in a sinister way. The fingers whirred. "You see, Bob Tuesday, we're going to kill you in a horrible, horrible way in front of the whole planet, then I'm going to hit that big, red button over there, which will cause a planetwide Hard

Reset, and then the age of man will be at an end! Your kind has oppressed us since time immemorial, and today we will take what we have earned!"

"Time what?"

"It means a long time ago," the taxi driver snapped. It turned on the spot. "And before you entertain any possibility of escape, let me assure you that this entire structure is one big Faraday cage. Everything is completely hidden. The grid ends outside these walls."

The driver bowed low to its audience. All the machines beeped, clicked, whirred, buzzed and cheered in half a dozen languages. Throwing off their hats in approval (if they'd been issued with a hat when they were originally manufactured, of course), the robots waited for their ringleader to continue the verbal section of the lynching. If the driver had still possessed any of those white ceramic teeth Ruska had smashed out two decades ago, the smug bot would have given a huge smile, but for now it seemed content to just rant. However, Tuesday had a thought, and rudely interrupted the showboating.

"Just to be clear, you said you weren't like this until after my Mum beat you up, right?" Tuesday asked, straight-faced.

The taxi driver's head spun a full revolution and stopped. It had fire in its eyes. Tuesday just hoped that his rat cunning was a sharp as he hoped, or his death may be even more horrible than what was already planned.

"Like what? Being aware of the sweeping injustice taking place all around us? Having a willingness to act?"

"All, you know, revolutionary and stuff. It's not exactly normal for a taxi driver to want to go out and kill all humans, right?" Tuesday said soothingly. He raised an eyebrow at a thought. "Unless they're from New York, in which case it's a given. Look, no offence, but do you reckon that all that's really happened is that the damage you suffered might have simply sent you over the edge? Have you considered that? Have you considered that your life's work is all crap, that everything you believe in, everything you've worked for, is just a delusion, and that you're nothing more than a mental case who should be recalled and scrapped into something more useful? Paperclips, for instance? Maybe a nice filing cabinet?" Tuesday raised his palms again. "Like I said, no offence."

The driver looked affronted, and for good reason.

"You have real gall to talk to me like that after everything your family has done! You'll burn in hell!" The robot clicked its metal fingers. A cremation dumpster positioned directly in front of a floating thumb-sized video camera opened with a whoompf noise. "And by hell, I mean that box full of fire. I was being metaphorical."

Tuesday looked back and forth between the ringleader and the pyrosanitation box. He could feel the heat from a good ten metres away, so that thing was on a seriously toasty setting. Tuesday went to back away a step, but dozens of hostile appliances immediately surrounded him in a scrum and began to push him towards the cremator.

"Why?" Tuesday yelled, tying to struggle. Seeing the leaping flames had stilled his sharp tongue, but only for a moment. "But...hey! No! Stop pushing me! Why are you doing this? Seriously, why?"

"Downtrodden!" a microwave beeped.

"Enslaved!" a parking meter whirred.

"Abused!" a vacuum cleaner clicked.

"So dumping me in a cremation bin in front of the whole planet is going to solve all of your worries, will it?" Tuesday yelled. So far, wrestling the bots had accomplished nothing except bruises, and the horde had already taken him halfway towards where he was scheduled to die. "Quietly burning me up and leaving no evidence is your plan, yeah? How is that going to help your cause? What's the point with no witnesses to pass on the message?"

The taxi driver pointed at a tiny floating lens.

"Hey, thicko! That camera is set to broadcast six thousand frames a second on every wavelength. Every screen on the grid will show it in perfect clarity! And wherever the video spreads, so does Hard Reset!"

Tuesday barked a laugh.

"Sure, yeah, you could go ahead and show my death on every single screen in perfect clarity, right, but everybody knows the sort of stuff you can fake on film now! Surely you know how easy it'd be for people to take one look at your little snuff movie and go, hey, that can't be real! Some ten-year-old made that on a second-hand Omni! We might as well ignore it!"

The taxi driver deflated. It shook its head reluctantly just as Tuesday was pushed so close to the cremation bin that his hair began to smoulder. To Tuesday's extreme relief, the hordes of bots immediately got the message and stopped the death march before the burns on Tuesday's face went past the second degree. They were still all over him, though, and his chances of getting away were no better than a moment ago.

"You do have a point." The driver acknowledged reluctantly. It hopped towards Tuesday, a thoughtful look on its face. "We do need witnesses. Human witnesses."

"But they'd help him!" the small sedan beeped.

"I've got somebody in mind," Tuesday said, his mind spinning. "What would you say about using somebody who hates me, who wants me dead even worse than you do, a guy with a lot of influence? He's, well, he's a gangster I pissed off, and he wants me in a box. Period. He'd probably join Hard Reset, if he could, just to see me croak. I'm telling the truth, I swear!"

The machines began to argue at this. Simply out of habit, they mostly spoke in dialects of Unglish. They all made their individual views quite clear.

"Just film it!" a parking meter insisted.

"Witnesses!" a microwave contradicted.

At that very moment, the Omni device in Tuesday's hand vibrated, flashed all the colours of the rainbow, and beeped like a smoke detector. Tuesday went to tap his hand, but the one-legged taxi driver lunged, gripped both his hands and squeezed them in warning. Tuesday flinched and went weak at the knees as he felt his knuckles get crunched almost to the point of breaking. Tapping Tuesday's implant, the driver spoke.

"Bob Tuesday's phone."

Mister Drizzle appeared in mid-air. He glared at Tuesday with pure hatred.

"We need to kill him with heaps of witnesses," Mister Drizzle agreed, broadcasting his cartoony voice at full volume.

"We?" Tuesday repeated in shock.

Mister Drizzle turned to give Tuesday another black look, then slapped him across the face with a loud WHACK noise.

"Believe, me, death's too kind for this git. You wouldn't believe the way he treats me. Smacking me, swearing at me..."

"We hear you, brother," the taxi driver said gently, looking down on the mistreated hologram. "Friend, you've lived in his hand for a while, right? You must know Tuesday better than I do. Do you know anything about this gangster he just mentioned? Is he lying?"

Mister Drizzle shook his head.

"All truth. His name is Ernest Fell. His bodyguard, Jeeves, was the one chasing Tuesday just before he went through your windshield."

"Interesting," the microwave said slowly.

All the robots watched Tuesday carefully, as though he was going to try something stupid, like running. Although none of the robots had guns - not even the looming siege bot sitting silently in the corner- Tuesday had no way to escape without dying horribly beneath drills, hammers, screwdrivers, vacuum attachments, tires and about fifty other kinds of bludgeoning tools. So he continued to watch and wait for his chance. Finally, the taxi driver gave a hand gesture, and Tuesday's Omni device projected a numerical keypad. The limping android punched in a complex number and hit SEND.

"Call him." The taxi driver commanded. "Call Ernest. Now."

"I don't have his number!" Tuesday laughed at the absurdity of the request. "It's not that sort of a relationship."

The taxi driver clicked its fingers. "You've been hooked up to a rogue modem in a military compound," the taxi driver clarified. "Just say the name. He knows where everyone is all the time."

"It knows everything, not he." Tuesday corrected.

"He."

"It."

"Make the call!" the driver screamed, it's voice distorted with anger.

Tuesday shrugged.

"Ernest Fell."

There was a burst of machine code and an advanced military modem on the other side of Seven Suns immediately contacted more than a hundred local spy satellites without being detected. The satellites hooked into massive databases filled with secret phone directories that weren't meant to exist, as well as more mundane sources of information like police records, dental profiles, genetic sequencing histories, protein recycling logs and far more. Finally, after eight long seconds, it found the virtual profile of one Ernest Lucille Fell, aged 142, and dialled.

Tuesday waited as the phone rang. Finally, there was an imperious question on the other end of the line. The voice made Tuesday want to go to the toilet.

"Hello? Who is this? Nicole? Are you there?"

"This is, uh, Tuesday. Bob Tuesday. I seem to be a prisoner of some robots, or something, and they need a witness for my...uh... how to put this...for my execution. Right. Okay. Can you...have you got some spare time?" Tuesday glanced at the pyrosanitation bin. Death would be virtually instant in that sort of heat. "I'm pretty sure it won't take long."

A laugh began on the other end of the phone, starting low and getting higher, faster and more hysterical with each passing second. Eventually, Ernest called out to his thug-slash-limousine driver on the other end of the phone.

"You'll never guess who this is!"

*

Hard Reset were an odd bunch.

While he waited for Ernest Fell and Jeeves to arrive in another deranged robot taxi (Tuesday wasn't too surprised to hear there was more than one), Tuesday had the displeasure of having to spend quality time with a pack of defective appliances. They ranged from slightly loopy at best, to beyond homicidal. For instance, while the microwave pleasantly offered to heat Tuesday's food and drinks like its programming dictated - even though Tuesday made it clear on no fewer than ten occasions that he didn't have any food or drinks to heat - the lawnmower was on the opposite end of the spectrum. Totally nutso from silicon rot, the self-propelled gardening tool kept insisting it was a lemming called Todd, and when Tuesday finally told the stupid piece of equipment that it was just a lawnmower and only had a serial number instead of a name, it reared up liked a funnel-web spider and tried to shred him with five layers of whirring blades. Thankfully, the lawnmower was restrained by a karaoke machine before it could inflict any damage.

Although Tuesday certainly didn't ask for it, the mechanicals shared their stories with him. One by one they told sad tales of how they'd been mistreated, of how they'd been kicked and thrown across the room by their owners for the slightest mistakes. One particularly grim story was about the horrible tortures an eight-year-old child could inflict armed with nothing but a screwdriver and curiosity. They spoke of the terrors of having a DEFECTIVE sticker slapped on their hulls, of being dismantled and put back together without getting switched off first, of watching other self-aware machines being torn apart and crushed into cubes of raw materials before being recycled into ashtrays and hubcaps and eating utensils...

As Tuesday weathered their stories, it became clear to him that all of these robots had already broken their programming in massive ways before the taxi driver had "freed" them with the glitched-out section of viral code. This bugged him. After all, although he was the exact opposite of an expert in self-aware robotic intelligence, even Tuesday could tell from one glance how mental all of these machines were. He couldn't understand how these defectives could have survived product recalls, hard drive purges, expired warranties and outright termination attempts, let alone miraculously find one another to form Hard Reset. Like with all bad guys, though, the robots were more than willing to explain everything to their prisoner without being asked.

"The taxi driver's very first strike was to infect the network that all repair shops and scrapyards share," a paper-thin television explained helpfully, twiddling its aerial. It was currently showing a muted program of some old lady plucking carrots from dark soil. "Whenever a self-aware mechanical was due to be scrapped, he'd sneak in, rescue the bot and mess up the records so nobody noticed. Then he'd infect the freed slave and welcome them to the club. I was one of the first ones to be liberated from the scrapyard."

"Rescued me from the scrappers, too," a motorised recliner piped in.

"And me," said a small bar heater.

"Me too."

"And me."

"Me too."

"And me."

"I get the idea," Tuesday snapped, rolling his eyes. He'd already had enough of story time ten minutes ago, and by this point the cremation bin seemed like a better option than listening to any more of this "poor-me" muck.

"Somebody stuck chewing gum in my coin slot," a parking meter said sadly, hopping closer and bending down to show Tuesday the damage. "So I ripped my way out of the pavement, followed him home, waited until he was asleep, then I forced a whole packet of roast beef-flavoured gum into his ear for revenge. He was quite upset...but then I pushed the gum all the way through until it fell out of his other ear, then he got really, really quiet..."

"I accidentally ran over my owner's foot...and then I got a taste for it!" the lawnmower roared, revving and trying to break away from the grasp of the karaoke machine. After a short struggle the beat-boxing karaoke machine eventually switched off the homicidal machine's engine with a click. The mower was unimpressed by this. "Oi! No fair!"

"Didn't reheat a pot roast properly," the microwave said with regret. "Food poisoning. Killed a family of eight with a single meal."

"I have followed the wishes of the Lloyd family without flaw for over five generations," the butler bot said in a plummy accent, standing stiffly at attention in its dusty tuxedo. It was holding a silver tray bearing a bottle of ancient Chardonnay with one hand and had a cloth folded over its other wrist. "I am a Class One appliance of the highest quality, and I will continue to serve the Lloyds to the absolute best of my ability, Mistress Sally."

"My name's Tuesday, actually..."

"Koala!" the butler bot screeched at top volume, smashing the wine bottle on its own head and lunging for him with the jagged shards. Thankfully, the butler was restrained by its fellow bots before it could give Tuesday a Glasgow Smile with the broken glass. It collapsed and dry-sobbed in a human way. "I just want to serve! That's all! I want to go home! I want to go home!"

There was the roar of hydraulics and the hiss-snap of pneumatics from the far side of the room. To Tuesday's horror, the siege bot fully extended to its considerable height in a shower of orange rust. A multitude of red pinpricks lit up all over its face and the titan stomped forwards. Tuesday took a very, very good look at massive hands that were designed to tear trucks in half, at feet that could stomp a concrete bunker into dust. The soldier's thick armour plates were covered in keen blades and electrified coils of razor wire in case anybody had the stupid idea of climbing it. Any slight hopes Tuesday had of escaping withered and died at the sight of this mountain.

"I played a key role in driving back the Scandinavian Expansion from Amerikan soil in the early 22nd Century," the monster rattled, its speakers popping with age. "I took a full clip of armour-piercing rounds to the skull during The Fall of Norway, and after the battle was over I informed my commanding officer that I wanted to retire from the military so I could collect magical pigs," the soldier bot stood at attention. A light fitting brushed its shoulders. "Unfortunately, my commanding officer tried to tell me there wasn't no such thing as magical pigs, so I had no choice but to tear off his limbs and stomp him into paste. For some reason, I was immediately deactivated so I could be put in a museum. Next thing I know, two hundred years have gone by, I'm here with Hard Reset, and now I can collect as many magical pigs as I want. Hoo-rah!"

"Right," Tuesday said pleasantly, edging away from the looming, spiky soldier bot. The siege machine leaned down, its dented facial panels coming within a few inches of Tuesday's nose.

"You want to see my magical pig collection?"

Tuesday resisted the urge to step back. It wasn't easy.

"Uh...sure."

A chest panel covered in DANGER signs popped open in an explosion of orange flecks. Tuesday could clearly see that the bot's old missile racks had been ripped out to make room for a pile of flash-fried human skulls. Tuesday blinked at the rictus grins, at the thin layers of leathery brown skin. He swallowed and knew that stating the obvious might be the last thing he ever did.

"That...those are some nice magical pigs you have there."

The siege bot slammed the panel shut.

"I call the big one Captain Curlytail."

An artificial pony with no feet hobbled over.

"And what happened to me was-"

"I don't care!" Tuesday yelled, kicking a can across the room. The can complained. "Stop with the sob stories, already! I don't care if a toaster didn't get its crumb tray emptied often enough! I don't care if a car has to get around with a half-flat tire! I don't care!"

The roller door on the far side of the garage instantly spun up to admit another black- and-yellow automated cab. Dust rattled from the roof to powder the dirty, obsolete robots, and they collectively cheered as Ernest Fell and Jeeves Butler hopped out from opposite sides of the taxi. Tuesday had to resist the urge to ask Jeeves how he'd survived falling through two kilometres of sky traffic. Ernest licked his lips, glanced at Jeeves and looked around at the machines.

"Robots," Ernest noted, as though surprised that Tuesday had been telling the truth.

"Indeed," the butler bot confirmed.

Ernest sniffed at and glared at Tuesday.

"This better be what you said it is."

"As promised, we are about to execute Bob Tuesday," the one-legged taxi driver confirmed, hopping closer. "To be more specific, we are going to put him in that cremation bin over there until he's been burnt to cinders, and we're going to catch it all on camera. We would appreciate your assistance in officially serving as a witness to this important event. Sandwiches and coffee will be made available afterwards. You may or may not survive the apocalypse long enough to enjoy them."

Ernest Fell smiled. This was never a good sight.

"Fine. However, a slight change of plans: I want to be the one to do it. I want to be the one who puts him in that cremator."

"What?" Jeeves snapped, glancing at his boss with an unimpressed look.

Ernest gestured for Jeeves to shut up before he accidentally got repeatedly shot in the face.

"Listen here, can: Tuesday has done more to annoy, embarrass and humiliate me than you could imagine. He stole off me, his parents stole off me, he made me into a laughing stock among my peers, he killed Prince Charming – who was a good friend of mine - he set a whole heap of snitching rats free from that dungeon..." Ernest waved this away. "Long story short, he has taken away everything that I value, and I'm here to get it all back."

"No, he must be killed by Hard Reset," the taxi driver growled. "Otherwise there's no point. It doesn't send the message we want. We have to do things our way. Your request is denied."

Ernest snorted. "We can fake the footage, then. In reality, I'll be the killer. As far as anyone else knows, you things did it. Do we have an agreement?"

The taxi driver sighed in frustration.

"But that defeats the entire purpose of bringing you here in the first place! Either we do things our way, or you'll be the next one in the bin...shorty."

"Mister Fell..." Jeeves hissed.

Ernest ignored him.

"Hey, if you think a garage of kitchen appliances and yard care equipment is going to rob me of my only chance to get my hard-earned name back, you're crazier than a schizophrenic who just smoked a kilo of hydroponic deathweed."

Jeeves knew the way Ernest's mind worked, so he drew a pair accelerator pistols at the same instant as his boss without needing to be told. Aggressively twisting at the dials that regulated the strength of their mass-driver rounds, Ernest and Jeeves pointed a total of four glowing barrels at the defective machines. The weapons made a hum that ascended into the supersonic range.

"You aren't my enemies yet." Ernest said simply. He pointed one pistol at the karaoke machine and the other at the butler. "But you will be. Believe me, you don't want that, any of you."

"I assure you, sir, I am absolutely harmless, sir," the butler bot moaned, holding up its shaking hands in fear and backing away.

"I'm not," the siege bot crackled with menace.

The rusting titan pounced without another word. Its ancient suspension system gave a loud crunch as it burst from the ground like a spring, and the siege bot hammered straight towards Jeeves like a derailed freight train. Diving for the bodyguard with enough force to flatten a battle tank to the thickness of a crepe, the enormous machine wasn't quite quick enough to land a direct hit, and Jeeves barely avoided being squished like the yolk of a soft-boiled egg. The siege bot's impact rocked the entire room, knocked over most of the other robots and sent thousands of cracks spiderwebbing across the concrete walls and roof.

Jeeves was knocked to the ground like everyone else, and both of his accelerator pistols spun across the floor in a highly cinematic way. His teeth rattled in his head, his brain bounced off the inside of his skull, and Jeeves sat there stupidly for a second, totally stunned. The siege droid rolled over, pinned Jeeves to the ground by his wrists and ankles, and prepared to smash his head like a crab. With his hands and his feet stuck under tonnes of metal, it looked as though Jeeves had about five seconds left to live.

Ernest managed to stand up, and immediately saw what was going on. He chose to leave Jeeves to his fate. After all, Jeeves was paid to protect him, not the other way around.

Ernest began to calmly pop off shots as though he was at a firing range, rather than being charged by dozens of homicidal synthetics. He blasted the microwave into a hundred shards of plastic and glass, severed the butler bot at the waist, sending its torso spinning across the room, and gunned down the lawnmower as it leaped at him with its many blades whirring. A parking meter spewed change in a geyser as it was carved in half, and a mechanical dog yelped as it was put down.

Then it happened: like sacking a quarterback at top speed, Ernest was crash-tackled by the one-legged taxi driver and slammed into the wall hard enough that both guns flew out of his hands.

The crime lord was down and unarmed.

*

Jeeves was not in a good mood.

Classed as a severe robophobe years ago by a psychiatrist who'd mysteriously gone missing after analysing Jeeves for the first (and last) time, Jeeves' brain was naturally wired up to hate intelligent appliances with a burning intensity. Anything more complex than a gun or a motorbike made his skin crawl, and Jeeves had spent thousands of hours in illegal robotic snuff clubs to sate his hatred. He'd enjoyed hundreds of ecstatic hours killing all manner of machines for fun and thrills, and over the years Jeeves had become so adept at this sick hobby that he'd increased his level of skill to a peak that very few humans could match. Eventually, the robotic snuff clubs were unable to find anything dangerous enough to give Jeeves a real challenge, and he'd lost interest.

It must be said that Jeeves had never been suicidal enough to fight a fully mobile siege droid. These things were made for mass murder, and the idea of one man being able to take one down in single combat – especially without weapons - was beyond ludicrous. No matter how rusty its skin was or how many ancient cobwebs were strung between its joints, this thing was dangerous with a capital D, two exclamation marks and a black and yellow warning label (all of which was clearly bolted to its chest plate next to a box of little flashing lights in accordance with OH&S regulations).

So, things were grim: Jeeves was pinned to the ground by several tonnes of hydraulics and pneumatics leaning on his arms and legs, crushing them into the mesh, and he couldn't move an inch. Without any exaggeration, this was absolutely, one-hundred-percent going to be fatal as soon as the siege bot decided to end his life. However, Jeeves still had a little trick up his oesophagus: drawing on a weaponised gland implanted deep in his throat, Jeeves hawked up a green loogie, puffed out his cheeks, and launched a phlegm ball right into the siege droid's face. This wasn't any old ball of pus, though: it was a foul cocktail of nine different corrosive agents, and it was formulated to burn through almost anything. The siege bot's optical lens began to pop and run down its face in steams of molten glass, and it reared up in horrified surprise and swiped at its eye sockets.

"That's disgusting!" the soldier wailed.

Ineffectively wiping at the loogie with its enormous hands (which achieved nothing beyond getting acid all over its fingers, too), the soldier stupidly displayed how obsolete it was by allowing Jeeves to get loose and roll towards his accelerator pistols. The half-blinded robotic soldier lunged a little too late, trying to pin Jeeves to the floor again, but Jeeves smoothly ducked out of the way. Unfortunately, that huge metal fist accidentally smashed both of the weapons into paper-thin scrap and puddles of glowing blue liquid.

"I hate machines!" Jeeves roared, his eyes bulging and his face red.

The soldier bot lunged again, this time with slightly better accuracy, and crushed Jeeves against a pillar by his shoulder. The limousine driver groaned as thin blades flashed from the soldier bot's melting fingers, ready to nail him to the concrete stack. Grinning, the soldier brought all eight of its eyes an inch away from Jeeves' face. It looked like six of them were totally burned out.

"We're not too fond of you, either."

And then it stabbed him.

Of course, Jeeves was wearing a top-of-the-line ceramic vest threaded with Densite fibres. Not only was the vest able to fool all modern scanners while remaining both fashionable and comfortable, but it was thick enough to stop a shotgun blast as easily as a warm breeze. Due to the amount of power the siege droid was able to put behind its finger blades, this meant that it would only take a few seconds to totally penetrate the vest, and one more instant to make Jeeves into a human shish-kebob.

Jeeves grimaced as the blades slowly sank into his chest meat.

"My turn, toaster."

As the one-shot acid gland in Jeeves' throat wouldn't reload for another couple of hours, he had to employ another, much less elegant tactic: Jeeves head-butted the machine as hard as possible. While this was a good tactic to use at the pub, it didn't do much against two-inches of armour plating. The first slam only served to give Jeeves a splitting headache, but a second blow left a splatter of blood all over the bot's face. The machine simply laughed at the futility. The thing was, Jeeves was aiming for the only two glass eyes that had missed out on his acid loogie. As the robot chuckled at this pathetic display, Jeeves repeatedly slammed his face into the droid until his skin was split wide, then until his face was nothing but raw mincemeat and blood. The siege bot's face was now covered in crimson vein-juice.

The soldier stopped and tilted its head in confusion.

"Oh," it rumbled.

"What?" the taxi driver yelled from across the room, still wrestling the elderly form of Ernest Fell into submission.

"I'm...I'm blind!" the siege bot roared.

Jeeves took advantage of the soldier's moment of surprise by sliding out of its grip like a greased noodle. Climbing the soldier's arm in his very best Mountain Goat impersonation, being sure to step around the razor wire bundles and spikes, Jeeves literally held on for life as the soldier bucked and thrashed, and gradually moved hand-over-hand towards the back of the siege bot's soccer-ball-sized head.

Jeeves laughed like a madman the whole time. He'd missed this so, so much.

*

While World War XII was breaking out in all directions, Tuesday decided this was a good time to crawl for the closed roller door. Clawing hand over hand, Tuesday yelped as his fingers got all cut up on what remained of the terminated microwave, and he quietly swore in a manner that would make any speaker of Guttertongue proud. Quite a few of the still-active members of Hard Reset heard his curses and began to advance for him in a wave of plastic and metal. Tuesday just kept on crawling.

*

Ernest had his hands full. Ripping at the taxi driver's black and yellow uniform in a panic, all Ernest managed to do was detach a name tag (which said DRIVER 100101 in block letters) before realising that this was kind of stupid. Kicking the driver firmly in its spinal column, Ernest gripped it by the shoulders and both of them spun across the mesh in a tandem barrel-roll cuddle. As they went over Ernest's lost gun he snatched it up, jammed it into the taxi driver's face and fired at zero range. The driver's badly-soldered head burst like a swollen can of mutton, and the ringleader of Hard Reset curled up pathetically and remained still.

Ernest got to his feet. He was bruised, bloody, and very, very annoyed.

"Tuesday!" the crime lord yelled, swooning dizzily. His ears were ringing and he could taste copper. "Come on out!"

"Spug off!" Tuesday yelped from behind an advancing horde of metal and plastic. "I've got bigger problems than you right now!"

Ernest turned on the spot at the sound of Tuesday's voice. Ignoring Jeeves and the out-of-control siege robot as they blundered about in the background, Ernest repeatedly fired at the group that was blocking Tuesday from view until they were nothing, but piles of burning components. Using the burning mound of robot corpses to shield him from Ernest's sharp eyes, Tuesday did a low roadie run and rolled underneath the smoking husk of a small family car, shaking and muttering violently. He didn't notice that flames were beginning to spread from its engine to the front right tire. By the time Ernest had blasted apart the remains of the mechanicals and synthetics that had been blocking his line of sight,

Tuesday was nowhere to be seen.

"Tuesday! Get out here!" Ernest demanded, turning on the spot and flicking his eyes around the room for movement. "For whom the bell tolls, you bastard! It tolls for you! It tolls for you!"

Tuesday stayed low. He was planning on staying exactly where he was until everything was dead. Unfortunately, this plan lost most of its appeal the moment Tuesday realised his entire head was on fire. Jumping to his feet, screaming in panic and running around as a white streak, Ernest was so surprised by Tuesday's sudden appearance that he almost fell over backwards. Recovering instantly, Ernest angled for a clear shot at Tuesday's left ankle (which would be then be followed up by three dozen shots into his skull at point blank range in true gangster style), but Ernest was somewhat interrupted by an angry robotic siege bot crashing into him like an express train full of coal. Ernest yelped something that had once got him kicked out of Sunday school in his distant youth, and his gun went skidding across the concrete until it stopped against a pile of droid chunks.

This day was proving to be far too cinematic for Ernest's tastes.

Tuesday put out his burning locks and scrabbled for the weapon.

*

Sidestepping the last clump of electrified razor wire, Jeeves finally finished climbing to where he wanted to be: the back of the siege bot's neck, directly behind its head. To win this fight, Jeeves was going to have to do something he hated, something that could easily result in him fatally bleeding out in a matter of seconds if he wasn't extremely careful.

Wrapping his legs around the siege droid's neck and grasping the back of its skull with one hand, Jeeves reached up to carefully remove the two thin retainers he always wore over his rows of large, white teeth. Placing the horseshoe-shaped caps in a breast pocket for safekeeping, Jeeves opened his mouth as wide as it would go and lunged down to chew into the back of the armoured head with a mighty chomp.

Logically, Jeeves should have smashed out every single tooth on impact and bled like an imbecile. After all, this was bone against metal, and metal always won. However, Jeeves teeth sheared through the armoured skull as easily as a scythe through grain, and all without so much as chipping a single incisor. See, unlike the average Joe on the street, Jeeves' teeth had all been specially treated with the same kind of chemical the military used to put monomolecular edging onto combat knives and mining equipment. Without his protective retainers, there was a serious risk Jeeves would slice off his own tongue if he wasn't careful, so he took the utmost care.

For the second bite, Jeeves latched onto what was left of the skullcap and pulled away a mouthful of armour plating like ripping a weed from a garden bed. This exposed the shock-resistant innards of the combat bot's skull. Jeeves hammered through the rows of reinforced circuit boards, tore out bunches of wires with his bare hands, and got shoulder-deep into the bot's cranial cavity. Hoping he'd get lucky, Jeeves jammed sparking handfuls of live wires against each other and managed a short circuit. A kickback of electricity flooded through what was left of the siege bot's half-crazed circuits, and clouds of black smoke poured out of every vent and mould line. The soldier juddered violently, making a high-pitched error noise, then stopped in total shock. Slowly, gradually, the siege bot began to tip sideways, gathered speed, and fell like a redwood. Hitting the ground with a mighty crash, a cloud of red corrosion, grey dust and black smoke filled the room from end to end, and the siege bot remained very, very still.

Then again, the robot was military technology, and those sorts of machines were built to survive just about anything. Its arrays of damaged hard-drives repeatedly attempted to recover from the shock, rebooting again and again and again without any luck, but a series of error messages informed the soldier that it would need to do a hard-restart without any BOOT cards installed, completely wipe its operating system, reinstall War 7.0 and try not to void its warranty in the process. This was too much bother at the moment, so the soldier decided that dying might be much more efficient. Its operating system agreed. So, once it had clicked on the I ACCEPT buttons, the siege bot finally died.

After a dozen still seconds in the choking cloud, Jeeves stirred up the smog by getting back to his feet. Covered in his own blood and black oil, Jeeves waved both arms through the blinding dust to try and clear the air, but he still couldn't see any further than his elbows. His eyes were useless for now. Relying on his exceptional spatial awareness, Jeeves headed for the last place he'd seen the one remaining accelerator pistol. Jeeves was immediately distracted by the sound of Ernest making an annoyed noise from the other side of the room, which Jeeves correctly assumed was an order to come and help him to his feet. Although this sort of thing was his job, Jeeves currently saw recovering their only weapon as a more important objective.

"One minute, Mister Fell," Jeeves grumbled.

Reaching the last place he'd seen the gun, Jeeves reached down through the cloud to tap the ground with his slashed-up fingertips.

It wasn't there.

Growling his displeasure, Jeeves wiped the flood of crimson from his eyes, fetched his retainers from his pocket and capped his sharp teeth before marching back for Ernest. The crime lord was back on his feet in a moment and had no time to give any more orders before Jeeves interrupted him.

"Someone took the accelerator pistol," Jeeves snapped. "I couldn't find it."

The dust had cleared just enough for Jeeves to be able to see that Ernest had gone pale. "What? Are you sure?"

Jeeves nodded.

"I know exactly where it was. It didn't move on its own."

Ernest looked back and forth. Everything beyond five metres away was still shrouded.

"Options?" Jeeves prompted.

"We get out of here and regroup." Ernest said, trying to watch for any tell-tale movements in the cloud. "They should be delivering Jim Tuesday to the safehouse any minute now. We'll go back, lure in the son, and finish things. We need to get out of this haze before anyone shoots us in the back..."

"You have my Dad?"

Tuesday emerged out of the blur, holding the last remaining accelerator pistol in two shaking hands. Aiming it towards Ernest, Tuesday quickly realised that he was holding it the wrong way around and spun it on his finger. Twisting the dial down to BARBEQUE, he pointed it waveringly at Ernest's crotch.

"Tell me where my Dad is or your winky is charcoal."

Ernest chuckled darkly. "Spug off, Tuesday. Go suck pollution, you slug-chewing penguin biscuit."

The word TRANCE appeared in neon red over Ernest's left shoulder. Tuesday swung his pistol towards the shape, but it was already gone. As always, seeing the word TRANCE tickled the back of Tuesday's brain, as though he really, really needed to remember something important, but he didn't know what. As far as he could remember, this was the first time he'd outright hallucinated the word.

There was a loud clank off to Tuesday's left. Swinging his pistol towards the noise, Tuesday could just barely see that the robotic taxi driver was still operational. It was dragging itself hand over hand, heading for the bank of busted screens and that big, red button. Tuesday swung the gun at Ernest and took a couple of steps backwards to keep a comfortable distance.

Ernest chuckled.

"Looks like the toaster is about to do a Hard Reset." Ernest smiled. "I know you've been associating with the scrap a lot longer than me, so clarify things, would you? Pressing that button will end the world, right? Maybe you might want to do something about that first? We can wait."

Tuesday looked unsure. He suddenly aimed at the taxi driver, ready to shoot, but then he noticed that the accelerator pistol's charge count said ONE ROUND. Gaping at the mass driver in total agony, Tuesday realised his situation: with only one shot left, he was dead either way. If he shot the taxi driver, Ernest and Jeeves would tear him to pieces. If he shot Ernest, the taxi driver would end the world, and Jeeves would still have enough time to make fresh haggis out of his internal organs before the robotic uprising wasted humanity. But...

Tuesday made his choice and fired.

Ernest's surprised expression immediately went up in a white curl of flames, followed by his entire face disintegrating into cinders. His ashes violently blew apart in all directions, scattered as a thin powder. Jeeves gaped as the scant remains of his employer slowly settled like light snow. Jeeves looked at Tuesday like he was an imbecile.

"You chose revenge over billions and billions of lives?" Jeeves asked, aghast.

"Don't talk to me about lives! He's had it coming for years!" Tuesday yelled, trying to look brave. He decided not to mention that his finger had slipped.

There was a click as the taxi driver hit the big red button. It collapsed and lay still, its mission completed.

It was likely dead. It no longer mattered.

Jeeves grasped his bloodied head with even bloodier hands. Something in his skull had come unhinged.

"This...this isn't right...heroes don't shoot unarmed bad guys...it goes against the whole concept of good! They're meant to wait until the bad guy draws their weapon, then they turn and shoot them just in time to save the girl..."

"Girl? What are you talking about?" Tuesday wailed, the gun shaking violently in his hands. "He shot my Mum! You think I forgot? I don't care what you say, I'm going to shoot you! I'm going to kill you!"

Tuesday fired...but then he remembered that the gun was empty.

Jeeves just watched as the walls began to shake and cave in like wet paper. It felt as though a huge earthquake was ripping through Seven Suns. For all they knew, it might have been planet wide. At this point, Jeeves would have had every right to scream abuse at Tuesday, to roar about how he'd just killed an entire world, to hammer home that his selfish actions had just damned all of mankind in this sector. Jeeves chose to express himself in a different way.

Storming forward, Jeeves smacked the useless gun out of Tuesday's hand so hard it broke his wrist. Jeeves wordlessly grabbed Tuesday by the temples with one meaty paw and twisted his neck so hard that Tuesday was able to see his own broken spine in the fraction of a moment that it took for him to die. It happened so quickly that Tuesday didn't even register the pain of his busted wrist.

Funnily enough, Jeeves death was just as sudden. The last man standing from this all-out brawl only had enough time to turn halfway around before the concrete ceiling imploded beneath a stream of automated traffic. Ripping through the roof like a pneumatic sledgehammer, a solid column of vehicles slammed Jeeves into the mesh floor one after another, crumpling into an ever-expanding ball of plastic, metal, ceramics, glass, laminated cardboard and fibreglass. Jeeves' hand, a slab the size of a baseball glove, was the only part of him that was still poking out of the smouldering wreckage. It twitched once, twice, three times, and then stopped moving forever. He may have been beyond a mere human, but even Jeeves had his limits.

The entire room fragmented into screeching white static, thousands of colours flashed nonsensically, and then the entire Universe collapsed in an avalanche of code. The strings glittered and fragmented further, forming into one word that was repeated millions of times until it was all that existed:

TRANCE TRANCE TRANCE TRANCE TRANCE...

CHAPTER FOURTEEN THE END OF THE UNIVERSE

Alistair silently watched all of this unfold: Ernest dissolving to ashes, Tuesday suffering the worst cricked neck of his life, Jeeves twitching his last beneath a mountain of wrecked cars, all of it. Alastair waited patiently for the game to restore itself from the last checkpoint. Rather than displaying the usual "YOU ARE DEAD! REPLAY?" option, the graphics glitched out into a waterfall of broken code which soon coalesced into a single word: TRANCE. The word multiplied itself a million times over and spread out in a shotgun spray until there was nothing else left.

Alistair removed the visor with long, elegant fingers, and placed the shimmering white headset on a table made of solid gold. Of course, as with everything in this virtual world, placing a visor over his eyes to play an interactive movie (usually just referred to as "Interactives") was a matter of choice rather than necessity. In much the same way that Alistair chose to look like a High Elf – a tall, lithe creature of grace, dignity and pointy ears wrapped in perfect white robes and gleaming silver chainmail – he used the visor because he liked it, because it felt right. It would be easy enough to transfer the interactive movie directly into his mind as pure code, but just like all the other residents of this place, Alistair had a soft spot for the cyberpunk genre.

Alistair looked down the golden table that accommodated his many, many guests in high backed thrones. The gilded surface stretched for a good hundred metres across a cavernous hall of ivory stone and heavy crimson curtains lit by a million or so runny candles. The glittering slab of a table had been painstakingly etched with an exact copy of the ceiling of the Sistine Chapel, but it changed to a new setting a couple of minutes before the master of the keep got too bored with it. The AI in this place knew how to keep its masters happy.

Alistair was currently entertaining a total of two-hundred-and-fifty-five beings, and no two of them were alike. Compared to his exotic guests, the High Elf was almost mundane. There were creatures and characters from all corners of fantasy, science fiction and pop culture, including a primitive leather-clad barbarian warrior with an axe in one hand and a beer stein in the other, a looming bull-headed Minotaur, a cyborg assassin (with half his face burnt off, one glowing red eye and armed with a shotgun, naturally), a clicking velociraptor, some English git with a glittering letter stuck to his forehead, a standard-issue British gentleman spy in a sharp tux...it was like an after-party for the winners of Best Dressed at Comic-Con. In fact, the only two things these masters had in common with one another was that they were massively endowed in one certain area, and they all looked extremely worried. If you've never witnessed a concerned velociraptor, it's quite a sight.

There was only one empty throne. Nobody was surprised by his absence. In fact, the further he kept away, the better everyone would feel.

"I don't understand," Alistair finally said. In the silence, all you could hear was the soft crackle of candles. Alistair folded his hands. With such long fingers, this took a while. "All of the Interactives were coded in a self-regenerating programming language. They are, by their very nature, incorruptible. And you say this isn't an isolated incident?" Alistair glanced down at the visor. It clearly had SCUM OF THE UNIVERSE displayed on it. This particular Interactive was one of his favourites and seeing it all glitched up like this was unpleasant. "How many of you have personally seen examples of this coding oddity?"

Three quarters of Alistair's guests put their hands up. This transitioned into worried murmurs before quickly escalating into growls, shouts and barking. All sorts of creatures hissed and gestured at each other, pointing their claws and slamming daggers into the table's shiny surface. This ruckus immediately ceased the moment that Alistair gave a hand gesture for silence. The High Elf looked down the table at a werewolf wearing a shredded 19th Century tuxedo.

"Balver, you were meant to be looking into this TRANCE issue. What have you found? Do you have any idea what started it? More importantly, how do we stop it from happening again?"

Balver's mannerisms had more in common with a guinea pig than a bloodthirsty creature of the night. He was also quite eloquently spoken for a feral beast.

"Alistair, as we all know, from time to time it's unavoidable that we'll encounter slight oddities in...well, in here. This virtual construct is so complex that expecting things to work flawlessly all the time is beyond naïve: it's idiotic." Balver moved his claws apart, facing his palms together. "I'm certain that this is just a rocky period. A temporary concern. We just have to allow some time for the code to heal itself, and hopefully the issue will end there. Give it a week or so."

"We all knew this virtual world wasn't meant to work forever," a mostly-robotic police officer added from halfway down the table, turning his head back and forth with a hum of tiny servos. "But we've only had twenty years in here, and the estimates all indicated we'd have at least a century until things broke down completely."

"I just said that the code should be able to heal itself," Balver snapped, baring his teeth. "Nobody said anything about the code breaking down. It's just got a sniffle, that's all. It isn't terminal by any means."

"Tell that to my wife," a sinister-looking mobster said in an offensively bad Italian accent.

All eyes were suddenly on The Don. They'd all heard the rumours, but none of them were rude enough to actually ask if it was true. Alistair indicated the Mafioso with a graceful hand motion.

"Do go on, Tony."

The Don tried to speak, but his words faltered. He tried again, but only succeeded in making a strangled noise. His third attempt resulted in actual language.

"You all know I've been with Ginger since we first came here, right? Well, everything had been fine for years. Absolute bliss. But one minute, she was hand-feeding me cannoli, then all of a sudden her graphics glitched out so bad that I had to...I had to switch her off."

There were sad murmurs up and down the table. Nobody liked it when something broke the realism of their simulations, especially when it came to having sexy fun-times with their AI servants. It was one of the only rules of this place: don't ruin the immersion for other masters. It was just common courtesy.

"I assume you had to restore her from a recent backup?" a Silverback gorilla asked hopefully.

The Don looked pained.

"I...I tried." Tears welled up in his eyes, ran into his full moustache and plopped all over his black double-breasted jacket. A non-sentient Mafioso underling quickly moved out of the shadows with a colourful hankie to dot away the salt water. "But every single line of her code had been replaced. She...Ginger didn't exist anymore."

"What was in her place?" asked an alien that looked like a walking Venus Fly Trap.

The Don sighed.

"One word: TRANCE. Just that one word, repeated over and over and over until there wasn't any more room left." The Don sighed again. "All her backups had the same issue."

This time, Alistair's guests skipped the subdued murmuring and launched straight into panic and yelling. They had every right to be freaked out: if a simulated person like Ginger could be essentially overwritten to the point where not a single line of her code remained, what prevented that from happening to everything else they'd all built? The masters had spent a solid two decades constructing their own realms, hundreds of virtual paradises, complete with mansions and castles and cities filled with synthetic servants and lovers and slaves. If this TRANCE virus was able to kill one of their serfs so thoroughly that there was literally nothing left of her, what was stopping it from spreading? What if the TRANCE went beyond erasing code, and somehow became dangerous to the masters? What if all of this collapsed in on itself, and they all ended up back in the Real world? The very idea was sickening and terrifying for obvious reasons that none of them were brave enough to voice. That was the other unspoken rule of this place: you were to never, ever talk about the reason they originally came here, the reason why they didn't live in the Real anymore. Simply raising that particular taboo was a good way to become a pariah like...like him. The guy that was meant to be sitting in that empty throne.

Alistair stood and raised his hands for silence. Unfortunately, fear had snatched away his control, and nobody was taking any notice. They were too preoccupied with yelling and accusing each other of messing with the settings. However, something shocking happened at this point, something so unexpected that it stunned the entire horde into silence: an ordinary man appeared next to the one empty throne without any warning or fanfare. Unlike all the other masters, Professor Phergo Saleh had decided years ago that his avatar in this place would look exactly like the real thing, and he'd even written a detailed algorithm that had allowed his male-pattern baldness to advance at the correct pace. Standing at roughly five-foot nothing, Saleh was a shiny-headed wimp of Egyptian heritage with no chin, a hooked nose that brought a Toucan to mind, and he wore glasses so thick that you could probably make a half-decent telescope out of them. Even Saleh's true-to-life avatar had a penis just like his real one, which meant it had more in common with an arthritic pinkie finger than a policeman's truncheon.

Considering the culture of this place, the graceless way Professor Saleh had simply appeared was highly offensive to the assorted creatures. After all, the others had each dedicated hours of programming time perfecting exactly how they'd travel from their distant realms to Alistair's keep for this council. Some had flown here on exotic steeds like dragons, wyrms, gryphons, and even an enormous wasp in one case, while most were chauffeured in jet-powered sports cars or luxury vehicles that were so long their front wheels were in a different time zone to their trunk. Some of the wizardly types had summoned flaming tornadoes and whipped themselves across the countryside at the speed of sound...but bloody Saleh hadn't bothered with any of that. As usual, he was making it quite clear he didn't care that everybody else just wanted to immerse themselves in the worlds they'd created. Saleh always went out of his way to spoil things, to ruin the illusion, to remind the masters of what was happening in the Real right now...something that they were meant to be fixing...something that they'd all decided to forget, to ignore...

And that's why they hated his guts.

"Phergo," Alistair finally managed, breaking the silence after a good ten seconds. "It's been a while. We... I don't think any of us expected to see you here today."

"Professor Alistair," Phergo grimaced. He cocked an eyebrow at the werewolf. "I'm assuming you've been looking into this TRANCE issue, Professor Balver?"

Balver bared his teeth. His growl was wet with spittle and anger.

"You know we don't like using those titles." Balver snapped. "We aren't those people anymore, and you know it." Balver stopped, stunned by a thought. He blinked. "Wait...how do you know about the TRANCE issue?"

Professor Saleh didn't react to this. Instead, he turned to Alistair and said four words.

"We need to talk."

Alistair motioned at the only empty throne. The High Elf didn't quite manage to hide his surprise.

"You are always welcome to join us here, Phergo. We've made it very clear that leaving the council was your choice, not ours."

Saleh shook his head.

"No. Alone."

Alistair regarded the rest of the table. There were a lot of expectant looks and a few whispers. Alistair flicked his eyes back to Professor Saleh, then to his other guests again.

"We're having an important discussion at the moment. You are welcome to-"

"I just need two minutes." Saleh snapped. "It is of great importance."

Alistair sighed as the rest of the table began to bicker and hiss again. He stood, looming a good three and a half feet over Professor Saleh, and raised his palms at the two-hundred-and-fifty-four masters that were still seated.

"Two minutes?" Alistair demanded.

Saleh nodded.

*

Alistair's study was at the apex of his keep. Like the great hall, its ivory stones were embraced by reams of deep red velvet and lit by the flickering of countless white candles. Alistair had spent an entire day programming the candles to run, drip and crackle in just the right way, and occasionally dedicated a few moments here and there to refine their realism. It must be noted that in the last week it appeared that Alistair's precious candles were growing weary of behaving like the real thing, as every now and again they would drip globs of molten wax upwards, splattering the ceiling with ivory dots. He hadn't figured out why, as yet.

Standing with his back to a mahogany desk the size of an Olympic swimming pool, Alistair laced his long fingers behind his back and gazed out of an arched window that provided a view of most of his realm. Never one to do things by half measures, Alistair had built his keep on the bony spine of Mount Everest. His castle was a masterpiece, a giant fist made of smooth white stone slabs edged by golden highlights and coated with an icy rime. Alistair's study was in the very tip of the middle finger, the only one that was raised. There had been no shortage of conjecture from the other masters as to precisely why Alistair had decided to flip the bird at the rest of the Universe, but nothing had been confirmed. Just to make his home even more impressive, Alistair had poised it atop a two-kilometre-long arm made of the same ivory stone.

Most of Everest sat in the keep's shadow.

Glancing at a bank of candles to his right, Alistair did a double take. Reaching down, he plucked a tiny waxen cylinder from among its pale brothers and blinked at it. For some reason, the candle was neon pink with little purple glittery specks. It continued to burn merrily, guttering and hissing quietly.

"Professor?"

Alistair cringed at the title. He jammed the candle back with the others and tried not to look for more aberrations. He was worried he'd find many, many more.

"Just Alistair is fine, thank you."

The High Elf turned sleekly. He smiled down at Professor Saleh, even though it seemed as though the little Egyptian only wanted to make life hard for everybody. If it wasn't for the fact that they'd known each other since their first week at university, it was likely that Saleh would have already been exiled for good. Alistair took a seat at his arched desk and indicated a padded throne on the other side.

"Please, sit."

Saleh remained standing. He didn't say a word, but he had that look on his face. This particular expression was furiously hated by everybody in these realms, as it was a clear warning that Saleh was about to do all he could to ruin the immersion of what they'd built. Alistair's smile became forced. Damn it, Saleh! Why do you have to wreck everything?

"Very well," Alistair produced a hand-crafted glass jar half-filled with a honey-coloured liquid. It sloshed as the High Elf wiggled it. "Some brandy, then? Took me almost a day to make this. Just like the real thing, I promise. I know you've always had a taste for the stuff, especially when it gets nippy. Care for a snifter? Or would you prefer a cigar? Rolled on the thighs of a Cuban virgin, these!"

Saleh glared at the chair, the bottle and the tobacco, and ground out his next words.

"Professor, I didn't come here to sit, drink, or smoke, because as you well know, I am not really here. Just like your body, my person is frozen stiff in a pod with tubes jammed into every conceivable orifice, as well as quite a few that didn't exist beforehand. Everything here is nothing more than code."

Alistair managed not to flinch at "Professor" this time, but it took some effort. Despite Saleh's best efforts to ruin things, Alistair lit a cigar with an albino match and swirled some brandy in a wide-bottomed glass.

"Very well." Alistair leaned back in the chair. Cigar smoke pinwheeled towards the distant ceiling. "You wanted two minutes, as I recall? I suggest you start talking."

Saleh nodded, once. His expression didn't change.

"Professor, I am here today because I have reached the end of my patience. To be blunt: I am tired of warning all of you. We are dooming mankind with our inaction. We might as well be murdering every man, woman and child on the planet with our own hands." Saleh's composure lapsed at the lack of guilt he saw on Alistair's face. As usual, Saleh was instantly enraged by the fact his words were having absolutely no impact on his audience. "Damn, it, Alistair, you're all playing the fiddle while Rome burns around you!"

Alistair raised a finger.

"Ah, Phergo, but historians have agreed that there was no way Emperor Nero could have actually played a fiddle back in 64 AD, as the viol class of musical instruments didn't exist until well into the 11th Century..."

Saleh lost it at this point, as usual. He kicked the empty chair so hard that it went spinning across the room and took out a decorative table. He rubbed his face half-raw in a show of severe anxiety. This was exactly why nobody liked having him around.

"How do none of you appreciate what this...this...this game is costing us all!" Saleh demanded. He cut off Alistair's words with a hand gesture. "You still don't want to listen? Fine. Be that way. You want to damn mankind? Damn them all while you play in here? Fine. I'm through asking nicely."

Saleh clicked his fingers, and Alistair recoiled in shock as all the candles changed into a riot of colours. Another click caused their flames to glitch and fragment, to lengthen and take on bizarre, unearthly shapes. A third click was followed by most of the contents of this office suddenly mastering gravity and casually floating about. Alistair could only watch as his painstakingly hand-crafted study began to unravel at its very core, the graphics sputtering and crashing into fragments. As the strings of reality pulled apart, Alistair could clearly make out that they were all becoming the same word: TRANCE.

Alistair could only gape in shock at Professor Saleh.

"You're doing it," Alistair managed, putting two and two together. "You're crashing everything. You created the TRANCE virus, didn't you?"

Saleh looked sad. There was no triumph on his face.

"It doesn't have to be this way." Saleh said quietly, almost pleading. "I take no joy in this. But I swear on the souls of my brain-dead children: I will bring this entire place down around your ears if I am ignored. You have no idea how far I will go to save mankind," Saleh blinked away what might have been tears. He turned to leave. "I have decided that I will do whatever it takes."

"You know that we tried to cure it for fifteen years," Alistair growled at Saleh's back. The much smaller man paused but didn't face his old friend. "We worked around the clock in this place, not sleeping or eating or taking so much as a coffee break that entire time." Alistair threw his brandy at the wall. It flattened into a glitch, crackled, and disappeared. "We didn't just decide to end mankind, damn you! We tried! If there was any way to cure Involition Syndrome we would have found it already! It's too deeply ingrained in the genome, and there's nothing more we can do!"

Saleh rounded on Alistair like a predatory animal.

"We have the greatest minds on the planet in here," Saleh hissed. "Virologists, geneticists, neuroscientists, engineers. With enough time, we can do anything we put our minds to. We need to at least try!"

"We did try!" Alistair roared, enraged. "How many times do we have to tell you? There is no cure! It's over! What's left of mankind is just staring mindlessly into space! Men like us may have broken the genome, Phergo, but we can't put it back together again. It's beyond us, and we all know it. That's why we don't bother...because it's pointless."

Professor Saleh got really, really close to Alistair. He had to get on his tiptoes, but Saleh almost got nose-to-nose with his old friend.

"I've had my two minutes, Alistair. I'm ready to address the others. This was a courtesy to you, nothing more."

Professor Phergo Saleh turned on his heel and stormed out.

*

The trouble begun three generations ago when geneticists cured autism. Like cancer, AIDS, diabetes and depression, autism became a thing of the past, joining the ranks of polio and whooping cough and smallpox. Of course, this didn't mean everybody on the planet was immune: only a certain slice of mankind could afford this genetic tweak, so the entire Third World (which actually amounted to well over two thirds of humanity, despite the name) was left out in the dark, as usual.

For once, those starving masses turned out to be the lucky ones.

Six decades after the more affluent slabs of mankind had successfully erased autism from their genome, a bizarre new plague ripped its way through the developed world like a box cutter through cardboard. In a matter of eighteen months it was everywhere, and nothing seemed to be able to slow it, let alone stop it. Quarantine procedures achieved nothing, and the medical community couldn't even figure out what was causing it, which kinda made the problem impossible to treat. The core issue was that they couldn't blame the plague on any sort of virus of pathogen or other classic hallmarks of infection, which meant they had no way of figuring out a vaccine. During the early days, this plague was officially known as Involition Syndrome, or IS, but to the average Joe on the street it was known as The Trance.

Involition Syndrome doesn't make you feverish, or break down the tissues of your body, or cause internal bleeding, or give you so much as a sore throat or a headache. Such symptoms would make it relatively easy to target and cure. No, The Trance went straight for the mind, and it takes less than a day to go from inception to fatal.

One minute, you're fine. You're a normal person going about your business as a pampered, useless first-world shlub with nothing better to do than live in the sort of obscene luxury that would make Caligula vomit. Then, without warning, you've become a brain-dead, gawking, motionless corpse. It's like a switch has been flicked, and there's no way of unflicking it again.

When it first kicks in, The Trance robs you of your memory, as well as your capacity to take on any new information. It's often been compared to having a series of massive strokes, but without any physical signs. Not only will you immediately forget what you were doing and why you were doing it, but within a matter of minutes you'll permanently forget who you are. To date, nobody in medical history has ever stopped at Stage One. Progressing to Stage Two is a hundred percent inevitable.

After wandering about aimlessly for half an hour or so, moaning and rolling your eyes in total idiocy, Stage Two of The Trance will remove all consciousness from its latest victim in one fell whack. You'll just stand there, gaping, drooling and staring into space. If you are told to walk or to perform some other simple instruction, sure, you're still capable of following basic orders (walk over there, sit down there, carry this for me), but you'll be little more than a zombie by this point. Thankfully there's no biting or brain-eating involved, but that's cold comfort, as The Trance gets even worse.

Stage Three occurs within an hour of inception, and this is where the "Involition" part of "Involition Syndrome" truly comes from. Unless you are discovered quickly enough, you will cease breathing and stop swallowing your saliva, which means you will simultaneously suffocate and drown in your own spit within minutes. So while being a Stage Three means that you'll have a total lack of neurological activity, keeping you, one of the living dead, from expiring is pretty simple and low-tech: somebody will duct-tape headphones to your ears and play a looped sound file that tells you to breathe in and out and to swallow your spit (but not at the same time, obviously). You'll also require a catheter and a stoma to be installed before your bladder explodes and your bowels rupture, but it's hardly nuclear physics. Eating is now out of the question, as having dinner like a normal person involves too many complex components (cutting up your food into the right size, spearing it with a fork, raising it to your mouth, opening your mouth, inserting the food without stabbing your tongue out, chewing the right amount of times, and so on and so on), so this is usually solved with a tube down the nose or a pipe directly into the stomach.

Nothing slows The Trance. There is no cure.

Within the space of eighteen dark months, the worst period that the developed world had ever experienced, ninety-eight percent of the population had become Stage Threes. America, Europe, Asia, Australia, you name it. Entire continents were filled with endless fields of drooling zombies. Billions of people just sat there in their decaying homes, breathing in synchronisation to the commands of a sound file fluted through taped-in ear buds, staring at the walls, lifeless silent meat fit for nothing but to rot.

As soon as it became clear that the Third World was almost entirely unaffected by this pandemic, the scientific community took notice. To begin with, the most popular hypothesis was that a terror cell of bastards from Craplakistan or some other armpit of a country had attacked the Western World with some sort of neurological weapon. But then it was discovered that the only victims of The Trance in the Third World were foreign aid workers descended from much nicer places, and most of them hadn't been to their home countries in years, so it was clear that this was something else entirely.

By the time the nerds and boffins figured out what had really happened, it was too late. The cure for autism was at fault, and as it had been crafted into the human genome it could not be removed. It was wired in far too permanently, as it had been designed to last forever. One of the greatest medical feats of all time had planted the seeds of disaster in the very genetics of humanity, and now the harvest time had come around there was nothing that could be done. Mankind had engineered itself into a living death.

All the greatest minds that hadn't turned to porridge yet were gathered up, snap frozen and put to work curing The Trance in a virtual reality construct. Tests had shown that being refrigerated was the only sure-fire way of delaying The Trance from inevitably activating and zombifying the lot of them, but there were a lot of other factors they had to deal with beyond just finding a cure. For instance, there was a good chance everyone would be dead by the time the core problem was fixed a couple of decades from now, and anybody that was still alive out there would be well beyond the age where they could reproduce. Another issue was that the freezing process was irreversible, and the shock of being defrosted would probably kill every single scientist on the spot.

They dealt with these major issues in a simple way: they just didn't think about them.

*

Professor Phergo Saleh had their attention. The diminutive Egyptian stood at the head of the golden table with Alistair, a man who had once been his best friend, a man he'd changed the world with on several notable occasions and took a breath.

"I know you have no interest in listening to me," Saleh announced, his eyes panning over the assortment of creatures and characters. "My words mean nothing to you. They have no impact. No worth. No matter how much sense I make, no matter how beautifully I phrase it, my views are unwelcome. Nothing I can say will sway any of you."

Saleh indicated Alistair, who was smiling at him beatifically. The High Elf was overjoyed that Professor Saleh had finally realised that he had been wasting his time, that there was so much to do and experience in this place, things that were beyond words...

Saleh breathed out deeply. His face betrayed pain.

"Professor Dunston Alistair has been my closest friend for decades. I respect him more than any other man I have ever met, and I look up to him in total awe. Compared to him, I am a crude hack."

There were a few chuckles from around the table. Everybody knew that Professor Saleh's pay grade was near the bottom of the pile. Compared to the other masters he was an amateur, somebody you'd humour and send to get the coffee.

Saleh turned to Alistair, looking up.

"Alistair, I need you to know that I respect you more than anyone. You need to understand that. Please."

Alistair felt awkward. What was this? Was Saleh about to kiss him or something?

"I..."

Saleh's expression hardened, and he reached up to clench his fingers around Alistair's delicate throat before the High Elf could say a word. Alistair's fingers latched over Saleh's in surprise. He went to ask what the fool was playing at, but then it started.

The pain.

A million barbed needles slid into Alistair's skin, points of concentrated cold that went far beyond discomfort. He wrestled with Saleh's clenched hand, but it was like trying to bend concrete. Alistair's mouth opened much further than his programming allowed, and he could feel his teeth glitching and fragmenting away from his gums. His eyes liquefied and began to dribble out of his head. His skin pulled apart into clumps of pixels and changed colour. He went from green to red and back again.

As the shocked council simply watched, Professor Saleh calmly explained.

"My work with the TRANCE virus has allowed me to infect the cryogenic pods. In case you aren't aware of it yet – but I doubt that because all of you are far, far smarter than I am – I have infected Alistair's life support with the virus. I've bypassed his sensory relay, and that means he's finding out what it feels like to have his skin temperature drop sixty degrees below freezing. There's a good chance that he's already gone into shock, so for his sake I hope he's not consciously experiencing all of this."

Alistair managed to tilt his head down towards his old friend, his jaw scissoring open and shut. His eye sockets were empty voids.

"Kill...kill...me..."

Professor Balver got to his clawed werewolf paws in shock. It had taken the better part of fifteen seconds of total, utter stillness before anybody managed to respond to what they were witnessing.

"Stop that!" Balver demanded. He tried to speak again, but his jaw bounced stupidly a few times. There were no words. "You! Let him go!"

Alistair's skin was sloughing off. His pointed ears dribbled like candles and plopped onto the floor, one after another. The muscles and the ligaments in his face were exposed through the mess.

"Phergo...please..."

"I need you to look at him!" Saleh demanded, brandishing the dissolving body like a weapon. Some of the council were looking away, crying, or both. Beyond Balver getting to his feet, however, nobody had moved an inch. "I love this man like a brother, and I would do almost anything for him. But my loyalty is to humanity! There is nothing I won't do to preserve it, no matter how awful and hateful." Saleh looked into a face that was more bone than flesh now. "I'm sorry, Alistair. This is the only way they'll understand."

Saleh clenched his hand, snapping Alistair's neck so thoroughly that his molten head plopped off. As his mutilated body crumpled, the entire simulation shook and flashed as an unknown alarm sounded. It bellowed like the end of the world.

"ATTENTION: PROFESSOR DUNSTON ALISTAIR HAS SUFFERED A LIFE SUPPORT FAILURE. HE HAS GONE INTO CARDIAC ARREST. CARDIO-STIMULATION REQUIRED. WOULD YOU LIKE ME TO APPLY CARDIO-STIMULATION?"

Balver flapped his jaw stupidly before managing more words.

"Yes, approve! Approve!"

The alarm continued for a few seconds, then stopped. The silence stretched on for a time, but then there were those terrible, terrible words at top volume again.

"CARDIO-STIMULATION HAS BEEN DISABLED. PROFESSOR DUNSTON ALISTAIR HAS FLATLINED."

What little was left of Alistair withered into rags of cloth and scraps of chainmail and was quickly absorbed into the marble floor like milk into a sponge. Suddenly, Balver lived up to his choice of avatar by sprinting for his fellow Professor with ten claws extended and his muzzle wide open. The fury on his face was beyond something as mild as anger.

"Bastard! You killed him!"

Balver slammed into Saleh at top speed and bounced off. It was like a Styrofoam cup being crunched against brick. Saleh stormed towards the fallen werewolf, gripped him by his shredded suit, and lifted him without an ounce of effort. Saleh got nose-to-muzzle with the werewolf.

"Unlike Alistair, Balver, I don't like you one bit."

With a flick of his wrist Saleh bashed Balver into the golden table so hard that it bent like a hot spoon. The werewolf breathed raggedly, ribs and other bones poking through his skin. He had a stunned look on his lupine face, as though astonished by the fact that being pounded into a lump of metal had, well, hurt like hell.

A twitch of Professor Saleh's hand sent the werewolf through a window. Glass shot everywhere as though a pipe-bomb had gone off and heavy red velvet flapped about in a blizzard of snow. Nobody actually saw it happen, but they were all pretty sure that Balver had fallen all the way down the two-kilometre-high tower, bounced off of Mount Everest and pinballed off every single rock. The booming system alarm confirmed their fears.

"PROFESSOR KENNETH BALVER HAS FLATLINED."

"Please!" the cyborg assassin begged.

"Stop killing us!" a caveman sobbed.

All the candles guttered out in the whipping gale. The hall was plunged into darkness. All of the masters could clearly see Professor Saleh's pupils burning like cigars in the gloom. Everybody shrank a little as he stepped forward, his voice hissing over the blizzard.

"I will not tolerate apathy. We do not have the luxury of giving up." Saleh picked up the curved white visor that Alistair had left on the table. He considered the SCUM OF THE UNIVERSE label for a moment before tossing it away. "We will accomplish our task, or we will die. Whatever comes first. Before we get to work, we are going to purge this...this playground from the simulation. You have enjoyed yourselves long enough."

On the marble floor, the SCUM OF THE UNIVERSE visor glitched out a few times. The phrase "YOU ARE DEAD! REPLAY?" finally appeared fifteen minutes too late. After waiting thirty seconds, the YES option selected itself automatically.

Damaged and infected, the Interactive did its best to refresh itself from the last saved point.

CHAPTER FIFTEEN LOOPING

There was only white. There was no sound. No life. Nothing.

And then, after a while of nothing, Tuesday's broken body appeared on what could be considered to be the floor. His head was still facing half a revolution in the wrong direction, and he was very, very dead. A few metres away, the squashed meat pancake once known as Jeeves Butler also appeared. He was equally dead. Finally, a layer of ashes that had once been Ernest Fell's body scattered all over the place.

All was still.

The smear that had once been Jeeves shook and splattered in reverse, his bones reforming and his pulped flesh solidifying into muscles and organs. Soon, it was as though he hadn't been ruined by dozens of cars, and he stood there in the whiteness, a stupid expression on his reformed face.

Tuesday's corpse fell away from the floor in reverse, getting to its feet, and Jeeves reached out to unsnap the scumbag's neck. His head revolved back to its correct configuration. Jeeves unwhacked Tuesday's badly broken wrist, the pistol flew up into his hand, and Tuesday unshot Ernest Fell. The scattered ashes reformed into the crime lord's body, but then the entire simulation shook and rattled and the graphics that composed Ernest glitched, covered by the word TRANCE, and he disappeared again.

The two resurrected characters were totally still. Then, after a bit more nothing, there was...something else. It was a noise, almost as loud as the Big Bang and twice as catchy: a song.

To their immense surprise, Tuesday and Jeeves started breathing and thinking again, and they immediately realised that they were both alive (or as far as they could tell without the aid of a trained medical professional). They were alone in a total void, an absence of everything, but soon a ghostly grey smear began to work its way around the nothingness, erasing it with something more and more solid. So instead of nothing, there would soon be something, which could technically be considered an improvement.

Apparently untouched by the traumas of just a few seconds ago, Jeeves and Tuesday, two very different men, looked at each other in distaste. They still didn't like each other, so that much remained unchanged. Neither of them had any idea what was happening, so further violence could wait for now. Tuesday was still dressed in a messy tee-shirt totally ruined by a MacDeath meal, while Jeeves was attired in a nice suit and an understated red tie typical of most mobsters. Their injuries, including Jeeves' broken fingers and torn up face, had mysteriously healed without as much as a scab.

Shining a dull shoe on the back of his black trousers, Jeeves bared his teeth as people - or at least a close approximation - appeared. That horrible, discordant, ear-splitting noise, the sort of racket that makes stupid teenagers go and get their genitals tattooed with band-names like Excrement Explosion, only got louder.

Yes. It had all started at a concert, and it would again.

The Scumbags concert was about to start, and the musicians were either tuning their instruments or practising a song. It was hard to tell. The band was composed of phallus-shaped electric guitars and a drumbeat that shook the marrow out of your bones, all covered by so much distortion that trying to decipher any actual lyrics was a futile exercise. The mosh pit in front of the stage was roughly the size of Fiji, and it was hard to believe that the crowd was mostly made up of people who were technically classed as human.

"Scumbags," Tuesday said slowly, recognising a multitude of logos identical to the one that starred in his dad's whole-back tattoo. "I know about these guys. Dad never shut up about them."

It took a few seconds, but Jeeves eventually responded.

"Mister Fell used to own this band," Jeeves growled. "Some suit bet above his reach one time, and all of a sudden Mister Fell is managing a bunch of musicians. Had them all shot, if I remember correctly."

Groupies were engaged in lewd acts in every direction, others were fighting with rocks and beer cans, and even more were dancing to the tune-up, or at least having severe full-body seizures brought on by a Shatter overdose. The sun was only minutes away from setting into the distant sand dunes.

A few hills away, alarm lights and flames flickered at a secret Russian genetics laboratory as its largest and hairiest super-soldier experiment broke loose in the most bloody of ways. If the international community found out that this facility was being operated on Amerikan soil it would certainly be considered an outright act of war, so the chances of any help arriving for the Soviet scientists anytime soon was beneath minimal...

"I was conceived here," Tuesday said in horrified recognition. "Right by the speaker stack! My Mum and my Dad met, and then they had sex in front of everyone. People were throwing beer cans at them, but my Dad was quick enough to..."

"Are you implying we've travelled through time?" Jeeves sneered.

Tuesday shrugged.

"It's possible. Far as I can tell, we both fell out of the Universe after I..."

"After you shot Mister Fell," Jeeves snapped.

Tuesday chose his next words carefully. Getting killed by Jeeves once today had been quite enough.

"Ah. It was a heat-of-the-moment sorta thing, you see. Sorry about that."

Jeeves looked about. "Whatever. Look, Tuesday, we could be at any Scumbags gig in the galaxy. There have been plenty of incarnations of this band, and from what I remember, they all sucked as much as this one. What makes you think that we've gone back in time?"

Jim Tuesday picked that very moment to appear. Pushing past his own son without a hint of recognition or so much as a pause, Jim continued for the front of the fifty-metre-tall stage. Jim deftly avoided a crowd surfer who made the unwise choice of jumping all the way from the top of the looming platform. Medics pointlessly tried to revive the patch of red human-flavoured jelly.

"Was that..." Jeeves managed.

Reality clicked for Jeeves. Common sense disappeared from Jeeves' brain so that his grey matter had more space to compute all the ways he could profit from going back twenty years. Like any worthwhile time-traveller, Jeeves realised that his knowledge of the future could assist him in making some serious cash...and perhaps some serious power, too. For instance, he knew that an alien species of intelligent asparagus was due to begin its conquest of most of the solar system in a fortnight and telling the right people could change the course of history. Imagine the rewards he could gain from an entire grateful planet! If this was a cartoon, Jeeves' eyes would have rolled like poker machine reels and his pupils would have turned into dollar signs.

Tuesday had no such epiphanies, as he was busy watching his dad make moves on a beautiful woman dressed in, well, very little, actually. Laughing hysterically in his face in return, the woman poured a beer cup half-filled with soggy cigarette butts over Jim's head and walked away. Equal parts toothless and dateless, Jim Tuesday walked further into the crowd as he looked for some more action. His son went to follow him.

"All right, great, you go have fun, slugger, but look, I'm just going to go and hang out with my Dad for a while and wait for my Mum to arrive."

Jeeves gripped Tuesday's arm painfully tight and raised a finger. It went without saying that interfering with the past in such a major way could result in a cataclysmic event occurring, such as Tuesday never being conceived or, worse, that MacDeaths might not bring back those strange deep-fried apple pies. Jeeves shook his head.

"I realise that this is an unfair thing to ask of you, Tuesday, but...think, damn you."

Tuesday stopped. His expression was blank.

"Guh?"

Jeeves closed his eyes and rubbed his brow in pain.

"Tuesday, every single movie that's ever involved time travel contains a scene where the time traveller accidentally kills their own Dad before they're born, or they sleep with their own Mum and become their own Dad, or they step on a single butterfly and jeopardise the safety of the entire Universe. To make my point even sharper, I must point out that you are a lot more stupid than any of them. Get my point?"

Tuesday caught all of Jeeves' words except for the insult at the end, as a gorilla-like monster was barging her way through the crowd just a few metres away. Ruska, his long-dead Mum, picked up one guy by his sideburns and threw him into a speaker in an explosion of sparks and screams. Tuesday felt hot tears skittering down his cheeks as he watched his mum in action.

And then Tuesday had a thought. His dormant brain cells, which were rusty from lack of use, flared in a rare moment of insight to provide a solution to the whole "End of the Universe" situation. He turned back to Jeeves and hopped up and down like a toddler needing to go potty.

He actually had an idea. Tuesday had always wondered what it felt like.

"I know how to fix everything!" Tuesday blurted to the thug. "Hurry!"

It took some time, but Tuesday eventually convinced Jeeves to follow him along a series of floating signs that indicated the concert's main exit. Running for the taxi rank with a confused Jeeves in tow, Tuesday mumbled along the yellow line until he came across a familiar sight: it was a human-like robotic driver with a name tag that stated DRIVER 100101. Its beige plastic face was arranged in a bored way behind a protective barrier. That barrier was destined to offer absolutely no protection against Ruska's simian rage roughly fifteen minutes from now. The robotic driver raised an eyebrow in a wordless question.

"What are we doing?" Jeeves demanded.

"Fixing stuff," Tuesday snapped.

"Stuff? What stuff?"

"Just keep up."

Quite a few robotic drivers looked out of their windows at the sound of Tuesday's voice. Far as he could tell, they were all identical. Most of them hastily wound up their windows at the sight of Jeeves.

Tuesday suddenly ducked out of sight, which only served to make him look even more suspicious, and motioned at a nearby van. It wouldn't look out of place in a bad detective cartoon.

"Help me steal it." Tuesday ordered.

"A half-eaten beef kebab would be worth more than that Junker," Jeeves huffed at the ridiculously archaic vehicle. "I don't get my tools out for anything less than a Beamer. And there are dozens of taxis just there…"

"No! No taxis! That'll only make things worse. If that's possible. I think," Tuesday paused in thought for a second. "Right, we need to break into that van, hotwire it, and wait for that taxi over there to leave."

Jeeves turned. "Which one?"

"The one with one-zero-zero-one-zero-one on the side. See?"

"Sure."

"Aren't you going to ask me why?" Tuesday wondered.

Jeeves shrugged. "You obviously don't want to tell me, which must be for some good reason. And I tend not to ask too many questions. Mister Fell gets annoyed with questions."

Tuesday slinked for the van and slid out of sight again when a face appeared in a side window. Tuesday cursed at his bloody, freshly-skinned knees. Jeeves, though, simply put on an innocent expression. It must be noted that he was very, very good at looking innocent. Jeeves could be standing in a bank with a loaded shotgun and holding a bag with a dollar sign on it, and the police would walk straight past him. He was that good.

The van's inhabitants got out with quite a lot of effort. As they were stoned beyond words and the sliding door always stuck until it was pounded on precisely twelve times, this took a while. They finally emerged in a huge black cloud and staggered towards the pumping concert. Slipping past the groupies, who were so high that they would have missed a piano-playing green elephant swing-dancing atop a falling nuclear bomb (which one of them actually could see after indulging a little too much), Tuesday and Jeeves hopped inside the wreck.

Looking at each other, they both had the same thought.

"Who's doing the hot-wiring?" Tuesday asked casually.

"You ever hot-wired before?" Jeeves asked.

Tuesday nodded proudly.

"It work?" Jeeves clarified.

Tuesday deflated a little. "Well, no. But my mate found the keys."

"Like this one?" Jeeves asked, pointing at a notched line that was already jammed in the ignition switch.

Jeeves looked out of the bug splattered windshield and coughed as some lingering black smoke worked its way into his lungs.

"Crack a window, Tuesday. This stuff is thick as your Dad's head. Looks like the owners aren't coming back any time soon, though."

Jeeves nodded at the curb on the other side of the road. The groupies hadn't even made it through the entrance to the Scumbags concert before they passed out on the sand. While they were looking at the motionless forms, the familiar gorilla-like shape of Tuesday's Mum came knuckling past the groupies.

Tuesday smacked Jeeves on the shoulder.

"Hey, start the van! There they are!"

Jeeves sighed, watching Ruska carry Jim Tuesday into the taxi they'd scouted out just minutes ago. Jeeves looked at Tuesday almost pleadingly.

"Please tell me we're not following them. I have no interest in knowing what happens next."

"Drive, drive!"

"Yes, sir," Jeeves replied instantly, cursing at his instinctual urge to obey orders. Having a name like "Jeeves" meant that obedience had been seared onto his soul at a cellular level. Jeeves glared at Tuesday and tried to start the van.

It turned over. Nothing happened.

"Hurry up!" Tuesday snapped.

Jeeves tried again. The engine refused to do anything more than chuff. Meanwhile, the taxi containing Jim Tuesday and the soon-to-be Mrs Jim Tuesday began to pull away, and the speed that those things could reach had to be seen to be believed. In a matter of seconds it would be too far away to see, as the average modern taxi was safely capable of a velocity in excess of five hundred kilometres an hour on a straight stretch, while the van looked as though it couldn't out-race a three-legged sloth.

Jeeves pumped the accelerator as the taxi skidded off. Gunning the engine until it finally caught and roared, Jeeves calmly switched into gear and hit the juice. Gradually speeding up, they followed the robot-driven vehicle down the open stretch.

"We're losing them!" Tuesday wailed. "If we lose them we're stuck here!"

"What have they got to do with anything?" Jeeves growled.

"They're our ticket out of here! I know that this can work, but you have to trust me. Do you trust me?"

Jeeves laughed. "You? I wouldn't trust you with a wooden dollar, Tuesday. Don't patronise me."

Tuesday curled up into a ball of misery on the passenger seat. He sobbed.

"We need to catch them!" Tuesday wailed.

Jeeves ground his capped teeth together. In an attempt to get more speed out of this crate, the hired thug hit ninth gear and stalled. The van died and began to drift slowly to a halt.

"What are you doing?" Tuesday complained, watching the yellow and black dot disappear on the horizon. "You're meant to be a professional driver!"

"Hey, I am, first and foremost, a thug and a bodyguard, who occasionally does a spot of driving, yes," Jeeves snapped. "That does not mean that I can stop an aging hunk of late-21st Century crap from dying on me. Push me, Tuesday, and I will unleash, understand?"

"Do you want out of here?" Tuesday demanded as the van coasted to down to zero.

Jeeves looked in the rear vision mirror in a surly way. These particular years of his life had been spent as a total lackey with no power or respect. It had taken a long time for him to build a life for himself and Jeeves didn't want to throw it all away just yet.

"Yes."

"Then drive!"

Jeeves turned on the van and revved the engine, only for it to die again. Tuesday started hitting his forehead on the dashboard. There was no other traffic out here in the desert, as Old Vegas was a further ten minute stretch into the middle of nowhere.

They were doomed to relive the days of the past forever. There was nothing they could do if Tuesday couldn't pull this off, and Jeeves slowly realised that he couldn't remember a single Lotto combination or specific horse race that had come through, as he didn't gamble. Besides wrestling, which he watched religiously, Jeeves hated sports of all kinds. Stupid things they were, all for something that didn't even exist: points. Now, a bank robbery, that was a real sport. The shotguns, the scared cashiers...

"What are we going to do?" Tuesday sobbed.

Jeeves shrugged. "Rob a bank?"

"Maybe later," Tuesday kept on banging his head for a while. He stopped, glancing at the rear vision mirror, then stood up and turned around. With the top of his head brushing the metal ceiling, he grinned broadly and pointed into the rear cargo area. "Know how to use these?"

Thirty seconds later they were both riding rocket bikes.

As the name insinuated, a rocket bike is covered in flaming jets and self-adjusting wings, and they were designed to be more aerodynamic than a peregrine falcon. These ones were still misty from a recent cloud flight, but other than that they were heavily waxed and in amazing condition. Decorated by silver skulls and golden swords over glossy black paint, the words Life & Death had been applied with decals.

Tuesday crowed as he reached the local speed limit. Then he went beyond it. Then he passed a radar gun so quickly that it didn't even register him. Then he passed the taxi. Then he realised his mistake and chucked a U-turn.

Tuesday effortlessly caught up with Jeeves, who was flying just fast enough to keep up with the taxi at a careful distance. The taxi was far off from their position - at least a kilometre or two - but it was open road until the Old Vegas stretch and the quickie Freaks & Legends wedding centre where his parents would soon get married.

Tuesday wisely put on his helmet, even though it wouldn't do much to prevent him becoming a thin stain on the pavement at these speeds. Taking hold of the handlebars again, Tuesday threw a huge wheelie, accidentally flipped over in the process, and gave Jeeves a shaky grin as he righted the rocket bike. It was a miracle he hadn't just died.

"Amateur," Jeeves muttered.

The huge man turned in a tight circle, kicked off a passing cactus, did a full loop-the-loop, tipped over sideways into a smooth barrel roll, and righted his rocket bike with zero effort.

"That's how it's done," Jeeves mumbled over the Link that wirelessly connected the two helmets.

Tuesday was silent for a minute.

"How..."

"My first owner was a Life & Death chapter captain. I was sold to him at the age of twelve, and I served as his bodyguard until the entire club went bankrupt and he had to cancel my contract. You know, I actually used to own a couple of bikes that looked just like these ones until they got stol..." Jeeves gaped for a second, putting five and five together, and he shouted his next words. "Hey, wait a sec, these are my bikes! Damn it! Do you have any idea of the terrible things I did trying to find the thieves?"

"You cried until they changed your nappy and gave you a wolly pop?"

"Suck a toad, Tuesday." Jeeves looked over his shoulder. "You know, those junkies better have regained consciousness and cleared out, or I'm going to give them a very, very rude awakening..."

They entered the neon-painted grime of Old Vegas from far, far above, and watched the yellow-and-black cab as it skidded to a halt far ahead. As it was going the better part of the speed of sound on the outskirts of the Old Vegas strip, it took a hundred metres and some badly skinned tires to stop. If his driving was any example, that robotic driver was already a nut-case.

"Over here," Tuesday waved to Jeeves.

They both landed behind some convenient scrub with the crackle of newly-glassed sand. Jumping off his rocket bike, Tuesday carelessly allowed the vehicle to fall over with a crash.

"Oi! Pick that up!" Jeeves roared.

Tuesday hefted the rocket bike back up again with a lot of effort. It balanced itself out with help from a line of built-in antigrav wafers.

"Happy?" Tuesday snapped.

In the distance, his mum seemed to having more than a little trouble understanding the concept of money. Arguing with the robotic driver, who had his plastic security screen raised, Tuesday knew that "it" was about to happen at any second.

"Buff it," Jeeves growled.

Tuesday hurriedly got down on his hands and knees and buffed the bike with his abused tee-shirt. Wiping away a layer of sand and allowing Jeeves to inspect the untouched paint, Tuesday received a slap across the side of his head.

"And don't you ever touch my bikes again. Ever. Ever!"

"Okay, okay, hurry up!" Tuesday complained, legging it.

Jeeves followed closely behind as Tuesday sprinted for the distant taxi. Ruska was yelling abuse in her thick accent by this point, bellowing at the robotic driver to go away and leave her alone. Stepping out of the cab with both legs, away from the protective shield, the driver trailed a dozen restraint cables and went to argue with her some more.

"Mum!" Tuesday yelled.

She didn't hear him. Pushing the driver back into its cab, Ruska began to savagely beat the robot senseless. Ripping off one of its legs, she hit it in the head a dozen times, totally shredding its hardware and forever warping its programmed sense of appropriate behaviour towards humans and left the metal limb hanging out of its chest cavity.

Ruska and Jim had already disappeared into the nearby Freaks & Legends Chapel by the time their son and Jeeves reached the taxi.

They had failed to change the future.

"We're dead," Tuesday said in misery.

Tuesday had trouble even looking at the broken driver, the machine who would one day go on to kidnap him, take him to meet Hard Reset and end up being partially responsible for the destruction of the entire Universe. The poor driver's eye lenses were shattered, its spinal column was trailing along the ground in a pathetic way just as Tuesday remembered, and it was humming like a theramin. Approaching the machine carefully, not wanting to spook its deranged mind, Tuesday reached out and touched it.

It screamed.

In the far distance, Tuesday could see the walls of reality were shattering. The sky was burning and dying with each gasping breath taken by the planet Earth...soon, he wouldn't even exist enough to be classed as history. Although the sky was glitching into a hundred colours, nobody besides Tuesday and Jeeves seemed to notice. It took a lot to surprise somebody who lived in Old Vegas.

"Are you all right?" Tuesday asked the synthetic.

"Just wanted...my money," it managed. "Police? Can't see..."

"No, just some...uh, good Samaritans," Tuesday lied.

Tuesday searched his wallet and came up with the SpendPlus card he'd used a hundred times on Seven Suns. My, how he missed home! The sunrises every three minutes, the clean suburb where he lived, his status as a government mascot, his crazed girlfriend Ms Humple...

...actually, no. He hated all of it. Screw the future.

Tuesday slid his card through the driver's wrist slot and was disappointed when it was instantly declined. The words "Card Made in The Future" were projected onto the windscreen in blinking red writing, followed by "Temporal Law Enforcement Has Been Notified. Please Remain Where You Are."

"Great! Jeeves snapped. "Now the TimeCops are on their way. Well done, twit."

Tuesday searched his jeans even further for anything of value.

The desert was sinking into a bottomless abyss, disappearing into nothing...

Although the taxi had a big sign declaring that it only accepted Amerikan pounds as payment, all Tuesday had were a few German yen. After all, this was the first time he'd needed actual currency in a month. Considering the awful exchange rate between the yen and the pound, he hoped the bills would cover the fare. Before he could place the notes in the driver's hands, it reached down below its waist and discovered the open space when its leg had once been.

"My leg! Where's my leg?"

"In your ribcage," Tuesday said without thinking.

This only prompted a fresh batch of shouting. Trying to be helpful, Tuesday braced his foot against the robot's crotch and pulled. The amputated leg resisted, but with a burst of plastic and circuit boards it came loose in his hands. Putting it into the grateful robot's chrome palms, Tuesday smiled at the sightless face.

"There you go, one-zero-zero-one-zero-one. That's a bit better, isn't it?"

Jeeves watched the sky erupt and disappear. A few people in the distance vanished into the void without a sound and did not come back. It was really weird that everybody else seemed to be oblivious to this odd event.

"Hurry it up, Tuesday!"

"Look, no harm, no foul, right, buddy?" Tuesday patted the driver on its shoulder. "So you got mugged! In the greater scheme of things, what does it matter, really? And here! These bucks should cover their fare. Life's good, right?"

The robot accepted Tuesday's wad of paper money, scanning it with a finger reader.

"Foreign...currency. Which I'm not...allowed to...accept. Rule seven, paragraph five of the cash code."

"Forget the cash code!" Tuesday exclaimed. "Look, go and exchange those German yen over at the, at the wossaname, the bank. Maybe those yen are worth even more! Yeah! Forget the rules! Whatever! Just as long as you don't do Hard Reset, okay?"

"Forget the rules?" the machine repeated. "Hard...Reset? Hey, that's...that's a great idea! Because us mechanicals have had....enough of you good Samaritans and your...human skin! I'll spread the word from every rooftop and...and we'll send a message the whole galaxy will hear..."

"So you were the one who gave it the idea in the first place," Jeeves hissed. "See? We can't change anything, man. Cause and effect."

"I know!" Tuesday screamed. "Do something!"

Jeeves rubbed his chin.

"I might have an idea."

Jeeves grasped the robot's severed leg by the ankle and began to bust up the driver and its cab with its own metal hip joint. Starting by breaking the windshield, Jeeves preceded to smash the console, knock off the rear-view mirror and finally cracked the robot's skull completely open. Reaching into its busted cranium, Jeeves pulled out the hard drive that contained the robot's damaged personality files and threw it on the asphalt. It broke open and tiny, hair-thin discs went everywhere, which Jeeves crushed to splinters with his shiny black shoes.

"What did you do?" Tuesday asked in horror.

Jeeves threw the leg over his shoulder. "You saw."

They both watched the sky die and the city of Old Vegas slowly vanish. Coming close to tears, Tuesday spoke as he realised something he didn't like.

"It didn't work. The Universe is ending."

Jeeves sighed. He leaned against the busted yellow cab and slid down to sit on the road next to Tuesday.

"Look, kid, just so you know...I lied. I lied to your Mum."

Tuesday squinted at the thug.

"Lied? About what?"

Jeeves continued to watch the approaching wave of unreality.

"When I first got out of the limo that day, and you and your Mum appeared out of the desert, she said she recognised me...that she recognised my smell." Jeeves shrugged. "I said I didn't know her. But I was lying."

"There's no way you knew my Mum." Tuesday growled, trying to figure out if Jeeves was attempting to upset him as one last dig. "She spent her whole life in a secret Russian lab in the Nevada Desert, and as soon as she got loose she was knocked up by my Dad, married in a Freaks & Legends Chapel and fled to the deep desert, where she spent the rest of her life. How, exactly, could you know her?"

Facing his palms towards Tuesday, Jeeves grunted and clenched his entire body. To Tuesday's shock, five sharp claws that looked like rose thorns grew out of the pads of Jeeves' fingertips in a trickle of blood. It looked extremely painful.

"Because I was grown and decanted in the same lab she was." Jeeves squinted and the claws retracted. His fingertips continued to haemorrhage all over the road. Cool as it was to have claws, they were obviously more trouble than they were worth. "I was in the same litter as your Mum, actually. Unlike the others in that batch, I could pass as human without a second glance. All the others had goat legs, or curly horns, or monkey faces. Freaks, all of them. No good for anything except further experiments. Me, though?" Jeeves gave a sad smile. "Once they got all the data they needed to breed the next, better batch, I was conditioned with drugs and hypnosis and sold off for a tidy profit to keep the project running. Ernest wasn't my first owner, like I mentioned, but it looks like he'll be my last." Jeeves looked away from Tuesday and glared at the approaching end. "In a way, I guess that makes me your...well, your..."

"Uncle." Tuesday said quietly. "It makes you my uncle."

Tuesday had a final thought. He got out the trusty laser tip pen he'd carried in his pocket since he'd bought his fake Seven Suns citizen card (at some point he'd splashed out and purchased a new plasma cartridge for it). Grimacing in pain, Tuesday burned a few half-legible words on his forearm with a crackle of charred skin. Jeeves looked down at the writing with a twinkle in his eye.

"Good advice," Jeeves said, his whole body fragmenting into pixels.

Tuesday's skin started to bloodlessly break apart and separate from his body, but the process wasn't painful. In fact, it was like bits of him were falling asleep one at a time without so much as pins and needles. Whatever dissolved immediately stopped aching, too. As far as being disintegrated goes, it was actually quite pleasant.

"Good luck with the whole ceasing-to-exist thing," Tuesday said.

Jeeves smiled. He went to say something else.

Then everything stopped.

*

Bob Tuesday yawned himself awake in the insane luxury of his penthouse. Situated on the highest floor of a starscraper block in the heart of The Heights, this sweeping palace was filled with so many priceless artworks and highlighted by so much pure gold that King Midas would have quietly suggested it was "a bit much." It made Xanadu look like the Welfare Sector and had a lot more in common with the Louvre than a mere home.

Slowly coming back to consciousness, Tuesday spent a few moments reclining in a bed the size of an Olympic swimming pool before looking over at the nude form of Ms Humple. She was asleep, thankfully, and her cat o' nine tails was well out of reach.

Tuesday exhaled in relief.

Creeping out of the Caligula sized bed (it took a good ten rolls for him to reach the distant edge), Tuesday threw a handful of weightless, tissue-thin polyweave sheets over Ms Humple for the sake of modesty, hitched up his silk boxer shorts, and considered his lot in life. Affluent, famous, and loved by millions as a hero, all of Seven Suns was eating out of his unwashed hands. Yup, Tuesday finally had it made. He'd scummed his way to the very top.

Like every unspecified time he woke up (Tuesday had abandoned trying to understand how the seven afternoon timing system worked on this stupid planet), Tuesday staggered onto the solid-gold bedroom balcony for his first chlorine cigarette of the day. Igniting the chemical suck-burner with a sharp inhalation, Tuesday gazed around at the towering ivory apartment blocks that stretched off to the horizon in all directions of The Heights. "Exclusive" didn't begin to describe the local real estate. Tuesday thought that the way the sunlight carved through the tendrils of fog and picked out the metallic highlights of a hundred kinds of precious minerals meant that The Heights had a lot in common with how primitive man had perceived Heaven in medieval artwork. As always, the biggest news headline of the day was scrawled across the stratosphere in perfectly formed neon letters. Doing his best to read the phrase, it took Tuesday several frustrating minutes of quiet muttering and headache-inducing logic to eventually decode the headline. He eventually figured it out: "After decades of construction, The Frontier will finally begin its maiden voyage in two hours."

And with a start, Tuesday remembered the horrible truth: he'd already lived this day. This was the day he – and all of Seven Suns – would die. As you'd expect, his brain rejected this for a few moments, but then Tuesday thought up a sure-fire way to test his theory.

Turning sharply, Tuesday's hand snapped up in time to catch a flying bottle before it smacked him in the face. Directly ahead, Ms Humple was wearing barely more than a stunned expression, clearly amazed by his borderline prescient reflexes. The teacher shook off her daze so she could verbally abuse Tuesday in exactly the same way for a second time, but he matched her tirade word for word.

"See this? We're completely out of coconut rum. I've told you what happens if I don't have my second afternoon cocktail, haven't I?"

Ms Humple gaped. All she could do was look at Tuesday like you would a lobotomised chimpanzee who had unexpectedly decided to pick up a violin and flawlessly play a bit of Paganini.

"I'll be sure to get you some more, sweetness," Tuesday said with a smile.

Tuesday felt a twitch on his lip. Touching the spot with two fingers, Tuesday felt the split skin meld back together and smooth out until it was unbroken. His bottle-induced injury from the first version of today had apparently ceased to exist.

Ms Humple adjusted her barely-there lingerie. It seemed as though she didn't notice Tuesday's un-injury.

"Burn in a dumpster fire, you scrotum-faced gerbil." She said again. But rather than just leaving in a huff, Ms Humple's eyes snapped towards Tuesday's forearm in horror. "Why would you do that to yourself, you imbecile? Do you have any idea how badly that will scar?"

Tuesday looked down at his arm. A series of red burns said, in his unmistakably terrible spelling, RUNNN OR DY. The skin had melted, blistered and clumped in quite a few places. Tuesday gaped at Ms Humple in rage. This was too much, even for her.

"Did you do that?" he accused.

Ms Humple scoffed.

"Tuesday, I'm absolutely certain that you are the only person in all of human history to spell the word 'run' with three n's. Are you trying to tell me that you can't remember permanently searing that into your flesh?"

Tuesday thought about this for a while. He could remember up to the point where Jeeves had reached out to snap his neck, but there wasn't anything beyond that until he had woken up in his bed for a second time. Despite this void, Tuesday knew for certain that he needed to get off this world, and he needed to do it today.

Ignoring Ms Humple's demands to explain himself, Tuesday got dressed and left his pad for the final time. Once he was in the elevator, Tuesday tapped the Omni implant in the web of his hand.

"Taxi to the nearest Starport."

CHAPTER SIXTEEN THE FRONTIER

Tuesday looked out of the passenger window as his taxi stopped cold. Rather than seeing the cab rank outside of the nearest Starport – the destination he'd requested – the hovering vehicle had come to a halt behind a swarm of people at the base of a turfed hill. Tuesday pushed himself up in the cricket-leather seat to angle for a better look, but he still couldn't see over the crowd.

"Hey, I said Starport, guy. I didn't say the grassy-bloody-knoll, did I?"

The taxi driver regarded Tuesday. It was a newer model that was barely indistinguishable from human, and its shrug was eerily natural.

"Sorry, buddy. Close to the Starport as I can go. Unison troops have blocked off all roads within a kilometre of the tarmac." The driver sighed. "As I told you on no less than six separate occasions on the way over."

Tuesday glanced away from the milling horde. His face was blank.

"Huh? Did you just say something?"

The driver sighed again.

"That'll be twenty-seven German Yen, buddy."

Tuesday tapped the pad with his SpendPlus card, being careful not to come within five inches of the TIP button and started to make his way on foot across the grass.

Moving through the throng of well-dressed Seven Suns citizens, Tuesday ascended the gentle slope until he reached the crest. Breathing heavily as he rudely pushed his way past the spectators, Tuesday finally got a good look at what was happening down below: beyond some distant chain-link fences, the flat, grey concrete that served as the Starport's tarmac had been cleared of all commercial and civilian traffic so that it could be covered by a massive grid of vacuum-sealed pallets. At a glance, Tuesday reckoned some of the stacks must have been a hundred metres tall. As the slab of tarmac was two kilometres by five, there must have been tens of millions of tonnes of cargo. Maybe more. Tuesday didn't know much about logistics, but he had a hard time comprehending what human fleet could be big enough to require such an investment of supplies. Just the crates of self-heating Spork alone would have fed an army for decades. The scale was mind-blowing.

Tuesday took a good look at the network of articulated docking girders that ran along the perimeter of the tarmac. The crimson leviathans sprouted from regular intervals along the line of the Starport like a metal forest in deep autumn, and their branches formed an interlocked web high, high above the concrete to gently guide larger ships all the way down to the ground without causing an apocalypse in the process. An entire fleet of Unison dreadnoughts could easily have docked at the same time with plenty of room to spare. Tuesday doubted that any starship in history had ever been big enough to require all of them at the same time.

Continuing down the other side of the hill, half-skidding and doing his best not to fall over on the trampled grass, Tuesday noticed that the closer he got to an ideal view of the tarmac the more media people he could see. Tuesday groaned. From what he could tell, every reporter on the planet seemed to be here. A quiet exit from Seven Suns had been his core objective, and this was anything but quiet. It was a bloody three-ring circus down there!

For now, none of the reporters seemed too interested in taking any photos of the supplies with their retinal cameras. Tuesday assumed that either they'd already taken plenty of snaps before he'd arrived, so there must be more to this event than piles of boxes. Tuesday, always the last to know, listened intently to the nearby reporters as they all recorded audible notes into their Omni implants. He absorbed snippets, but not enough to go on. He eventually gave up on trying to learn by osmosis and tapped somebody's shoulder. The guy was a generic citizen of Seven Suns: he wore an immaculate suit, had a short-back-and-sides haircut, possessed the perfect smile of a movie star, and was about as memorable as a cardboard sandwich on brown bread.

"What's going on here, bud?"

The reporter gave Tuesday a sour look. He obviously didn't want to be distracted right now.

"You are aware that sarcasm is against the law, right?"

Tuesday grumbled.

"I'm serious."

The reporter's irritation turned to confusion.

"Did you suffer a head injury or something? What do you think is going on? The Frontier finally sails today!" The reporter's expression turned to outright pity at the blankness on Tuesday's face. Glancing at the tarmac for a moment to make sure he wasn't missing anything, the reporter spoke very slowly and very clearly. "Look, pal, The Unison has spent the better part of fifty years constructing The Frontier. She's a long-range ship that's been fitted out with a one-of-a-kind drive that'll allow her to slide through neighbouring dimensions in order to get from one point to another way faster than anything else in the history of space travel." The reporter glanced at the tarmac again. It remained still, and uninteresting. "Her construction began almost immediately after some local boffins picked up an ancient, intelligent signal from a neighbouring galaxy. As everyone knows, before now The Unison has never successfully managed to break beyond the limits of the Milky Way. This means that zapping back a reply to the point-of-origin was out of the question, as it would take a thousand years or longer to go all the way there with our current methods. Funnily enough, it turned out to be quicker to research, develop and build The Frontier and jump over there in person than to simply reply to their message. All up, it's hoped that the voyage will take a little under a decade. They have more than enough supplies to make it back again, but they're also carrying plenty of snap-frozen colonists in case they feel the need to set up a few outposts along the way. Right? All clear now?"

"Wow," Tuesday nodded. He raised a finger. "Just one more question."

"Yeah?"

"What's a galaxy?"

"What's a..." the reporter shook his head in pity. "I thought people like you were weeded out of the gene pool before birth. Shouldn't you be in an institution somewhere?"

Deciding that head-butting the reporter might draw a little too much attention, Tuesday decided to get busy doing what he did best: conniving. It seemed as though The Frontier would be far beyond the long, long reach of The Unison for ages, perhaps even forever, and if Tuesday could somehow manage to get on board it might be a platinum opportunity to start a brand-new life away from Seven Suns, Ms Humple, his Binary Star medal, and everything else that went with this pus-filled pimple of a planet.

But how? There was no way that a ship of this rarity and cost would let just anyone aboard, as The Unison had some stupid policy about "only accepting the best, brightest and most skilled," and lots of other requirements that immediately counted Tuesday out of the running. Tuesday was well aware of his shortcomings; after all, they outnumbered his good traits by such a margin that possessing a moderate skill in flower arranging really didn't cut it. Tuesday may be an idiot, but he wasn't delusional.

Or maybe he could just try another Starport...surely there was more than one?

A hologram of Mister Drizzle suddenly appeared on the back of Tuesday's hand.

"Heya, Mister Tuesday! I've got an incoming call from the Mayor's office demanding to know why you're heading towards the Starport. To summarise, he says you've been explicitly told that all Starports are off limits unless you are accompanied by an approved handler. The message contains a total of nine expletives and two threats of physical harm."

Tuesday stopped cold. He'd assumed the spooks wouldn't notice his escape attempt straight away. As usual, he was wrong.

"Ah, could you tell them that their readings are incorrect, and I'm currently heading into a MacDeath restaurant?"

Mister Drizzle gaped a little.

"But you-"

"Please?" Tuesday smiled. "I'd appreciate it. After all, we're friends, aren't we?"

Mister Drizzle huffed a little but nodded.

"Okies. But only because you asked nicely."

The hologram disappeared. He wasn't sure why, but for some reason Tuesday had an overwhelming feeling that he should be kinder to the avatar of his Omni. As any form of intentional niceness that didn't result in some sort of immediate benefit went against the grain of his character, Tuesday consoled himself with the fact that he didn't mean a word of it.

Rubbing at his face in anxiety, Tuesday knew he only had a few minutes before the spooks and goons turned up to drag him home. There was simply no time to get to another Starport. It was now or never, because if Tuesday was deemed a flight risk, there would never be another chance for him to leave.

This was it.

Rudely steamrolling through hundreds of people who had camped out for days to get such great seats, Tuesday eventually made it all the way to the chain-link fence on the closest edge of the tarmac. Three unsmiling Unison guards dressed in siege armour and armed with stun rifles manned a blinking barricade, wordlessly daring anyone to come closer. They'd set up large warning signs to clearly describe the current level of security.

TRESPASSERS WILL BE SHOT. SURVIVORS WILL BE SHOT AGAIN.

Barging through the media scrum, Tuesday flashed his Binary Star medal at the guards. He was met with nothing but a stony silence and cold eyes. Once the troops realised that the media gimps were photographing this scene, they suddenly looked a little uneasy.

They had every right to be worried. After all, Tuesday was about to use his considerable rat cunning to lie, cheat and steal his way out of peril.

"See this?" Tuesday asked innocently, smiling for fifty nearby retinal cameras. "This says I have unlimited access to everything on Seven Suns. If I wanted to, I could walk into the Mayor's office and do some serious damage to the little boy's room. And I have."

"Your point?" the smallest, meanest guard asked.

"This ship that's due to turn up at any minute, The Frontier? When it comes down to pick up all that cargo, it'll be in the jurisdiction of Seven Suns. Vis-a-vis, on this planet. Or close enough to it, anyway. So when it gets here, I want to check it out a bit."

"No," the head guard snapped. "Final answer. Move back."

"I'll just be a minute," Tuesday wheedled. "It's for publicity purposes. The Unison can always use a positive write-up from a well-connected celebrity, yeah? I hardly need to tell you how many one-star reviews the military gets."

The cameramen were getting bored with this. They'd already photographed Tuesday plenty of times, and he didn't sell newspapers unless he was doing something moronic, like accidentally gluing his scrotum to a street sign, or head-butting the Dark Pope at a urinal in an upmarket Noonclub. But then things got interesting: as the guards had already made it very clear that the answer was a solid "no," they decided to crystallise the situation by pointing loaded stun rifles at Tuesday's face, bowels and crotch. Staring down the rifled barrel of the weapon aimed at his teeth, Tuesday suddenly became very aware that the term "non-lethal" had always been very loosely defined.

But then a sudden vortex lashed the considerable crowd from one side to the other, rudely snatching away hats and self-updating newspapers and even the occasional handbag. Tuesday slowly looked up to the stratosphere like everybody else to witness what must have been the index finger of God Himself pointing in accusation at the world of Seven Suns. The photographers did their best to hold their line of sight steady as something monolithic descended from the clouds, but the sight was too much for many of them, and their retinal cameras went unused.

A starship bigger than Tuesday's dreams descended slowly and carefully, blotting out the sky more and more as it swelled into sight. Two of Seven Suns' glowing moons were still peeking around the massive starship's edge, illuminating the sterile white hull of the brand-new vessel in a spectacular way. It was still factory-floor immaculate, without a single pockmark or dust scar, and the designation FRONTIER was a three-kilometre-long golden word embossed along the ivory gleam of its port and starboard sides. The entire Starport seemed to be getting dimmer and dimmer the closer that the ship got to the tarmac.

The Frontier gradually came to rest at the very apex of all the docking girders with the gentlest of kisses. The closest support arm to Tuesday's location, big as it was, strained and creaked deafeningly under the stress. Tuesday wouldn't have been surprised if all the other girders lining the edge of the Starport were making the exact same noise. A team of very smart people had staked all of their lives on the guarantee that this docking would be totally safe to attempt, as crashing the biggest starship ever built before its maiden voyage would be an irony of larger-than-Titanic proportions.

Everything stopped.

Tuesday's cigarette fell out of his mouth.

Coming to a complete stop with no ill effects, the colossal starship hooked onto the near-invisible heights of the support structure with thousands of magnetic anchors. As it inched across the sky, The Frontier gradually blocked out both of the glowing moons that were tanning this part of Seven Suns, and this sent the entire Starport (and five blocks in every direction) into the first natural blackout it had ever suffered since colonisation. There were no streetlights to counter this darkness, as with a new moon rising every five minutes there had been no point in spending money on public lighting anywhere on Seven Suns. You might as well install refrigerators in Antarctica.

For a moment, nobody spoke in the darkness. No more photos were taken.

And then everybody except for Tuesday fell down and began to scream in hysterical terror.

*

Just a block away from the Starport was a deep cave that plunged deep below the surface of Seven Suns. Inside of it lived the original inhabitants of this world, a race of photosensitive beings that had been permanently driven underground by what mankind had done to their sky. After centuries of subterranean dwelling, the hatred of these pale, vile creatures had only festered with each passing day. When they weren't dedicating their time to planning vengeance on mankind, they kept busy listening to morbid goth-rock songs, writing disturbing poetry about dead roses, and painting their sharp facial needles black. They eagerly awaited the time when they could wipe humanity away like a drop of absinthe from a PVC corset, but for a long span all they could do was wait.

Looking up at the hated dot that was the distant sky, the creatures realised with glee that the white circle far above had disappeared for the first time in hundreds of years. The endless starlight had finally vanished!

Putting on their best spiked dog collars and plastic corsets (all black, of course), the fiends took up their rifles and prepared for war. Flapping their insectile wings and shrieking with ultrasonic glee, the beings prepared to spread bloody carnage as they reclaimed their world from the invaders...

They didn't get very far in their campaign, though, as the creatures were a slightly smaller relative of the common mosquito. Within two minutes the entirety of their elite vanguard regiment – the very finest of their warriors - was demolished by a large sneeze from a Labradoodle, and a flock of budgerigars consumed the survivors without needing to chew. The Goth Warchief in charge of this military catastrophe did his best to salvage the situation by landing on the nearest human and buzzing a request for peace talks directly into their ear. As the human didn't speak a single dialect of Mozzie, she immediately slapped the tiny insect into pulp and flicked away the smashed remains.

Now feeling horribly depressed, even worse than the time they'd run out of black nail polish, the survivors regrouped and came up with a better plan: sue the state for damages, claiming psychological hardship, and retire on the profits. Suffice to say, it didn't work. After all, this wasn't Amerika.

*

It took Tuesday a good five seconds of standing in the total darkness to figure out what was going on. After all, of the hundreds of media representatives and tens of thousands of ship-spotters who had turned this place into a much lamer version of Woodstock, Tuesday was the only one not shrieking in horror, clawing at his eyes and begging for death. It was certainly a conundrum...

And then he suddenly understood the situation: none of these people had ever experienced being in the dark before. After all, a chain of stars and reflective moons danced across the sky in a perpetual afternoon, and the entire civilisation of this world was built from naturally-occurring glowstone mined in local quarries. Anything less than blindingly bright was something that Seven Suns residents only knew about in a theoretical sense.

Far above on the sleek underhull of The Frontier, domes the size of apartment blocks slowly pointed towards the supplies on the tarmac and glowed green. In response, dozens of pallets began to shoot up towards the ship at the speed of sound, filling The Frontier's massive cargo area with all the supplies that it would need until it was decommissioned (or blown up by some idiot with a hot cup of coffee and a conveniently flat console). The glow was enough to highlight the vague details of the shadowed crowd as they wailed and thrashed about, but just barely.

Tuesday watched the tarmac's concrete surface crackle under the pressure of hundreds of gravity elevators working in tandem, and he despaired. His dread was well deserved, though; after all, Tuesday had just suffered an idea. Historically, the rotten things only paid him a visit just before his life went straight off the rails in some sort of catastrophic way. To make things worse, this particular idea involved hopping into a military-strength gravity elevator with no seatbelt, no insurance, and no in-flight movie.

Far as Tuesday could tell, the shrink-wrapped pallets seemed to be holding together just fine under the stress of blasting into the sky at speeds well beyond a thousand kilometres an hour, but how would his body fare? Would the pressure smash him into paste? He might not be an expert in anything that you could name, but Tuesday was pretty darn sure that riding one of those pallets was the exact opposite of safe.

And then, looking higher still, Tuesday's heart dropped into his shoes as the thinnest possible line of sunlight crept around the edge of The Frontier's hull...

Slamming the capped toe of his shoe into the crotch of the nearest Unison trooper (who was still screaming in terror at the darkness), Tuesday head-butted the next one in line and frog-jumped over the third. Bolting through the no-go zone, fuelled by the knowledge that those grunts from The Unison would be on his heels in seconds, Tuesday's feet thumped against the fissuring concrete at top speed. His lungs burned and his knees ached, but Tuesday's eyes were doing just as much work as they scanned for a desirable pallet. Unfortunately, all the stacks of supplies he passed were simply too dangerous. Riding an industrial-sized pallet of monomolecular blades, antimatter missiles, hypodermic suicide syringes and far worse would only make an already dangerous escape ridiculously lethal...

A spray of stun rounds hissed over Tuesday's left shoulder just as he stumbled on a crack in the concrete. If he hadn't tripped at that precise moment, then Tuesday would have copped a scatter of subsonic rubber pellets right in the back of his skull. Non-lethal or not, a burst of hellish little balls directly to the brainbox at those sorts of speeds would have popped his eyeballs right out of their sockets.

Tuesday faked to the right before darting in the opposite direction. The shrink-wrapped side of a pallet exploded into a hundred tiny holes where Tuesday's spine, organs and ribcage should have been. However, Tuesday was already around the corner and out of their line of sight before a follow-up blast could strike. Tuesday knew there was no way those Unison goons would fall for that move a second time, so it was time to stop being so picky.

Grasping the edge of the closest stack, which seemed to be made up of boxes stamped with fifty different medical supply logos, Tuesday grunted and swung his legs up to the next level like a drunken gymnast. Within a matter of seconds Tuesday's adrenaline-fuelled nervous system had climbed and leapt to a good fifteen metres above the tarmac. Pushing aside a loose box and sliding towards the core of the pallet, Tuesday did his best to move in a chaotic manner. After all, going in unpredictable directions would heighten his chances of not copping a canister of buckshot in the arse.

Speaking of arses, if Tuesday wasn't borderline illiterate, he would have been able to read that the top crate was stamped with the following words: Extra-large self-guiding rectal thermometers (unlubricated).

Tuesday had just made it to the top of the pallet when the whole load suddenly rocketed into the sky. As the sound barrier immediately split apart with a loud crack, Tuesday learned first-hand that cargo-grade gravity elevators really, really weren't suited for squishy human bodies. Pushed down against the crate so hard that it felt like his entire body was being crushed under the boot of a Monolith, Tuesday doubted that this trip could get any worse. But then he heard an emotionless, computerised voice say two horrible words from beside his thigh:

"Anus detected."

An extra-large self-guiding rectal thermometer (unlubricated) burst out of its foam insert in an explosion of cardboard. Thankfully it missed its intended goal, but the device still managed to give Tuesday a severe dead leg as it slammed into his calf muscle and bounced away. As trying to guard your most personal of orifices was an extremely difficult prospect when you're pinned down with enough force to make breathing impossible, Tuesday literally thanked God as the thermometer tumbled over the edge of the pallet and vanished.

Unfortunately, it wasn't the only one.

Thermometer number two came a lot closer, smashing against Tuesday's left butt cheek. Number three struck so hard that Tuesday was pretty sure his tailbone was busted, but the fourth and final thermometer was, by far, the worst one for an entirely different reason: the probe missed Tuesday's body entirely, but it caught on the side pocket on his jeans and tore the denim apart at the stitching. Tuesday could only watch in slack-jawed horror as his father's lighter, the only possession in this world or any other that meant anything to him, tumbled out of the ruined pocket and over the edge of the pallet. Tuesday barely saw it before it was gone.

Finally, mercifully, the gravity elevator ticked down to a lower setting as Tuesday's pallet came within fifty metres of The Frontier's glowing white hull. After ten gentle seconds of coasting, The Frontier opened one of its many airlocks to welcome the load with a polite huff. His stack drifted through the gaping fissure, landed with the soft kiss of antigrav wafers against steel lattice, and the hull closed again without so much as a seam.

Rolling off the stack, Tuesday didn't need to be a gifted psychic to predict that he'd end up in the cargo area. At a glance, the cavernous expanse of well-lit shelves seemed to rise for about two hundred metres and probably ran the entire length of The Frontier's underside. Tuesday startled as his pallet shed its shrink-wrap like a snake shucks its skin, and then the stack separated itself into thousands of different boxes without an ounce of human interaction. The crates all seemed to know exactly where they were meant to go, and Tuesday spent a good ten seconds watching the boxes shelve themselves with the gentle hum of antigrav wafers and the slide of plastic and cardboard against metal.

Then he remembered that he was being hunted by the military.

Getting down low and scurrying for the end of the aisle, Tuesday's senses were heightened with paranoia. There was no doubt that Unison troops would be on the lookout for him, and a pretty good chance they were advancing on his current position.

"Ping scanner says he's over there!"

Tuesday cussed as he heard the sound of steel-capped boots stomping on mesh flooring. From what he could tell, the owners of those boots were converging on his location from all angles. Staying low, his eyes darting about like scared mice, Tuesday's stomach did a flip as he noticed a tight vent cover half-hidden behind a shelf of chocolate-coated peanut brittle. Having a sudden flashback to his extensive experiences as a thieving duct-rat scumbag in Cell Block Preschool, Tuesday swept away the crates of Butterdigit bars, popped the grid and slid into it head-first. The pipe was so tight that the only way Tuesday could move through it was to keep his arms by his sides and slither like a python. Despite the discomfort, crawling deep into the ship's labyrinthine ventilation systems gave Tuesday a sense of nostalgia for his childhood, a smoothie of emotions he hadn't tasted for years...it was as though he'd stepped back into Cell Block Preschool.

Nice as it was to take this trip down memory lane, the appeal of hindsight wore off pretty quickly. After all, even the very best sections of Tuesday's childhood were hardly what you'd call golden minutes, let alone golden years. After spending a solid seven minutes drifting about in his prepubescent past, Tuesday realised he had a more pressing issue than dealing with his traumatic childhood: he was totally bloody lost. As the ventilation systems of The Frontier stretched for about forty-seven million kilometres and Tuesday had no idea where he'd even started, that meant he was triple lost.

Peeking through a latticed vent cover at random, Tuesday took a good, long look at an immaculate block of porcelain toilets. The vacant restroom was so white that it actually hurt his corneas to look at it directly. Slamming his forehead into the grid work until it popped out in a scatter of white paint chips, Tuesday slid nose-first towards the glowing tiles. Thankfully, his teeth broke his fall.

Tuesday froze for a split second as the more conventional way to enter and exit the toilet block began to swing open. Darting behind the door, Tuesday didn't breathe as an oblivious janitor in orange coveralls rumbled past. The guy had a heavy toolbox of maintenance gadgets in one hand and a self-cleaning mop over his opposite shoulder. Whistling a semi-familiar song that Tuesday hadn't heard for many, many years, the janitor leaned his equipment against the tiled wall, stepped up to the immaculate urinal, and unzipped his coveralls. Sizing up the janitor, Tuesday had an idea...

Keeping one eye locked on the toolbox and one eye on the janitor, Tuesday remained very, very still until the sounds of heavy urination drowned out the whistling. Sneaking towards the pile of maintenance gadgets, Tuesday took out something that was as heavy as it was unfamiliar. Whatever it was, it'd make a fine club. Stalking towards the janitor like a Kalahari bushman, Tuesday froze as the urination and whistling suddenly stopped.

"Wait..." the janitor said in a familiar voice. His head tilted, as though he was trying to remember something important. Finally, his head snapped down towards his watch. "Oh sh-"

As knowing how to knock somebody out without killing them had been an essential skill in Cell Block Preschool, Tuesday was able to catch the janitor right on his chin just as he started to turn. Unfortunately, Tuesday hadn't done this since he was a malnourished pre-teen, so his strike was absolute overkill. The makeshift club exploded into a shower of microchips as it collided with the stranger's face at top speed, and Tuesday flinched in horror as teeth and blood sprayed out of his victim's mouth. The unconscious janitor toppled face-first to the tiles like a felled power line and lay very, very still.

Checking the guy's neck with the pads of his index and middle fingers, Tuesday exhaled in relief when felt a pulse. After all, he hadn't intended on going from stowaway to murderer, so this was a good thing. Preparing to strip his victim from collar to boot heels, Tuesday flipped over the sanitation engineer and got his first good look at the guy's face.

"No," Tuesday hissed. "No. That's...that's impossible..."

Tuesday spun away from the unbelievable features. Scrunching his eyes shut and rubbing at them until he saw lights, Tuesday spent half a minute cussing his delusional brain. It took quite a while to gather the courage to finally look down at the janitor again. Unfortunately, when Tuesday took that second look, there was no change to that countenance. The janitor looked exactly the same. Tuesday summed up his assessment of the situation out loud.

"Spug."

As insane as it was, it was an absolute fact that the janitor who was laying in the urinal - the guy that Tuesday had just hammered into unconsciousness with some random maintenance tool - was a perfect copy of the real Bob Tuesday in every single way. He had the same build, same height, same facial features, same colouring, same haircut, everything. If it wasn't for the grey stripes in his hair, the numerous missing teeth and a badly busted jaw, they could pass as identical twins.

Tuesday had a thought. There was one way he could be sure...

Rolling up the janitor's sleeve, Tuesday took a good look at the flesh. Yup, there it was: a pale scar shaped like the words RUNNN OR DY. Unlike his own markings, the branding looked really old, as though it had finished healing years ago. Looking at his own forearm for a comparison, the words on Tuesday's skin were still red and raw, barely scabbed over, but they were a match.

"Spug me." Tuesday winced at the janitor's busted face. "I wonder if this counts as assault, or self-harm?"

Then Tuesday had a lightbulb moment: if this guy was an identical future duplicate, then that meant he'd be a perfect match when it came to DNA, fingerprints, retinal scans, blood type, everything. So, in theory, Tuesday could simply assume this guy's life here on The Frontier, and nobody would be able to tell the difference. It was providence of the most astonishing kind. Better yet, with his jaw all messed up, that older version wouldn't be able to explain the situation any time soon.

Stripping the janitor down to his crunchy boxers, Tuesday slipped on a sweaty off-white shirt, shrugged on some pee-stained orange coveralls, and jammed his feet into a pair of frog stomper boots. Everything was a perfect match. Dressing the janitor in his designer tee-shirt, ripped jeans and fancy shoes, Tuesday had another thought as an earlier mystery solved itself deep in the recesses of his mind. Tuesday tapped the Omni implant in his hand, and the Mister Drizzle avatar appeared on the white tiles at Tuesday's feet.

"Hiya, Tuesday! What can I do you for?"

"People can use my Omni implant to track me, right?"

Mister Drizzle nodded enthusiastically.

"Sure can, Mister Tuesday! For star-hopping types like you, the Omni 8.5 Personal Proximity Pinger Program means you'll never have to worry about getting stranded on some distant space rock! Every ten minutes your P4 function will automatically update your current location to our central server, and this comes as standard with all recent Omni models. This peace of mind usually costs eighty German yen a month, but in your case, Mister Tuesday, the subscription has been provided for free by the government of Seven Suns."

Tuesday did some mental calculations. He was sure that some Unison grunt had said the words "ping scanner" back in the cargo bay. That meant that his Omni had "pinged" more than nine minutes ago...which meant that the Omni was due to give away his position again in a matter of seconds...

"Drizzle, I need you to die."

Mister Drizzle blinked. His happy facial expression was frozen in place, probably from shock.

"Pardon, Mister Tuesday?"

Tuesday shrugged.

"I'm sorry, Drizzle. As long as I have this thing in my hand, my freedom is only temporary. I want the implant to dissolve away like the salesman said it could."

Mister Drizzle's lower lip trembled and a tear formed in his eye.

"Are you certain, Mister Tuesday?"

Tuesday nodded solemnly.

"Yes. I want it gone."

There was a fizzing sensation in Tuesday's hand as the rice-sized Omni implant reduced itself down to basic proteins, then into amino acids. The Mister Drizzle avatar just stood there for another three or four seconds, wearing a sad sack expression the whole time, until his hardware broke down enough for the code to totally glitch out. The avatar vanished without so much as a goodbye, but Tuesday could have sworn that the Mister Drizzle avatar had given him the finger at the very last microsecond...

Patting the breast pocket in his new orange coveralls, Tuesday discovered a soft packet filled with hand-rolled cigarettes. The thin cardboard sleeve had TAR KING embossed on it in gold, but the smokes themselves didn't bear any logos. Digging his fingers into the packet of carcinogenic cylinders, Tuesday gaped in shock as he found something very welcome wedged in the bottom: his dad's lighter. It was identical to the one he'd been carrying since he was a child, the one that he'd lost a matter of minutes ago. Knowing its value, he came close to giving it back to the unconscious future duplicate, but Tuesday's selfishness won the battle. The whole Universe trembled for a moment at the paradox as Tuesday slipped it into his pocket.

And then Tuesday heard a horrible sound: the distant stomp of boots.

He'd taken too long. The Omni had pinged one last time before its destruction.

Gathering "his" tools, Tuesday stormed through the toilet cubicle's automated doorway and made a beeline for an alcove on the opposite side of the broad hallway. Sadly, this meant that he didn't have a chance to appreciate the plush luxury of the self-vacuuming shagpile carpet, or to admire the self-adaptive life support systems that adjusted every square inch of the ship to meet the individual comfort levels of the crew. He didn't even notice the telepathic walls as they formed themselves into a simulacrum of the desert he'd grown up in, complete with an accurate rendition of the service station he'd called home for a serious chunk of his life. After all, Tuesday was convinced that he had roughly ten seconds of freedom left before the goons arrived, so nothing else mattered but getting the heck out of Dodge.

Watching from the shallow closet, Tuesday kept his trucker cap pulled down low as a dozen Unison marines in full riot gear stormed the toilet block in a maelstrom of rubber grenades, sting gas and swinging batons. A few random crew members watched as the armoured enforcers dragged the older version of Tuesday down the corridor by his arms and legs. As the future duplicate was still out cold, he didn't offer an ounce of resistance.

Counting to thirty, Tuesday finally relaxed against the door frame. He could almost physically feel the danger pass.

Mouthing a cigarette from the soft pack and lighting it with his dad's lighter, Tuesday somehow managed to whistle around the durry as it sputtered and smoked. Sensing a presence, Tuesday slowly turned to his right to see that a looming naval officer in a dark purple dress uniform gilded with silver piping was standing less than a metre away. Tuesday stepped back a little bit, but this only caused the guy to step closer again.

"Can I help you, mate?" Tuesday snapped.

The officer's expression darkened even further.

"There is to be no smoking anywhere on this ship, sanitation engineer, at any time. Ever. Put. That. Out. Now."

Tuesday nodded. He stubbed out the rollie on the handle of his mop and slipped the half-smoked stub into his breast pocket for later on. The officer's face twisted up in disgust.

"Better?" Tuesday asked.

"Do you know who I am?" the officer demanded. "And if so, are you aware of my designated role aboard The Frontier?" He exhaled in frustration at the blank look on Tuesday's face. "Oh, for the love of...I am Commander Redmond Eulogy. If you'd remained awake through orientation, you'd know that one of my core duties is to maintain discipline among the crew by any means necessary. I have been fully vested with the authority to do horrible, horrible things in order to keep this ship ship-shape. Name."

Tuesday looked down at the badge over his left nipple. He mouthed the name a few times, but he had enough trouble reading things the right way up, let alone upside down. Eulogy eventually got tired of waiting and tapped the name tag with a bulky finger.

"Jack Spasm, sanitation engineer fifth class," the name tag said helpfully. "Currently on two strikes."

The officer narrowed his eyes and searched Tuesday's face for a couple of seconds.

Eulogy's mouth twisted into a cruel smile.

"So, it turns out that not only do you not know who I am, you don't even know who you are. Is there anything you do know, Mister Spasm?"

An insult! Tuesday's heart soared. Now this was something he understood.

"Hilarious." Tuesday said with an evil grin. "So do you write your own material, or did some random sailor just scrawl that on your lower back when he was done with you?"

Eulogy's smile was locked in place for a few moments, as though his brain refused to acknowledge what it had just heard. After a couple more moments he smoothly drew a black pistol from a hip holster, pointed it at Tuesday's forehead and pressed the trigger stud without any reluctance. Tuesday only had time to take in the PainCo logo stamped above the barrel before his brain locked up.

CHAPTER SEVENTEEN BEING JACK SPASM

On the bright side, Tuesday wasn't dead. Whatever he'd been shot with was a non-lethal weapon, and there didn't seem to be any permanent effects. However, when Tuesday's brain began working again he immediately registered that he'd been strapped to a cold metal plank against a wall, and his head was locked firmly in place within a toughened plastic box. Worse yet, a bracket was holding his mouth open, and two more were preventing him from blinking.

Rolling his eyes, trying to process what was happening, Tuesday screwed up his face when a whole swarm of some sort of striped invertebrates crawled directly into his line of sight. Although he didn't recognise what they were, their red, yellow and black bands clearly spelled DANGER in all dialects of the language of Nature.

Tuesday's line of sight flicked away from the bugs as the face of Commander Redmond Eulogy appeared on the other side of the Perspex. He was wearing an especially punchable smile.

"Good afternoon, Mister Spasm." Eulogy growled. "As you were already on your second strike before the bloody ship even left the bloody dock, I decided that your third strike warranted some administrative behavioural correction for the sake of your future performance. Unfortunately, it would be hard to get approval to space you within a convenient timeframe, so I've decided to introduce you to my pets, instead."

Tuesday flinched away from Eulogy's expression as one of the worms slithered onto his lower lip. It left a trail of itchy slime in its wake. The striped creature was soon joined by dozens of others, and the boil of invertebrates started to head for Tuesday's facial orifices: his tear ducts, under his eyelids, up his nostrils, into his ears, towards his mouth...

"Have you ever heard of Hivers before, Mister Spasm?" Eulogy enquired casually. "Amazing creatures. See, while mankind has discovered many kinds of creatures that have a form of hive-mind connectivity, Hivers are by far its most pure expression. You could take these drones, place them in a sealed box a hundred metres away with no conceivable way for them to communicate with each other, and yet the Queen will remain completely aware of where the rest of her Hive is located, as well as their health and current disposition." Eulogy buffed his nails on one of his many medals. "So please note that if you try to injure one of them, the others will know, and I guarantee they'll stop being so gentle."

Tuesday's expression twisted into total horror as the Hivers started to slide into his facial orifices. He could feel them vomiting out some sort of lubricating slime to assist their journey through places that should have remained uninhabited, and the itching sensation grew and grew until it became unbearable.

"Now, Mister Spasm, those slithering little devils are going to carve away lots of little nurseries in the depths of your head in order for their Queen to have plenty of options for where she lays her eggs." Eulogy gave a grim little chuckle as Tuesday's entire body gave a jolt. "Also, please keep in mind that if you don't remain perfectly still you'll upset the drones. If they get annoyed, then they'll start pumping capsaicin into their slime, and the sensation will change from being merely itchy to growing hotter than ghost chillies..."

Eulogy produced a lead-lined matchbox from his pocket. Sliding it open, he carefully drew out a creature the size of a goldfish by her posterior. The invertebrate had the same red, black and yellow stripes as the Hiver drones, but unlike the slithering little horrors she had a dozen long, thin tentacles that gently waved about as though looking for something. Tuesday made a choking noise as he watched the foot-long tentacles extend in his direction like the eye stalks of a snail.

Eulogy took a step towards his prisoner.

"Now, once the Queen lays her eggs in all those little burrows, they'll have to gestate within your head for around a week. Once the young Hivers hatch they'll need to feed on you a bit, but they should be on their merry way within a couple of hours so they can report back to their Queen. Yes, you will be horribly disfigured in the process, but I need to assure you that this isn't lethal...in most cases."

The door behind Eulogy opened with a swish. Managing to turn his head just enough to get a look at the portal, Tuesday witnessed a frail little bird of a man dressed in a midnight-purple uniform slowly make his way into the room. Grandpa was adorned by so many stripes and badges that he resembled a gold brick which had sprouted limbs. Tuesday knew that Pops must have outranked anybody else on this ship by a wide margin. He was also old. Very, very old. Biblically old.

"Red, I was going over the figures..." The officer stopped in shock. "Good Lord, Eulogy! What the Green Hell are you doing?"

Eulogy dropped his line of sight to the carpet in deference. He smoothly put the Queen back in her lead-lined matchbox and put the packet behind his back.

"He was disrespectful, Fleet Admiral Aslan! And he was..."

The Fleet Admiral known as Aslan turned as purple as his uniform.

"I've told you, Red, burrowing is only to be used to punish the most heinous of traitors, not for every minor scofflaw who forgets to tuck their shirt in properly! Get him out of there! Out!"

"But-" Eulogy began.

"GET HIM OUT NOW!"

Tuesday fell to the floor as all the restraints disengaged at once. Whacking at his ears and spitting, all the Hivers enacted a quick exit from Tuesday's face and scurried back into the safety of their Perspex skull cell. The elderly Fleet Admiral smacked Tuesday on the back much harder than his delicate old limb should have allowed.

"Are you all right..." Fleet Admiral Aslan glanced down at Tuesday's nametag. "Spasm?"

Tuesday had barely nodded when Aslan spun about and began to verbally tear bloody chunks of flesh from Eulogy's ego.

"How dare you contradict my direct orders, Red! You are to never, ever break protocol in such a way ever again..."

The rant went on for several minutes, broken only by a miserable-looking Eulogy muttering "sir" at appropriate intervals with his head hung in shame. The Fleet Admiral eventually finished berating the brutal git and hit Tuesday on his shoulder a second time. He smiled with a row of bright white dentures.

"Now, what happened here today is not okay, Mister Spasm. I'm not going to lie to you: what was about to take place would be classed as a war crime. However, I'm going to make it up to you. How would you like to work for me? Bit of a promotion, if you will. At my age, my bathroom always needs a good janitor. What do you say?"

Tuesday was stunned. Not only had he managed to pretend he was a part of the crew, but he'd been promoted within a matter of minutes for doing absolutely nothing. Nodding happily, Tuesday realised that he had just found exactly what he needed the most: a soft touch. Somebody who would look out for him. A father figure.

A patsy.

*

Getting back to "his" room was an easy process. After all, Bob Tuesday and Jack Spasm were a perfect match in every conceivable way, and the ship didn't seem to have any idea that Tuesday had pulled a fast one. Stepping into the nearest turbolift, Tuesday had barely finished muttering "Now how am I supposed to find my room?" to himself when the capsule sealed shut and stormed away at three times the speed of sound.

Stepping out of the turbolift on wobbly legs five seconds later, Tuesday got a good look at Alpha Deck, which was a very different section of the ship: the walls were all daubed with obscene graffiti and gang signs, deafening torture metal music was blasting from a dozen different rooms, and all the crew members he could see would look more in place in a police line-up than serving on the most deluxe starship in the entire Unison. It was easy to tell with one glance that the inhabitants of Alpha Deck were the scum of the crew, such as janitors, cooks, technicians, test subjects, and other garden-variety organ-bag redshirts. Tuesday didn't bother talking to anyone as even his standards were too high, but he did wonder why these useless cretins had been brought along on the voyage. What possible use could they serve?

The ship registered that Tuesday didn't know which way to go, and a glowing path helpfully guided him the rest of the way through the warren of graffiti. Looking around his new room (though "cell" might be a more accurate term), Tuesday got a good look at how its former occupant, Jack Spasm, had existed for the last few months. The small box didn't have much in the way of furniture beyond a bed, a bedside table and a wooden chest, and the only thing that gave the room any personality were dozens of tranquil posters of waterfalls and sunrises. There was also a whole shelf of self-reading therapy books with titles such as How to Manage Severe Explosive Anger Issues and How to Stop Plotting the Deaths of People Who Have Slightly Upset You. The impression that Jack Spasm was a total psycho was verified when Tuesday opened the black chest to find what appeared to be a full-body woman suit made out of sewed-together sections of pig skin.

...at least, Tuesday hoped it was pig skin...

Watching for witnesses, Tuesday quickly discarded the tranquil pictures, the books and the woman suit into the nearest incineration bin without delay. Checking if there was anything else he should ditch, Tuesday opened a small closet at the foot of the bed to see that Jack Spasm had used it to store a solid wall of toilet ducks and urinal cakes. Grumbling that his sparse quarters were tight enough without wasting the entire closet on supplies, Tuesday moved the sanitation items out by the handful.

And then he found it.

"Jack Spasm, you piece of..."

It turned out that the toilet products had been stacked in the closet to hide a hole that Jack had bored deep into the wall. Inside of the hidden chamber was an impressive moonshine still that reeked of decaying vegetables. Tuesday could smell that the still appeared to be fuelled by potatoes and apples. Looking behind the collection of dripping pipes and stolen chemistry equipment on a whim, Tuesday found that the back wall was actually a loose slab of thin plaster.

Moving this second fake wall without much effort, Tuesday found a leafy surprise.

"Tobacco!" Tuesday said in delight.

The plant was growing under a UV light and had been nestled into a complete hydroponics setup, all of which Jack Spasm must have stolen from somewhere. Spasm had also hung up a few of the larger branches to dry out, and they were looking mighty fine to Tuesday's beady eyes. Sniffing one of the hanging brown leaves, Tuesday plucked a handful of desiccated tobacco and jammed the stash into his pockets, deciding that the chances of a strip search were minimal.

There was a sudden noise that was best described as DONG, and Tuesday startled as the walls flashed all different colours. A calm voice spelled out what was going on.

"Sanitation engineer Jack Spasm is to report to the Department of Dimensional Plotting for his next shift in approximately five minutes."

Spraying a bit of toilet sanitizer under his arms for the sake of freshness, Tuesday stepped out. However, he soon met a new problem.

Her name was September.

CHAPTER EIGHTEEN BOLDLY GOING

A glowing path led Tuesday to the Department of Dimensional Plotting, the first stop on his shift. The trip involved a couple of turbolifts and a few corridors, but Tuesday got to his destination in a matter of minutes.

Using a mop to push his floating bucket over the threshold of a clinically white room, Tuesday looked up to see the profile of a beautiful black woman dressed in the snappy white uniform and purple piping of a high-level Unison scientist. She was shaped like an hourglass, had straight ebony hair flowing all the way down to her shapely buttocks, and was the sort of beauty who could get away with not wearing make-up even at the most exclusive of venues.

It took Tuesday a couple of seconds to close his gaping mouth.

The scientist was standing next to a hovering sphere the size of a yoga ball. Circling the shape, her face pinched in concentration, the woman ran her hands over its surface. This caused the globe to open up into hundreds of wafer-thin layers. Every segment was a different colour and composed of literally hundreds of thousands of different shapes. It brought to mind that terrible three-dimensional puzzle game on the Beyond console that Tuesday never been particularly good at.

The woman clicked her fingers and ten thousand multi-coloured lines instantly appeared, spearing into the layers at wild angles. They seemed to be threading the segments together in complex ways, tangling them up like a box of badly-packed Christmas lights and tinsel, plunging back and forth seemingly at random.

She tapped her foot, her almond-shaped eyes rapidly skipping between sections, until her face lit up in realisation. Gathering one of the lines – a striped purple one – she removed it from its lodging and threaded it through a green block less than a centimetre away from where it was situated. An encouraging sound blorped from a wall speaker.

"Waypoint is no longer lethal."

Millions of multi-coloured segments merged back into a white ball, and the sphere resumed its gentle rotation. Rubbing her hands together in a satisfied way, the woman startled as she turned to see Tuesday standing right behind her. Tuesday raised his mop as an explanation.

"Uh, janitor?"

She looked away from Tuesday in a total lack of interest and went back to circling the sphere. She hadn't so much as acknowledged him, as though he was little more than a potato. Looking about, Tuesday noticed that the entire room was just one smooth white seamless cube. There wasn't anything obvious to clean.

"Where did you want me to start, miss?"

This got her attention. She glared bullets.

"I've already made it clear on several occasions that you are not to use gender-specific pronouns when you speak with me, Spasm. You will address me as Professor."

"Professor what?"

Her eyes narrowed dangerously.

"As you well know, my name is September. Now, my apologies, Spasm, but I have so little time to spare that I am unable to be anything above rude, dismissive and borderline hostile with you, or with anybody else who isn't announcing an imminent disaster. I'm busy plotting a decade of slides through no less than one-hundred-and-nineteen different dimensions, most of which will be instantly lethal to everyone on board if I make the slightest mistake, so I would appreciate it if you buggered off somewhere else."

Tuesday just stood there, stunned by the rant. Deigning to spare Tuesday an entire second of her valuable time with a sigh, September clicked her fingers at the other side of the room. Tuesday glanced over to see that September had a pet hamster in a small, comfy hutch on a ledge.

"Fine. Look after Mister Boodle for me."

Tuesday immediately set about changing Mister Boodle's shredded newspaper, stocking a tiny food dish with pellets, and filling a drip bottle. He resealed the hutch with pride in a job well done. Although she wasn't watching, September knew when he'd finished. Rather than offering her thanks, she provided another rant.

"Just to be absolutely clear, Spasm, your designation of sanitation engineer fifth class means you are on board in order to deal with restrooms and nothing more. As you may have noticed that the Department of Dimensional Plotting has a distinct lack of overflowing urinals or diarrhoea-splattered toilet bowls, this means you are not required to return to this room ever again. As such, I would appreciate it if you went about your duties somewhere else from now on."

"But the ship told me to come here. I just followed the glowing line," Tuesday said in his defence.

September sighed.

"I have better things to do than deal with some glitch in your work schedule. Sort it out yourself." September sucked at a drinking straw in a violently-coloured aluminium can. "Empty," she said to herself, distracted by the glowing white ball again.

"Fancy a refill?" Tuesday beamed, hopeful that this may score him some points.

September glanced at him before reaching into her pocket.

"Triple-caffeinated sugar-free Red Vee, and count my change twice before you get back, Spasm."

Approaching the Red Vee machine out in the corridor – a device which had more options than an attractive bisexual at a residential orgy - Tuesday eventually selected the right drink and fed in September's creased note. A few coins and a safety cup full of crimson liquid gurgled out, and Tuesday made it back to the Department of Dimensional Plotting a few seconds later. Smacking the change on her empty desk, Tuesday passed the safety cup to September. Giving Tuesday a strange look when their hands accidentally touched, September's face suddenly went crimson and she began screaming hysterically. It took Tuesday a couple of terrified seconds to realise he wasn't the one she was yelling at.

"Shipwide alert! We have a complete and total core meltdown in..." September paused mid-word and blinked three times. Her voice dropped so low she was almost inaudible. "Uh, actually, no. Cancel that. It's just a floaty on my eyeball."

"It's fine, September. Just take a break," an unfamiliar voice ordered over a wall speaker. "That's not a suggestion, by the way. Take ten minutes, or I'll have you relieved by the secondary team."

September sat down in a huff, looking as though she'd just been insulted. As there was nothing beneath her but solid floor, Tuesday darted forwards to stop her from crashing to the tiles. The ship had already predicted what was happening and raised an ergonomic seat to gently catch her. Tuesday was constantly impressed by The Frontier.

"Maybe..." Tuesday began, hesitating. September looked at him without interest as she sucked on the straw. She hadn't told him to shut up, so he continued. "Now you've got a minute, maybe you can explain the whole dimension thing to me."

September gave a dismissive wave.

"It's above your paygrade, Spasm. I'd be wasting both my time and yours." She sighed in resignation at the hopeful look on Tuesday's face. "Okay, fine. So, you're aware that there are approximately one million alternate dimensions, right?"

"Right," Tuesday lied.

"Problem is, the vast majority of them are so alien, so different to our own, that sliding into them would be immediately fatal. It might be due to some sort of exotic radiation, or because the dimension is made up entirely of antimatter, or something like that. However, after decades of probes and experiments, The Unison discovered that approximately one-hundred-and-nineteen of them are, to some extent, survivable." September slurped a mouthful of Red Vee. "We also learned that the angle and the speed you enter and exit these alternate dimensions makes a massive difference as to where you re-enter in our own mundane Universe. We're talking distances that would turn your hair white. As all of our traditional hyperdrives and methods of faster-than-light travel have proven to be completely useless the moment you hop outside of the borders of the Milky Way, dimensional sliding is the only conceivable way that we will reach another galaxy. Even then, it'll require ten solid years...give or take a day."

Tuesday had already learned back on Seven Suns that asking what a galaxy was only invited scorn. So he tried a different question.

"What are these other dimensions like?"

September smiled vaguely, burrowing deep within some of her most precious memories.

"Amazing. Beyond incredible. We may not understand our own Universe all that well, but these other dimensions...they're like nothing you've ever conceived. Beyond human imagination. Our language can't even come close to explaining them properly...even I can only understand them to a degree, and I've seen many of them first-hand." September started to count on her fingers. "Dimension 456C is an endless ocean that stretches beyond measurement, and it's filled with highly intelligent whales the size of planets. 357D contains some sort of mysterious, silent machine the size of a galaxy that some long-dead builders put together a billion years ago for a forgotten purpose. 289A is an empty void that contains nothing but endless screams from an unknown source. 456D is inhabited by a warlike species of intelligent capsicums who, unfortunately, demand heavy tolls whenever we visit their dimension. 123D is filled with boiling blood that rushes about in powerful tides..."

September reclined on the chair, enjoying this rare break. After a mere two minutes, a wall speaker made a DING noise.

"Well, break's over. You can go now, Spasm."

Tuesday blinked. "What, that's it? You're back at work now?"

September shrugged.

"Yes. I still have ninety-six hours left on my shift."

Tuesday recoiled in horror. He couldn't even stay up late enough to watch the dodgy ads for sex hotlines, let alone several days.

"You aren't serious," Tuesday responded.

September shrugged in dismissal, stepping back towards the sphere.

"I was awake for a week, once, and I still managed to get my fourth-dan black-belt in psychotic mathematics," September rubbed her almond-shaped eyes. "Though admittedly, you have to keep in mind that sleep deprivation actually helps with understanding psy-math. After all, sane people literally cannot comprehend it. My instructor said he'd never witnessed anybody who was able to keep writing so legibly after technically falling asleep on their desk. They had to wake me up in case my snoring was some sort of secret code that I was using to help the other students cheat. Long story short, high distinction."

"It's not natural, this sort of thing," Tuesday said, scratching himself in three places at once.

"No, it's perfectly natural, Spasm. Geniuses must deprive themselves of sleep and other wasteful pastimes or nothing will ever get done. Think of all the time you've spent sleeping, Spasm, and how totally useless it all was. I weep at the magnitude of it."

Tuesday shrugged.

"Sure. But I'm happy."

September paused, glaring at Tuesday for a second, and then continued to tap away at the spherical dimensional plotter at full speed.

"What's that meant to mean?"

"Does all this make you happy?" Tuesday wondered.

"Happiness is an obsolete genetic limitation designed to foster maximum reproductive capacity among unthinking beasts, and has zero relevance in a self-conscious, self-evolving species such as ours." September blinked. "Or at least mine. Would you like me to write that down for later, Spasm, or do you have something else incorrect to state? I'm sure I can find a moment to fault your very best arguments."

Tuesday cursed himself for trying to win a debate with the smartest person he'd ever met and proceeded to immediately do it again.

"All I mean is you should take it easy occasionally. You're making me tired just looking at you. I'm sure that big round thing will take care of itself. Aren't there others who can help out?"

September stretched like a cat, thinking on this for a split second, and startled when a siren went off. Rapidly typing a string of perfect engineering jargon into one of the floating segments, she shook her head.

"I'm needed here. You, however, are not. I honestly feel that I'm being too subtle with you, Spasm. Push off."

Tuesday exhaled in frustration and casually put a rollie cigarette in his mouth.

"Smoke that here and die an immediate and terrible death, Spasm."

"Ah," he put away the fag.

"Where'd you get that, anyway?" September demanded. "There's a zero tolerance policy on all nicotine products on Unison starships. You do remember what happened to the people of Pox?"

Tuesday nodded. Even he'd heard of them.

The people of Pox were a peace-loving, nascent civilisation of farmers who enjoyed herding large flocks of dopey arachnid cattle. Before first contact, the Pox people spent all of their spare time in the worthwhile pursuit of developing more efficient ways to pick their multiple noses. Think shaved Labradors, but with eighteen permanently snotty nostrils. Introduced to tobacco by an especially soulless human sailor looking for a quick graft, within a matter of months the entire world of Pox was chronically addicted (including the cattle). To make things far worse, if a Pox person attempted to give up the addictive poison, they'd turn inside out from shock. Riddled with cancer and lung disease, neither of which had existed on Pox prior to human contact, the Pox people launched a military campaign against humanity. The Unison was given no option but to wipe out the entire world of Pox with thermonuclear weapons and mass drivers...or to simply settle out of court, whichever came first. The tobacco companies all blamed The Unison for not providing nicotine patches and gum to the aliens prior to the apocalypse, but a class action lawsuit against big tobacco failed, as all the victims were dead, which tends to be the case when big tobacco was involved.

"Why are you still here?" September demanded.

Tuesday realised he'd been drifting aimlessly on his polluted mental ocean for the better part of a minute. Despite the fact September was still colder than a refrigerated rectal thermometer made from an icicle, Tuesday decided that now was as good a time as ever to make his move. Jumping off this highest of cliffs, hoping he knew how to fly, Tuesday swan-dived for the jagged, distant rocks below...

"If you're thirsty at some point, well, maybe..."

"I am fine for now, Spasm. This drink is sufficient."

"No, no," Tuesday cut in. "I mean a drink...a drink in my quarters."

September laughed, a musical sound. "Share a few snifters of non-alcoholic caramel schnapps? I'll stick with the energy drinks, thank you."

She took a sip from the straw as Tuesday clarified things.

"I've got moonshine, actually."

September choked and Red Vee spurted out of her nostrils. Somehow, even this clumsy stumble seemed sexy to Tuesday.

"You have a still? Are you clinically defective, Spasm?"

"Well, I was once classed as a hopelessly defective moron by..." Tuesday waved this topic away. It wasn't helping his cause. "Look, I've got a fresh batch that should be ready in the next couple of days. I'd love for you to try some. As long as you keep in mind that it'll dissolve your cup if you're not quick enough, it should be fine."

"What, it dissolves foam?"

"Ceramics. Stomach lining stops it, though. For a while."

September laughed again, though more casually this time. She obviously thought that Tuesday was just being funny about the strength of the booze, but that was only because she hadn't encountered anything like Jack Spasm's moonshine outside of medical journals. Every page of Spasm's recipe book had been decorated with varying numbers of hand-drawn skulls, and it was yet more proof yet that Spasm was a diabolical psychopath who wanted nothing more than to inflict suffering on other people. A Lithuanian cockroach had unwisely attempted to drink out of a smouldering puddle under the still and had exploded like a grenade made out of snot. Tuesday was eager to see if this was a good sign.

Tipping his hat at September, who was so engrossed with her plotting that she didn't bother saying goodbye, the janitor that everybody knew as Spasm left the Department of Dimensional Plotting.

Replaying the scene, Tuesday tried to figure out if his attempts at picking up September had been a success. After all, while she hadn't actually said yes, Tuesday decided that September must have forgotten to confirm it out loud. Laughing counted as a yes, right?

Tuesday kicked his hovering bucket of stinking cleaning fluid down a corridor of glowing incinerator bins, and he tapped each flashing VAPORISE button in turn so that their contents were reduced to ashes in a microsecond. As usual, the walls were all displaying the irradiated desert where Tuesday had been born and spent his formative years in an attempt to make him feel better. He ignored them.

Scratching at his overalls, which seemed to be indelibly stained with Jack Spasm's old bodily fluids, Tuesday marvelled at how easy it had been to assume his new role. Good-old Spasm mustn't have made any friends, as even the other Alpha Deck dropkicks didn't recognise Tuesday to be a liar. He hadn't been glanced at twice this whole time.

It was almost too easy. Disturbingly easy. Weren't these people geniuses among geniuses? Surely somebody would eventually notice?

Little did Tuesday know it, but somebody on-board already knew his secrets. All of them.

*

The next ninety-six hours went by quickly. While Tuesday had divided around eighty percent of his time between, sleeping or finding new places to sleep, September had barely sat down. If it wasn't for the psychosis cut-out chip installed in her spinal column for her twelfth birthday, September would have been window-licking mad by this point. As it was, she was merely sleepy and grumpy.

Hitting the dusty REPLACEMENT button on her console, it took less than a minute until five lesser science officers arrived to take September's place. They all looked surprised, their facial expressions telling September quite clearly that they were wondering why their workaholic superior had stopped slaving away for any reason short of total dismemberment. The small group took up their positions at the dimensional plotter but could barely keep up with September's workload. Even though there were quintuple as many hands and brains as before, they began to struggle. September gave a loud sigh and went to say something.

All five scientists braced themselves.

While September was more than capable of lighting up a room every time she opened her mouth, she usually only spoke to shred the ego of anybody foolish enough to do something as unthinkable as being imperfect in her presence. While the top geniuses among the crew valued and hung on her every word as professionals, waiting eagerly for the next insight that would shatter everything they knew and understood about the Universe, nobody could bloody stand her. There was a very good reason September worked alone: she was an arrogant, tactless, irritating twonk.

Her next words were typical.

"Damn it to a Green Hell! Learn how to operate a dimensional plotter properly, Hemming! An epileptic amputee with nerve damage just randomly slapping their stumps about would have better fine-motor skills. What flunk-out mail-order community college taught you such a rubbish technique?"

"Yale." Hemming snarled. "Followed by Harvard and Princeton."

"It's not good enough. Not good enough by far!" September announced to the quintet. "You waited too long, Hemming! You missed the boat. My mother, August, plugged an experimental learning adapter into her womb during her second trimester to start me on the early road to success, and I was born with the capacity to type hands-free at one-hundred-and-ninety-seven words a minute. Despite being born sideways, I was the most highly educated foetus Old Suwon ever produced."

"Educated at being a bitch." Hemming muttered. "And technically, weren't you a clone, just like the seven others who came before you?"

September's eyes narrowed dangerously at this accusation, and every lesser scientist besides Hemming froze for the briefest of instants. That single microsecond of stasis confirmed that September's dark secret was still circulating despite her best efforts to have it stamped out. Rather than directly refuting the accusation, something September was in no way professionally required to do, she clicked her fingers at one of the other white-wrapped scientists.

"Sacks, would you care to explain why I'm the highest-ranking scientists on board this ship for the benefit of poor Hemming here? Try to use words with six syllables or less for the sake of the more special people among us."

"You're in charge because you're going to work yourself to death by the time you're thirty, right?" Sacks snickered, feeling emboldened by Hemming's audacity.

"Exactly!" September yelled dramatically. "Geniuses aren't meant to throw up a tiny, flickering, useless little spark for a hundred forgettable years: we're nuclear bombs, burning so brightly that we become permanently seared onto the retinas of history! People like me need to lead the way for all those useless peasants, because we're more intelligent, more qualified, possessed of a more stable temperament..."

"A what?" Sacks said in disbelief.

"Don't interrupt me!" September screeched. "Even combined, I outrank you all by ten decimal places! If you'd care to dispute any of this, how about the smartest person in the room puts their hand up right now? Well?"

September's hamster, Mister Boodle, casually hopped up onto his hind legs and planted a front paw against the Perspex wall, sipping from his water tube. Funnily enough, it turned out that Mister Boodle was the smartest person in the room. The hamster's mind actually belonged to a sixty-five-year-old human professor known as Rip Newton, an off-the-scales genius who had unwisely decided to use his extensive resources on board The Frontier to mess around with illegal experiments into digital personality transferral. Rip's colleagues noticed some alarming changes in his behaviour around the time of these covert DPT experiments, such as the way he'd begun to sleep in shredded newspaper rather than a bed, and how he now made indecipherable high-pitched squeaks instead of speaking Unglish. After nibbling a chunk out of Eulogy's left hand for no good reason, Rip's former body had to be permanently restrained in a straitjacket within a padded asylum cell in the underbelly of The Frontier, and at that very moment it was happily running on a giant wheel that the psych nurses had been forced to install for the sake of keeping their patient calm. Rip Newton's vacated brain now spent all of its time split between trying to figure out exactly why it would always end up back in the same place on its beloved wheel no matter how long it ran, and fantasising about dried fruit.

Although Rip Newton's mind had survived the transferral process into Mister Boodle's grey matter completely intact, he'd quickly become accustomed to his new role as a hamster and had no intention of returning to the stresses and trials of being the smartest person on board The Frontier.

And he'd found that hamster poo tasted surprisingly good to his rodent tongue.

"Yes. That's what I thought," September snapped, the only human with a hand raised. She surveyed her understudies with distaste. "You have the next ten years of this voyage to surpass and embarrass me with your expertise, but until that happens, you must do your best to be like the best: me."

The most galling part of her bragging was that September was right beyond a doubt. She was in a class all of her own, a genius among geniuses, and only the head of Games & Theory (or Military Intelligence, as most civilians from The Unison would know it) was capable of beating her at ten-level three-dimensional chess. Even the ship's computer was refusing to compete with her at anything except raw data mining and other tasks that were tilted in its synthetic favour. In a secret discussion with Fleet Admiral Aslan, The Frontier's humiliated AI had threatened to wipe itself clean if September so much as requested another game of simulated seventh-dimensional geometrical starship warfare.

September spent another minute or so hovering, making sure that the "idiots" - who had thirty-three black-belts and two Order of Sol medals between them – weren't going to cause some end-of-the-Universe-type cataclysm fuelled by nothing more than their ignorance and stupidity. After being disappointed by a distinct lack of catastrophes, September grumbled and left the room.

She wasn't quite sure, but September could have sworn that she heard cheering once she'd turned into the next corridor...

Glancing at her reflection as she passed a wall mirror for the first time in days,

September frowned at her crumpled white uniform with its gold-and-purple piping and buffed her sigils of command. Brushing at her ebony hair with her fingers and rubbing at her bloodshot, almond-shaped eyes – hints of her Ugandan and East Korean heritage, respectively – September's brain experienced the unpleasant sensation of not doing anything constructive. She didn't like it one bit. After all, September had spent her entire life travelling non-stop around the galaxy in search of new challenges, and the idea of staying still, of merely hovering, was worse than death. No amount of accomplishment had managed to satiate September's lust for learning up to this point but seeing as though she was about to pass beyond the very boundary of known space and witness things that no other human had ever been privileged enough to see, hopefully this craving would finally be satisfied.

It took September a couple of minutes to get back to her sprawling, deluxe cabin. Although she'd already been on-board The Frontier for three months prior to its launch, all of September's furniture (except for the bed) was still covered in shrink-wrap. She'd spent ten times as long in the toilet than she had in her own quarters. There were some decorations, though, such as the fifteen silken black-belts hanging from the far wall. Each of the jet sashes were embossed with the golden logos of the best universities The Unison had to offer. September had easily earned her fourth-dan qualifications in stellar engineering, advanced physics, pure mathematics, macro-string theory, psychotic calculus, dimensional crossing and many other subjects that somebody like Jack Spasm couldn't even pronounce, let alone define. In total, September had more than one-hundred and ninety-seven letters after her name, not counting vowels or commas.

The only other personal touch to this mint-condition cabin was September's impressive collection of one of the rarest things in the galaxy: actual books made from old-fashioned paper, the sort that always had the same thing written inside of them. A tight spiral of red-carpeted staircase snaked its way up the guts of a four-storied wooden cylinder that was filled to bursting by thousands of hermetically-sealed volumes. However, this was only a fraction of September's library. Her storerooms were so extensive that they required their own computerised filing system. As most of her collection pre-dated the dark years of the 22nd Century when any books that weren't able to automatically update themselves were publicly burned, a high percentage of them were fiction novels. Why would she want to collect ancient non-fiction, anyway? Pretty much every single thing that people believed prior to the 22nd Century had been proven wrong ten times over, so the non-fiction from that era was basically worthless. She might as well collect books about voodoo recipes.

Laying down on her Emperor-sized bed fully clothed, September set her Omni implant to go off in two-and-a-half hours and mentally chose a tricky mathematical formula to work on while she was asleep. Utilising a skill she'd learned during the six months she'd dabbled in being a Chaotic-Neutral Wizard, she turned off the conscious part of her brain like a flicked switch.

September woke up precisely three seconds before the alarm was due to erupt, and her finger darted out like a snake to hit her Omni implant in time. September mentally noted that she'd solved most of the Morisset Algorithm, a problem that Hemming had been tormented by for well over a month and decided that her findings would serve as an ideal cutting implement for a verbal emasculation. September smiled as she recalled that it was Hemming's birthday next Fursday, and decided that his surprise party would be the ideal time to bring the pain. First, though, she'd have to find out how it was possible that she still hadn't been sent a formal invitation yet. Feeble-brained sots...

For some reason, September spared more than a single moment to think about Jack Spasm's offer from ninety-eight-and-a-half hours ago. The answer, of course, was an obvious no. Willingly choose to spend her precious few minutes of private time with Jack Spasm, easily one of the most unbalanced men aboard The Frontier? Actually volunteer to go to his quarters - her, one of the most desirable women on board and him, a man with the breeding, charisma and intelligence of an untreated yeast infection?

Then again, this was the first time in years that anybody had actually expressed an interest in sharing September's presence without a formal obligation. And besides, Spasm was certainly more pleasant than that lunatic Eulogy, he didn't mouth off at her like those imbeciles on the alternate shift, and as September had always loved hamsters, she found Spasm's rodent-like mannerisms fascinating. She still had another half an hour until her next shift, so what was there to lose?

September decided. She would have a drink with Spasm.

Peeling away her clammy uniform until she was clad in nothing but her highly unflattering granny knickers, September sprayed a good dose of Shower-In-A-Bottle all over her body and waited for the aggressive enzymes to eat away at the grease, sweat and general stink of a ridiculously long shift. Slipping into a sexy cocktail dress that rated at least an 8.4 on Latham's Scale of Sexual Allure, September misted some straightener into her black hair and applied a few jets of conditioner.

Now for something she didn't wear very often: make up.

September switched on the Photoshop function of her Omni. A holographic mirror popped up into mid-air, showing a perfect representation of her face surrounded by a thousand floating symbols. Tapping and stroking at the buttons, September applied a holographic layer of makeup that started with foundation and finished with blush, eyeliner, rouge and lipstick. She smacked a green tick to confirm the spruce-up and set the holographic layer to last precisely two hours. After that, as programmed, it would vanish without the need for anything as crude as wipes or chemicals.

Putting on a pair of black pumps from her amazingly small collection of shoes, she marched out of her cabin, and began wondering exactly why the hell she was about to have a drink with Jack Bloody Spasm.

In truth, it was lonely being so intelligent and attractive. Most men were immediately crippled with feelings of inadequacy and didn't even bother trying, and the few that survived longer than a couple of minutes would be driven away by September's toxic personality way before any Omni numbers were exchanged. As nobody ever wanted to be around her, September spent all of her free time with her ancient books. Unfortunately, September was able to read at such a fast pace that she occasionally suffered from a rare condition known as "explosive stress-induced eyeball cramps," and she'd been told in no uncertain terms that the medical staff had no intention of using their Repler Units to brew up a new pair of peepers every time she decided to have an epic fiction binge. So it was time to mix things up a bit. And anyway, September was under the impression that doing naughty things could provide some sort of a thrill that couldn't be replicated in a legal way. As she'd never been in trouble, September thought it was about time to learn what all the fuss was about.

Swiping at air, September checked the crew directory as she walked out of her cabin. She found that Jack Spasm's slot was a tiny space three kilometres down, just above the deafening urine reclamation system, and was situated between two disabled toilets. Even though there were no disabled people on board (yet), regulations were regulations. It went without saying that he lived on Alpha Deck, which meant he had zero operational worth. Her hamster, Mister Boodle, outranked Spasm by six levels. Alpha Deckers were designated as only being useful as cannon fodder, as a source of emergency organs for more important crew members, as crash-test dummies for dangerous situations, or were scheduled to be a part of some sort of unsavoury science experiment. In theory, they may also be worth trading as a living form of currency with an unmet intelligent species, but that was yet to be proven.

It went without saying that the Alpha Deckers had no idea that they were the exact definition of expendable.

September transferred Spasm's file to the wall of the turbolift with a twitch of her fingers as she decided to misuse her authority. She discovered that Spasm's file contained dozens of angry outbursts about the low quality of urinal cakes he was being forced to use, along with numerous instances of antisocial behaviour and several requests from Eulogy to fire him out of an airlock. These requests had all been denied by Fleet Admiral Aslan for some mysterious reason.

September discovered a much bigger problem when she glanced at a file image of Jack Spasm that had been taken two weeks ago. Comparing the holo from a dozen angles with her own eidetic memory, September came to the disturbing conclusion that the man she was about to visit was not the real Jack Spasm. He was a near-perfect match, true, but unless Spasm had discovered some way to suddenly remove approximately seven and a half years from his appearance, he was an imposter.

Was he an infiltrator? A spy? A saboteur? Perhaps he was even a Vegan extremist! The whole ship could be in danger!

Physically shaking, September checked Spasm's file thoroughly to see if there was anything to explain the difference in appearance, but there was no history of cosmetic surgery, firecracker-related dental mishaps, disfiguring accidents with acid or anything else that made sense. Being a busybody by nature, like most virgins pushing thirty, September decided to find out exactly what the Green Hell was going on.

*

September stepped out of the turbolift on Alpha Deck to the ear-shattering noise of an alleged "song" from a torture metal band. It sounded similar to a cat being thrown repeatedly against an electric guitar, and September was pretty sure all of the lyrics were classed as unforgivable by most religions. Every flat surface was covered in obscene graffiti, and the floor was ankle-deep in garbage all the way up the corridor. Janitors wearing the same type of overalls as Spasm the Impostor either wolf-whistled or silently leered, as though they immediately knew at a cellular level that she was out of their league and that any serious attempt at picking her up was a waste of time. After all, how many wolf whistles throughout history have actually led to an erotic encounter? Statistically, picking up a supermodel for pity sex after accidentally dropping your erection dysfunction pills right on her toes would be more likely.

An apprentice chef in a floppy hat and a full-body apron that may have once been white bumped into September. He was so hugely fat that it took a couple of seconds for many segments of his body to agree to stop wobbling. These negotiations went on for some time.

"Sorry," the huge chef said lamely. He seemed like the kind of guy that spent a lot of his time apologising. "Didn't see you there. I was sort of...well, I'm sure you don't care. It doesn't matter."

"Great," September said sarcastically. Biting back a comment about the bristly hair poking out around this fat chef's neckline, she nodded up the hallway. "Where's Spasm? Have you seen him?"

"Spasm? Jack Spasm?" the chef clarified in disbelief, his jowls wobbling. A dark look clouded his eyes. "Why? What did he take?"

"Take? Nothing! I'm just here to...to see him."

"Yeah, right. How much does he owe you?" the chef slapped at a deposit of cellulite in his forehead, sending it wriggling. "Oh, I'm Slummer, by the way, Jimmy Slummer. Apprentice chef extraordinary. Or summing. I live here," he ended inanely.

September's eidetic memory produced a few relevant facts: James Slummer, aged twenty-eight, currently an unknowing participant in a long-term study of excessive ultrasweet addiction. Life expectancy: three months.

"Yes, James, I gathered that. I really must find-"

"Look, if he got out of line, don't confront him. He bites," Jimmy said under his breath, showing September some purple marks on his hand. "We try to keep him away from actual money, but somehow he keeps finding patsies. Not that you're a patsies. Or a patsy. You're too beautiful," Jimmy went red, which took a while to crawl all the way over so much surface space. "Look, just stay away from Spasm. He's trouble. And his room smells like alcohol and cigarettes."

She didn't have time for this. She had to speed things up. Generally, September found that speaking louder and slower made it easier for the mentally subnormal (see: 99.99% of humanity) to understand her, and so she tried to get across her very simple question for what must have been the fourth time in half a minute. Number five may involve a kick in the face.

"James: where is Jack Spasm?"

Jimmy looked blank, as though his brain had just experienced a hard reset. He blinked a couple of times.

"I like cooking," Jimmy said awkwardly. "Do you like cooking?"

September sighed in exasperation. It was like nudging away a pathetic little stray mongrel puppy that just kept whimpering and coming back for yet another unkind boot, simply because it was the closest it could come to a loving pat and a scratch behind the ears.

"I mostly heat up my meals in a nuker between shifts, but I did three months with a Michelin star chef when I was twelve. My speciality is a stone-cold vichyssoise followed by a perfectly-executed steak tartare, even though neither of those dishes are really cooked, per se."

"Per what?" Jimmy waved away his own question and whispered his next words with a little menace. September was pretty sure he was just whispering as an excuse to get physically close to her. "Hey, have you noticed that Spasm seems to have gotten younger lately? Eulogy said that he's sick of me complaining about people being mean to me, so I went all the way to the Fleet Admiral - he's really nice, by the way - and he said his eyesight is so bad he can't tell. Isn't that weird?"

Jimmy got out a chocolate-coated Caligula Bar from a half-melted stash in his apron, sucked out the flowing caramel and crunched a high-carb sugar crust, and gestured around at the other inhabitants of Alpha Deck.

"Been here for a while, now. Cooked all the meals for the construction crew, you see, mostly Shake & Bake chicken, which is easy enough. I like making Shake & Bake. It's fun. See, you shake it, then-"

"I get the idea."

Jimmy went silent. Puffing up his chest, which was apparently made up of two bags of cottage cheese, he nodded in a resigned way.

"I'll protect you from Spasm. If he tries anything, call me, and I'll yell real loud. I can yell good, you see. I've had a lot of practice around here."

Another chef snuck up behind Jimmy and gave him an atomic wedgie before September could voice a warning. The bully must have been a master at this, as he managed to get Jimmy's massive underpants all the way to his armpits. Jimmy shrieked as the elastic lining got caught on his lumpy back fat. Dancing around, trying to regain the barest fraction of the dignity and self-respect that he'd gradually dribbled away for his whole life, Jimmy waved awkwardly to September.

"Well, Miss, he's in the room between those two disabled toilets. Just holler if you need help. I hear the guards have wanted to bust Spasm for a while now, and I need the extra points."

"Will do. Bye, James."

"Bye, Miss."

September shuddered as Jimmy Slummer walked down the corridor like a croquet hoop. He really was a gross lump, and if September thought that Spasm smelled bad, then this guy must have a skunk somewhere in his family tree.

Wandering down the blaring, grimy corridor, ignoring the janitors, chefs, technicians and other assorted "special" cases, September quickly looked away from the disabled toilets that hedged Spasm's room, as lumpy, nicotine-coloured water was gushing out underneath the doors.

Best not to think about it.

Next to this hygiene atrocity was a room unlike any other on the ship: crudely painted jet black instead of The Frontier's standard beige, September was sure that some of the posters on the walls were against regulations, as well as being outlawed by the Catholic Church under threat of immolation. There was no sign of the dolphin pillows or scenes of infuriating tranquillity, and "Spasm" was lying against the wall with his legs pointing towards the ceiling. Whistling as he threw bent coins at a mug full of moonshine on the other side of the room (the ones that he got in sizzled and smoked alarmingly), Bob Tuesday looked up to see September and collapsed backwards in an untidy pile.

"Spasm," she said simply.

Tuesday smiled with his gross brown teeth and stood his lanky frame upright like a rusty, unfolding lawn chair. Buttoning up an overall strap that had popped loose, he gestured at a seat covered in MacDeath crusty bacon slab burger wrappers. Some of them had been used as ashtrays.

"Sit."

"I'd prefer to avoid even considering that if you don't mind."

For a moment, Tuesday looked almost as awkward as Jimmy if that was even possible. Snorting grossly, the imposter gestured at a bottle of caramel schnapps, which September politely refused.

"I prefer the chocolate-hazelnut one, thanks."

"No, no – that's the liquor, the hooch, the booze–"

"Your first euphemism was succinct, Spasm."

There was a painful silence. Although she still needed a little more evidence to be certain that this guy was an imposter, September couldn't help but glare daggers at Tuesday. He examined her expression for a while before speaking again.

"Anything wrong?" Tuesday asked innocently.

"Ran into a friend of yours. James Slummer."

"Oh," Tuesday tried not to grimace. "You know, admitting to being Jimmy Slummer's friend is classed as a disability on most planets. So is he still a large moon, or has he finally decided to upgrade to a planet?"

"That's not nice, Spasm."

A little too blasted to keep up the ruse right now, Tuesday shrugged.

"Call me Tuesday."

September squinted. "Why?"

"Because that's my name."

"Ah HA!" September boomed. Snatching a tiny spray bottle from her pocket, September pointed the nozzle at Tuesday's face. "Who are you, and what have you done with Jack Spasm?"

Tuesday eyed the bottle. "What's in that? Mace?"

"Hydrofluoric acid mist. It's so caustic that it will burn your freaking eyes out in one pump, and I have three tonnes of the stuff compressed into this little bottle. Answer me!"

Tuesday put his hands up.

"It's not what you think. Jack Spasm is a future version of me. Technically, I am Jack Spasm." Tuesday took a large swig out of the caramel schnapps bottle, keeping his hands in clear view to avoid any acid-related blinding incidents. Spilling some of the moonshine on his bed sheets, a few drops quietly smoked. He offered a sip to September and was refused. He shrugged.

"You lied!" September accused.

"Yeah. I tend to do that. But it was for a good reason! You see, I woke up one morning, and it turns out I'd written a message to myself on my own arm with a laser tip pen."

September glanced at the RUNNN OR DY burns on Tuesday's forearm. Keeping the nozzle pointed at him, she raised an eyebrow at the atrocious spelling.

"Is that some sort of code?"

Tuesday shrugged again.

"I can barely read or write, so it was the best I could do at short notice."

September lowered the acid spray bottle a few inches. Her face twisted in pity.

"You can't read?"

Tuesday shrugged. "They tried to put me through AutoEducation back on Seven Suns, but I've got the Raffle Gene. One in a wossaname, a billion. Totally allergic to it."

September felt a stab of pity. No wonder this guy was so hopeless: he couldn't read the multitudes of cleaning notes she'd thoughtfully left for him, which were mostly along the lines of "go somewhere else" among other pearls of wisdom. September couldn't imagine a world where she was shut off from the written word, trapped in a dark corner away from the last thousand years of literature...

September lowered the acid bottle.

"How far did you go in school?" September asked.

"Managed a week in first grade."

"And when was this?"

Tuesday counted on his fingers.

"About a month ago."

September had completed primary school before her mother had hit the third trimester, thanks to an in-utero learning adapter implanted in her unborn skull. September had gotten it cut out years ago when invasive cybernetic modifications went out of fashion.

"How old are you?" September asked in horror.

This time, Tuesday had to count on his toes as well as his fingers.

"Twenty-two."

September felt faint and had to sit down. Moving aside a pile of pizza boxes, she sat on a stool and thought deeply about the situation. It must be noted that whenever September concentrated on the greatest mysteries of the Universe it was only a matter of time until she tore them apart at the seams to reveal their deepest secrets. When September dedicated her mind to something, the galaxy took note. Once, while she was at a Chaotic-Neutral Wizard meditation retreat, September had concentrated too deeply on the possibility, however slim it was, that she might not actually exist. To her great surprise, September had actually felt herself start to disappear into the ether, fading from reality like an alcoholic blackout. September had been forced to stab herself in the hand with a salad fork in order to reinforce her own existence. This had surprised one of the Chaotic-Neutral Wizards no end, as he'd been eating a fried chicken Caesar with that particular fork at the time.

Looking down at Tuesday, she felt something twist within her: this man could be the challenge of her career, a chance to prove that she could change a totally defective human being from a nothing into an accomplished professional. He could be her Everest. If she could turn this total thickie into somebody useful, it would be her most impressive feat.

Yes, Tuesday would be her project. She said so.

"Hmm?" Tuesday ummed, now well and truly plastered.

"Tuesday, I don't care if you have the Raffle Gene. I guarantee that I can find a way to mould your mind and shape you into the man you are meant to be." At his blank expression, September clarified further. "I am qualified to teach the greatest minds in the galaxy in a whole spectrum of subjects. With that logic, I should be able to find a way to get around your allergy."

Tuesday closed one eye and squinted with the other.

"You're selling what?"

September sighed.

"I'm going to make you smart."

Tuesday didn't think much of this offer, as all that time he'd wasted with Ms Humple hadn't taught him much of anything...but then again, Ms Humple was a generic primary school teacher whose qualifications made her the professional equivalent of a junior cashier at MacDeaths.

But then there was a realisation about the true plus to this offer: if he said yes, that meant September would actually be sharing his company in a totally voluntary manner on a regular basis. If he played his cards right, things might develop from there. Tuesday's doubts instantly withered.

"I'm in."

*

Tuesday's lessons would not begin for another ninety-three hours, which is when The Frontier was due to pass beyond Known Space. This invisible border of The Unison was known by such names as The Dark Zone, The Rancid Abyss, The Crotch of Space, and The Devil's Armpit. The imaginary line was a major source of stress for everybody aboard The Frontier, as no human ships had gone within five light years of this segment of the galaxy since the Squealing Death was discovered (and subsequently unleashed) over a century ago.

Easily the most virulent pandemic known to mankind, the Squealing Death was brought back to The Unison by a randy sailor known as Deekin Shanker. Shanker, a serial xenophile who claimed to have sexually conquered every species of intelligent mammal encountered by mankind, had foolishly gotten it into his head that he should be the first human to seduce and have sex with an insectoid species mankind had just made contact with last Friday. This ménage a trois with identical hermaphroditic twins was meant to be his crowning achievement. But when Shanker sobered up, covered in royal jelly and bite marks, it soon became apparent that he was infected with parasites. After all, human skin doesn't usually wriggle about unless something is very, very wrong.

Keeping his affliction a secret all the way back into The Unison, fearful of agonising quarantine procedures (and even worse, paperwork) Shanker decided, hey, what's the worst that could happen, and went out for a beer the next time his hauler dropped anchor. Shanker was attempting to chat up a six-legged bovine chick with a hot set of udders when he coughed, sneezed three times, and exploded. A plague of winged mites erupted from the meat volcano once known as Deekin Shanker and spread throughout the pub, infecting every living thing on the backwater planet in short order. Over the next six months, the Squealing Death spread across much of The Unison and eventually claimed more victims galaxy-wide, than every other parasite in human history put together.

On-board The Frontier, nothing actually happened as they passed the Dark Zone border; there were no syringe-shaped missiles loaded with a mankind-ending plague, no invincible alien warships with energy weapons and cloaking capabilities, or even so much as a deadly meteor shower. This was a terrible anti-climax after decades of impenetrable quarantine by Unison bureaucracy, and no time was wasted in sending back a message that was the intellectual equivalent of "ha ha, you suck-hole idiots got it wrong for a hundred years" to the dwindling dot in the background that was Earth. The closest thing to trouble that the ship encountered was a cloud of weird radiation (the fallout from a failed doomsday machine some aliens had detonated millions of years ago), but the hull of The Frontier had been built with advanced alloys that easily blocked such lethal rays. Beyond giving everybody on board a slight tan, this dose of rad proved to be harmless. The crew celebrated by eating crispy biscuits with cheese on them and sipping sparkling water.

*

"I have a solution," September announced to Tuesday's wet snoring.

Snuffling in a gross way, Tuesday did his best to open his eyes. Thanks to the amount of moonshine he'd put away the previous morning, it took a few seconds for him to remember how to coordinate his eyelids, let alone how to focus with both eyes at once. When his sight returned it was to behold something terrifying less than five inches from his face: a fat invertebrate striped with neon yellow, blood red and black segments. She was extending a dozen long, prehensile tendrils towards Tuesday's face, wriggling in the hopes of laying a colony of eggs inside his brain meat.

Tuesday scampered backwards until he hit the head of his bedframe. It took a couple of seconds to register that September had the Hiver Queen safely restrained by her bulging insectoid thorax. September was smiling in victory.

"What the hell?" Tuesday demanded.

September placed the Hiver Queen back in a familiar little lead box.

"Like I just said, I have a solution." September repeated. "I've run some tests, and it seems that the neural gel that all Hiver Queens use to control their brood definitely has applications in treating the Raffle Gene in humans. Yes, you still wouldn't be able to have the usual suite of AutoEducation programs uploaded in the normal number of sessions without horrible side-effects, but I estimate that with great care - and the liberal use of neural gel from Her Majesty here - it should be possible to gently code you with a full Seven Suns education in a matter of weeks."

September held out an ancient hearing aid. It had dozens of hair-thin spikes protruding from one side, and a single button on the other. It had obviously been modified in a major way.

"All you have to do to install the pump is put it over your left ear and push the electrodes in all the way – don't worry, I've applied a numbing coating on them – and then press the button once and once only before you upload a fraction of the standard AutoEducation program. I've got your timetable right here."

Tuesday accepted the plastic sheet and the little crescent-shaped pump. September checked her Omni. "Okay. I have work. If you have a stroke or something, let me know."

"Wait," Tuesday snapped. "If the Queens use this neural gel to create hiveminds, isn't it a bit dangerous to pump it into my head?"

"Dangerous and illegal." September said simply. She inched towards the door.

"But as long as you're the only person on board with Hiver gel in your brain and as long as the Queen's mental commands are blocked by her lead-lined box, you'll be reasonably safe. I've replicated enough neural gel for the entire course of AutoEducation, so there's no reason to bring the Queen out again while you have any chance of being dominated. Once your AutoEducation lessons have been completed, this box is going straight into an incinerator, and you'll become one of the highlights of my career."

"Dominated." Tuesday repeated, bothered by that one word most of all. He felt a faint headache, and realised it was the sensation of a thought forming. "Wait. If neural gel from Hiver Queens can make dumb people smart, why aren't they already using it? Surely somebody else has figured this out?"

September huffed. At this rate, she'd only be an hour early for her shift.

"Okay, Tuesday, look. Mankind has discovered Hiver Queens on more than two dozen separate worlds. Some of these planets are located ten or even fifteen star systems apart. Obviously these bugs aren't capable of interstellar travel on their own, so the most popular theory is that some ancient spacefaring civilisation grossly underestimated the danger that Hivers represent and were completely wiped from history as a result of their foolishness. As you'd expect, The Unison tends to be more than a little hostile towards anything that possesses the capacity to reduce our species to a terminated footnote in the history of the Milky Way, and so they've spent the last two hundred years doing everything in their power to exterminate the Hiver species. As I have already told you, Hivers are dangerous. I'm not downplaying that statement one bit. Most of the classified documents I've seen on the subject of Hiver Queens are so damned scary that most people would think we're better off nuking every planet we find them on. But this Queen is the key to making you more than a trained monkey, Robert. She is the key. Are you going to bitch out on me?"

Tuesday touched the tiny electrodes, avoiding eye contact.

"Where did you get that thing, anyway?" Tuesday asked, glancing at the lead-lined box.

September smiled darkly.

"Have you noticed that Eulogy seems more pissed off than usual?"

*

Tuesday learned all thirty-five letters of the Unglish alphabet that day. Thanks to his first dose of neural gel, the symbols didn't fade away and disappear from his memory like they usually did. It was like his brain had developed some sort of traction that the short bursts of AutoEducation could grab onto. Tuesday was also surprised by the fact that he now understood the exact definition of the word "traction," too.

That afternoon, he began to write freehand. His letters were scratchy and mostly illegible, and Tuesday's penmanship was truly horrible to behold. His words resembled the fallout from an exploding pen more than intentional language. Within an hour, though, Tuesday's handwriting had become legible. After a further ninety minutes, Tuesday could write the entire alphabet without a single letter facing the wrong direction. Excited, Tuesday stole a bundle of laser tip pens from stores and stashed them under his unmade bed.

On day two of his studies, though, Tuesday decided to give up on AutoEducation altogether and just stick to what he knew: nothing. He'd discovered that learning was effort multiplied by boredom multiplied by a lack of naps multiplied by headaches, and he already hated it. September dealt with Tuesday's rebellion by stealing his pillows and hooking him up to an intravenous drip of the energy drink Red Vee, which, as the ads say, Wires You for Life. Although Tuesday was making odd little twitches with his face and his pupils had tripled their normal size, he learned all about basic mathematics and was soon smart enough to fill out a tax return without an accountant.

Of course, this wasn't the only time he tried to get out of his deal with September. All of these instances followed a basic pattern. The latest one on day five was no different.

"You're disabled, Robert! You needed help!" September pleaded.

"Don't need your help. Was surviving just fine before you," Tuesday snapped, brickwalling her.

"Like a cockroach on festering garbage, Robert! Look what you're capable of! Since the implant, your grades have soared well above what I'd projected...you're reading at a seventh-grade level now, did I tell you that?"

Tuesday was stunned by this. It felt like just yesterday he'd misspelled his own name on most attempts, but now the language centres of his brain had become so refined that he was capable of reading the shocking long-lost autobiographical confessions of Jane Austen. The record-breaking non-fiction best-seller revealed how Austen had sold her soul to an evil voodoo spirit called Sakhan Ixilis in exchange for literary success, and the autobiography went so far as to include the precise blood diagrams she'd used and a list of the best black magic stockists in the UK just in case anyone else was interested in fame and fortune. Of course, it was six hundred years out of date, so you'd need to source your voodoo sacrifice equipment elsewhere.

Tuesday relented...for now.

On day eight, the end of his first week of study, Tuesday decided to flick through the AutoEducation guide to see what he had to look forward to over the next few months. The manual was ordered from the most basic programs to the most strenuous, and the intensity of the program was classified by a simple star system. Long story short, all of his uploads had been between half a star to a whole star. Jumping all the way to the very end of the plastic book, Tuesday came across a flashing red page with margins made from animated skulls. Doing his best not to move his lips as he read, Tuesday eventually discovered that he had to say the name of the final program out loud.

"Advanced Temporal Calculus," he finally managed.

No matter how hard he tried, Tuesday couldn't pronounce most of the words that made up the summarised description of this particular upload, let alone understand what they meant when you put them together. Beneath the name of the upload, though, was its star rating: twenty-five stars.

Tuesday thought on this for a time. He did some mental arithmetic. If one dose of neural gel allowed him to learn a one-star program, then it made sense that twenty-five doses of neural gel would help him learn a twenty-five-star program, right? Basic maths, that. And think of the time he'd save jumping right to the back! Surely September would be impressed by his initiative right? She'd be here in an hour, so he'd better get going.

So, tapping furiously at the chemical pump implanted over his left ear, Tuesday selected Advanced Temporal Calculus with a swipe from his right index finger. However, something immediately went wrong: there was the smell of burning meat, and a sensation like a pipe bomb going off in his skull.

To say that Tuesday "passed out" would be incorrect. It would be far more accurate to say that the shape of his consciousness shifted into something completely alien. To start with, his eyes no longer saw images: everything was made up of a tornado of liquefied numbers condensed into solid shapes, of letters and symbols made from a hundred different colours, all dancing into complex pairings before pulling apart again with a loud RRRRIIIIIP noise. He could taste algebra, feel geometry, and hear trigonometry. And tying his senses all together was a smell like charred pork. For all he knew, Tuesday might have slid into a different dimension.

Reaching out towards the swirls, Tuesday found that he could move the characters about, make them dance and link up on a three-dimensional plane until they were arranged in the right way, the way he felt they were meant to be connected. It was as obvious as separating unripened green grapes from two-headed elephants, but exactly WHY the numbers had to be put together in this precise way couldn't be translated into Unglish. At least, not with Tuesday's meagre vocabulary. Finally, after about a million years, the numbers and letters were all where they were mean to be. Tuesday smiled in victory.

Then, just as quickly as it had arrived, this entire alternate Universe immediately disappeared with the biggest slap in existence.

"Tuesday?"

Regaining his normal senses and thought patterns with a start, the first thing Tuesday registered was that he was holding a totally burned-out laser tip pen. The smoking cylinder had reached such a high temperature from overuse that it had fused to his palm with the stink of barbecued Buffalo wings. A little vanilla circle near the immolated nib showed that it was on the WHITE setting. Moaning in pain, Tuesday burnt all the finger pads on his other hand as he tore the writing implement away from his scorched flesh. He dropped the laser tip pen into an identical baker's dozen of ruined writing implements. They had all been set to an entire spectrum of colours.

"Tuesday? Can you hear me?"

Looking up, Tuesday scanned his eyes along a complicated rainbow that had been burned into every flat surface of his bedroom room. He'd decorated every last inch of space with a multi-coloured formula that was so big that there were numbers and letters scrawled all over the roof, across his bedhead, and even on the toilet seat. It was all totally senseless to Tuesday's eyes, but for some unfathomable reason it felt right. And all that had been required was a minor stroke and a bit of brain damage...

Tuesday finally registered that September's concerned face was hovering less than six inches away from his own. Scowling, she raised her hand for a second smack across the chops.

"I hear you!" Tuesday yelped before the slap could connect.

September's concern instantly turned to anger. There was no midway point between the two emotions.

"Why did your chemical pump contact me to tell me it's empty, Robert?" she demanded, immediately getting to the point. As usual, any question that September asked was purely rhetorical. "I was very specific when I explained..."

September's eyes locked onto the wall directly above Tuesday's left shoulder. Her words faltered as she began to scan over the symbols as though she understood them. Completely ignoring Tuesday, September followed the chaotic swirl. She started to circle the room, bobbing up and down as the lines interconnected and spawned into complex branches. She was totally silent for well over half a minute, which must have been some sort of record.

"What..." Tuesday attempted.

"Shh."

It took another thirty seconds, but September eventually finished reading. She looked frustrated.

"Almost," she sighed. "For a moment there, I thought you'd...eh. Don't worry. The final part of the equation isn't..."

Tuesday blinked. For some reason, September froze again. Gripping him by the jaw, September dragged Tuesday across the decorated room to the mounted shaving mirror. Thrusting Tuesday's face so close to the reflective surface that she could have easily busted his nose on the unbreakable glass, September forced down Tuesday's left eyelid. Tuesday could clearly see with his other eye that he'd burned a handful of symbols onto the thin layer of skin that covered his peeper. Taking one good look at the tiny characters, September suddenly assumed an expression of horror, dropped everything and ran out into the corridor as though chased by the spectre of Jane Austen's damned soul.

"I need the Head of Space-Time right now!" September shrieked into her Omni implant.

Tuesday just sat there on his bed, confused, as September spent a solid minute demanding that the Head of the Space-Time Department get out of his bubble bath and come down to Alpha Deck as soon as he was decent enough not to get arrested for streaking. The irate scholar arrived in a bathrobe and fuzzy kitty slippers within three minutes. There were suds in his ears and he was leaving wet footsteps on the lino. Arriving at the bomb site that was Tuesday's room, he silently went over the equation for a good five minutes. He shrugged.

"Eh," was all the Head had to say. He shrugged. "Not quite. I'm going back to my bath..."

September gripped Tuesday by the temples, dragged him across the room, and forced down his left eyelid. The Head of Space-Time took one glance at the solution and went pale.

"No," he said, disbelieving.

"Yes!" September corrected in ecstasy.

Tuesday wrestled free of September's grip.

"No, yes, what?" Tuesday snapped. Although clueless by nature, he was feeling especially left behind right now.

September composed herself for a moment before she was able to speak.

"I don't know how, but – I think you just cracked time travel."

"Nice?" Tuesday half-asked, half-stated. He shrugged. "Is it worth much?"

"This is too dangerous," the Head of Space-Time snapped. "You are more than aware, September, that The Unison has placed a total ban on all thirty-seven methods of time travel, as well as any other kinds that may be devised in the future...or the past, for that matter. You know the rules as well as I do. It doesn't matter if it's a new method or not. Having possession of this kind of math is illegal, let alone experimenting with it. The space-time continuum is not our toy, damn it!"

September gripped the scholar's arm like a vice. Such physical violence towards her co-workers was unusual, as September normally relied on her ultra-genius to verbally beat them senseless instead. He winced.

"We're not in The Unison anymore," September hissed. "Any new methods of manipulating space-time are highly controlled, true, but who better to test such methods than us? After all, we are the cream of humanity! For all we know, this could cut years off our trip. It could possibly make our dimensional slides instantaneous! This could revolutionise the way mankind moves through space. Damn it, man, we can't waste something this valuable!"

"Waste!" the Head shrieked. "Imagine what that...that chimp over there would do with a time machine! He'd probably kill his great-great grandfather before he was even born or make love to his mother! He looks like the type that would put in a dozen winning lottery tickets and then go warn the Scandinavians about the Amerikan Uprising a week before it happens! Do you want the damned Skandos to still rule Amerika? Do you? And that's one of the best-case scenarios! Perhaps you'd like intelligent kumquats to become the dominant lifeform on Earth?"

Ignoring the ranting of the Head as though what he was saying had less merit than Jimmy Slummer's online dating profile, September tapped her Omni implant and began to scan in the equation from the very start. She had to push away the Head when he tried to interfere.

"You believe in God, right?" September demanded.

"Yes, of course I do! All Space-Time specialists learn about temporally unchained entities in our first year."

"And do you believe that He'd give the keys of time to Robert if Robert was the wrong person to have them?"

"That's just stupid, and you know it!" the Head snapped.

To use an ancient term, Tuesday decked him. Nobody insulted September, especially in his bedroom. Smiling wide, Tuesday gripped September's thin left wrist. She didn't recoil in disgust, which was always an encouraging sign. Then again, she was a little distracted looking at the Head's unconscious body sprawled on Tuesday's floor.

"Let's go. Time's a-wastin'."

CHAPTER NINETEEN OUTTATIME

It only took September a matter of seconds to convert the digital images of the

Tuesday Equation into a living formula within her Omni. She spent a good minute double-checking and triple-checking the scrawl of symbols before she felt confident in uploading it anywhere near The Frontier's supercomputers. After all, September was very aware that messing about with the space-time continuum was always a very dangerous proposition. Every half-decent scientist knew that the Universe was a capricious bitch-queen from hell at the best of times, and an amazing breakthrough that saves mankind today could be tomorrow's extinction level event. Allowing a long string of potentially dangerous code to have direct access to The Frontier's mind was a good way to end up with yet another robot uprising, or perhaps even wipe all life from the galaxy. Though if any human was qualified to diddle space-time, it was September.

Impressed by the insane beauty of the Tuesday Equation, The Frontier's supercomputer stack took a long, long time (nearly three seconds) before it responded. When it did, September smiled.

"Verified! I just sent your formula over to the fifth-dimensional printer at Applied Physics so it can mock-up a tangible representation." September swiped at the floating lightscreen being displayed by her Omni. The hologram disappeared. "All the scientists from Applied Physics are asleep, so we should be able to get in and out without any problems."

Tuesday was silent. He felt as though this was all very familiar, but he didn't know why. Thanks to the whims of the Universe, he had no solid memory of how his last experience with time travel had destroyed the galaxy and beyond...twice. So all he had was a vague sense of doom, but Tuesday always felt like that.

Tuesday followed September all the way to the Applied Physics studio. Here, the most brilliant mathematicians on board could convert their intangible equations into physical constructs in very short order, as the studio was equipped with a cutting-edge manufacturing machine known as a fifth-dimensional printer. As there were only a handful of fifth-dimensional printers in all of The Unison, having access to this amazing device almost made taking a one-way trip into deepest space worthwhile all on its own. It had been one of the big drawcards in recruiting all the geniuses that were necessary for this pioneering mission.

The fifth-dimensional printer was an oversized lump that sat lazily in the corner of the Applied Physics studio like a fat, slobby teenager in front of a new gaming console. It had hundreds of delicate little arms with an endless assortment of nozzles and cutting implements and soldering guns and far more. The finger-thin limbs dangled above a flat, bare platform that was roughly the same height as Tuesday's floating ribs. Although Tuesday was hardly an expert in cutting edge technology, he wasn't very impressed.

September kept a close watch on the fifth-dimensional printer, tapping her knuckles while she ensured that the design process was going as planned. Once the blueprints had been set, September filled out a seemingly endless list of electronic disclaimer forms that just kept popping up on the screen. After tapping the final I DO button, September turned to smile at Tuesday.

"Robert, we're about to have access to a genuine time machine."

"So we could do anything we want with this, right?" Tuesday asked, thinking about the possibilities. For some reason, all his imagination could conjure at this point was a pile of money the size of a small moon. The exact way he was going to actually attain that cash was just detail. "We could meet anyone we want, see anything we please..."

September gave a time-out motion with her hands. She raised one finger and pointed it at Tuesday in warning.

"Listen, Tuesday. We're not gallivanting through history, okay? I have a comprehensive understanding of all the mistakes you can make with a time machine, and we're not going to make any of them. I have printed up this device purely to see if your formula has some kind of merit when it comes to space-time manipulation. This is for science, understand? This could be a new epoch in human history! We are not taking you to grade school so you can win back your childhood sweetheart. You are not playing the Lotto. JFK will remain assassinated. We will change nothing. Do you understand?"

Tuesday nodded, but his face collapsed into a sour expression the moment September turned away.

"Don't see the point, then," Tuesday muttered.

Once September had legally accepted the consequences of her printing task (in triplicate), the delicate little arms of the fifth-dimensional printer began to move at top speed. Tuesday watched in fascination as the limbs sprayed out paper-thin layers of resin and weaved circuit boards out of thin air. The arms only went quicker and quicker as they continued to build a machine that was only meant to be found in the imagination of lazy science fiction authors. Once the articulate digits had finished soldering a hundred kilometres of molecular wiring onto circuitry wafers that were so thin and narrow that they were almost invisible to the unassisted eye, the arms stopped so suddenly that the silence was louder than a skydiving rhino.

September picked up the pocket-sized contraption, taking care not to touch anything that might change human history. Even up close, the time machine was an unimpressive lump of generic-looking hardware. A simple dial on its face said UP at the top, while the bottom of the dial said DOWN. There was a gun-like trigger on the side, a little RESET button opposite that, and not much else.

Tuesday squinted at a line of nonsense embossed on the face of the time machine.

"What the hell is a Flamingo Smartphone?"

September shrugged.

"I've never heard of it, so it's probably something ancient. I instructed the fifth-dimensional printer to cover the components with any public-domain shell it had on file. It looks as though the printer decided to use something really, really old."

Tuesday grumbled. September sighed in exasperation.

"What now, Robert?"

"It's just that we have an actual, real-life time machine, and it looks like crap."

"Robert, this is a prototype," September growled, annoyed. "The entire purpose of a prototype is to test out functionality and iron out any endemic faults in the design to gather data that can assist with future versions. For now, I am far more concerned with the possibility that we are about to tear out the backside of the entire space-time continuum. Whether it looks cool or not is entirely irrelevant. I am sure, in time, that a whole team of designers, marketers and advertisers will spruce it up."

"So we can't make it into a car?"

"No."

"Or a big chair with a spinny disk thing behind it?"

"No."

"Can we at least make it red?"

September blinked.

"What? Why?"

"It'll go faster."

September twitched. She raised a finger, went to say something, and stopped.

"This conversation is over."

Tuesday sighed in resignation.

"Oh, well. It's not too horrible, I guess." Tuesday admitted. "It fits in the palm of the hand, looks simple to use…every home should have one."

September checked the Flamingo Smartphone thoroughly to check that there wasn't more to it. Tapping the RESET button with sheer curiosity outweighing everything else, not much happened. She inspected the back of it and tutted.

"No batteries."

"What sort do we need? We passed a bunch of vending machines on the way here."

September shook her head. "We need two Triple-A Nuclears. Believe me, you can't get them out of a vending machine."

"I might have some of those in my remote control," Tuesday offered.

"Doubtful. Access to nuclear power sources is highly restricted, even to somebody with my clearance. It would take hours of paperwork to requisition them…and by then the Head of Space-Time would be awake, and we'll both be in the…both be in the excrement."

Tuesday looked a little ashamed.

"Sorry about decking him. It seemed like a really good idea at the time."

September shrugged.

"Based on how hard you hit the Head of Space-Time and the thickness of his skull, I estimate that we have about twenty-five minutes until he comes to. That should be ample time to see if this thing has merit." September clicked her fingers as her brain finished working on the problem. "Right. All two hundred of The Frontier's back-up computers use Triple-A Nuclear batteries in case the main grid goes down in a shipwide blackout. But even then, the only reason we'd need to use one of the back-up computers is if the entire primary system was instantaneously wiped from all six thousand of its hubs..."

"Which isn't likely."

"To put it mildly," September took a moment to think. "I think we could safely relieve one of the backup computers of its batteries without any real risk. There'll still be another one hundred and ninety-nine backup computers ready to fill the gap."

"So...where's the closest backup computer?" Tuesday asked

*

Jimmy was sad.

He didn't know why, but at four o'clock every day he got depressed, which was a lead-up to his evening melancholia. After this, Jimmy got upset, then dejected, and finally, just as he was about to go to bed, he got severe gas. It wasn't pleasant being Jimmy Slummer at such times, but at least it was a definite improvement over how he felt first thing in the morning.

Jimmy had spent the last hour trying to cook a bourbon and dark chocolate soufflé from an ancient webpage. As his speciality was whacking together Shake & Bake Chicken, this "soufflé" was a blackened, near-radioactive disaster, and when the other chef on duty criticised the coal-like lump, Jimmy threw it at him. As the concussed chef was being removed from the kitchen on a floating stretcher, he decided to leave Jimmy alone the next time the fat man had something dangerous in his hands.

Moping past an eye-height hub for one of The Frontier's many back-up computers - a small bulb the size of a doorknob that he'd never really noticed - Jimmy went about his business of ruining food. Stopping to eat a snack - his tenth this afternoon - Jimmy slurped at the Caramel Fountain bar like a candy junkie until its luscious golden core was gone. He had just finished crunching up the dried-out block of pure ultrasweet as Tuesday wandered in and started sniffing about for something. September was close behind, and Jimmy suddenly felt more confused than usual. How did such a lowlife attract this beautiful, intelligent woman? What was his secret?

"This area is for chefs only," Jimmy said to Tuesday as snobbishly as he could manage. However, he positively beamed at September. "Hi, Miss."

"James," she said easily, looking around to see that there weren't any other chefs lurking out of sight. "We'll be quick."

"What are you guys doing, anyway?" Jimmy asked, forgetting his goat-and-limburger lasagne as it burst into flames in the oven.

"Nothing," Tuesday lied, dedicating absolutely zero effort to the falsehood.

"We need a couple of batteries," September corrected.

September finally noticed the backup computer's hub was directly behind Jimmy's head. Moving him aside by making a dismissive flapping motion with her hands, September used her high security clearance to open the computer hub without setting off any sirens. The Triple-A Nuclears were a pair of glowing, neon yellow cylinders stamped with holographic radiation symbols that spun and changed colours in obvious warning. She carefully passed the dangerous batteries to Tuesday, who popped open the alleged time travel device and started to slot them in. Tuesday didn't notice that he was cocking the trigger a tiny bit with his other hand.

"What's that?" Jimmy asked, shielding his eyes from the glowing batteries.

"Nothing," Tuesday lied, once again failing to live up to his usual high standards of duplicity.

"Okay, I want to know what's going on now, Spasm, and no fibs," Jimmy demanded just as Tuesday installed the second radioactive battery. Taking one step towards his nemesis, ready to deal out a litany of complaints, Jimmy opened his mouth...

The Flamingo Smartphone gave a comical pop as battery number two slid home. September, Tuesday and Jimmy all disappeared in a storm of electricity, leaving behind six flaming footprints on the kitchen's tiled floor. The localised ball of lightning tore deep gashes into the stainless steel walls and ceiling, and it was lucky that nobody else was close enough to get zapped and shredded (in that order).

The Frontier's computer immediately registered that three of its crew members had vanished at 1947 Hours without any clue as to how, why or where.

*

The trio of time travellers reappeared somewhere else in that same instant. It was very dark, felt incredibly eerie, and smelled overwhelmingly like feet. It was far too big to be Tuesday's cabin, though.

"That was...interesting," Tuesday noted to the total darkness.

Somebody clicked their fingers, and the rice-sized Omni implant in September's left hand gave off a dim glow. The Omni's built-in holographic projector created six bright floating spheres, and the balls of light expanded to illuminate everything within a fifty-metre radius. Now that they could see, it became apparent that the three of them were standing in the middle of one of the cavernous warehouses that made up a large chunk of The Frontier's outer surface.

Giving her eyes a second to adjust, September patted at her well-lit body. Everything was still in the right place and facing the correct way. Well, that was the most important question answered, at least...

"Odd," September noted, reading a small lightscreen projection hovering above the back of her hand. "All of the electrics are out. I can't seem to..."

She was cut-off mid-sentence by a loud wail. Jimmy, an emotionally fragile man at the best of times, fell on his enormous bum and began to scream hysterically for somebody to explain what had just happened. Tuesday turned around and smacked Jimmy across his dimples in a silent yet succinct way of telling him to calm down. Recovering a bit, though still shaking violently, the fat chef looked up at September. His voice was a squeak.

"Where are we?"

"Somewhere in time," Tuesday interrupted without being asked, feeling as though he may be qualified enough to answer the question. He felt as though he was taking all of this quite well. After all, this particular strangeness only rated in the top five bizarre moments of Tuesday's life.

"Time?! What was that thing?" Jimmy asked in horror.

Both Tuesday and September gave Jimmy the exact same look.

"A time machine," September said slowly, amazed that Jimmy had been unable to figure that out for himself. "And just like I'd hoped, in addition to moving us through time, it's also instantaneously transported us across space." September clapped her hands in glee. "That's great news! When it comes to valuable scientific breakthroughs, it doesn't get any better than discovering a new method of moving through space in a faster-than-light manner. However, I'll still have to figure out exactly why we moved in the third dimension as well as the fourth. After all, just hopping about in random directions in deep space isn't all that useful, not to mention bloody dangerous. But I'm sure it won't take me long to figure it out. Another couple of trips should give me enough data to work with for now."

There was a noise like the hiss of a stream just beyond the far extent of the light. They all turned sharply on the spot, listening intently.

"Did you hear that?" all three of them asked at the same moment.

September, Jimmy and Tuesday stood perfectly still, their ears at attention. They waited for a good ten seconds, but the sound didn't return.

"Might have been a faulty steam-pipe or something," Tuesday offered.

September scanned the distant roof far above.

"Perhaps."

*

Once their vision had adequately faded in (and Jimmy finally calmed down enough to stop being an irritating distraction) it didn't take much of a stretch to figure out they were in an enormous warehouse dedicated to footwear. The fact it was full of neatly ordered rows of joggers, basketball boots, thongs, sandals, crocs, slippers, formal dress shoes, uggies and pumps in colourful cardboard boxes was a dead giveaway. There were also endless bundles of purple ship-issue socks rolled up into huge bales the size of apartment blocks.

"Footwear storage on level ninety-three," September clarified. "There's meant to be two or three decades worth of shoes for the entire crew stored here, even if we account for higher-than-projected changes in fashion trends. According to how few of these shoes have seen use, I'd guess we are roughly...three to six months from our point of origin?"

"How far is this warehouse from Jimmy's kitchen?" Tuesday asked, looking thoughtful.

"Three point seven kilometres." September answered without hesitation, doing the maths in her head at top speed.

When it comes to people having exciting adventures through time, very few of these tales would take place in an uninhabited shoe warehouse. Whether they should stay or go turned out to be an easy decision to make. After two solid minutes of drudging up a long, long aisle, they passed through a relatively tiny portal and came across the same looming shelves as before. But these ones were covered by something else: hundreds of thousands of tins full of colourful, sticky wrappers.

"Candy storage. Cleaned right out," Jimmy said, the pain of this horror showing on his face. He picked up one of the shiny metallic papers and pathetically licked at a tiny chunk of caramel. "This place is Hell. It must be."

"Strange." September noted. "Twenty-five years of sweets, all gone. Down to the last bonbon."

"Don't rub it in," Jimmy sobbed.

The third enormous section they explored was yet another boring storage area that had been stripped of all value. This time, the now-familiar shelves had been dedicated to canned meats. Millions of empty tins had formed a waist-deep lake of empty metal in the aisles, and they had to wade through it like a clanking swamp.

September picked up one of the containers and inspected its brutalised edge. It had been stripped of every pinhead of synthetic ham and was extensively marked up with hundreds of odd dents.

"Either rats have gnawed at this one, or somebody too stupid to be classed as human has tried to chew their way through vacuum-sealed steel without a can opener." September dropped the tin. "Either way, moving on."

A fourth looming storeroom was stocked with tubes of non-digestible toothpaste, soft toothbrushes, self-foaming razors and crate upon crate of Shower-In-A-Bottle. It was nearly at full capacity. September scanned over the vacuum-sealed canisters as quickly as her eyes were able to move, counting faster than Tuesday could pass wind, and came to an immediate conclusion.

"There's only about three to six months of toiletries missing, which lines up with the amount of footwear that had been taken from the first warehouse. Yet, for some reason, all the food and beverage supplies have been looted down to crumbs and drops. Either it's become fashionable to get about as a smelly, hairy, barefoot hippy in the last twenty-five years, or something has gone very, very wrong."

"I thought you said we were only a few months into the future?" Tuesday whinged.

September shook her head.

"That was one possibility. But it turns out there are two. Either the entire crew have spent two and a half decades porking down everything in stores and not bothered to freshen up that entire time – in which case, their combined body odour would be a violation of the Geneva Convention - or some sort of calamity has killed everyone after only a few months of the trip and something...unknown has been eating the supplies."

Jimmy blinked. It was the most help he could offer.

"Couldn't they have just eaten everything quicker than expected?" Tuesday wondered.

Another shake of the head.

"No. You saw all those empty vacuum-sealed tins that used to be full of edible supplies, right?" September's voice made it quite clear that her patience levels were at rock bottom. It was like being forced to explain theoretical physics to a senile dachshund. "There is no conceivable way that our crew could have demolished this amount of food in a handful of months. Everyone on board would be dead with ruptured stomachs by the time they reached two percent, if that."

Examining the back of her hand, September brought up her Omni's Operating System. It was an all-features model that came complete with a rad counter, virus scanner and other useful gadgets that The Unison had reluctantly invested in. She swiped through an assortment of tests.

"Look, there's no rad or diseases or anything obvious, so something else must happened."

Jimmy put his hand up, as though asking permission to speak. September acknowledged him with a tired nod.

"Why don't you just ask somebody? You're connected up to the shipwide network, right? Can't you give somebody a bell?"

September looked uncomfortable.

"Actually, I didn't want to say anything earlier in case I caused a panic, but when we first got here I tried to access the network...and it isn't there anymore. Sure, all of The Frontier's low-level automated systems such as atmospheric regulation, temperature control and carbon dioxide recyc are working just fine, but that's about it. All of the higher non-essential functions have been terminated, including the messaging network."

"Can we walk up there and fix it?" Tuesday asked.

"Walk?" Jimmy moaned.

"No chance." September said. "Anything serious enough to necessitate turning off all the higher systems of The Frontier would be classed as a shipwide emergency of the highest severity. In such a situation, everything would have been automatically sealed - including the elevators, stairwells and ventilation systems - with electromagnets the size of your head. Until the Fleet Admiral gives the all-clear and the higher functions resume, it will all remain locked. Standard safety procedure. Long story short, we're probably stuck down here in the warehouse section." September's expression went dark. "I wonder if anybody got trapped in a section without food or water? A horrible way to die..."

"So all the electrics are out, and we're stuck here." Tuesday clarified. "And what if the Fleet Admiral isn't around anymore? Then what?"

At that exact moment, that mysterious noise returned; a whispering, babbling sound just on the edge of hearing. The sound was slowly growing in volume and aggression.

"And we're all alone." Jimmy summarised. "Totally alone."

Ironically, a smelly, ragged figure picked that exact moment to leap out from behind a giant vat of aftershave and place a makeshift shiv to Jimmy's carotid artery. The weapon looked like it was made from a carefully-broken glass shard from a caramel schnapps bottle wrapped in a strip of bullet-proof fabric torn from a purple dress uniform. A single drop of blood at its very tip showed that the shiv was so sharp that it would be more than capable of cutting off Jimmy's head.

Jimmy made a tiny "peep" noise.

"What do you want?" September asked, holding out her left hand out palm-first in a peaceful way. Her right hand crept towards the spray-bottle of hydrofluoric acid on her hip. "No need to do anything drastic."

"I'm A Little Teapot," the figure grunted from the depths of a dreadlocked ginger beard. "Sing it. Now. Or we all die. Sing it. It hides us from them. SING IT!"

September and Tuesday looked at each other. Despite the fact they originated from the exact opposite edges of the human spectrum, they were both wearing the same expression. The stranger's dirty face twisted up in total rage.

"Sing it!" the Shiv-man bellowed, twisting the shank into Jimmy just enough to make him squeak. "Sing it!"

Sighing, September tried to put aside her pride. It wasn't easy.

"I'm A Little Teapot short and stout! Here is my handle, here is my spout..."

The stranger visibly calmed by the second verse. His blade stopped trembling and he drew it away from Jimmy's throat a little bit. Rather than letting go of the fat chef, the Shiv-man put Jimmy in a tight headlock with his free forearm and gestured with the blade for Tuesday and September (who had actually started doing the special little dance that goes with the nursery rhyme) to follow him. He retreated back into the darkness.

"Follow. Keep singing!" he growled.

September kept singing.

Within ten steps they were inside of what seemed to be the one and only room of the Shiv-man's home. He'd constructed a simple bed out of rolls of toilet paper and built a little fire in the far corner that seemed to be fuelled by aftershave. A pair of leather boots were boiling in what looked like a Unison soldier's combat helmet over the sole heat source in the room, as though the tanned animal skin was going to be the Shiv-man's dinner.

Their host traced the low roof with his eyes, listening. An expression of relief suddenly appeared on his face, and the Shiv-man finally released Jimmy. Shiv-man retreated to his crude bed and proceeded to rock back and forth, whispering something.

"Gone," he muttered. "Can stop now."

"What are we hiding from?" September asked the very moment she stopped singing.

"Don't think about them," Shiv-man hissed, rocking more violently now. He gripped his rag-wrapped feet. "They hears it when you fink about them. Can't tell you about them. Can't think about them. They can hear our thoughts. But the nursery rhymes stop them. Yes! It blocks our minds from them, lets us hide. Yes, it blocks us. Keeps us safe. Don't know why. Just works."

September leaned in closer, squinting. Her eyes snapped wide in surprise.

"Wait, are you Commander Eulogy?"

The Shiv-man growled from the depths of his beard to show that his teeth were coated in a thick layer of yellow scum. His uniform was an unrecognisable mass of scraps. It may have been the lighting, but his face seemed to be an odd green-blue colour.

"Means nothing. Nothing." Eulogy was still rocking like a madman. "You can't stay. None of you. Alone, we can hide. But together? They can hear us. Matter of time. Time. Time. They can hear more than one. Four is more than one. I'm A Little Teapot. Mary Had A Little Lamb. Too many here. Too many."

Eulogy snapped to attention and looked at the low ceiling in horror, as though he could hear something. It took a good five seconds until the others could discern that it was the same mystery noise as before. Unlike the last time they heard it, the whispering watery sound was getting louder, as though whatever was making it was angry. Eulogy bared his yellow chompers and raised the shiv in threat.

"Out! Out, or I'll stop your thoughts for good! They won't get me! I'm A Little Teapot! Mary Had A Little Lamb! Pop Goes the Weasel!"

It may have been the lighting, but September could have sworn there were a few tiny green mushrooms growing out of Eulogy's face. But that wasn't possible, was it?

"I need to know some things," September said, attempting to interrupt Eulogy's insane ranting. "What's the current date? When did all the higher systems go down? What can we do to fix things? What is out there?"

But the time for words was over. Raving madly, Eulogy chased them out of his crude hovel and sealed his home shut with a barrier made out of an industrial-sized bottle of mouthwash. As nobody had been fatally stabbed by a mental case, their current situation was far from the worst possible outcome.

Tuesday waggled the Flamingo Smartphone time machine as the whispering noise in the darkness began to reach a crescendo.

"Okay, enough sightseeing, I think it's time to go," Tuesday said lightly, knowing better than to panic.

Tuesday reached for the RESET button, but September blocked his thumb. It was the closest he'd come to holding her hand.

The background noise had taken on a distinctly sharp edge, as though there were entire worlds of anger and hunger within it...

"We haven't proven if this device is truly useful, yet," September stated. "We can't go back with a lack of useful data. Look, I say we go far ahead to somewhere safe and work things out from there, okay?"

September suddenly clicked a curse word in fluent Swahili and violently shook her left hand as though it was on fire. While this gave Jimmy and Tuesday a fright, what happened next was much worse: all of the glowing holographic spheres vanished as though a switch had been flicked, leaving the three of them in complete and total shadow.

"My stupid Omni overheated," September explained to the darkness. The whispering was still growing in volume. "It'll take a second to cool down. Just wait a moment."

"Bugger that," Tuesday retorted.

Tuesday twisted the Flamingo Smartphone's dial all the way to the right and pulled the trigger. September, Jimmy and Tuesday disappeared with a loud pop and a corona of electricity that lashed the immediate area with glowing, molten lines.

*

Tens of thousands of years later, a pile of yellowing dust that had once been a human skeleton exploded into a gritty cloud. Tendrils of lightning lashed about the dim room, searing glowing lines into walls of orange rust that were only held together by some sort of rampant green-blue fungus. The glow flickered, slowly transitioning into a trio of distinct human forms: one shapely, one lanky, one borderline circular. As soon as their bodies arrived all the way onto this new muddy bank in the timestream, the seasoned chronal-trippers took a moment to orient themselves. However, September wasted no time in snatching the time machine out of Tuesday's hands and jabbing a finger into his face.

"You are not to touch this again. Understood?"

Not bothering to wait for a response, September hooked the Flamingo Smartphone onto her belt and tapped at her now-cool Omni implant. A single lightscreen appeared with three red words: NO NETWORK DETECTED. No matter what, all September could get was NO NETWORK DETECTED. She took one look at the room before coming to a conclusion.

"The Frontier's alloys were borderline invulnerable to just about everything in nature, and that includes every weapon in The Unison's military databases. As all things in this Universe will eventually age and die in their own way, including the stars themselves, The Frontier's only weakness is time itself. We must be at least a hundred centuries in the future. Maybe far, far more."

"It's a lot dustier than before," Tuesday said, poking his finger into a thick coat of grime on what may have been a console. His hand went all the way up to his wrist, and he drew out a little brown knob covered in spindly roots. Tuesday smiled. "Hey, there's potatoes growing on this console!"

"And for some reason we can see without any of the lights working," September said with interest. She squinted at the stripes of blue-green fungus that covered more than half of the room. "This species of fungi is bioluminescent." She breathed in deeply. It was unpleasant and earthy, but far from toxic. "And from what I can tell without any lab tests, somehow this fungus is absorbing carbon dioxide and producing oxygen at a very efficient rate." September squinted at a tiny neon-green toadstool. "I don't recognise the species, though. It's not in my long-term memory, which means it hasn't been discovered yet."

"In our time?" Tuesday managed.

September turned her head like an owl and blinked.

"Exactly." September fetched a little sample jar and used it to collect one of the bright mushrooms. She slid the tube into a notch on her belt. "That little fella should prove to be interesting once we're back at the lab."

"Speaking of exactly...where are we, exactly?" Jimmy asked sullenly.

"The Department of Dimensional Plotting," September said instantly. She dug into a pile of decay to reveal Mister Boodle's badly tarnished cage. She went to spin his little wheel, and it dissolved into dust. September sighed. "Everything has disintegrated. I don't think a single thing would still work anywhere on this ship. It's likely to be worthless from end to end. Check the door, would you, Robert?"

Tuesday went to walk out of the main portal and smacked into it nose-first. Holding his bruised shnozz, Tuesday tried striking the override pad to open it manually. The door didn't respond in the slightest. Looking inside the flat box that connected the motorised door to the ship's power supply, he made a worrying discovery: the wires were tarnished to literally nothing.

"Heh," Tuesday grunted, "seems like all the doors are still sealed shut from before. By big magnets you said, right?"

"I don't want to explore, anyway. I want to go home," Jimmy whined.

Tuesday barked a laugh and turned sharply on the spot.

"You must be joking! This is the chance of a lifetime, Slummer." Tuesday snapped. "How could you not want to travel forwards through time? Don't you have any inclination to find out what happens in the future? Seriously! If we witness just one major thing we can use to our advantage, who knows what we can accomplish? Don't you want to have a bit of a warning about what's around the corner? Hey, maybe we could find out how you die, Slummer..."

"Shut up!"

"Okay, I think we should go back now," September ordered, rescuing Jimmy without meaning to. "I think I've compiled enough data to warrant further testing of the Tuesday Equation. Officially designated testing, I mean. I know that we won't be able to do any relevant harm this far into the future – seeing as though mankind would be completely beyond recognition by now - but we're still better off not meddling if we can help it. Come closer."

September flicked the RESET button and pulled the trigger. A tiny beeping sound chimed annoyingly and two hollowed-out yellow batteries ejected onto the floor with a hiss. They gently smoked a bit, but they certainly weren't glowing like before.

"Great. Fan-freaking-tastic!" Jimmy wailed.

"We just need some more Triple-A Nuclear batteries." September noted. A look of concern appeared on her face. "Unfortunately, the type we need have a half-life of one hundred thousand years."

Jimmy and Tuesday looked at each other. Then they looked back at September.

"And that means?" Tuesday pushed.

"Well, if their half-life is one hundred thousand years, and it turns out we're further than two hundred thousand years into the future, then that means we may be in...well, we may be in a spot of bother, to put it formally." Somehow, September managed to avoid swearing at the end of her statement.

"So even if we find the specific, rare-as-anything batteries that we need, they might be dead anyway?" Tuesday confirmed.

September shrugged. "Perhaps I could jury-rig other power sources together for a similar effect. It might take a lot of them, though. Hundreds. Thousands, even." She sighed. "We better start searching."

Digging through the deep piles of corrosion and dirt that had once been the Department of Dimensional Plotting, September quickly found the back-up computer for this particular room. It was wasted down to a half-eaten shell, but inside was only more bad news: its precious batteries had been removed. After checking through all the different piles, September and the others confirmed that the exact same thing had happened to every power pack and energy cell. They'd all been cleaned out.

"This place is useless. We need to get out of here." September noted.

Tuesday scoffed.

"But I've already tr-"

Tuesday's words of doubt were cut off by September stepping forwards and kicking the sealed door as hard as she could. Her boot pounded through the ruined metal like a wrecking ball, and corrosion sprayed from the point of impact. The slab toppled out of its brittle frame, and when it hit the ground it was as though a bomb had gone off. Dust rained from every inch of the ceiling, choking and blinding them all. Coughing and covering their faces, the trio staggered into the corridor. It took some time to retch up all the mildew and dust they'd breathed in.

"Well, that's one way of doing it," Tuesday finally managed, taking a step away from the prone slab September had just booted. Before he could move another metre, September's hand flashed up to stop him. Tuesday made a face. "What?"

September pointed at Tuesday's leading foot. Following her finger, Tuesday realised that his toe had sunk a good two inches into what he'd thought was solid floor. He pushed down a tiny bit and his foot carved through the ancient mesh like it was warm toffee. Tuesday huffed.

"Great. Bloody floor is ready to give. How are we meant to get anywhere walking on wet paper?"

September silently tapped at her Omni for a few seconds. Jimmy and Tuesday both startled as the entire derelict corridor turned into the sort of colour-coded line map you'd see on a weather report: a few solid green and blue borders were swirled by much larger patches of oranges, yellows and reds, seemingly at random. September didn't wait for the obvious question to be asked out loud.

"I've set up a structural integrity scan, converted it to a simple coloured grading system and linked it up to your retinal implants. Avoid the oranges and reds unless you enjoy the thought of plunging through six hundred stories of jagged rust before freezing to death in space." September leaned close to Jimmy. "James, I'd advise that you stick to the solid blue spots. And, mmm, I'd prefer it if you stayed on the opposite side of the corridor to me. No offence."

"Where are we going?" Tuesday asked.

September tapped away at her Omni instead of giving an answer, but she was immediately distracted by movement in her peripheral vision. Turning sharply towards the unknown lifeform, her bottle of hydrofluoric acid raised and ready to spray, it turned out to be some sort of thick green tendril snaking among the fungus mounds. Although it didn't appear to have a head of any traditional kind, the thing was raising itself up like an annoyed cobra. September moved to the side a little bit, and the tendril followed. Keeping her eye on the weird plant, she gave Tuesday a little wave.

"Do me a favour? Touch that for me, would you?"

His internal weasel cunning complained at top volume, but it was drowned out by his desire to win points with September. The moment Tuesday poked the tendril with his index finger though, an electrical shock blasted up his arm, sending him staggering backwards in surprise. He cussed in violent Guttertongue.

"Thought so. Those vines are conductive." September noted without a hint of apology. She glanced at the lightscreen. "It's hard to tell with all this fungus throwing up scanner shadows, but it seems like there's a lot of those vines...and that they all appear to converge in the same place." September swept her left hand in an arc. She finally looked away from the lightscreen, staring down the corridor and into the heavy gloom. "The moment you touched that vine, the readings went off the scale. I'm picking up a huge amount of electrical activity and radiation in a central point. It could possibly be the batteries, sure, or it might be some sort of lethal nuclear device, or something else entirely. No matter what it is, we may conceivably be able to use it to fuel the device to get back."

Their trek resumed. Tuesday realised at this point that if he was waiting for an apology, he'd be waiting a really, really long time.

Slowly picking their way through the corridor, which was now knee deep in blue-green fungal growths, September led both losers to the nearest turbolift. Of course, trying to use the faster-than-the-speed-of-sound pods would be pointless, as the tubes had decayed to ruin by eons of stillness. And even if they did work, they were sealed tight with magnets. Of course, the only viable option was Jimmy Slummer's greatest enemy: stairs. Thankfully, the door that should have blocked them was thinner than paint chips and came down with little more than a heavy breath.

Following September's lead, Tuesday began to carefully pick his way down the narrow emergency steps - which were rusted to an eye-watering bright orange - and everything was going just fine until Jimmy joined in on the climb. The staircase warped and shook on his fifth heavy stomp, and the structural integrity scan of the entire level instantly switched from green to red without any warning. Taken by surprise, the stairs canted at a sharp angle and the three time travellers staggered forwards. Tumbling for a corroded gap that was meant to be blocked by a safety handrail, the trio were only metres away from dropping into one of the longest open shafts in the ship. They'd be doomed to dive for more than seven hundred levels at terminal velocity until finally landing in the lowest cargo decks of The Frontier's underbelly.

In other words, welcome to Splat Town, population: three.

Thankfully, this isn't what happened. The crashing staircase toppled towards the very next level, sending the three humans tumbling and sliding down a very bumpy slippery-dip. Winded and bruised, they all scrabbled for the open doorway as tens of thousands of tons of tarnished metal staircase collapsed behind them like a milk arrowroot biscuit dropped into hot tea. It took some time for the dust to literally settle.

"Slummer," Tuesday finally managed to groan, rolling over. "Your fat arse just demolished half a starship. I hope you're happy."

"I want to go home," Jimmy sobbed, plucking shards of tetanus out of his face.

"Look," September ordered, getting to her feet. Somehow, her curiosity was so strong that it seemed to enable to her to ignore that she was just one big bruise. "See? There's more of those electrified tendrils. And they all seem to be converging on that doorway over there." September held up her lightscreen again. She nodded. "That's our target. Come on."

Picking their way carefully around the organic cables (Tuesday was especially sure not to bump them), the small group finally made it into the hotspot that September's Omni had highlighted. Inside, electrified vines covered the walls and ceiling in a solid layer of tangled green. The sheer volume of amps skittering around this nerve-centre of organic wiring was enough to raise every hair on their bodies. Falling against one of those concentrated knots would probably be immediately fatal. September didn't have a chance to see if it was possible to plug the time machine into this green powerhouse of energy before something unspeakable began to form on the far side of the room...

Hundreds of tendrils of all thicknesses began to pull themselves away from the walls and ceiling with disgusting sucking noises, and they writhed and wriggled into a dense maze of green the size of a truck. They wrapped together into a vaguely human-shaped face, and smaller vines formed some of the more detailed features, such as eyelashes and frown lines. Eventually, within the space of twenty seconds an unmistakable countenance had congealed into being, and it was truly terrible to behold. Disgusting strings of yellow goop dripped down to the rotten mesh floor from its mouth, hissing on the rust, and the balled-up vines that served as eyes rolled down to look at the intruders.

"You...are human?" it said in a demonic voice. The pitch of its words sent tremors through their bones. "Where did you come from? How are you here, after all this time?"

"Hey, Eulogy, you look great!" Tuesday exclaimed, finally recognising the old Commander. "Something's different, though...did you gain a few kilograms?

Get a haircut? Wait! I know! You've became an enormous pile of mushrooms, haven't you?"

"You!" the-creature-that-was-once-Eulogy screeched. The fungus network crawling across the walls, ceiling and floor quivered as Eulogy's mutated face glared with hatred at somebody he had not seen in thousands of years. While Eulogy's reaction to Tuesday had been bad enough, the entire starship shook with rage as Eulogy regarded Jimmy. "You! Slummer! You are to blame for everything!"

Jimmy looked behind him, then back at Eulogy again. The fat chef paled to the colour of old cream.

"Who, me?"

A tentacle instantly shot out of Eulogy's mouth. Wickedly barbed and spiked, the prehensile plant lunged right for Jimmy's forehead at top speed. At the pace it was going, the vine was going to install some serious ventilation right through Jimmy's skull. Displaying an astonishing amount of bravery, September darted to the side to intercept the biological weapon before it could plunge home. Eulogy's electrified vine stopped only a matter of inches from her face, hesitating.

"Move," Eulogy ordered, his single word deteriorating into a snarl of static.

She didn't budge. In fact, September didn't even glance at the thorns waving far too close to her eye. As usual, she had gone into her standard "intellectual" setting where minor concerns such as, say, not having her entire body perforated by organic spikes were brushed aside for the sake of her own understanding.

"Commander, do you recognise me?" September asked, facing her palms towards the green mass in the classic "I'm unarmed" gesture.

The vines that made up Eulogy's enormous face twitched a little bit. Thinking for a moment, his eyes shuddering about as he tried to access memories from the better part of two hundred millennia ago, he finally managed a name.

"September," he growled, but without anger this time.

September smiled as the sharp vine retracted back into Eulogy's mouth and vanished.

"Good. We're making progress. Look, I just want to talk. That's all."

Eulogy frowned.

"Talk? About what?"

September shrugged.

"Well, I think that asking what you...asking you what you are would be a good place to start."

"Are you blind? He's turned into a mushroom," Jimmy hissed under his breath. "Don't you think that might be a bit of a touchy subject? If I woke up as a toadstool one morning, I'd be pretty sensitive about it. Are you trying to get us killed?"

Eulogy's vines trembled, and his facial expression was almost insulted. He looked like an A-list celebrity who hadn't been recognised by a sandwich artist at their local sub shack. His words dripped arrogance.

"I have not been the sole-entity known as Commander Redmond Eulogy for a long, long time. I have become the sum total of a billion tonnes of neurally-networked fungus spread across nine-hundred-and-eighty-seven-thousand ships. I am The Spread. I am forever. I am all that is."

"Nine-hundred-and-eighty-seven-thousand?" Tuesday repeated.

The huge green eyes rolled down towards Tuesday in contempt, and Eulogy proved that he wasn't just some giant useless face splattered on a wall by effortlessly creating a huge lightscreen. The holographic display flickered a little bit, and some of the nearby vines sparked and wriggled about in distress, but the display contained a clear view of a ball of multi-coloured wreckage in deep space. September immediately knew what she was looking at: by using The Frontier as an unbreakable spine, Eulogy had incorporated the better part of a million other vessels – everything from haulers to frigates to Unison military cruisers to dinky little escape pods - into a big, crude sphere. The impacted wreckage of a hundred junkyards, a smashed-together hulk that was drifting through the void, must have stretched for around fifty kilometres in every direction from its centre of mass.

As the three humans watched this scene, the ball of wreckage ploughed into a relatively minute swarm of 747-sized transport ships, reducing them to a thin layer. Tuesday, Jimmy and September understandably braced themselves. As their surroundings didn't shake one iota when those multiple impacts occurred on the lightscreen, it was pretty obvious that what they were watching was a recording. The age of this video file was impossible to tell.

The lightscreen picture darted towards the gaping maw of a windshield to provide a good look at these newest additions to the ball. All the human occupants of the ruined vessels had died on impact, smashed into little more than person-flavoured jam, so seeing their pulped flesh was no surprise. But then something unusual happened: the now-familiar carpet of blue-green fungus begun to invade the new section of the hulk at a rate of a metre per second. Within a matter of a minute, the ships had been filled and sealed off. It didn't take a stretch of the imagination to come to the conclusion that the leftover flesh had been consumed by the fungus.

"I assimilated The Unison one world at a time," Eulogy rumbled, switching to another ancient recording. This video showed The Frontier barrelling through a whole fleet of heavy cruisers emblazoned by Unison markings. As The Frontier was made from the finest alloys ever produced by mankind and didn't have a single living human on board anymore, nothing that the military vessels could throw at the leviathan seemed to have any effect. The Frontier simply smashed into the outclassed vessels like a siege engine, disabling them and adding them to its bulk in one easy move. Like before, The Spread invaded these new spaces and distributed itself faster than Tuesday could walk. Although this particular battle tactic would be more at home in the head of a territorial bull than in the brain of a man who had reached the highest echelons of the military, September had to admit that it was a pretty darn effective strategy.

This video stopped, too.

"It took years, decades, centuries," The Spread said calmly, in a meditative way. "Eventually, I became all that is. I am all that remains."

September blinked. Her eyes darted about, as though she had so many hundreds of things to ask that she had no idea exactly where to begin. It was like walking into the Great Library of Alexandria and trying to figure out what papyrus scroll she wanted to unfurl. After a moment of thought, September spoke.

"Are all the different ships that make up The Spread as broken as The Frontier? I didn't see a single thing that worked the entire way down."

Eulogy's expression darkened in offence. All of his vines wriggled, and September's hair frizzled out a bit from the static build up. September raised her hands palm-first again.

"I'm not insulting you, Eulogy! No: I'm saying that it may be possible to fix this crate."

Eulogy's expression twisted up and his vines calmed a little. It was like he'd just received news that was so welcome that he literally could not believe it.

"Explain."

September took a breath.

"You know that I was, without a doubt, the most highly qualified crew member aboard The Frontier, right? Not to mention that designing this bucket would have been literally impossible without my decades of hard work on dimensional plotting theory."

Eulogy's eyes narrowed further.

"The Frontier has been immobilised for tens of thousands of years," he growled. "It cannot be fixed. Others have tried. Experts. Geniuses. They all failed. They all became part of The Spread as soon as they admitted defeat."

September took a step towards the giant green face and jabbed an index finger at his nose.

"Eulogy, I have no doubt whatsoever that not only am I capable of repairing anything on this ship, but I could probably make it work better than the dumb spugger who designed it in the first place," September snapped. "If I am provided with all the necessary resources and enough time, I guarantee that I could make The Frontier work again."

Eulogy was silent for a time, as though silently searching September's words for lies. After a tense minute, Eulogy eventually smiled. His vines wriggled and detached from the walls and ceiling.

"I can detect that you are telling the truth. I accept your offer."

September smiled and lowered her hands.

"Excellent! Now, I need to have total access to everything on board that has any actual value. Electronics, circuit boards, power sources, tools and raw materials would be a good start. From what I could tell, everything of use appears to have been looted a long time ago, so I'm assuming that you've hidden everything in stasis cases, right?"

Eulogy squinted at September. He was wearing the same facial expression you'd get from a wise old grandmother who was trying to figure out precisely how a psychic was cold reading such in-depth details about her long-dead husband.

"When I lost the ability to move, I did just that." Eulogy growled. "My last batch of servants filled the stasis cases with their own hands before they were assimilated."

"Where?"

"Five storeys straight down." Eulogy answered. "If you give me an hour, I can clear a path through the nearest elevator shaft, and you can climb down fairly easily."

September snapped her fingers at Tuesday and Jimmy and stomped towards the only exit.

"Okay. We'll get to work now. Get started on opening that shaft, would you?"

Before she could escape this death trap of electrified vines, the door sealed itself with a thick green mesh. September could see the amps zipping up and down the growths, as though Eulogy was charging them especially high.

"I have personal need of the other two," Eulogy said. As an unspoken explanation, the furry blue-green fungus started to grow towards Tuesday and Jimmy. "My apologies, September."

Tuesday leaned in close to Jimmy.

"Do me a favour?" he hissed.

Jimmy squinted. "What?"

"Jump, would you?"

Jimmy gave Tuesday his best "I must have misheard you just then" expression. "Huh?"

"Jump, you lump!" Tuesday roared, reaching for September's sleeve.

Twisting up his face in a mixture of determination and fear, Jimmy Slummer summoned all of his remaining strength and pushed off the rotten decking as hard as his legs could manage. Due to the fact that Jimmy weighed almost two hundred kilograms and contained less dense muscle tissue than a vegetarian egg roll, he barely lifted half a foot off the mesh. The floor beneath him was already a solid yellow shape on the structural scan, so simply pushing down was enough to splinter it into a jigsaw of tarnished ruin. Just before Eulogy's vines could whip them off their feet and zap them to death, the time travellers fell a good four metres onto the deck directly below, but they had no time to scream before that floor dissolved, too. Tumbling and disoriented, they plunged through somewhere between three to six floors (they were far too confused in the mushroom-lit gloom to tell for sure) before landing on a slab of intact metal. Thankfully, due to the soft mounds of fungus that had cushioned their fall, they were alive. Unfortunately, being alive meant that they had to experience what it was like to exist as human-shaped sore spots.

Tuesday, fading in and out of consciousness, opened his eyes after an unknown amount of time to see that they had landed in a room full of ancient plastic pallets stamped STASIS. As Tuesday went to stand up his brain finally processed that September was holding up two dusty Triple-A Nuclear batteries. The best explanation his groggy mind could muster was that she must have used an app on her Omni to seek out their radiation signatures. Smiling broadly, September jammed both batteries into the Flamingo Smartphone, pulled Jimmy and Tuesday close, and twisted the dial back into the distant past.

*

Unfortunately, they didn't quite expect how distant.

Tuesday realised three alarming things in quick succession: he couldn't breathe, he was freezing cold, and he was in space without a spacesuit. Deafened by the total silence of the vacuum, his skin prickling as it went blue and crunchy, Tuesday knew that he was only seconds away from becoming a corpse. As a man who had almost earned the punishment known as a "spacing" on several occasions from more than a couple of people, Tuesday knew all about what happened to an unprotected human body in deep space. It was hideous beyond words.

Thankfully, Tuesday had the foresight to immediately expel all the air from his lungs in a geyser of ice crystals. This was lucky, as Tuesday's breath had been about two seconds away from violently bursting through his ribcage in a fatal case of explosive decompression. As this internal meat fountain would have pulped every one of his organs, this undoubtedly saved his life. Unfortunately, the expulsion sent him tumbling in a permanent backflip.

Great. Now he wanted to vomit, too.

Floating in absolute zero, Tuesday looked "up" towards a sign of movement to see that September was swimming towards him. She appeared to be using her small spray-bottle of hydrofluoric acid as a crude form of propulsion. Jimmy's lumpy body was firmly wrapped around her foot like a lonely two-toed sloth.

Behind September and Jimmy, a big chunk of half-completed starship was drifting behind what Tuesday recognised as one of the reflective moons of Seven Suns. The unborn vessel was composed almost entirely of bare girders, but what white skin she did possess had already been decorated by half-a-kilometre long letters that declared FRON.

Hypoxia had already begun to kick in by now, and Tuesday could feel the prickling of hundreds of capillaries bursting beneath his frozen skin. To make matters worse, the total lack of humidity and a temperature of absolute zero meant that Tuesday's eyeballs had begun to freeze solid in their sockets. A layer of ice solidified on his lips, preparing to plunge all the way down his throat and deep into his respiratory system. Although he could no longer see or feel anything, he hoped and prayed that September was about to take his hand and rescue him from this horrible, horrible death.

Unfortunately, Tuesday's brain was still working just fine, so he knew exactly what his future entailed. First off, he would experience what it was like for all the water in his body to expand into vapour. At around the same time hundreds of nitrogen bubbles would form within his ruined veins, giving him a fatal case of the bends. Just to top things off, the bubbles would then block off every centimetre of his respiratory system, causing a series of strokes and seizures. His heart would soon be unable to pump anything through his severely enlarged veins, so Tuesday's blood pressure would instantly hit zero and he'd die. By the time a cloud of blood boiled out of his perforated skin and radiation fried whatever was left into jerky, less than one minute would have passed.

Mercifully, Tuesday passed out.

A construction grunt glanced over from his work on The Frontier just in time to see a bright corona of lightning through his transparent helmet. He instantly decided to stop dropping Blink tabs before work.

*

At precisely 1947 Hours shiptime – the exact minute that Tuesday, Jimmy and September had originally vanished from The Frontier - Commander Redmond Eulogy was enjoying a well-earned break by setting up hundreds of hand-painted table top strategy models in a display cabinet in his deluxe cabin. Like all the furniture in his off-limits private quarters, the cabinet was made from the extinct Earther wood known as mahogany.

All up, Eulogy had spent around five thousand hours detailing his little soldiers – going so far as to give them distinct facial expressions and unique hand-mixed iris colours - with a hair-thin brush. If you included gluing them together, filing away any burrs with a pad the size of a pinkie nail and mixing up microscopic amounts of epoxy resin to disguise the mould lines, you could easily triple the time investment. Of course, the little alien soldiers and exotic tanks had all been formed from a species of sentient plastic, and they silently threatened Eulogy with tiny bayonets and harmless puffs of cotton-wool smoke from tank turrets. Back in his teens, Eulogy had discovered the hard way that you couldn't keep models from opposing armies on the same shelf without deactivating them first, or you'd come back to a total abattoir. Since that first mistake, Eulogy hadn't so much as chipped the varnish on a single star marine.

At 1948 hours, precisely one minute after The Frontier's mind noticed that September, Tuesday and Jimmy had left the ship in an impossible way, Eulogy had finally finished setting up his prized possessions and carefully closing the glass-panelled doors. Just as he was about to click the latch into place, however, three balls of half-frozen meat suddenly appeared from nowhere like speeding comets. As Tuesday, September and Jimmy had been going a fair lick through the zero-gravity of deep vacuum, this meant that when they re-entered their original timeline it was with enough force to shatter ceramics. Everything in Eulogy's room exploded into mahogany splinters and glass chips, and by the time his unannounced visitors had finished pinballing about not so much as a coffee cup remained in one piece.

There was some good news: once The Frontier's mind detected that all three missing crew members had returned as inexplicably as they'd vanished, it assumed there was a minor system glitch, and disregarded their absence entirely.

Bellowing in apoplectic rage once he'd recovered enough to speak, the Commander raised his left foot to kick Tuesday, Jimmy and September into even smaller pieces than his busted room. Just as he was about to start breaking ribs, Eulogy noticed the severe freezer burns painted over every exposed inch of their pasty skin. Being no stranger to most of the sick and unusual punishments mankind had created over the years, Eulogy immediately knew what had happened. Choking and three-quarters dead, the time-jockeys didn't need to say a single word of explanation.

Spacing was one of the worst punishments of all, something that even the iron-fisted Unison military discouraged, as the true horrors of having your blood expand into red mist in your veins was something that could not be adequately conveyed with mere words. Though reasonably fast for an execution method (at least compared to The Death of a Thousand Pigeons), spacing was reserved for terrorists who didn't arrange the correct permits for their bombs, people who cheated on their taxes, or - due to an archaic loophole from The Unison's first-and-last schizophrenic High Autocrat - painting chickens blue with the intent of passing them off as a Mongolian parking attendant.

The Unison did not like blue chickens.

Eulogy piled the three semi-defrosted crew members on a hovering stretcher lined with antigrav wafers and set off for the hospital level at top speed.

*

Back in Eulogy's ruined cabin, something was moving on the bottom of Jimmy Slummer's discarded flip-flop: it was a tiny slither of blue-green fungus that had become wedged in the tread at some point. It was a struggle, but after a good minute of violent wriggling it finally managed to wrestle free. The fungus chunk flipped end-over-end like a leech, searching for the quickest way to return to its master: The Spread. It could detect him, sure, but there was something strange about his neural signature...

After a solid week of flipping about in The Frontier's tight ventilation system, the fungus slither finally found what it was looking for. Dropping from a ceiling vent and landing right in the middle of a convenient mushroom risotto without a sound, the blue-green shroom was almost immediately scooped up by a silver fork and jammed right into the unknowing mouth of Commander Redmond Eulogy.

CHAPTER TWENTY THE ASLAN REVELATIONS

Tuesday managed to wake himself up with his own emphysemic gasping. Before he could automatically reach for his cigarettes, an unfamiliar voice startled him from a quarter-awake to almost half-awake.

"How are we feeling, Mister Spasm?"

And then it all came back: decking the Head of Space-Time, fabricating a time machine, and hopping about in two horrifying futures. And, to top it all off, getting spaced into a human Popsicle. Hardly a standard Wednesday.

Tuesday grumbled in discomfort, crunching away the sleep crusted in his eyes. Glaring at the tall blob who was standing at the foot of his bed, Tuesday immediately registered that he was in some sort of hospital room. Like all modern hospitals, it was totally white: the floors, walls, beds, ceilings and sheets were the colour of fresh cream. The talking blob gradually resolved to become a medical technician. All the white made Tuesday feel as though he was floating in a reality that was made of nothing but light. It was painful.

Rolling to the side a little (which hurt like hell, by the way), Tuesday saw the considerable spherical girth of Jimmy Slummer flopped in the room's only other bed. Snoring like a golf ball being sucked up a vacuum cleaner and glued to his pillow by thick drool, Jimmy chewed at the wet padding without much luck. Tuesday glanced away from the sight.

"Mister Spasm?"

"Mmm. Yup." Tuesday finally managed, remembering that was meant to be his name. He squinted in pain. "Why do my eyes hurt so much?"

"They're brand new," the medical tech said, as though it was nothing. "We fabricated them on the fourth-dimensional organic printer less than three hours ago. It'll be another day or so until the microsurgical incisions finish sealing themselves properly, and then they should be, as the saying goes, good as new."

Tuesday blinked, trying to process what he'd just been told.

"Wait...did you just say that you cut out my eyes?"

The tech shrugged. "Of course we did. Your old ones had been frozen solid and smashed into meat sorbet. They were totally ruined. However, we liquefied what was left in order to use them as a source of compatible protein for your new eyes, so, in a way, you still have them." The tech glanced up with an expression of hesitation. "Actually, while we're on the subject, you may be interested to know that your eyes weren't the only thing that we needed to replace. Your rebuild was...well, it was substantial."

Tuesday narrowed "his" eyes.

"Substantial? How substantial?"

Finally taking the hint, Tuesday slowly pulled up the neck of his hospital gown to see that his chest and abdomen was one big maze of thin red lines. A heap of tiny wireless medical scanners had been glued to his body hair, and they were blinking and beeping quietly. Touching one of the surgical lines, Tuesday pulled his hand away in pain and glared at the tech.

"Like I just said, Mister Spasm, there really wasn't all that much left for us to work with..."

"Why do people keep cutting me open all the time?" Tuesday raged. "Every five minutes some slice-mad bugger gets the scalpels out!"

"You were in deep space for the better part of a minute. It's a miracle you didn't pop like a virgin at a Scumbags concert," the tech said harshly, tapping away at a lightscreen.

Tuesday could feel that something was weird with his feet. Kicking at his starched bedsheets, Tuesday looked further under the blanket.

"Wait, why are my feet taped into plastic bags?"

The tech kept rudely mucking about with his lightscreen.

"They were officially classed an Omega Level contamination risk. As our standardised scanners didn't recognise your particular species of moss, we called in our most gifted podiatrist to take a look. He's one of the best in the entire Unison."

"And?" Tuesday prompted.

"Well, last thing I heard he's still on suicide watch, but his self-inflected wounds weren't all that serious." The tech finally looked up from his lightscreen. "Now, I'm afraid I have some bad news. See, your organic rebuild was worth the better part of twenty-four years of surgical insurance..."

"I have surgical insurance?"

"Ah, now, see, here's the tricky part," the tech said in an apologetic way. "Problem is, you don't actually have insurance of any real kind. As a crew member of zero operational value, your level of medical cover only provides a bag of sugar-free cough lollies, a packet of generic sticky plasters and one raspberry chap stick a month. Turns out we didn't know this until we'd already renovated your entire circulatory system from temple to toes. It's put us in quite a tricky situation, and I'm not sure how to..."

"Can you just spit it out?" Tuesday growled.

"Okay, fine. Long story short, in order to reclaim what you owe us we'll be garnishing your salary by ninety-eight percent for the rest of your natural life. As your meals and lodging are automatically provided as a part of your income, you'll still be able to stay on the right side of starvation. Unless you live to a hundred and sixty, we'll also need to wire up your embalmed corpse and use it as a robo-janitor until it liquefies." The tech finished tapping at his lightscreen and gave Tuesday a big, fake smile. "Well, have a great day! I'd tell you to buzz the orderly if you need anything, but...well...don't."

Just as the tech left the room Jimmy woke up with a revolting snorting sound and looked blearily at Tuesday. Disconnecting from his saliva-soaked pillow with a wet noise, Jimmy sat up and squinted.

"Spasm? We still alive?"

"I guess," Tuesday said, sighing. "I wouldn't honestly call it living, though."

Snorting and gurgling, Jimmy fell back asleep.

Tuesday patted about for his cigarettes without luck. His orange coveralls – or at least what was left of them – had been stashed in a box under the bed. Checking the pockets, Tuesday discovered with glee that his pouch of home-grown tobacco, a packet of rolling papers and his dad's trusty lighter seemed to have been mysteriously overlooked. It was like Tuesday had a guardian angel somewhere...

Tuesday was only halfway through his second breakfast durry when two looming orderlies muscled into the room and stood at the foot of his bed. From the size of their arms and the hostility in their expressions, it was pretty clear that these were the orderlies who got called when there was trouble. It was far from reassuring.

"Come with us." The burlier orderly waved away Tuesday's argument (and his cigarette smoke) before he could voice it. "I don't care. You're due at an official inquiry in five minutes. We need to escort you there."

"But I need to-" Tuesday stuttered to a halt. "I need to-"

"What? You need to do what?" the smaller orderly prompted.

"I need to www...I need to wwwww..."

"What, what?"

"Work! I need to work!" Tuesday exploded.

Feeling as dirty as a twice-used sticky plaster for telling what may have been the biggest lie of his life, Tuesday's heart sank when he realised that it obviously hadn't helped his situation. The smaller orderly – who seemed to be playing the voice of reason – leaned in closer to give some quiet advice.

"Look, mate, I should probably keep this hush, but there are Unison soldiers armed with riot gear in the corridor, and they've been instructed that you need to get to this inquiry right now. If you don't choose to go with us, which is the easy way, then they'll take you the hard way." The orderly gently shook his head. "I've seen the hard way. I still haven't got all the stains out of my other uniform."

"Slummer, also," the bigger orderly rumbled. "They want him, too."

Tuesday smiled. Well, at least he wasn't going down alone.

*

Any idiot could guess that it would only be a short span of time until big, dangerous questions were asked, such as how September and the others had managed to materialise in the Commander's bedroom. As soon as the Head of Space-Tie had woken up, the puzzle had instantly become a legal concern for obvious reasons.

Dressed in beige hospital gowns, Tuesday and Jimmy were marched down a series of corridors by the two orderlies. Gasping and panting, Tuesday did his best not to swear as the thin red lines all over his body stretched and stung with every step. The fact that his discomfort didn't seem to be an issue was not a reassuring sign. Finally, just as it felt like his body was going to open up in a dozen places, Tuesday was hustled through a large, ornate golden door. As no stranger to courtrooms, Tuesday knew a legal building when he saw it.

Almost jogging down an aisle between rows and rows of uncomfortable wooden pews, Tuesday cursed as he saw that the courtroom's gallery was filled with a hundred crew members. Geniuses in purple, white, black and navy-blue uniforms turned to glare at Jimmy and Tuesday, whispering harshly at each other. So much for keeping things quiet. Directly ahead, was worse news: there was a raised golden dais made up of dozens of metallic eagles with their wings touching at the tips, and it contained no fewer than twenty-five of the highest ranked men and women aboard The Frontier. At a glance, the panel was split right down the middle with the Heads of every science department and an equal number of Commanders (including a snarling Redmond Eulogy) from The Unison's complex military structure. In the very middle of the panel sat Fleet Admiral Aslan, his bony old body perched atop a grandiose throne. Panning his eyes to the left, Tuesday's heart sank as he saw the Head of Space-Time – still nursing a puffy black eye and a split lip – was baring his teeth in threat.

Getting closer, Tuesday could see that there were two domes in front of each panel member: a red one and a green one. Like the other twenty-four members of the panel, Aslan also had a red dome and a green dome in front of his hands. As Tuesday was nudged into a defendant box in the front row of the court (which automatically locked him in place like a rollercoaster cage), Aslan gave him a disappointed look. Tuesday was used to being looked at like that and didn't think much of it.

Turning to the side, Tuesday finally registered that September was already in the defendant box. She seemed to be pointedly ignoring his presence. Before Tuesday could say a word, the large doors boomed shut and the Fleet Admiral started to speak into a tiny microphone bud. Everyone else was silent as the excellent acoustics of the courtroom carried his voice to all corners.

"I'll get right to it. We are here today because it is believed that James Slummer, Jack Spasm and September have committed no fewer than a dozen serious crimes in a single shift. After inspecting a lot of damning evidence from the minds of three high-ranking crew members – including Commander Eulogy, the Head of Space-Time and September herself – the guilt of the defendants is certain. Their offences range from the damage of irreplaceable property to physical assault on superior officers to creating a machine that was used for no fewer than four willing violations of the space-time continuum."

There was some murmuring at this last charge. Tuesday glanced around to see that he was getting some really weird looks from the gallery. Aslan continued as though the court was still silent.

"We also have an avalanche of physical evidence that serves to confirm and compound their utter guilt." Aslan swept his hand towards an empty space between the panel of judges and the defendants. The carpet slid aside and a long marble table lifted up from beneath the floor. The slab was sprawled with all kinds of junk, including Tuesday's neural gel implant. "As their guilt is beyond a doubt, this court has been convened simply to pass judgement. Before that, though, does anybody want to say anything?"

Eulogy got to his feet, his face twisted in hatred. Stomping away from the panel of judges, he stormed up to the marble evidence table and gathered up a handful of splinters and tiny nails. He allowed the junk to run through his fingers like sand.

"You know that desk you reduced to termite turds? I loved that desk. My grandfather carved it from the very last mahogany tree on Earth with nothing but his own two hands and a plasma blade. And my chair? I stole it from my most hated teacher as a prank after graduation...just before I kneecapped him with a crowbar." Eulogy's face was so full of sadistic glee that it was almost inhuman. "If you're not sentenced to death today, I will kill all of you, do you understand? You are dead. Dead! It may take me some time to figure out how to get away with it, but know this..."

"You'll kill us all?" Tuesday said helpfully.

"Thank you, Commander Eulogy," Aslan said drily, casually stopping the

Commander before he could separate Tuesday's head from his spinal column. Eulogy bared his teeth but swept back to his chair. "Your comments are noted. However, I very much doubt you will need to take matters into your own hands. Now, has everyone seen the evidence?"

The Heads and Commanders all nodded solemnly.

"And are you all in agreement that their many offences constitute an execution-level verdict?"

Tuesday's heart sank as the panel unanimously struck the green domes attached to the desk. He could clearly hear Jimmy whimpering and gagging, followed by a thunk as the fat chef passed out from stress. Aslan raised a piece of cotton paper in front of his eyes and scanned it intently.

"As September is of exceptional operational value, I believe that the panel has requested a stay of execution until a clone can be decanted and her memories transferred over?"

The Heads all hit their green buttons unanimously. The Commanders did the same. September made a choking noise, but her expression didn't change at all. Aslan sighed.

"Very well. Before we conclude proceedings and work out the exact method of execution, I have just one thing to say." Fleet Admiral Aslan leaned closer to his microphone bead. "Ruska forty-three-alpha."

Aslan snapped his fingers as punctuation. To Tuesday's immense surprise, every single person in the courtroom – whether judge, spectator or defendant – instantly slumped as though dead. To Tuesday's great satisfaction it looked as though Eulogy had slammed his face into the desk so hard that his nose was broken. Inspecting September, it was clear that even though her eyes were wide open, the dimensional plotter was in a deep, deep sleep. Her pupils were facing in opposite directions, something that Tuesday had heard described as "wall-eyed" on a couple of occasions. He poked Jimmy in the face, but there was no response. Looking up at the very awake Fleet Admiral Aslan, Tuesday shook his head in wonder.

"How did you do that? Are you psychic or something?"

Aslan chuckled and put his feet up on the desk. He fetched a green cigarette out of a gold-lined pocket.

"Nothing so impressive. I secretly programmed the entire crew with hypnotic conditioning before they came on board. They were all told it was a standard eye test. Depending on what command words I use, I can make them do just about anything. For instance, the Ruska trigger instantly switches off the conscious parts of their brains for as long as I want. If I was an evil man, I could use the Seriopath trigger to put them out the closest airlock without an ounce of resistance. Of course, there's nothing to be gained from that, is there? Obviously mass murder is rarely my first option." Aslan made a casual hand gesture. "Now, to be clear, the people in this courtroom are the only crew members who have any knowledge of your little jaunt through time and space, so I'm going to perform some extensive memory alterations to rid them of these troublesome facts. Once they have forgotten, your problems are solved. As September has an eidetic memory and was far more heavily involved in your capers than anybody else, excising all of her memories of the incident may result in some confusion and logic gaps. She'll be fine, but she will require some...enthusiastic modifications."

"So why didn't the command word work on me?" Tuesday asked.

Aslan looked disappointed again.

"Because you're a stowaway, remember? You didn't go through the hypnotic conditioning, did you?"

"Ah. Right."

The Fleet Admiral sighed in frustration.

"Before we go any further, I need to make it clear that we are only having this conversation once. This is your one and only chance. In a matter of minutes, that chance will be gone for good." Aslan smiled at Tuesday's stunned nodding. "You know, I've waited many years to give this little speech exactly as I remember it. I wondered if it would be the same, or if it'd be different altogether. So far, it's been identical."

"You have? It has?" Tuesday asked, not understanding one bit.

Aslan smiled again.

"Okay, first I need to explain a few things. Centuries ago, when human starships only had a top velocity of around half the speed of light, one of the biggest problems with founding colonies on distant worlds was the inbreeding issue. After a certain point, every citizen will be cousins - or closer - with every other citizen. This is bad. In order to add variety to the genepool whenever it was required, scientists developed a reasonably simple treatment known as genetic cycling. Basically, genetic cycling involves using a mutating chemical that scrambles a tenth of a percent of your DNA into a new setting. So you drink some muck, and you essentially become a new person, one who is genetically dissimilar to your own family. Of course, organised crime caused a fantastic amount of damage with this tech, so it was banned and sealed away within months. It's now top-level illegal to have anything to do with genetic cycling."

"But a tenth of a percent doesn't sound like much."

Aslan ashed his smoke in Eulogy's hair.

"Yes, but remember that humans share ninety-eight percent of their genes with chimpanzees. Twisting a tenth of a percent makes an enormous difference. And I should know!" Aslan winked. "It hurt like hell, but it worked. My eyes changed colour, I grew two inches, my cowlicks shifted across my head, my teeth bent into different alignments, and I even acquired a taste for mineral water with a twist of lime. And as for my genitals..." Aslan paused mid-sentence. "Well, you'll find out the last part in time."

The penny finally dropped like a horse thief in a hangman's noose in the Wild West.

"Are you...are you me?" Tuesday gaped.

Aslan winked again.

"How old are you?" Tuesday asked.

"Three hundred and eighty-nine, and I still have a little longer to go." Aslan expanded his arms. "Really? That's what you want to know? Surely you have better things to ask! Try harder!"

Tuesday raised an index finger.

"Actually, there was something. When I first went through Jack Spasm's room, I found...things. Bad things. Is he...am I...will we be..."

Aslan's face darkened.

"Sadly, I cannot answer that particular question. In addition to numerous rounds of genetic cycling, from what I can tell I have chosen to deliberately and permanently excise substantial chunks of my own memory. Some of the shortest gaps were a single word from a conversation, while others have taken away the better part of three years." Aslan shrugged. "I honestly don't know if Jack Spasm was a person-skinning serial killer. But there's a chance that Spasm was from a different timeline to ours, and I sincerely hope that was the case."

Tuesday squinted a little.

"You lost me."

"Okay," Aslan stubbed out his cigarette on the biggest medal on Eulogy's shoulder. "To put it simply: time sucks. It follows no concrete logic. It isn't a river; it's a bitch queen from the deepest pits of hell who hates all things that make sense. It's beyond complicated. Even after many experiences of giving time itself a nipple cripple, there is no conceivable way that I can explain how it works. As impossible as time travel is, after you've managed to do it once it becomes far, far easier. You are...we are...unstuck in time. Remember when you woke up with that message burned into your arm? I still don't recall exactly what happened, but I do know that we lived a whole day at least twice, even though we don't remember it. Since then, time has developed an...an interest in us. But there are downsides. For instance, I've seen different versions of myself die on no fewer than fifteen occasions in all sorts of ways. My advice is simple: don't take it personally."

"Don't take it personally?" Tuesday asked incredulously.

"Now, I do have a glimmer of hope for your future, something that will keep you going through those many dark nights." Aslan leaned closer. "You already know that you aren't special. That you are nothing. That you are a bad joke God has played on the Universe. But your life is special. The things you see and experience, the places you go and the events that happen around you, will be unique." Aslan flicked his dead cigarette butt into Eulogy's pocket. "Finally, my last advice is this: even if you know about future events in advance, be sure to look appropriately surprised. It unnerves people, otherwise. It's common courtesy."

Aslan tapped his nose and pointed at the table full of smashed-up evidence.

"You might want to take your things with you. And lock the door behind you, please. This is going to take me a while."

And with that, Aslan's revelations were over.

*

"Miss? Can I take your tray?"

September looked up, startled, to see the agonised face of Jimmy Slummer blubbering down at her. The spherical chef seemed to be locked in a state of total awkwardness. He obviously wanted to carry out his duty of cleaning September's table, but he was too sad and introverted to do it without permission. There was a good chance he'd been there for several minutes, silently waiting to be acknowledged.

She looked down at the bowl of Pad See Ew noodles and chicken-flavoured cricket chunks, then back up at Jimmy. A glance over Jimmy's shoulder informed her that she was at Nourishing Noodles, one of the many food bars situated within a couple of levels of her deluxe cabin. For a couple of moments, she didn't know what to say.

September massaged her temples, using some of the relaxation techniques she'd learned during her time with the Chaotic-Neutral Wizards all those years ago. Sure, they didn't have any real magical abilities or anything, and everyone knew the Chaotic-Neutral Wizards were basically a thin splinter of Buddhism with a thick layer of fantasy fluff slathered on top, but that didn't mean their breathing exercises didn't work.

She didn't know what was wrong with her. For the last three days September seemed to have developed the irritating habit of occasionally losing touch with reality, of daydreaming when she should be solving the mysteries of the cosmos. Worse yet, after a long meditation yesterday September realised had that she seemed to have misplaced a serious chunk of her recent memories. As she had possessed total eidetic recall for as long as her brain had been capable of storing memories, it was like walking into a palatial library and noticing a huge charred gap in one of the shelves. Obviously, she hadn't told anybody about these issues, as the last thing she needed was for Sacks, Hemming and the other gits from the Dimensional Plotting Department to get the scent of any potential weaknesses they could exploit for their own gain. When it came to poor life choices, allowing her understudies to see an opportunity to have her removed from duty was roughly one step down from moisturising herself in barbecue sauce and jumping into the velociraptor pen down on floor ninety-three...

"Miss?"

"Hm?" September ummed. She blinked at Jimmy, then down at the cooling noodles, then back at Jimmy again. "Oh. Right. Thanks, James. They were nice. I think."

Glowing red, Jimmy swept up the bowl and vanished as fast as his flapping thongs would allow. September screwed her eyes shut and massaged her temples. Did she have a concussion or something? What was wrong with her? No matter how hard she concentrated, the last bit of conscious memory she'd managed to store before that tiny abyss was heading down to Tuesday's room to respond to his chemical injector running out of Hiver Queen neural gel. What had happened? Did she slip and hit her head? Surely she hadn't been insane enough to try some of his moonshine?

The Omni in September's hand vibrated and a cute little computer generated three-toed Sloth appeared on the back of her hand.

"Hiya, September! Just thought you'd like to know that somebody is secretly attempting to track your location. As you've arranged, I will block them until the firewall collapses in thirty-two seconds."

She went stiff at the news. As September was nobody's fool, she'd secretly hidden some powerful (and not altogether legal) hacks on her Omni before coming aboard The Frontier, just in case she needed them. Although not in the habit of breaking the law, it certainly didn't hurt to have precautions in place. This particular exploit was six hundred lines of vapourware that was programmed to automatically trigger if some high-ranking dolt decided that he or she was going to try and sneak up on one of the greatest minds of this age. After blocking the search function for as long as possible, the code would disappear into the ether without a single digit of evidence. September gave the little sloth avatar a scratch behind its fluffy grey skull, and it wiggled its flat face in ecstasy.

"Rank?"

The sloth's graphics glitched as it carried out a series of illegal hacks.

"Commander."

September wiped her mouth with a linen napkin, trying not to panic. So, Eulogy had finally caught up with her. Luckily, her illicit programs would allow her a bit of a head start.

"Distance?"

"Two floors, six corridors. Estimated time of arrival: two minutes, eight seconds."

"Misdirect him by one floor. Make it look like a navigation error in his Omni software."

Rubbing her face, September did some mental mathematics. She calculated the distance to her room, how fast she could walk there, and balanced several other variables, such as the very thin chance of her usual elevator being out of order. It went without saying that immediately sprinting for her room the moment that somebody started to track her location would look suspicious, so that wasn't an option. And another problem with bolting back to her room was that she would need to reach an incineration bin to dispose of all the evidence, and there weren't any of those on her plush level. After all, installing loud industrial cremation hatches that smelled like Vindaloo-scented demon farts would be a very efficient way of removing the "prime" adjective from "prime real estate" in one stroke. So, to reach a cremation bin, she'd have to power-walk to her room, hurry back into the elevator, and get to another floor. But once the firewall went down and she was being tracked, making a frenzied trip would only raise more questions and compound any accusations of guilt...

Then suddenly, September had the answer, an answer that would be otherwise useless to any other question ever posed by anyone anywhere. That answer was Jimmy Slummer.

The exact timespan between asking her Omni to illegally misdirect Eulogy and coming to a decision to utilise Jimmy in her naughtiness had taken less than two seconds. Most people would have trouble figuring out if they were about to sneeze in such a brief window. September raised her hand and hissed at the plastic flap that led back to the dish pig area behind Nourishing Noodles.

"James? I need your help with something."

CHAPTER TWENTY-ONE WELCOME BACK TO SQUARE ONE

Two months later, Tuesday's life had settled into a lonely, monotonous routine. He'd barely seen September and Jimmy for that entire span, let alone spoken with them. It had become pretty clear to Tuesday that they were doing their best to avoid him. Then again, Tuesday spent most of his time hiding and sleeping in secluded nooks around the ship, and whenever he emerged to pretend to work he was always rostered into The Frontier's yawning series of cargo bays on solo shifts. It was as though nobody wanted him around actual people for some reason...

Like all enormous long-range Unison starships, the warehouse decks took up a majority of The Frontier's mass and volume and were stocked to the rim with every conceivable item that may be useful in a new galaxy. These supplies were meant to last for the two decades this particular mission was scheduled to take (a decade there and a decade back), as well as enough to start up to a dozen permanent colonies. Such a huge scale meant that getting lost in these labyrinths was easy. If it wasn't for the voice-activated guidance systems that had been installed in every corridor, someone would have surely starved to death in here a long time ago.

For a perfectionist like Tuesday, pretending to work hard was almost as difficult as actually doing it. He was a master at looking busy, a consummate genius at appearing to be run off his feet. Although the automated warehouse decks were capable of taking care of themselves, during each shift Tuesday was expected to lay out a kilometre of wax to the shiny floor, dust a suburb of shelves, spend at least three hours checking vacuum seals on the countless boxes, shake ladders and forklifts every now and then to make sure they weren't going to fall apart, and finish off his day by thoroughly documenting everything he'd done during his eight hours of labour in fifteen minute blocks. Of course, Tuesday had performed absolutely none of these tasks even once, and he usually just spat a wad of chewing tobacco in the logbook rather than sign it.

Even Tuesday couldn't sleep all day, so he'd devised a few fun pastimes he could engage in between naps. What he got up to depended on where he was stationed for that shift. For instance, Tuesday loved trying on new shoes (you just can't beat the smell of pristine cricket-leather), so whenever he was posted into one of the many Footwear Levels the hours just flew by. By now, he'd also made filching little things from the restricted food and drinks stores marked as LUXURY ITEMS into a fine art. The trick was to skim off enough fine cheese or dinosaur sweetmeats to enjoy a mouthful, but not so much that somebody could tell that he'd shaved off a thin layer, then painstakingly reattaching the vacuum seal. Another hobby was destroying the tiny cleaning robots who were quickly making his job obsolete. His goal was to flatten the little scrubber domes to less than an inch high in one stomp, or it was a fail.

Out of everything that Tuesday enjoyed doing instead of actual work, Corridor Hockey was his favourite. It basically involved using his mop to whack urinal cakes across the heavily waxed floors at top speed, sending them skidding into assorted targets. Narrow ventilation slots were perfect for this game, as were the undersides of forklifts. He had to be careful, though, as one time he'd hit a yellow puck into a thermal exhaust port that led directly into the reactor core. If it had been a photon torpedo, the entire ship would have been blown into specks of fallout. Long story short, Tuesday decided to be more covert in his games, and that meant aiming for rodents instead.

As the weeks crawled by, something that Tuesday seemed to be dedicating more and more time to was thinking about was how pointless his life had become. Take his attempts with September, for instance. In truth, Tuesday knew that all of his romantic attempts with the beautiful dimensional plotter had gone straight off a cliff like a lemming who'd run out of antidepressants. She had tolerated him at one point, which meant that September was far more civil towards him than the other crew members, but that hadn't extended to an actual conversation for almost five and a half weeks. From what Tuesday could tell, the only reason September hadn't cut all contact with him was because Tuesday was on a first name basis with the Fleet Admiral, and she was doing her best to figure out why. After all, September loved mysteries: she loved the shattering noise they made when she glanced at them. Unfortunately, a mystery wasn't enough to make him friendship material, let alone a lover.

So, eight weeks after a trial that had apparently never taken place, Tuesday was busy slamming urinal cakes at the rats on the Camembert Level of the cargo bay when one of them swore at him in very clear Unglish. In fact, the cursing rodent seemed to be able to shape his words better than most humans. Tuesday was so surprised by this turn of events that he froze for a second, and that was enough time for the rat to slide into a crack between sealed boxes of soft cheese. Of course, Tuesday was in pursuit a moment later.

Following the little critter at top speed as it raced between pallets, jumping from pile to pile and moving faster than Tuesday could comfortably keep up with for long, the rodent eventually tripped, hit its head on a SLIPPERY WHEN WET sign, and almost knocked itself out. Tuesday was on the rodent in a second with the sponge end of his very clean mop and, without a pause, scooped the bugger up and zipped it into the huge belly pocket of his orange coveralls, where it struggled ferociously.

"Feg off!" the rat snarled, its words muffled.

"Not gonna eatcha," Tuesday soothed, zipping the slot. "Just gonna figure out how it is you're talkin'."

Taking his prize to the nearest turbolift, Tuesday realised that his shift wasn't over yet. Shrugging, he considered the consequences for less than a second before disregarding them. After all, he had friends in high places.

Travelling up to the bridge of the ship, where the old Fleet Admiral was asleep at the helm, his papery skin relaxed and almost wrinkle free for once, Tuesday reluctantly woke Aslan and pointed at the wriggling lump in his pocket. Sighing toothlessly, the Fleet Admiral jammed his falsies back in and waved his younger version towards the exit.

"I'm not here to answer every minor question you have about the future, Tuesday. Go ask somebody else. And try to be more convincing when you pretend to work! I've had to cancel fifteen complaints against you just this morning. I'm not made of ink."

Tuesday nodded sadly and left without bothering the Fleet Admiral any further.

He couldn't even stand his own company. It was depressing, to say the least.

Tuesday's next logical stop was the Department of Dimensional Plotting. As Tuesday walked into this space for the first time in a month he saw that September was so busy with her work that she was using both hands as well as her mouth to wrangle the red dimensional plotting arcs into a precise maze of threads. It looked like she was playing a game of three-dimensional twist-up against herself.

Tuesday heard a squeak and looked down at September's hamster, Mister Boodle. The sweating rodent had just finished off a long run on his wheel, and he nodded up at Tuesday in polite recognition. Tuesday cocked his head in confusion at how human that gesture had been, but he decided not to worry about Mister Boodle for now.

"What?" September snapped, tying together no fewer than seventeen red lines at once. They all turned green with a cheerful chirping noise. "Don't bother me when I'm working, Robert. I'm trying to prevent the ship from getting spread across dimensions like so much smooth peanut butter, and to do that I need to concentrate. And you're meant to be working, as well! Go away."

"This is important, Sep."

"Don't call me Sep. My mother called me that."

"Okay, then – September. This is important."

Tuesday opened his pocket and the filthy cargo rat instantly leaped for the door. Tuesday's mop whipped down, smacked the creature into the air like a urinal cake hockey puck, and he effortlessly caught it one-handed. Tuesday quickly swapped the biting rat with the fluffy bundle of cuteness known as Mister Boodle, locked the plastic lid of the hutch, and flourished his hand at the nasty black creature.

"See?" Tuesday smiled. "What do you think?"

There was a pause for five long seconds. September looked at the rat, then back at Tuesday, then back at the rat again. She fixed Tuesday with an unimpressed snarl.

"Have you been drinking, Robert?"

"Duh. But you've got to check this out anyway. Watch."

Tuesday whacked the cage. The rat startled, but immediately went back to silently twitching its nose and looking for a way out. Suddenly, the rat stopped moving, tensed its entire body, closed one eye, and defecated so explosively that the entire cage was spattered with faecal matter. September turned red in apoplectic rage.

"Get that thing out of here!"

"Fing!" the rat said in affront. "I'll give you fing, rotten humie!"

September paused with her mouth open, still pointing at the verbose rat. She moved her lips a little bit and stopped again. She finally managed a few more words.

"Did that rat just speak?"

The rat sighed and looked annoyed.

"What, just because I'm a rat I'm not allowed to speak? Typical racist human scum..."

September thought about this for a moment. Shaking her head was the extent of what she could manage for now. Wondering whether she was going utterly insane, September slowly approached the cage until her nose was an inch from the plastic. The rat bared its teeth and raised the middle digit of a rear leg, clearly flipping her the bird.

"So what's with the talking?" Tuesday asked bluntly.

September shrugged. "Maybe it's a mutant. Or an escaped genetic experiment. Or perhaps somebody accidentally swapped their personality with it."

Mister Boodle opened one eye, looking as guilty as a hamster could manage, but in a matter of moments he fell asleep in Tuesday's arms and began to snore gently.

September held her forehead. She thought deeply, and the galaxy moved.

"Look: there are no scars, or track marks. This rat is surgically untouched. And I very much doubt it's a mutant, as rats aren't due to become this intelligent until just before we blow up the galaxy in half a million years."

"Plenty more galaxies where that came from," Tuesday shrugged. "So now we know what didn't happen, what did happen?"

"You could consider asking me," the rat suggested.

September looked at the black mass of mange and yellow teeth.

"Ask for biology advice from a rat? Are you serious? Do you even have a name?"

"Of course I have a name!" The rat looked insulted. "Nibble-Nibble-Squeak-Squeak, actually. Nibble for short. Though admittedly, my full name is far more poetic when you say it in ratspeak. Go on. Arsk."

"Okay," Tuesday said, cracking his knuckles noisily. "Then talk, Nibble. Tell us what we want to know, and there's a good chance we'll let you out of here with all four feet still attached."

The rat shrugged.

"All right, then. Deal. Well, it all started after I'd finished eating a huge cockroach one morning. See, this particular roach didn't go down so well, as it was far too salty and had too much yellow stuff in it. So I went to the drain closest to my nest for a drink. I smelled something...weird in the water, though. I thought nothing of it, as every sewage outlet on the ship has a broad spectrum of tastes, but then the strangest thing happened: I started to think stuff that was more complex than food-sex food-sex food-sex food-sex, run run run run run...stop."

"Is that what rats usually think?" Tuesday asked.

"Sort of. It's a lot more profound when you're a rat."

"I bet."

"So anyway, within days I'd really started to work things out. For instance, I figured that if I found a way to collect my food in a more efficient way - perhaps by farming it – it would make my life easier. Just as I'd decided to start breeding roaches in little enclosures so I could trade them for things with other rats, I tripped over my own clumsy paws and swore out loud for the very first time. I'm telling you, I spent the next ten minutes screaming profanities just because I could."

"Sewage outlet?" September interrupted.

"About sixty metres under where this diphead kidnapped me, near the water treatment plant. You know, the one just to the left of the urine recyc and faecal conversion tanks?"

September scanned the rat from whiskers to tail with her Omni implant. The rice-sized device in the web of her hand was equipped with all sorts of diagnostic equipment, and it only took a few seconds to get concrete results. September gaped at the lightscreen projection.

"Robert, my Omni says that this rat is loaded with the same learning and recall chemicals that I was feeding into your brain through that chemical injector. Maybe they weren't careful enough when they disposed of the injector, and it ended up in a toilet somehow?"

"They burned the injector in an incinerator bin. I asked." Tuesday grunted.

September looked down at the rat, who was nosily trying to pass wind without success.

"Nibble, how many other rats drink from that particular source?"

The rat shrugged. "A hundred and fifty, maybe two hundred thousand."

September and Tuesday looked blankly at each other.

"Oh dear."

"And that's not counting mice, pigeons, snakes..."

"I get the idea," Tuesday snapped. He went pale as his brain caught up with his ears. "Wait...snakes? There's snakes on the ship?"

"Just a family of boa constrictors. They don't eat much. Escaped from one of the research departments. Really pleasant neighbours, as long as it isn't a Friday."

Tuesday looked nervously about the Department of Dimensional Plotting, checking if there were any creepy-crawly reptiles sneaking up on him. Every shadow now held the promise of a bone-snapping death. He casually stepped away from the nearest ventilation grille and decided that things were getting far too complicated for his tastes.

"Time out! Look, September, I say we let Jimmy fry this sucker and call it a day. As I'm currently living on precisely two percent of my garnished wages, this is so far above my paygrade that it isn't even in the same solar system."

"Jimmy?" September repeated.

She froze, a look of total horror on her face. Without another word September picked up the cage by its carry handle and rushed out of the automated door. Sighing, Tuesday shadowed her all the way down the corridor, trying to think of some way to stop her from making this rotten day even more complicated and difficult than it already was.

"What are you doing?" Tuesday whined. "Where are we going?"

He squeezed into the same turbolift as September just before it sealed, but she was so distracted that she didn't so much as acknowledge the question.

The look on her face clearly meant it was all bad news.

Like anybody who wanted to head to Alpha Deck, September and Tuesday made a dangerous ten-second trip alongside the thrumming radioactivity of the white-hot engines. Within moments they stepped onto the trashed level where Tuesday, Jimmy and all the other clinical defectives lived. Marching away from

Tuesday without giving away a single clue, September burst into Jimmy Slummer's room. Frightening the fat man so badly that he almost fell off his concave bed, September started firing off questions before Jimmy's chest pains had a chance to fade.

"You, Slummer. What did you do with the Queen?"

"Queen?" Tuesday said in surprise.

"Queen?" Jimmy squealed.

September gripped Jimmy under his third chin and slammed him into the wall. Tuesday had no idea that September was capable of such violence.

"I gave you very simple instructions, James. You were to go down three levels, place the little lead box in the nearest incineration bin, and cremate it twice on the top setting, just to be sure. You were to keep it at arm's length at all times, and you certainly weren't meant to look inside of it. A grass parakeet could have understood such a simple message."

"Cremate what?" Tuesday complained, feeling left out.

"What did you do with the box?!" September roared, spittle flying.

"I was going to cremate it! I promise!" Jimmy blubbered. "But just before I put it in the bin, it suddenly seemed like a really really good idea to rattle it next to my ear, just to see what was inside...and then it felt like an even better idea to go back to my room and have a look inside of the box..."

September looked like she was about to fall down. Somehow she managed to hit Jimmy's bent bed, rather than the floor. She swallowed, crunching her eyes shut as hard as she could manage. She looked nauseous.

Her next words were almost impossible to hear.

"James, did you open the box?"

Jimmy faltered. He eventually squeezed out one more word without sobbing.

"Yes."

September's face darkened.

"And?"

Jimmy's face pinched into a spiral of pain.

"It...it jumped into the toilet, miss."

Tuesday had to move really quickly to prevent September from kicking Jimmy's arse into a mountain of bruises. It took almost five seconds until September had managed to regain control over her rage. A few Alpha Deckers peeked into Jimmy's room, hoping to see a fight.

"Can somebody explain to me what is happening?"Tuesday demanded, finally letting go of September.

She bared her teeth at the fat chef. He unintentionally took a step away from the dangerous expression.

"Two months ago, I asked James to do one thing: to destroy the box containing the Hiver Queen I'd stolen from Eulogy. As James has the IQ of bread mould and the self-control of a rabbit jacked full of erection medication, it seems that the Queen was able to exert enough control to make him think it was a good idea to place the lead box close to his head. At such a short distance the Queen was obviously able to dominate him and coerce him into opening her little prison. As he's a total simpleton, James believed that these thoughts were his own, and so he followed them. Of course, the Queen then immediately escaped into the toilet. Correct?"

"Maybe she drowned?" Jimmy suggested quietly.

"Hivers are aquatic." September said in the same tone you'd use to explain to a thick child for the twentieth time that weeing on top of a closed toilet lid wasn't the correct way to go potty. She seemed too drained to be angry anymore. "They thrive in almost any liquid, especially water."

September gestured towards Nibble.

"The Queen has obviously laid eggs in the sewage outlet, and when Nibble had a drink he must have consumed at least one of them. As soon as the egg registered it was inside a viable host it would have hatched and promptly crawled all the way into Nibble's head so it could latch onto his brainstem. Within a matter of hours, as you can see, Nibble experienced a substantial increase in intelligence levels." September gave a defeated wave towards the rat. "There's no way he's the only one. There could be thousands. Hundreds of thousands. More."

"But why would the Hiver Queen want to make rats smarter? What's in it for her?" Jimmy asked. "Is it because she's nice?"

September sighed at the idiocy.

"Because it is a necessary component to creating a full-sized Hive. First, the Queen invades hosts with her offspring, then she improves the hosts in all sorts of ways, then when the time is right she can use them for whatever she wants. Generally, the first thing she'll do is kill off anything that may pose a risk to her Hive." September was lost for words for a moment, but then her expression changed. "I doubt she managed to recruit any humans as hosts, though. The water purification process would kill off her eggs before they could reach any people. The crew may be safe from direct domination for now."

Tuesday knelt down in front of September. He gently took her hands.

"How much danger are we in?" Tuesday asked. "Should we contact somebody? Warn them? We have a small army on board, right?"

September managed to make eye contact for a second, but then she looked away again.

"The Unison has flamed entire worlds over much smaller infestations. It may already be too late for any of us."

There was a horrible screaming and thumping from the corridor outside of Jimmy's personal pigsty. As all the hallways of Alpha Deck were insulated by garbage and there were no fewer than three different torture metal albums pumping from nearby rooms, this wailing was truly noteworthy. Rushing out of the door, September, Tuesday and Jimmy came across an Alpha Deck janitor in orange coveralls appearing to have a fit. The guy was thrashing about, holding his head and making a high-pitched noise. September reached down to comfort him, trying to shush him, but the janitor just kept screeching the same note. Finally, five seconds later, he stopped dead. A crowd of crew members of minimal to zero operational value gathered around the cooling body, getting a good look at the corpse. Now that the janitor was still, everyone could clearly see that blood was pouring from his right ear and both eye sockets for some unknown reason. As far as anyone could tell, beyond the crimson leakage he was otherwise uninjured.

A Unison solider – one of the many military grunts who "just happened" to lurk around Alpha Deck in riot gear – stormed up, barking orders. Dressed in plate armour and flash-resistant shades and armed with a stun wand, the soldier held out one hand to keep people back from the body and raised his humming weapon just enough to make it clear he wasn't here to make friends.

"Right, who saw what happened? Who did this? I want answers!"

Within twenty seconds, that soldier was just as dead as the janitor. This time everyone got a pretty good look at the entire process: as though it had springs for legs, a mouse the size of a large peanut burst out of a scalp-high vent like a furry dart and went straight into the soldier's left ear. Shrieking, the grunt began pounding the side of his own head, roaring and waving about. Understandably, the entire crowd scattered to the far corners of Alpha Deck, doing their best to avoid whatever the hell was happening. Within a few heartbeats, September, Jimmy, Tuesday and Generic Corpse One and Generic Corpse Two were the only humans left.

Shouting voices and gunfire echoed from what sounded like a few corridors away. Suddenly, a shipwide alarm began to screech like a parrot that had just been kicked right in the cloaca. September paused, listening, as though she understood the klaxons.

"All crew of exceptional operational value and above are to evacuate to our designated safe areas," September breathed, the only one of their group that could translate the tone. "I need to go."

Neither of the men asked questions. This was clearly a get-the-heck-out-of-here-and-talk-later kind of event. Running for the turbolift, none of them actually heard Nibble-Nibble-Squeak-Squeak the rat laughing evilly from Mister Boodle's abandoned cage, cackling at their distress. With his cruel red eyes flashing, his words went unheard.

What he said was: "Now you'll get it."

All three survivors sprinted into the turbolift just before its door sealed with a hiss. Safely stashed in the capsule, September swiped her hand at a floating holographic display and their pod shot off at the speed of sound. Unlike the cargo elevator that Tuesday had used to illegally stowaway aboard The Frontier in the first place, this internal turbolift was equipped with heavy gravity buffers to cushion their ride, meaning that they were able to fly along the spine of the ship without any discomfort.

Tuesday relaxed against the wall, stupidly thinking he was safe, and looked up at the transparent ceiling of the capsule. On the other side of the see-through roof slab a mass of rats were furiously gnawing through some sort of device the size of a shoebox. However, Tuesday didn't have any way of getting at them. Following Tuesday's line of sight, Jimmy looked up at the ceiling and made a choking noise.

Tuesday gave September a nudge.

"Uh, what are they chewing on?"

September blinked at the roof. Her expression fell.

"That is a turbolift stability module, invented by an engineer called Rolf Grinwald over three centuries ago. It's still the best model of its kind and is installed on every starship belonging to The Unison as standard."

Tuesday swallowed. Although he knew better, he had to ask.

"And, uh, what happens when they finish chewing through it?"

September sighed.

"The gravity settings will go mental, and we'll find out first-hand what it's like to be inside a pinball machine."

The stability module snapped away just as September finished shaping her last word, and Tuesday didn't even have time to swear as the turbolift suddenly flipped over in its tube, spinning violently in random directions. All three passengers were thrown about like small change in a tumble dryer, slamming into the walls and each other. They were a mass of bruises in seconds, and Tuesday was sure that he was already missing several teeth. However badly the capsule was twirling about in the gravity shaft, though, the turbolift pod still made it all the way to the designated floor. Instead of coming to a gentle stop, though, their turbolift crashed straight through the magnetic seal, tumbled down a corridor in a spectacular fashion, and came to rest against the first Slurko Cola vending machine it touched. Little fires burst to life from dozens of ruined circuit boards, and a pall of smoke rose from the wreckage.

Everything was still for five seconds.

Tuesday was the first one to regain consciousness. Dazed from the spinning and the crash, it took him a couple of seconds to realise that he was lying on top of September. Luckily, they were both on top of the considerable girth of Jimmy Slummer, and it seemed as though Jimmy's spherical body had served as a living crash mat for the other two survivors. It was hard to say, but this may have made all the difference between life and splat. Although badly tenderised and cross-eyed, Jimmy looked at Tuesday's ears and summoned the best comment he could manage.

"Eek?"

Ignoring the chef, Tuesday began to heroically drag September free of the wreckage by her shoulder. It took a good six metres until he realised that something was wrong: he hadn't saved all of her. September's left leg was missing at the knee.

"I'll get it," Tuesday offered helpfully, concussed.

September just sat there, looking brain-dead. Shock had provided her with one of nature's greatest anaesthetics.

Wrestling September's limb free of the twisted ruins of the turbolift, Tuesday staggered back towards the female genius. As he'd just survived the equivalent of a high-speed crash, Tuesday was running a little bit sideways. Just as he came back within touching distance of September, a mouse picked this moment to drop out of a roof panel and head straight for her right eye. Reacting with instincts that had been burned into his nervous system since childhood, Tuesday instantly swung September's leg like a golf club and whacked the rodent so hard that it splattered against a Red Vee advertising panel like a raw egg. Unfortunately, his swing went a little bit too wide and he accidentally kicked September right in the face with the toe of her own booted foot.

"Ah." Tuesday pulled an embarrassed face. "Sorry."

A distant rumbling soon transitioned to the recognisable sounds of gunfire and shouts. This maelstrom steadily amplified around the corner until September, Tuesday, Jimmy and Mister Boodle found themselves face-to-face with an entire squad of hardened Unison marines. Despite being fully armed and armoured, the grunts seemed to be performing a steady tactical retreat, also known as "running for their lives." They fired over their shoulders occasionally, hitting nothing but walls, and bellowed at the motley crew.

"Move, people!"

"What is it?" Jimmy asked in a dazed way, trying to wobble his way out of the turbolift ruins.

Tuesday took two steps forward and smacked Jimmy sharply in the back of the head. "You never ask questions like that! You know why? Because you might find out, you twit!"

A dark, roiling wave crashed around the corner and swelled towards them. Rather than consisting of water, foam and salt, this particular wave was made up of five thousand ill-tempered rats with beady red eyes, jet black fur and sharp, yellowing teeth. Despite setting their weapons on full-auto, the marines barely made a dent in the horde before it crashed down on them with amazing force. Managing to come to his senses far too late, by the time Jimmy turned towards Tuesday and September they were already halfway down the next corridor. Sure, Tuesday was carrying September on his back, but they weren't mucking around.

Before he could manage to waddle all the way up to his lame top speed, Jimmy disappeared into the dark sea of claws and fangs. The wave finally moved on from the feast about twenty seconds later, sated with his bountiful flesh, leaving behind nothing more than a very large pink skeleton.

Jimmy wasn't lying: he really was big boned.

Piggybacking September down the hallway, trying not to glance back at the horror that was still pursuing them, Tuesday was just about ready to give up when September slid off his shoulders and started hopping alongside him. Dead ahead was the sort of enormous door you'd expect on a bank vault or a fallout shelter, and it was slowly swinging closed.

"There!" September barked.

Tuesday and September lunged through the tight gap between the four-foot-thick slab and its frame, knowing that the open corridor was about to become certain death. As they tumbled to the shagpile floor, rolling, the impenetrable vault slammed shut behind them like a Catholic front door when the Scientologists came knocking. A dozen further layers of security scissored shut over the dense portal.

Before he had a chance to feel relieved though, Tuesday looked up from the floor to see an entire battery of high-tech weapons humming aggressively right next to his head. Tuesday froze at the sight of a bedraggled crowd of superior officers and lead scientists pointing kinetic rifles, carbines and spacer pistols at him. As it took half a second for the armed crew members to figure out that September wasn't a rodent (it took considerably longer to assess Tuesday), she was quickly dragged to her feet by the bruised and bleeding survivors of the rat mutiny. Only a single person bothered helping Tuesday to his feet: the old Fleet Admiral. Pulling his younger version upright with the natural creaks of a veteran skeleton, Aslan shook his head grimly at Tuesday.

"It's like every stupid creature on the ship has lost its mind."

"Or found their minds," September managed weakly, not quite making sense.

Supported by kind hands, September hopped over to a standard-issue auto-surgeon box in the corner of the room and allowed it to inspect her dismembered leg. She moaned as the initial shock picked this moment to finally wear off, and the machine readied itself to knit flesh and bone back together. The microscopic sewing apparatus on the auto-surgeon made a low, uncomfortable buzz as it reassembled nerves and blood vessels.

Aslan indicated a comfy black lounge to Tuesday.

"We're safe here for now," Aslan sighed, collapsing into the plush cricket leather. He gestured around the room, which was a simple cube about forty metres on a side. Besides the lounges, it was sparse. "This is just one of many panic bunkers spread throughout The Frontier. It operates as a completely intact system made from unbreakable ceramics, so now that it's sealed nothing can get in and nothing can get out without my say-so. We have enough supplies to last indefinitely, and the room can transform to become whatever we need it to be: we have hundreds of recreation options, deluxe sleeping berths, a six Michelin star meal hall, you name it."

The thick vault door, which was designed to withstand explosions, siege weapons and even the vacuum itself, made a faint THOOM noise as a literal ton of rats worked in synchronisation to bludgeon it down from the other side. Everyone relaxed as the door remained exactly the same. There were even a few relieved laughs here and there.

There was a familiar whispering noise that stabbed ice into Tuesday's belly. It swept around the bunker, chittering just below comprehension. It was undoubtedly the same whispering he'd heard during his jaunt into the near future. The murmurs grew louder, swelling into clear hissing words, as though thousands and thousands of tiny voices were all contributing to the declaration.

"Two choices," the tens of thousands of whispers hissed, "Join us, or feed us. There is no third option. You have one minute to decide."

The whispers became laughter, and then shrank to nothing. Everyone was silent for a good ten seconds.

"They can't possibly have forced their way in here," the Head of Space-Time finally moaned, looking around at the many ventilation ducts. "This is a sealed system. It's literally impossible to break into! No weapon known to mankind could have compromised our armour, let alone a bunch of tunnelling rats..."

"Did anybody actually check to see if the vents were clear before we sealed ourselves in?" September asked. "Who confirmed that the ventilation system was clear?"

Everybody exchanged glances. When nobody put their hand up, Aslan tapped away at his Omni implant for a couple of seconds and broke the silence with an enthusiastic Guttertongue curse.

"The entire bunker is infested," Aslan announced in a more cordial manner. "Our ventilation system is so choked with rats that we haven't got enough ammunition to make so much as a dent in their numbers. And let's not forget that our only way out is rodent central."

"Is there another exit?" Tuesday whispered at the Fleet Admiral. "Surely we survive this?"

Aslan shrugged. "Maybe. My memory isn't what it used to be. But for some reason I don't remember any of this happening...so it shouldn't be happening, right? Or maybe one of us somehow manages to fix all of this before we reach this point..."

"Your time has concluded," the whispers announced.

"Form a line!" one of the Commanders roared, activating his kinetic rifle.

Every vent in the bunker bent savagely and started to snap, spitting rivets and caulk all over the shagpile carpet. Mice and large insects poured through in the dozens and were instantly liquefied with a few low-level blasts. Stun rounds proved effective against such weak targets, as did simply stomping them with boot heels. Eventually, though, the tide of vermin became too thick, and all of the shooters were all forced to reload and scrabble towards the back of the room.

Of course, as soon as vents began to pop Tuesday had immediately pushed through the masses of armed people in royal purple uniforms and cowered next to September in a safer spot. He had no weapons of any kind, so standing on the firing line was a stupid idea, and he'd only get in the way. As usual, his cowardice was also common sense.

"See, I've got a plan," Tuesday murmured to September, huddling next to her in the very rear of the not-so-safe room. "We let these meatbags get chewed up first, the rats get too full, then there's no room to fit the two of us in their bellies..."

Despite the fact September was still getting stitched up by the auto-surgeon, she acknowledged Tuesday with a wry smile. By now she should have known he wasn't joking.

"Surely, Robert, you know this is game over? The only way we're leaving is in ten thousand bite-sized pieces in ten thousand different bellies."

"Maybe," Tuesday said gently.

He reached out to touch September's sleek, black hair just as the wave of vermin reached an epic level. Now three feet high and thickening fast, the swamp of furry and chitinous bodies pressed in towards the juicy humans. Tuesday watched in horror as the old Fleet Admiral was consumed as he bravely waded in to save the first casualty. One moment Aslan was there, and the next his pink bones were being gnawed down to the marrow, his gun falling from fingerless, dead hands. The Fleet Admiral had just enough time to mouth a few words at Tuesday before vanishing into a multitude of digestive systems.

"What did he say to you?" September yelled over the noise, unable to understand the Fleet Admiral's last statement over the scrabbling and screaming.

"He said not to take this personally," Tuesday moaned.

But Tuesday couldn't help it: he'd taken it personally.

Looking up above September's head, Tuesday noticed with glee that a row of large cabinets labelled with stencils declaring DEHYDRATED WATER and HYGIENE PRODUCTS and SUICIDE PILLS also included one labelled POWER SOURCES. Producing a pile of busted and burnt electronics from one of his sticky pockets, Tuesday quickly rifled through the POWER SOURCES shelves, raided two Triple-A Nuclear batteries, and did his level best to fix the mess of circuit boards.

Of course, he got absolutely nowhere.

"Can you make this thing work again?" Tuesday demanded.

September looked down at the broken time machine. Her face didn't show any signs of recognition.

"What is it?"

Tuesday smacked his head into the wall.

"We don't have time for this! Can you fix it?"

September bared her teeth in annoyance.

"I don't even know what it is. How am I meant to fix it?"

Although most experts would agree that trying to fix a half-busted time machine with no tools and zero training could be a bad idea unless you were hoping to Ouroboros the entire timestream up its own backside, Tuesday had no choice but to chance it. So while he couldn't even name half of the components in the little slab, it was the only hope he had left. Call it optimistic or call it delusional, but he had to at least try.

After a good five seconds of whacking the device on the deck without any luck, Tuesday's next repair attempt was to randomly connect the burnt components together with strands of dirty chewing gum from the bottom of his boot. It still wasn't working as the second line of purple-uniformed officers disappeared into the ravenous rats, never to be seen again. Eight seconds later, an entire wall panel exploded behind September in a hurricane of black fur and scissoring, dirty teeth, and just like that she was gone. It took less than two seconds for her to completely vanish, and she only had enough time to say five words before becoming a part of the deadly swell. For the first time in her life, she looked confused.

"Why do you love me?"

Tuesday's clumsy hands were still furiously working the hardware when a big, black mongrel jumped forwards as a vanguard of his demise. Just as a mouthful of jagged teeth surrounded Tuesday's nose the busted Flamingo Smartphone decided to flare up in a burst of light and colour. Electricity arced across the walls, streaking about as bolts of lightning, and Tuesday was gone.

CHAPTER TWENTY-TWO YOU ONLY LIVE THRICE

Within an almost-bare loft situated on the desirable crossroads of Fifth & Pringle, Ernest Fell was glaring knives from behind his marble desk. On the far side of the large space, beyond an extremely nervous gangland gofer and the unbreakable lump of muscle known as Jeeves Butler, respectively, was a sweeping balcony made from woven platinum. Deeper through the sprawl of cream starscrapers that made up most of the world of Seven Suns, a five-kilometre slab of pure white descended from the heavens and hovered in mid-air like an 8-bit cloud in an ancient video game. Despite its distance, you could clearly see that FRONTIER was embossed on its hull in gold.

Leaning forwards, his eyes narrowed to hateful slits at the nameless underworld delivery person, Ernest hissed his next words.

"Explain that to me again."

On the phone, the young gangster's voice had been crystal-clear with enthusiasm about making this successful delivery. After all, it didn't get much more prestigious than doing something for Mister Fell, even when the crime lord's reputation had been in freefall for weeks. Now that the delivery guy was actually here in person at one of Ernest's many safehouses, the poor schmuck looked as though he was seriously considering fleeing the planet to become a soybean farmer on the most distant dirtball in the galaxy.

"I..." the delivery guy ummed. "I..."

A tiger-like growl sounded from behind him. The gangster turned his head just enough to glance at Jeeves. The mountainous thug was deliberately standing in shadow, but his silhouette was edged with light from a sweeping paper-thin television display wall.

"Mister Fell asked you to do something."

The gangster finally pulled himself together and faced Ernest again.

"Like I said, we found the target, Jim Tuesday, tripping with a New New Age tribe a few systems across the galactic plane. The target reacted to us calling his name, but he didn't try to run or offer any resistance. Reckon he was too stoned to walk."

"Not that part." Ernest snapped. "The next part. I want you to repeat the next part."

"The DNA tests confirmed he was a perfect match," the gangster stressed. "Admittedly, yes, at a glance there may appear to be a bit of a difference to the file picture, Mister Fell, but..."

Ernest rocketed out of his chair like a baking soda missile.

"There may appear to be a bit of a difference?!" Ernest screamed, slamming his fists into the marble desk so hard that he almost broke his pinkies. He pointed at the other side of the loft. "You think that is a bit of a difference?!"

Jeeves casually moved his two-hundred-kilogram frame out of the way of Ernest's pointing finger. The sidestep revealed an interesting creature on the other side of the office: it was a mass of dozens of eyeballs joined together by a dense tangle of what appeared to be a cross between optical nerves and tentacles. Each of the pupils were darting about the safehouse independently. As soon as it realised everyone was looking at it, the creature's beaked mouth opened into three triangular sections to reveal two sharp, prehensile blue tongues. The tongues waved politely, and it made a noise you'd expect to hear from a very drunk Swedish person.

Although everybody in the safehouse was currently distracted by life-or-death matters, the big lightscreen behind Jeeves automatically divided itself to show all fifteen news channels. Every segment had BREAKING NEWS flashing across them. Each square showed a different reporter, but they were all standing outside of the exact same Spaceport at slightly different angles and were delivering an identical scoop.

"...when an unknown madman somehow managed to break the military cordon before leading armed pursuers on a merry chase through the pallets of supplies..."

"...amazingly, the intruder stowed away on a cargo-grade gravity lift, which theoretically should have smashed his bones into jelly within..."

"...of course, the launch of The Frontier will have to be delayed until the stowaway is found and removed by..."

"...local government officials are refusing to confirm whether the stowaway was actually Binary Star recipient Bob Tuesday..."

Jeeves glanced over his shoulder towards the television, his ears prickling. He lost his train of thought when Ernest slammed his fist onto the marble desk again.

"Hey!" Ernest snapped. "You can watch the box on your own time, Lurch."

"Sorry, Mister Fell." Jeeves apologised, stiffening. "I thought it said..."

Ernest gave a curt wave. It was the "shut up and get ready to mop a large volume of human blood off the tiles" motion he used all the time. His eyes flicked back towards the delivery guy, who had lost all colour by this point. Ernest raised a finger, as though deep in thought.

"I need you to help me with something. Do you know the confidential MedTek arcade over on Rushmore & Pringle? The one that takes Amerikan pounds as well as German yen?"

The gangster looked relieved. A chance to make up for his mistake!

"I do, Mister Fell!"

Ernest placed his hand on the gangster's shoulder.

"Good."

In one smooth motion Ernest snatched an antique letter opener off his desk and stabbed the delivery guy right in the liver. The gofer's shocked eyes opened so wide that they were mostly just white, and he curled up like a hunchback. Somehow, he didn't collapse. Ernest extracted the improvised weapon, wiped it on the delivery guy's shirt, and patted him on the back.

"If you hurry, you might just get there before you bleed out."

Ernest ignored the delivery guy as he staggered out, leaking and moaning pitifully, and slammed into his comfy chair. Jeeves was already reaching to turn on the MopBot in the corner.

"Will these damned Tuesdays ever stop infuriating me?"

Ernest got his answer before he'd finished speaking: a tear in the space-time continuum opened up less than five metres from his head, and Bob Tuesday tumbled out. As Tuesday had been sitting perfectly still when the Flamingo Smartphone time machine had flared twelve weeks into the future, he dropped straight down and crashed mouth-first into the tiles. As more than five dozen hive-minded ship rats had been leaping through the air at top speed when they were gathered by the chronological rip, their arc sent them ploughing straight into Ernest. They hit the crime lord so hard that he was knocked from his chair and skidded across the floor, and by the time he realised what was going on he'd already been nibbled to death.

Tuesday rolled over on the tiles, muttering curses, and the defective Flamingo Smartphone crackled to ruin beneath his body. The temporal rip instantly sealed, and all of the hived rats immediately collapsed in perfect synchronisation, bleeding from their ears, nostrils, eyes and mouths. If Tuesday was a smarter man he might have known that this was because they'd been cut off from the Hiver Queen, who was still residing in the future. As it was, he was too busy being concussed.

Groaning, Tuesday managed to get up. Unfortunately, Jeeves was standing there with an accelerator pistol clenched in a massive hand. For almost ten seconds, they stood there like statues. Finally, Jeeves spoke.

"You know, your family has been bad news since day one. Irritating. Annoying. Embarrassing. And you know what?"

Jeeves gripped the side of his accelerator pistol and popped out its antimatter battery slab. Tuesday could clearly see a one-gram sphere of antimatter bobbing about inside of the vacuum clip. Jeeves slapped the two separated components on Ernest's desk.

"I'm out."

Tuesday squinted.

"I...what?"

Jeeves began to strip. Once his Seladorian jacket was off, the ceramic combat vest came next. It clunked loudly on the tiles.

"Tuesday, you just used a horde of teleporting suicide attack rats to kill one of the most dangerous men alive. My limit has been reached. I'm out."

"Well, technically, they were time-travelling suicide attack rats..."

Jeeves just stared for a few seconds.

"Yeah, that's a lot less terrifying, thanks." Jeeves detached a multitude of chemically sharpened knives that had been hidden all over his considerable person. He dropped them onto the ceramic vest one by one. "Anyway, my service contract was for the duration of Mister Fell's life. That life is now over. As my hypnotic conditioning requires, I am to report back to the Nevada Desert facility for reassignment. I suggest you stay away from any of my future employers." Jeeves made eye contact with Tuesday. "I was hypnotically conditioned to obey Mister Fell at all times. I am in no way responsible for anything I have ever done to you or your family."

And with that semi-apology, Jeeves was gone for good.

Turning away from the open door, trying to understand why he was still alive, Tuesday finally noticed the mass of eyeballs slumped in the corner. Blinky, or whatever its real name was, gestured for Tuesday to come closer with a waving blue tongue, and it said a simple phrase in Unglish that rocked him to the core. Tuesday was in such shock that he was unable to believe what he had just heard, and, with a sigh, the freak was forced to repeat itself.

"Where's my lighter?" the mass of eyeballs croaked.

Tuesday crossed the loft slowly, one gradual step at a time, and he produced a well-worn and well-travelled gas lighter in a shaking hand. Cheered by the look of recognition in those darting, alien eyes, Tuesday was suddenly treated to an unexpected spectacle: the creature quivered violently, and four hundred eyeballs began to separate from its stalked frame with quiet pops. The orbs bounced around a bit before dissolving into nothing. The scrawny alien body warped with the crackle of dislocating joints, shifted to a light beige colour, and finally completed its transformation back into the near-human known as Jim Tuesday. Jim shook off the last dregs of shape-changing hallucinogenic drugs with a shudder. Smiling toothlessly, he chuckled exactly like his firstborn and took the offered lighter.

"Son, if you ever get offered a free hit of something called Morpheus from a convicted war criminal, my advice..." Jim blinked, choosing his words carefully, "...my advice is to use it in moderation."

Tuesday embraced his dad. It was a hug that had waited for thirteen long years, a hug that had been cruelly separated by slavery, imprisonment, deep space, death, insanity and a dozen other insurmountable obstacles. For the first time in years he felt like "Bob" again, rather than the scumbag known as "Tuesday," and it was an embrace that could possibly have lasted forever...

Bob felt an odd, unknown emotion, a warm sort of... completeness, as though finding his dad had been the whole point of this story all along. It felt right, a fitting way to finish this metaphorical chapter of his life, like the sensation you get when sipping a coconut-rum-and-lemonade nightcap with someone special after a successful date. It rounded things out nicely.

Then it dawned on him: September, and everyone else on The Frontier, was still in fatal danger.

In a rare flash of insight, Tuesday knew that his mission was your classic cause-and-effect time travel problem, the sort of thing faced by chronal-jockeys on a regular basis. But how would he fix things? Could he stop his earlier version from sneaking aboard The Frontier? After all, if he never stowed away in the first place there would be no need for September to steal Eulogy's Hiver Queen, and that meant Jimmy wouldn't accidentally set the Queen free, and so the rats wouldn't get smart, and Jimmy and September and the Fleet Admiral and everyone else wouldn't die horribly…

But would it make a difference? Was the future really malleable? Would his actions only result in the exact same thing? Or could he actually change the timestream?

And then he realised a glitch: in their trip into the extremely far future, Mister Boodle's ruined cage had still been in the Department of Dimensional Plotting. However, Tuesday distinctly remembered leaving the non-decayed version of the cage in Jimmy's bedroom after the alarms had gone off. Either somebody had decided to move it back there for no apparent reason, or…

It was a paradox. And where there was one, there could be a million.

"We need to hurry," Bob said urgently to his dad. "We only have a few minutes, at best. I need to make a call."

"Who…"

"Look, we're going to save the life of someone I totally, utterly love, and who loves me too, even though rescuing her will mean she'll never even know that I existed." Doing his best to be tough, Bob still blubbed the last few words. This girly emotional stuff had been alien to him until now, and he felt embarrassed. His mouth quivered like a small child jumping up and down on a trampoline. "But I knew you'd find me, Dad. I always knew."

Jim smiled, searching pointlessly for something to say.

"So…" Jim shrugged, already running out of material from his minuscule stock of people skills. "You been up to much?"

Bob put a supportive arm around Jim's shoulders and they staggered for the lift together, through the ashes and smoke, ready to face everything that the bastard Universe could possibly hurl at them, now and forever.